Dear Reader:

Many years a_____
"Bill, it doesn't _____. What's important is to be the *best* William Johnstone you can be."

I've never forgotten those words. And now, many years and almost 200 books later, I like to think that I am still trying to be the best William Johnstone I can be. Whether it's Ben Raines in the Ashes series, or Frank Morgan, the last gunfighter, or Smoke Jensen, our intrepid mountain man, or John Barrone and his hard-working crew keeping America safe from terrorist lowlifes in the Code Name series, I want to make each new book better than the last and deliver powerful storytelling.

Equally important, I try to create the kinds of believable characters that we can all identify with, real people who face tough challenges. When one of my creations blasts an enemy into the middle of next week, you can be damn sure he had a good reason.

As a storyteller, my job is to entertain you, my readers, and to make sure that you get plenty of enjoyment from my books for your hard-earned money. This is not a job I take lightly. And I greatly appreciate your feedback—you are my gold, and your opinions *do* count. So please keep the letters and e-mails coming.

Respectfully yours,

William Johnstone

Years ago, when I was a kid, my father said to me, ...really matter what you do in life. I don't...

WILLIAM W. JOHNSTONE

RAGE OF THE MOUNTAIN MAN

WILLIAM W. JOHNSTONE
with J. A. Johnstone

BETRAYAL OF THE MOUNTAIN MAN

PINNACLE BOOKS
Kensington Publishing Corp.
http://www.kensingtonbooks.com

PINNACLE BOOKS are published by

Kensington Publishing Corp.
850 Third Avenue
New York, NY 10022

PUBLISHER'S NOTE
Following the death of William W. Johnstone, the Johnstone family is
working with a carefully selected writer to organize and complete Mr.
Johnstone's outlines and many unfinished manuscripts to create additional novels in all of his series like The Last Gunfighter, Mountain Man,
and Eagles, among others. This novel was inspired by Mr. Johnstone's
superb storytelling.

All Kensington titles, imprints, and distributed lines are available at
special quantity discounts for bulk purchases for sales promotions,
premiums, fund-raising, educational, or institutional use. Special book
excerpts or customized printings can also be created to fit specific needs.
For details, write or phone the office of the Kensington special sales manager: Kensington Publishing Corp., 850 Third Avenue, New York, NY
10022, attn: Special Sales Department; phone 1-800-221-2647.

ISBN-13: 978-7860-1907-6
ISBN 10: 0-7860-1907-7

First printing: January 2008

10 9 8 7 6 5 4 3 2 1

Printed in the United States of America

RAGE OF THE
MOUNTAIN MAN

1

Slanting sunbeams cast a pink glow on the higher snow-capped peaks of the Rocky Mountains which surrounded the lush valley that housed Sugarloaf, the ranch of Smoke Jensen. Smoke and his wife, Sally, had lived here most of their adult lives. They shared a fondness for the quiet, serenity, and wealth of resources of the fruitful basin.

At least, most of the time Smoke loved it. He had a terrible case of cabin fever. It had been a long, hard winter in the High Lonesome. Eight feet of snow, on the level, still covered a large portion of the Sugarloaf. Yet spring had loudly announced its imminent arrival in the clear, strident call of male cardinals and the noisy splash of invigorated trout in the clear stream that ran near the stout, squarely built log house. Smoke had taken to muttering to himself of late about the long, gray months of enforced inactivity. He did so now as he slipped the cinch strap to free his handsome roan stallion from the saddle.

"Okay, Dandy," Smoke said softly to the animal. "The nosebag comes next. One coffee box of oats."

A single large brown eye turned to examine the tall, broad-chested man with the thick mane of black hair and steely gray eyes. To Smoke's way of thinking, it held an accusing glint. *Only one box of oats?* it seemed to plead. Smoke's smooth, square jaw shifted right-left-right and a small, amused smile split his sun-browned, weather-toughened face. A sudden patter of small boots drew his attention to the large, open barn door.

Bobby Harris appeared a moment later. Pug nose in active motion over a scattering of freckles, mop of straw-colored hair sprouting wildly on a head still damp from the first spring sweat, the slender boy paused with hands held out to illustrate his exciting news.

"Mr. Smoke. Linc let me brand two of the new calves this afternoon."

"Well, now," Smoke responded, gently teasing the orphaned boy he and Sally had taken in. "It looks like you're about ready to draw a grown hand's pay."

"Aw, I ain't that big yet."

"Aren't," Smoke corrected.

"Yeah. I aren't that big yet." Bobby wrinkled his button nose. "That sounds funny."

"That's because it isn't proper speech. 'I am not that big yet' is what you should say. Don't they teach you anything in the school in Big Rock?"

Bobby looked sheepish. "They try. But it just goes over my head. I don't understand what they're talking about."

"Then ask questions, boy," Smoke raised his voice to say, putting a little heat in it. "You'll never learn if you don't have it made clear to you."

"Who needs all that educatin' stuff to work the Sugarloaf?" Bobby countered in childish defiance.

"*You do.* And you'll not be on the Sugarloaf all your life. There's a freight wagon full of opportunities outside this basin. Sally and I came here to find peace, and we did. But a young man needs his adventures before he turns to a more ordered way of life. Take my word for it."

"Yes, sir," Bobby chirped. "Like that time Sheriff Carson was tellin' me about when you shot up all those folks around Bury, Idaho?" Impish delight danced in the boy's big cobalt eyes.

Smoke Jensen did not have to fake the flash of irritation that warmed his insides. "What the hell is Monte doing, telling tales like that to a kid?" he snapped. "Well, no mind. The harm, if any, has already been done. I suppose you have a head full of wild tales about Smoke Jensen and old Preacher?"

Bobby looked solemn and nodded. "Yessir. But they just make me feel proud living here, being around you." He produced his most engaging smile.

Smoke fought back the agitation borne of the long days of confinement during blizzards and in their aftermath. With effort he produced a more lighthearted mood. "Well, time for you to take a dip in the horse trough to float off some of today's dust, then you had best change clothes. You're eating at the main house tonight."

Bobby brightened. "Am I? That's swell. Did Miz Sally bake any pies today?"

Smoke smiled warmly. This was one place he and the boy shared common ground. They dearly loved his wife's pies. "Yep. Apricot, I think. Made it from some of those we dried last summer."

Bobby's eleven-year-old eyes went big and round. "I *love* apricot."

"Seems to me you love anything, so long as it is spelled p-i-e. Now, get along with you and wash up."

Dinner had gone well. Linc Patterson, his vivacious wife, Cynthia, and their two young children had attended. Much to the delight of Bobby Harris and the Patterson youngsters, Sally Jensen had prepared two pies. Smoke was secretly pleased, too. There was nothing he enjoyed more than Sally's pies and biscuits—crusty and brown on the outside, light, flaky, and soft inside—or just about anything she cooked, for that matter.

Long ago, when he was not much older than Bobby, Smoke had learned to cook from old Preacher, the legendary mountain man who had taken Smoke in and raised him to manhood. Preacher's culinary accomplishments ran to the school of, "If it's small enough to put in the pot, stew it. If it's too big, or red meat, roast or broil it." Smoke's kitchen skills developed accordingly. To this day, he retained that first burst of gratitude and delight he'd experienced when he'd discovered that not only was Sally lovely to look at and saucy in temperament, but also a marvelous cook.

Not that Smoke Jensen doted on food like some eastern gourmand. Preacher had seen to the practicality of Smoke's education. He had become a devotee of moderation. That fact notwithstanding, or perhaps because of it, Smoke believed that when the best could be had, make the most of it. Now, as he lowered the wick in the last lamp in their living room, his mind turned to means to escape the tedium the long winter had engendered.

It centered, as most of Smoke Jensen's thinking did, on the things of nature. Perhaps a two- or three-day fishing expedition far up the valley, beyond the area developed for the ranch. Or a jaunt down to Denver. Just him and Sally, away and alone for a visit to the theater, visiting the livestock exchange and his old friend Silas Greene. Such things would have to wait, Smoke acknowledged, as he blew out the flickering yellow flame, until the calves and new foals had all been branded.

He had no way to know that Sally envisioned something entirely different for them. Despite the difficulty of traversing the miles to Big Rock, Sally had maintained relatively regular communications with her family back in Keene, New Hampshire. High on her list of concerns was the state of her mother's health. Her father's last letter had brought the welcome news of considerable improvement. It had also contained intelligence regarding the top priority for Sally Jensen.

She would have to broach the subject with Smoke at the earliest opportunity, in order to have any hope of success. That would come over breakfast the next morning, she decided, as she arranged herself in a suitably suggestive posture on the large, comfortable bed. Wavering yellow light announced the approach of her husband.

Smoke Jensen entered the room and peered beyond the saffron ball of candlelight. His lighthearted smile bloomed into a wide grin of anticipation when he saw his wife's position. "I'll undress and put out the light," he offered.

"No, leave it burning," Sally responded breathly. "I like to watch you make love to me."

Smoke Jensen lay beside his Sally in a deep, restorative slumber. His keen senses were finely honed by Preacher's constant advice and example, and he may well have noted the series of five soft crumps in the distance. A moment later, he definitely heard the sharp crack as a huge wall of snow and ice broke away from the mountain above their stout log house.

Smoke sat upright, fully alert, by the time the rumble of the avalanche reached his ears. Gently he shook Sally to rouse her. "Something's wrong," he whispered calmly.

"Wha—what?" Sally asked groggily.

By then, Smoke had analyzed the sounds that had reached him. "Something's happened to break off the snow wall above here. There's an avalanche. Put on shoes, wrap up in warm clothing. We have to get away from the house."

Alarmed, Sally came upright, one hand going to her long, golden locks in an unconscious feminine gesture. "Will—will it hit the house?"

"We can't take that chance," Smoke declared from his side of the bed, where he worked to pull on his trousers.

His boots came next, while Sally rushed to a large, old armoire to find a robe and a heavy coat. From outside, the faint thunder of cascading snow grew steadily louder. Smoke slid into a sheepskin coat and helped Sally into hers. They made their way to the front door.

Outside, the stars still shone from above. Their glow turned the Colorado countryside to silver. Slowly, small puffs and swirls of wind-borne white began to obscure the sky. Smoke took Sally by one arm and directed her away at a right angle to the avalanche. Billowing ice crystals and fairy-lace snowflakes pulled a black cloud over the heavens.

The sound of the descending snow made it impossible to hear words shouted next to one's ear.

Sally stumbled and Smoke gripped hard to steady her. He also chanced a quick glance to his left, toward the descending wall of snow. It rolled and tumbled, while great gouts shot into the air. The leading edge crashed into a sturdy old pine at the uphill end of a large boulder a hundred yards behind the house. Like the parting of the Red Sea, the tumbling snow and ice cleaved in twain around the huge stone obstruction.

It flowed unceasingly to either side, spread wider, and rushed toward the barns and bunkhouse to the right of the house. It sent small, rounded clumps skittering across the ground toward Smoke and Sally on the left. With a seething hiss, the avalanche passed some ten feet behind the Jensens. Slowly the ominous rumble stilled, saved only in the echoes from across the basin.

An even more alarming silence blanketed the Sugarloaf. Small streamers of still mobile snow made the sound of escaping steam as they poured on down over the white rubble that now covered the bunkhouse. Sally's chest heaved in great gasps. Smoke stood for a stunned moment before the realization of what he saw registered.

Faintly, as though from a mile's distance, he heard the thin, broken cries from the direction of the inundated bunkhouse. The sky lightened as the haze of particles thinned. Sally turned a stricken face toward Smoke.

"What happened to the bunkhouse? Where is it?" Smoke waved a hand in the proper direction. "It's . . . under there."

"The men—did they get out?" Sally asked, overcome with worry.

"I don't know. I don't think so." Then Smoke amended his statement when he saw movement within the snow and the dark silhouettes of heads and the upper torsos of men emerging from the deep bank of snow. "Wait a minute, some of them made it out."

"We have to do something," Sally urged. By some unusual quirk, their house had been spared, yet the hands remained in terrible danger.

Smoke nodded, thinking, devising a plan. "Go to the small toolshed. Bring shovels. I'm going to put these men to scooping out an escape route for the others."

One of the ranch hands stumbled toward Smoke and Sally. Gasping, he stopped before his employer and gestured behind him at the deep pile. "Thank God, there ain't many winders in that place. That snow slide knocked the building plumb off its foundation. If the walls had been weakened by a lot of winders, we'd all be goners."

"How are the men?" Smoke asked anxiously.

"All right, considering. There's bumps and bruises, a couple broken arms, one broken leg, but the whole crew rode it out. Believe me, it was worse 'n the hurricane deck of a mustang bronc. I cracked my head and wound up wedged under little Bobby's bunk."

Anxiety clutched at Sally Jensen. "What about the boy? Is he one of the hurt?"

"No, ma'am, just a few scrapes. He ought to be along in a minute or two. The boys are handin' out the ones hurt bad first."

Another rumble sounded from above and everyone froze, expressions showing their alarm. Smoke Jensen began automatically to tick off the seconds. Another crackling groan from the deteriorating snow, longer and louder. Only seven seconds. It could let go at any time. He turned to Sally, kept his voice calm.

"Go for those shovels. Only stay in the shed. It's good and strong. I'll send men to get the tools." Without waiting for a reply, he set off running toward the ruined bunkhouse.

"What about the livestock that was in the corral. . . that was over there?" the young wrangler ended wonderingly, eyes fixed on a ripple-surfaced bed of snow. Not even a fence post showed above it.

"We'll put men on it as fast as possible," Smoke Jensen directed.

Half a dozen men stood in dazed dejection outside the short tunnel through the rubble of the avalanche. Some shivered, and one stockman cradled a limp broken arm. Another head wormed up out of the icy tomb.

"Yer boy, Bobby, is comin' up next, Mr. Jensen," the next wrangler out of the hole announced.

"Good. Try to work faster here, and I want you boys to get started digging out the horses in that corral," Smoke commanded. "Go to the tool shed for shovels. Be quick about it, but take it easy. Some of them may be down on all fours."

With a strident crack and prolonged screech, another section of the snow overhang gave way and raced breathlessly down on the ranch headquarters. The men scattered—all except Smoke Jensen, who rushed to the opening in the mound to try to retrieve Bobby Harris.

To Smoke Jensen's perception, the decaying shelf of snow-pack remained in its place on the mountainside one second, and the next it smacked him in the back and drove him down the short tunnel into the engulfed bunkhouse. A cloud of crystals hung in the air as the rumble of the secondary avalanche died out. Smoke worked his hands under his chest and levered his torso upward. He shed snow in a shower. He found himself face-to-face with an anxious Bobby Harris.

"Smoke, are you all right?" the small lad asked.

"I'm fine. How about you?"

"We got bounced around some." Bobby indicated the half dozen ranch hands still inside.

"Likely we'll get some more if we don't dig our way out of here fast," Smoke advised.

Two of the wranglers began to pull heavy slabs of compressed snow off Smoke's legs. When most of the pressure eased, Smoke made a powerful thrust and broke free. He made a quick study of the shambles inside the bunkhouse.

"Can you get the door open?" he asked.

"Naw, boss. It swings out, remember?"

Smoke examined the hinge pins. "One of you take a knife and slip these pins. We'll pull the door down. It'll make a bigger tunnel to get us out."

Surprisingly, the potbellied stove had not been overturned. It sat skewed on its box of sand, emitting a cherry glow in the darkened room. The stovepipe had been scattered in sections on the floor, and a thick haze of smoke clung to the roofing above the rafters. Smoke realized they could suffocate if they didn't escape soon.

He searched the floor for what he wanted and came up with a tin dinner plate. "Once that door is out of the way, use your plates to dig in the snow," he instructed. "Move fast, but be sure to pack the upper surface as you go."

To set the example, Smoke Jensen was first to hack away at the white wall outside the bunkhouse. He hurled the snow behind him into the room and burrowed at an upward angle. Space factors limited the tunnelers to three, one crouched below Smoke and Sam Walker. At first they made good progress.

"Dang it," Sam exclaimed, after they had dug some three feet outside the door. "I've hit a big hunk of ice."

"Same here," Smoke advised. "We'll have to try to dig around it."

Tense minutes went past with little progress being made. To deviate would be to dig forever without a reference point. Or to tunnel beyond their source of air. When Smoke and his wranglers began to sweat, Smoke called for a change. Three others took their places at the barrier of white.

Smoke used some of the accumulated snow to douse the fire. One of the Sugarloaf hands made a grumbled protest. Smoke said nothing, only pointed at the thickening cloud over their heads. Looking chagrined, the wrangler said no more. He turned away to work at the window where the first escape had been made.

It looked mighty bleak, Smoke had to admit. Despite the hopelessness of their task, Smoke never lost his fierce determination to bring them all out of there alive. He joined the complainer at the window.

"You're right. This is the shortest way. Or at least, it was," Smoke told him.

"Do you think we've got a chance, Mr. Jensen?" His worried expression matched his words.

"Yes, if we keep at it."

"Can I help?" Bobby asked eagerly.

Smoke considered it. "I suppose so. When we break through, you're the smallest, so I want you to wriggle up to the surface and call for help."

"Will—will there be anybody out there?" Bobby asked.

"There had better be," Smoke stated flatly.

After twenty minutes more, with the breathable air supply dangerously short, Smoke Jensen began to hear muffled spurts of voices. Then came a scraping sound. He dug harder. A small, black hole appeared in the white screen before his eyes. Swiftly it grew larger. He could hear the hands talking clearly now. With a final jab of his tin plate, Smoke broke through into the open.

"There! There's somebody's hand," Smoke heard the shout.

He slid back and wrapped big, square hands around Bobby's waist. He hoisted the boy up over the windowsill. "Crawl on out of there, Bobby," he instructed.

A shower of icy flakes descended from Bobby Harris's boots into the face of Smoke Jensen. A ragged cheer came from the throats of the rescuers outside. Smoke relaxed for the first time since the avalanche had struck. It wouldn't be long now.

An alarmed yelp and muffled boom turned Smoke around. A thick, moving shaft of snow propelled the wranglers back inside the bunkhouse, partly burying them. The primary tunnel had collapsed.

2

With three quick strides, Smoke Jensen reached the nearest of the snow-interred hands. He made big, scooping motions with his arms until he could grab both ankles and drag the unfortunate man out of his frigid tomb. Spluttering, the wrangler sat upright and pointed to the mound of crystalized flakes.

"Zeke an' Harb are still under there," he gasped.

"Go to the window and crawl out if you can," Smoke ordered.

He went to work at once, helped by Sam Waters. They found Harbinson Yates quickly and yanked him free. Zeke Tucker had been driven back against the far wall. He sat in a semi-erect position, the huge slab of ice held in his lap. Smoke and Sam strained to remove the heavy object and it thudded loudly on the plank floor when released.

Zeke's color returned and he spoke through heavy panting. "I . . . think . . . the way is open. Th—this was . . . was the . . . cork in the . . . bottle."

"Glad you can take it so lightly," Smoke said dryly.

Yellow light from a kerosene lantern spilled down through the doorway into the bunkhouse. "You all right down there?"

"Nothing that warm, dry clothes and a couple of shots of whiskey couldn't cure," Smoke replied. Then he recalled the fragmentary report he had been given before the second snow slide. "Have those who were injured been taken care of?"

"Oh, yeah, boss. If none of you is hurt, we'll get you out in a minute."

"Hey, what about me?" Zeke protested. "I got the livin' hell squeezed out of me."

"So that's why your eyes are bugged out, Zeke," Smoke observed through a chuckle. Then, suddenly, everyone began to laugh, as the tension drained away with the danger.

From the ten-foot-high, nearly floor-to-ceiling, windows of the Café London, located on the top floor of the Windsor Hotel in Denver, one could not tell that the High Lonesome still languished in the final throes of the most severe winter on record. Golden sunlight slanted warmly into the room, while below, on the street, children ran noisily home from school, protected by only the lightest of jackets.

Mid-afternoon traffic flowed with its usual jumble past the five-story edifice, designed like Windsor Castle in England. A favorite, "must do" stop for Europeans visiting the West, the Windsor also catered to the discriminating tastes of the wealthier, more traveled easterners. At two o'clock the noon crowd had dwindled in the fashionable pub-style eatery. White-jacketed waiters mutedly took orders from the few late arrivals, and walked across the thick carpets soundlessly, as though on a cloud. Not even the rattle and clatter of the dishwashers and other kitchen help intruded on the two men seated at a table in a corner turret window.

Phineas Lathrop had a striking appearance. He was in his early fifties, and the widow's peak of his lush hair had not the slightest sprinkling of gray. What accentuated his remarkable good looks were two large streaks of white hair at his temples, shaped like the wings of a bird. He peered at his associate down a long, aquiline nose, through a pince-nez perched near the slightly bulbous tip.

"Well, Arnold, this is a far cry from Boston, I daresay," Lathrop declared, in jovial spirits.

"Yes, it certainly is that," Arnold Langford Cabbott returned; his words coated in the syrupy drawl of a New Englander.

A bit of a dandy, Arnold Cabbott wore the latest fashion, his vest as bright as the plumage of a scarlet tanager. A large, puffy silk cravat peeked from the V neckline, set off by a sea of snowy-white boiled and starched shirt. Junior to Lathrop by some seven years, he was the youngest of the five-man consortium established to engender Phineas Lathrop's grand project.

Lathrop leaned forward slightly, his deep-set eyes burning as usual with a fixed, glassy walnut stare. "What was so urgent that it brought you so far away from your bully-boys down on the docks?"

Such colorful reference to the men of his Brotherhood of Longshoremen caused Arnold Cabbott to wince. He reached soft, pallid fingers to the arched flow of his walrus mustache and stroked it absently. While he toyed with the silken light brown strands, Arnold considered how to break his news to Phineas. At last he sighed as their waiter approached with the old-fashioneds both had ordered.

Once the drinks had been put in place and the waiter had departed, Arnold leaned across the table and spoke softly. "There's a problem with our associates in New York. They are reluctant to commit the money. At least until our—ah—difficulties are resolved with that uncouth lout to the north of here."

"Ah! I see. Having the available funds is always a problem. However, we should be hearing about that other matter any day now. I dispatched my most trustworthy subordinate to deal with it." Phineas Lathrop paused and sipped from his drink. "Excellent," he pronounced it. "They are so much better with good Monongahela rye. Out here you have to specify or you get rough-edged bourbon."

Arnold sent the nervous glance of his watery blue eyes around the dining area. "What do you mean, 'deal with'?"

"You'll know when Wade Tanner returns from the high mountains," Phineas said, evading the issue. "I left word at the desk that we would be here in the event he gets back today." He broke off as the waiter approached again, order pad in hand. "Ah, yes," Phineas Lathrop sighed, his eyes giving a quick, final appraisal of the menu. "I'll have the medallions of beef in burgundy mushroom sauce. A side of potatoes Henri, some creamed leeks, and a salad of tossed greens."

"For today, we have a combination of chicory, dandelion, and lettuce from our kitchen garden, sir. Will that be satisfactory?"

"Certainly, certainly. Does that come with a dressing?"

"Yes, sir. Chef Henri's own rose-petal mayonnaise."

Phineas Lathrop all but clapped his hands in delight. "Splendid."

Arnold Cabbott ordered mountain oysters and observed to Phineas Lathrop that it was remarkable that shellfish lived at such high altitude and in such icy waters. Lathrop, who had been in Denver for more than two months and had learned the ropes, hadn't the heart to advise his associate of the true nature of the entree.

To the waiter, he did add, "We'll have a bottle of your best white wine with the salads, and a bottle of claret with the entrees."

Left to await the wine, Arnold Cabbott leaned across the table again and spoke with greater force. "Our friends in New York insist on immediate action. They will not release a penny until they know the obstacle keeping us from our achieving our goal has been removed."

Lathrop screwed the fleshy lips of his large mouth into a moue of distaste. "You're talking like a bloody accountant, Arnold. *I* am in charge in the West, and I'll decide when funds are to be released for the progress of the enterprise. If those penurious bastards in New York don't like that, they can be cut out altogether."

"We need their money, Phineas. Desperately. That's why I came here to appeal to you to return with me and convince them yourself. You convinced them once, I know you can talk open their pocketbooks now that we're in the clutch."

Lathrop's heavy black brows shot upward. "Aha! So that's what this excursion into the Rockies is all about. Are things really so desperate?"

"Yes, they are! You should know. That walkout on the docks is sucking us dry. We have to pay Sean O'Boyle and his longshoremen their pittance every week in order to keep them out. We can break the backs of the shipping companies and then move in and take over. But we must have the cash to do it, all of it! No bank would lend the money to buy a shipping company plagued by a wildcat walkout." Conscious of how unfashionable his ardor appeared, Cabbott caught himself, paused, then spoke through an indulgent chuckle. "And we can hardly confide in the bankers that we're responsible for the strike.

"So, to cover all of that, and continue to finance your acquisitions out here, we need the New York people," Arnold pressed his point. "You, more than anyone else, has the power to persuade them."

Phineas Lathrop sighed heavily and made to respond in agreement. Then he brightened as he caught sight of the head waiter striding in their direction. Behind that worthy came the most unlikely patron for the establishment. The sour expression on Reynard's face advertised his agreement with that evaluation.

Dressed in dust and sweat-stained range clothes, his scuffed boots clumping noisily on runover heels, a man in his early forties followed the fastidious maître d' to the corner table. He had cold, riveting black eyes that could be clearly seen from the distance, in an angular face topped by thick, slicked-back black hair, on which perched a coal-colored derby hat.

"Mr. Lathrop," Reynard spoke deferentially. "This— ah— *gentleman* claims to have an appointment with you."

"That's correct, Reynard. Thank you," Lathrop dismissed. To the newcomer, "Sit down, Wade."

"Always a pleasure to see you, Mr. Lathrop. And you, sir?" he asked in a cultured, courteous tone that belied his scruffy appearance and the menace of a brace of Smith and Wesson American .44s slung low on his hips.

"Forgive my manners. This is an associate from back East, Arnold Cabbott. Wade Tanner, my—ah—chief enforcer, shall we say. You have good news for me, Wade?

"A pleasure to make your acquaintance, Mr. Cabbott. Yes, Mr. Lathrop. That dynamite worked splendidly. You should have no difficulty obtaining the desired property now, and the others, without a rallying figure, should capitulate readily."

Arnold Cabbott blinked at this cultured speech pouring from under the large, wide nose, past rabbity teeth that heightened a certain rodentlike appearance. Tanner looked the part of the lowliest of common gunmen, yet talked like a gentleman. If only his boastful preamble proved true, their troubles would be over.

"You are absolutely sure of that?"

"Oh, yes, sir. Smoke Jensen is now just a memory."

For Sally Jensen, the avalanche was the final straw. She was not one to make issues out of frivolous discomforts, but the snow slide that had nearly claimed the life of her husband and many of his workers hardened Sally's determination to escape the rigors of the past winter. Hands still worked to dig out the imprisoned livestock and their damaged bunkhouse. With the stove dislodged, no cooking could be done in the men's quarters. Sally did double duty, helped by Cynthia Patterson, to serve hot, filling meals to the ranch employees.

She put down a skillet now to peer through the open rear

door and up the face of the mountain that, to her way of thinking, had betrayed them. Was that a blackened smudge she saw against the sparkling white of the snow ledge? Her eyes watered at the brightness and strain. There appeared to be two—no, three—dark spots. Her vision was no longer as sharp as when their children had been the age of Bobby Harris. Smoke would be able to tell, Sally assured herself. But first she must make it clear to him how badly she needed to get away from the basin.

Turning from the stove, she spoke with hands on hips. "Kirby, we simply have to get out of here."

That got Smoke's immediate attention. She never called him by his given name unless a situation had reached the critical level. "I've been thinking along those lines myself," he allowed neutrally.

"Well, I'm glad. Because I'm convinced we need to get as far away from these mountains and that dreadful snow as possible."

Smoke cocked a raven eyebrow. "Meaning where?"

Sally took a deep breath. "New Hampshire. My father's place. It's been years since I've spent more than a day or two there. Longer still since you visited. He would be so pleased, and so would mother."

Astonishment registered on Smoke's face. He viewed any country north, south, east, or west of the Rocky Mountains with suspicion. But particularly east. And he considered anywhere east of the Mississippi River with abhorrence. People didn't know how to live right back there.

Fact was, to Smoke they seemed only to *exist*. Odd creatures, they chose to spend their lives bunched up on top of one another in tall, narrow row houses, on tiny plots of ground not fitting even to grow a kitchen garden. And they had cities with two, three times the population of the entire state of Colorado. No, definitely not the place for them to go. He opened his mouth to say so, but Sally rushed on, eager to sell her idea.

"In his last letter, father grew almost poetic when he described the coming of spring in the Green Mountains."

Mountains? Smoke thought, faintly amused at the use of the term. *More like worn-down hills.* "I was thinking of New Orleans," Smoke managed to insert. He hoped to distract Sally from her temporary madness by offering a trip to her favorite city. Sally called New Orleans "the most civilized town in America."

For a moment, her blue eyes glowed as she considered the *Vieux Carré,* and all those tiny balconies with their ornate wrought-iron banisters and the gaily painted shutters at the narrow windows. The spanking clean carriages and hansom cabs that twinkled around Jackson Square. The French Market, with its heady aromas of spices, exotic coffees, and succulent vegetables. And, oh, the plethora of seafood: oysters, shrimp by the ton, redfish, crabs, and lobsters.

The latter were not so good, Sally had to admit, as those of New England. Yet she found the Crescent City enchanting. Who could not be charmed by the Garden District, where all the swells lived? And the constant rainbow flow of humanity and its many languages. From the palest, pampered milk white to coaly black, with cajuns, creoles, and red men mingled in for variety.

With conscious effort, Sally arrested her fleeting images and returned to her original campaign. "That would be very nice, dear," she answered Smoke's tempting blandly. "But Father has been growing more earnest in his urging for us to pay a visit. His last letter said he had a marvelous diversion in mind for you."

"You are all the diversion I need," Smoke teased, as he cleaned up his noontime plate of pork chops, beans, and cornbread. "We could rent a room in that big old house on Basin Street, and I could have you all alone to myself."

"It's . . . tempting," Sally admitted. "But father would be so disappointed. "I've all but agreed, needing only to confer with you, of course."

A perfunctory necessity at best, the ruggedly handsome

gunfighter admitted to himself. Sally Reynolds Jensen had a knack for getting around him on nearly anything. And why not? She had given him everything a man could want out of life: a home that had grown from a cabin to a sturdy, two-story log mansion; fine, healthy children; a partner in hard times, a nurse when needed, a companion, friend, and lover. That revelation brought to Smoke Jensen a sudden change of heart.

"All right," he drawled gently, albeit with a tinge of reluctance. "I suppose we can spare a couple of weeks to visit your father and mother. But I'm holding out for at least a week in New Orleans."

Sally's eyes went wide. "Why, that's wonderful. Only . . . it's so extravagant."

"What's wrong with that? We can afford it." Smoke simply stated the obvious. "When do you want to go?"

"Right now. Right away," Sally rushed to advise him. "I mean, right after the livestock have been rescued."

Smoke pushed back from the table. "I'll ride in to Big Rock this afternoon to telegraph John about our intended arrival, and also get the tickets for the train."

Sally Jensen hung her arms around her husband's neck and delivered a long, powerful, very wet kiss. "You darling, I knew you would say yes," she sent after him as Smoke headed for the out of doors.

Big Rock, Colorado, had grown considerably over the years since Smoke Jensen had first ridden into town. The main street had lengthened to three blocks of businesses, with an additional residential block at the north and south ends. Cross streets featured shops at least to the alley, with the central intersection extending the commercial area a full block east and west. Smoke concluded his business at the railroad depot by four in the afternoon.

With himself committed to the journey east, he decided on paying a call on Sheriff Monte Carson. They had not seen each other for two weeks. Although Smoke Jensen had hung up his gun long ago, he liked to keep in touch with what went on outside the Sugarloaf. Particularly which specific gunhawks or bounty hunters happened to blow through town.

A man could never be too careful, Preacher had taught him early on. In his wild, single years, Smoke had walked both sides of the law. He had never gone so far as to be considered a desperado. Yet he had made enemies. Some of them still lived, and carried around grudges the size of Pike's Peak. So, after his siding with the sheriff during the Valley War, Smoke Jensen had cultivated his friendship with Monte Carson. It had more than once saved his life. He walked Dandy along Berry Street, the main drag, to the squat, stone building that housed the sheriff's office and jail.

There, a deputy told Smoke that Monte had left for the day, and could be expected in the Silver Dollar. Monte liked his beer, as the slight rounding and thickening of his middle gave testimony. Smoke thanked the deputy and headed to the saloon anticipating their chat.

He entered through the batwings and spotted the lawman at the bar. One elbow resting on the mahogany, Monte Carson was turned three-quarters away from the array of bottles on the backbar. His left hand held a large, bowl-like schooner, its contents lowered by half. The other wiped idly at a froth of foam on his walrus mustache. A smile lighted his face when he made out the features of Smoke Jensen.

"Now, ain't that a sight," Monte brayed good-naturedly. "What brings you to town?"

"Cabin fever," Smoke Jensen responded, as he neared the lawman. To the apron, "Beer."

"Let's sit down," Monte invited, when the brew had been delivered.

They took a table off to one side. Settled in, their conversation ran to small talk, until Smoke mentioned the avalanche of the previous night. Carson asked for details and got them. He shook his head wonderingly as Smoke recounted the initial downfall of winter-packed snow. He literally gaped when Smoke told of the second slide.

When Smoke concluded, Monte asked with genuine concern, "Did you lose many horses?"

"Only one had to be put down. Broken leg. The others in the corral got bruised up by ice chunks and a right good chill."

Smoke went on to tell of the intended trip and suggested the sheriff might take a swing or two up to the Sugarloaf in their absence. Monte readily agreed. Smoke had started to launch into a colorful account of how he viewed matters in the East, when five youthful drifters entered the saloon.

They surrounded a table and glowered menacingly at the sole occupant until he rose and hastily departed. The apparent leader plunked into the vacated captain's chair and propped his boot heels on the scarred, water-ringed tabletop. The over-sharp rowels of his spurs punched deep gouges.

"Get yer ass over here and bring us a bottle," he growled in the general direction of the bartender.

Smoke and Monte exchanged meaning-loaded glances and the ex-gunfighter put their mutual understanding into words. "Looks like you've inherited someone else's troubles."

3

Monte Carson looked again at the five loud-mouthed punks. "I'd say we had a problem."

"Where do you get that 'we,' Monte? You have a chipmunk in your pocket?"

Monte didn't even blink. "You're here, you're packin' iron, and it's too far for me to go get a deputy."

Smoke Jensen gave a mock sigh. "You're slowing down in your old age, Monte?"

"I'm not that much older than you, Smoke."

"Hey, what'd you old farts come in here for, to take a nap?" another of the rowdies asked the usual throng of regular customers.

Wisely, the locals refrained from answer and tried to ignore the quintet so obviously on the prod. It did them little good as two of the testy drifters came to their boots and swaggered toward the bar.

"What's keepin' our whiskey, you bag of guts?" he demanded.

Tortoise-like, Opie Quinn's head appeared to pop down into the protection of his rising shoulders. Without a word, he pointed to a big, bold sign that read,

We Reserve the Right
to Refuse Service
to Anyone

"What? You think yer too good to serve us? Y'all think yer too good to drink with us? Waall, jist who do you think that is, sittin' over there? That's Red Tyrell. That's right, *Red Tyrell,* the man who gunned down three Texas Rangers in a fair fight, an' all at once."

Softly, from a table a dozen feet from Smoke and Monte, came a one-word appraisal of that astounding piece of information "Bullshit."

At once, the punk at the bar whirled in their direction. "You lookin' for an early trip to the boneyard? Which one of you gutless wonders said that? C'mon, 'fess up. We're reasonable boys. We're in a mood for some whoop-de-do, bein' cooped up all winter, so we're inclined to go easy. Leave y'all breathin' an' with all yer teeth."

"Locked in a jail cell, more likely," Monte said in an aside to Smoke.

Smoke gave him a momentary pained frown. "You do like living dangerously, don't you, Monte?"

Another of the saddle tramps rammed to his boots. "I heard that. Don't think I didn't. You sure don't know who it is yer raggin'. That's Randy Slate, an' I'm Buddy Harmes, an' that really *is* Red Tyrell."

Smoke Jensen rocked back his captain's chair and came to his boots. "Pardon me if I'm underimpressed," he stated dryly. "If you gentlemen will excuse me, I have to visit the outhouse."

With slow, deliberate insolence, Smoke turned his back on the quarrelsome punks and strode to the rear door. His disdain left Harmes and Slate slack-jawed. Smoke made it out the door before the first man to comment on their brags added fuel to the fire.

"Talk about big fish in a little pond."

Slate and Harmes rounded on him. They crossed to his table in three swift strides. "You're the one said 'bulishit,' ain'tcha? Now yer gonna have to back that up with iron. Come on, get up out of that chair and pull yer piece, you son of a bitch," Slate snarled at him.

Intimidated by the bulging muscles and harsh voices, the local stammered, "Bu—but I'm unarmed."

"Like hell!" Randy Slate snarled at him. "Buddy, give him a sixgun."

Their spouting off had gone far enough, Monte Carson decided. He flipped the lapel of his black coat away from his vest, revealing the five-pointed star he wore there. He snapped to his boots and advanced on the two agitators.

"That'll be enough of that. Back off, or spend a night in our jail," the lawman growled close in the face of Buddy Harmes.

Red Tyrell moved with the liquid speed and silence of a snake. He came up behind Monte Carson and laid the seven-inch barrel of his Colt Peacemaker alongside Monte's head, an inch above his right ear. The sheriff grunted, went rubber-legged, and dropped to the floor a moment before Smoke Jensen entered through the back door.

Monte's head had just bounded off the padding of sawdust by the time Smoke took in the situation. He flashed a broad smile he didn't feel and spoke in a calming tone. "Now, you've done a very unwise thing. Assaulting a peace officer can get in you some real trouble."

Like a winter-starved trout, the mouthy Randy Slate went for the bait. "What do you think killin' Texas Rangers could get us, sissy-boy?"

The soft gray of Smoke's eyes turned to steel. "Dead, if I know Texas Rangers, and I do."

"Dead?" Slate crowed, as though he'd never heard of such a thing.

"Yes. Exactly like you will all be if you don't pick up my friend the sheriff, clean the sawdust off him, and accompany me to the jail."

"You?" chortled an amused Randy Slate.

Smoke had grown tired of one-word sentences. "I've handled a dozen pieces of shit like you before breakfast and never turned a hair."

"That does it! By God, that does it," Red Tyrell shrieked,

an octave above where he wanted his voice to be. "Spread out, boys." To Smoke, "Fill your hand, you bastard!"

"Oh, hell, I really didn't want to do this," Smoke Jensen said, already in that dreamlike state where everything slows down when the action starts.

Red Tyrell and his four juvenile hard cases opened out into positions which gave them each a clear field of fire at Smoke Jensen. Trouble was, they were too stupid to realize that it also gave Smoke an open line on each of them. Tyrell led their way to the butt-grips of their six-guns. Then everything went terribly wrong.

Red Tyrell had not cleared the cylinder from leather when an invisible fist punched him right in the breastbone. Hot pain exploded in his chest and he experienced a rush of dizziness. Reflexive action brought his Peacemaker clear of the holster. But it had suddenly grown to weigh a ton. A brief struggle went on in his dimming mind as he tried to command the blue steel barrel to rise.

Like the pops of tiny firecrackers heard from far away, three more reports registered on Red's ears. Something twitched at the front of Randy Slate's shirt and the youthful gun hawk staggered backward. Red blinked his eyes. Feeling awfully tired, he sank to his knees as a great gout of blood and brain tissue erupted from the back of Chet Bolton's head. Red had scant time to marvel at the pattern it made in the smoke-thick air of the saloon as darkness rushed over him.

Smoke Jensen made a half-turn to line up on Buddy Harmes, who gulped and swallowed with difficulty, then blurted out as he released his revolver to thud on the floor, "No, don't. Oh, God, don't shoot me."

Easing down the hammer, Smoke swiveled his head to check out the fifth young hard case. He saw the boy sitting at a table, his .45 Colt on the green baize in front of him, head down, blubbering. A scraping sound from the floor cut Smoke Jensen's eyes to Monte Carson.

Holding his throbbing head, Monte sat upright. He eyed

the undulating layers of powder smoke and the scatter of bodies, then shot Smoke a querying glance. "Anything I can do to help, Smoke?"

"Smoke?" The word came as a strangled gasp from Buddy Harmes. "You aren't . . . you can't be . . . tell me you ain't Smoke Jensen."

"That's who he is, all right," Monte Carson informed the boy.

Buddy's face washed white. He began to tremble violently, big, wet tears streaming down his downy cheeks. "Oh—my—God, ohmygod, no wonder we never had a chance. I ain't—ain't never seen nothin' like it."

The sudden aroma of fear-loosened bowels filled the Silver Dollar. Monte Carson looked at Buddy Harmes, sniffed, and cut his eyes to Smoke Jensen. "Smoke, I think this little boy done dirtied his drawers."

A warm day had melted away much of the scattered snow of the avalanche. The hands had spread out across the Sugarloaf during the afternoon to tend to various duties, the foremost being fence mending. Smoke had not returned from Big Rock, although that did not distress Sally Jensen as she spoke with the smooth-talking stranger who had introduced himself as Buford Early.

Early had ridden in five minutes before and asked to speak with the "widow of Smoke Jensen."

"I am Missus Sally Jensen. There is no widow here," she had told him.

A strange light glowed in his eyes and he spoke with a smirk in his words. "I've been given to understand otherwise."

Sally had taken an immediate dislike to Early, even before he'd spoken in such a presumptuous manner. A dapper dresser, he impressed her as a bit foppish. An overabundant amount of pomade had slicked back his hair, made darker by its presence. Sally presumed it to be dark brown, rather than jet, when free of the goop. His business suit had not a trace of trail dust, which had been screened from it by the long white linen duster he had removed the moment he dismounted . . . uninvited, Sally noted for the second time. His high-button shoes gleamed like patent leather. Now he spoke to her unctuously, with the air of a superior adult to a slow child. That heightened her disapproval.

"I have been authorized by my principals to make a handsome offer for the Sugarloaf, Widow Jensen."

"Thank you, no, Mr. Early. The Sugarloaf is not for sale."

Early blinked his eyes behind rimless spectacles secured on a black ribbon, his expression perplexed. "This is a lonesome, I might say—ah—dangerous country of a woman trying to go it alone, Widow Jensen."

"I told you before, I am not a widow. My husband is alive and well, and should be returning from Big Rock at any time now."

"Ah, my, I understand. The first stage of grief is always denial," Early simpered. "Seriously, you must come to grips with the facts and plan intelligently for your future. Consider what you could possibly do if a gang of rustlers struck."

"Since we keep only ten head of cattle, mostly for table meat, and two milk cows, I don't think rustlers would be the least interested in the Sugarloaf. Prize horses are what we raise. And they are all marked on the inside of the lower lip in a manner that cannot be altered. So stealing them would be fruitless."

For all her bravado, icy tendrils of fear invaded Sally's mind. Any number of things could have happened to Smoke in Big Rock. An opportunist, like this wretch, catching wind of such an event, would be quick to move in, like a vulture.

"Come now, a young widow like yourself must face the facts. My offer is really quite generous."

"No. My husband is not dead, and the Sugarloaf is not for sale," Sally persisted.

Growing exasperated, Early blurted, "Face reality!"

Sally cut him off. "Mr. Early, what part of 'no' don't you understand?"

Again Early blinked eyes made owlish by his thick lenses. "I know for a fact that Smoke Jensen died in an avalanche just last night, here on this ranch."

Secret relief flooded Sally at this disclosure, which banished her worries about something having gone wrong in town. She had seated her visitor in the large parlor, and now she rose from the Queen Anne chair from her mother's home she prided. Listening in fascination to the little man spout misinformation, she edged her way toward the drop-leaf secretary in the corner.

"I must caution you, Widow Jensen—you certainly can't believe that some mere woman can hold out against my principals. They are determined men. With your husband so recently deceased, I can understand a certain hesitancy to act with reason, but one must strike while the iron is hot."

Sally's eyes narrowed as she delved a hand into the upper drawer. "Are you threatening me, Mr. Early?"

Unaccustomed to this much resistance, Early let his exasperation slip through. "I'm trying to get you to see reason," he snapped. "This is a difficult time, of course. But such a generous offer won't come around again."

Sally gave him an expression of wide-eyed innocence. "My goodness, is that so? From what you said a moment ago, I got the impression you intended to keep pestering me until I did what you wanted, no matter how often you had to come back."

Confounded woman, Early thought in silent anger. He had no time for this coy fencing. He reached into the inside pocket of his coat as he advanced on her across the large, oval Oriental rug.

"I have the papers right here. I'm going to put them on that desk and you are going to sign them."

Sally Jensen had her hand on the black hard-rubber grips of the .38 Colt Lightning that Smoke had given her for Christmas when she heard the scrape of boot soles on the porch outside. She looked over the shoulder of the infuriated Early to see Smoke enter the room.

"What is it you have in mind for her to sign?" Smoke's voice boomed in the room.

Early literally skidded to a halt. The powerful, masculine voice of Smoke Jensen caused him to dig his heels into the brightly colored Esfahan rug. That caused the carpet to slide across the smoothly finished and lovingly polished planks of the floor. His arms windmilled in his attempt to maintain balance and the papers fluttered toward the ceiling. His performance brought a throaty giggle from Sally Jensen.

"Who is this tinhorn?" Smoke asked his wife in a milder tone.

"His name is Buford Early. He came to make an offer for the Sugarloaf to the 'Widow' Jensen. I tried to tell him, but he wouldn't listen. Mr. Early," she went on, stifling her laughter. "Let me introduce Mr. Smoke Jensen."

Buford Early ended in an awkward position, bent half over, arms extended. He raised his head to gape at the new arrival. What his eyes took in left no doubt. The man was huge. Not in stature alone, but with thick shoulders, a long, square jaw, bulging arms, a trim waist. Below that he saw the gun, a big .45 Colt Peacemaker, in a soft pouch holster, tied down, gunfighter style, and . . . Early blinked in sudden fright. Another revolver nestled in a matching rig, on the left, slanted across a lean, hard belly. The safety thongs had been slipped from the hammers of both. Smoke Jensen, alive and well, and terribly menacing. Early cleared his throat and spoke in an uneven squeak.

"There—ah—there appears to have been some mistake."

"'Reports of my death are greatly exaggerated.'" Smoke took pleasure in quoting one of his favorite writers. "I'd be interested in hearing how and from whom you got this mistaken information?"

"I—ah—my principals prefer to remain anonymous," Early stated primly, part of his aplomb recovered.

Smoke Jensen reached him in two swift strides. He wound thick, hard fingers into the blossom of Early's cravat and yanked the small man upright. Bravado deserted Buford

Early as he hung on tiptoes from the silk stock around his neck. Smoke shook him once.

"I asked you nicely. I could do it another way. Who are you working for?"

Buford Early knew he had to come up with something or he might never leave the Sugarloaf. He knew the legends about Smoke Jensen, the man who had killed hundreds with those use-worn sixguns. Some said three hundred men. He knew those fists to be equally lethal. He swallowed hard around the fear in his throat and fought to stop his eyes from darting around to fix on the face of Smoke Jensen, to make his lie convincing.

"I—I, they will be terribly upset if I breach their confidence," Early stammered.

"Not nearly so much as I am right now," Smoke grated through clenched teeth.

Buford Early struggled to fix an expression of verity on his face. "If I provide you that information, you will see to it that I do not suffer as a consequence?" he bargained in a manner he thought convincing.

"What I do with the names is no concern of yours," Smoke told him with a cold smile. "And what happens to you is none of mine."

"Oh, my. Oh, dear," Early dithered. "I—I truly regret this unfortunate interruption."

"I'm sure you do. Now, the names." Smoke spoke pointedly.

Early sighed heavily, showing a sign of resignation. "My clients are Misters Armbrewster and Coopersmith of Denver," he lied, his eyes locked on those of Smoke Jensen.

"Thank you," Smoke offered sarcastically. "Being straight-forward always makes one feel better, don't you agree?" When Early nodded in agreement, Smoke thrust his next dart. "Now, tell me, how did you intend to get my wife to sign those papers?"

Smoke set him down and Early shrugged to ease the tension in his neck and shoulders. "Well, after all, she *is* a mere slip of a woman. I felt that the force of my person and the reasonableness of my argument would eventually persuade her."

Smoke wanted to laugh. "Just a 'mere slip of a woman,' eh? Sally, show him the pen you were reaching for to sign his papers."

An impish grin danced on Sally Jensen's face as she opened the drawer and took out the Colt Lightning. Buford Early blanched even whiter, if that was possible. He began to tremble.

"Consider yourself lucky I came back when I did. Otherwise, Sally may have punched your ticket to the monument garden. Together we have fought Indians, rustlers, and outlaws intent on carving a big chunk out of our High Lonesome, for more years than I care to count. We've even kicked hell out of more than our share of two-bit tinhorn upstarts like you. So far we haven't gone soft. We haven't even slowed down much.

"So, take word back to Armbrewster and Coopersmith if those are their real names," Smoke added. "The Sugarloaf is not for sale, will not ever be, for so long as Sally or I am alive. And I don't look for our children to sell it, either."

"Wh—what can I say?" Early bleated.

"Good-bye," Smoke informed him, along with a hard shove toward the front door.

After Buford Early's hasty departure, Sally Jensen looked admiringly at her husband. "That was some speech. I've never heard you string so many words together in all the years we've been married."

Smoke Jensen actually blushed. "That oily snake touched on something close to my heart. And he upset you." He drew a deep breath, changed the subject. "You'll be happy to know that we are due to leave in two days. We'll take the day coach to Denver, then a compartment on a private car all the way to Chicago."

Sally clapped her hands in enthusiasm. "That's marvelous. How did that happen?"

"Courtesy of a grateful Colonel Joshua Drew, president

of the Denver and Rio Grande. You recall I scouted for him some years back on a breakthrough route in the Rockies? Well, when Nate at the depot telegraphed our reservations to Denver, Colonel Drew learned of it and made arrangements. Nate's boy brought me word while I was visiting with Monte Carson."

Sally's beaming countenence darkened and furrows appeared on her high, smooth brow. "Two days? How can I possibly pack everything in such a short time?"

4

Phineas Lathrop sat fuming in the parlor of his suite in the Windsor Hotel in Denver. He glared heatedly at Buford Early. "You're positive?" he demanded. "It couldn't be just some man in her life?"

"He wore two guns, one of them in a gunfighter cross-draw. He picked me up off the floor without even a sign of effort. It was Smoke Jensen, all right. He all but told me that if I showed my face around there again, he'd kill me. I believed him."

"I'm sure you did," Lathrop told, him nastily. "Wade Tanner assured me that the avalanche accounted for Jensen."

Buford Early blinked. He'd heard the name before, but had no idea that Tanner worked for his employer. Tanner was reputed to be trouble on horseback. A real *malo, hombre,* as folks in southern Colorado would say. Then the meaning behind Lathrop's words struck him: the avalanche had not been an accident of nature.

It gave Early new insight into his boss. If Lathrop and his associates stooped to violence so readily, he had better carefully tailor what else he reported of his run-in with Smoke Jensen. Good fortune shone on him a moment later, when Phineas Lathrop waved a hand irritably and spoke gruffly.

"We missed him. We'll have to try again. Get out of here, I have plans to make."

After Buford Early's hasty exit from the suite, Phineas Lathrop summoned Wade Tanner from the hallway. He wasted no words.

"You're wrong about Smoke Jensen. Early locked horns with him at the Sugarloaf. He's still alive, Tanner. I want you to put men on changing that right away."

"You want me to go with them, Mr. Lathrop?"

"No. I have something else in mind for you. I'm leaving this afternoon for back east. There's much to be done in Boston and New York. I want you to take the rest of your men and start obtaining the smaller holdings in the high mountains. Proceed as though Jensen was no longer alive and everyone knew about it."

"What if they know better and won't sell?" Wade Tanner asked.

Coldness radiated from Lathrop's deep-set walnut eyes. "Then deal with the widows."

Spewing a huge, black cloud, the 4-6-0 mountain locomotive on the D & R G spur to Big Rock glided into the large, multitracked station at Denver. The engineer applied the brakes with a deft touch, then swung the big, brass lever over to activate the reverse control and change the direction of the wheels. White plumes of steam erupted from the escape valves in the cylinder heads and the pistons churned to drive the main rods, connecting rods, and walking arms.

Pale amber grains cascaded down from the sandbox to increase traction. The drivers spun a moment, then bit on the sand. A final touch of brake, then the throttle went off. Forward, the high, wide cowcatcher gleamed like carnival teeth, painted alternately in glossy black and red. Already the conductor had swung down off the first passenger coach, and now ran ahead to set his stepstool in place.

When the train stopped moving, it was aligned exactly

with the door. He climbed up and opened the lower half, exposing the vestibule. In less than a minute, passengers started to detrain. Then the ruddy-faced conductor began to chant his familiar litany.

"Denver. Denver. Passengers for the eastbound Santa Fe for Ellsworth, Topeka, Kansas City, and points east, cross over to Track Four. Southbound for Pueblo and Santa Fe, Track Six. Westbound passengers will find accomodations in the waiting room."

Smoke and Sally Jensen stepped down onto the platform with expressions of relief. Sally could not hide a girlish enthusiasm that made her look ten years younger than she had during the blizzardy days of January. Without livestock to worry about, although Smoke felt decidedly uncomfortable not having a saddle horse available, the couple crossed directly over to Track Four. They had been assured that their luggage would be transferred without need of personal supervision.

A clutch of other passengers had preceded them. More came from the depot, released from behind the wrought-iron gates by the ticket agent. When Smoke handed their tickets to the conductor, he glanced at them, then up at Smoke and Sally. He touched two fingers to the brim of his small, round, dark blue Santa Fe cap in salute.

"There will be a ten-minute delay, sir, while yer private car is coupled to the rear of the train. Sure an' I hope it's no bother."

Surprised by this revelation as much as by the conductor's deference, Smoke didn't know how to respond. He stood in silence until Sally gouged him in the side with an elbow. "Uh—that will be fine. Thank you," he blurted out.

Some of those close enough to overhear turned indignant glowers on the couple. "Damned robber barons. He's got no right to hold up the train. They all have too much money, if you ask me," one man with a distinct Boston accent grumbled loud enough for Smoke to hear.

Momentary anger flared in Smoke Jensen. He was

fiercely proud of his wild, free, albeit dirt-common years at Preacher's side. He had carried his weight, earned his keep. And the hardscrabble days with Sally, building the Sugarloaf, gave him just pride in his accomplishments He and Sally might be comfortable now, well off, truth to be told, but he had put hard work and sweat into it. Every bit was honestly made. Before Sally could exert her calming influence, Smoke took three strides forward and tapped the offensive man on the shoulder.

"Mister, you have a serious problem with that mouth," Smoke growled at him. "I'd be happy to rearrange it for you."

Bristling, the Bostonian reacted in a manner Smoke Jensen had not anticipated. He hunched his shoulders and balled his fists, then spun on his left heel as he cocked one, ready to deliver a sucker punch. His aggression speedily deserted him as he focused on Smoke's hard, set face, and the level, steely gaze of those compelling bullet-gray eyes.

For an icy moment the contenders took the measure of each other. The Bostonian broke off contact first. Deflated, he felt the color of his implanted class envy bleed from his face, then muttered something while he avoided further confrontation.

"What was that? I didn't hear what you said," Smoke challenged.

"Arthur, for heaven's sake," the diminutive woman beside him urged, as she tugged on his sleeve.

"Yes, Arthur, you had better listen to the little lady," Smoke suggested, his full lips twisted in a sneer.

Self-examination revealed to Smoke Jensen how much he resented just such an attitude in other men. Yet he had to admit he enjoyed this a great deal. He shook his head in resignation. *How would he ever put up with being surrounded for two weeks by thousands like this one?*

". . . uh—said I was sorry. I spoke out of line," Arthur mumbled a bit louder.

Smoke made himself be magnanimous. "That's all right. The offense is forgotten. Have a pleasant journey."

Some imp of rebellion lingered in Arthur from Boston. "Yeah, sure. I know *you* will."

Smoke chose to ignore it and turned to Sally. "How do they get so lippy?"

"It probably comes from living all crowded up close to one another," Sally opined. "And it might be because they have ordinances prohibiting people from going around armed. From even owning guns, in some places." She nodded to indicate the cartridge belt and the pair of Colts under Smoke's dress coat.

Smoke produced a rueful grin. "Yeah. An armed society *is* a polite society. Preacher always said that."

Sally dimpled with a conspiratorial smile. "I know. I have that cute little Lightning in my purse."

Cute? Smoke thought wonderingly. That Colt was an instrument of death. Sally ought to know better. Preacher had taught Smoke that one respected guns, cared for them, even might fear them in the hands of others, but you didn't personalize them or give them familiar names, like Old Betsy. He took Sally's arm and helped her onto the vestibule platform.

They started through the first of two Pullman cars when Smoke had to grab Sally's elbow to steady her. A sudden jolt and loud, rumbling crash of metal against metal came from the rear of the train.

"Don't hump that car, you dizzy idiot!" the conductor shouted to the yard goat engineer. "The colonel will have your balls for that."

"It appears our coach has arrived," Smoke said through his amusement.

Although well-accustomed to train travel, Sally Jensen had never seen anything quite so opulent as Colonel Drew's private coach. Entering, they encountered a narrow passageway past the lavatory, storage pantry, and kitchen. A narrow, cell-like space provided sleeping accommodations for the cook, his helper, and the butler. Next came the doors to four sleeping compartments. Beyond that, the dining room, which had opened out to full width, its forward and rear walls covered with crystal mirrors in mahogany frames. A cut-crystal chandalier with Tiffany reflector hung over a large, oval cherrywood table. Matching chairs, with plush seat cushions, provided seating for eight.

Graceful columns of polished mahogany formed an archway into tile sitting room. Overhead, pressed tin ceiling covers depicted scenes from mythology, the details picked out in gold foil. Comfortable wing chairs, a loveseat, and a chesterfield sat in casual disarray among low tables and smoking stands in the sitting room. A small bar graced the wall that screened the dining room. Stained glass bordered the windows and a domed cupola that admitted light. Sally drew in a delighted breath.

"It's so beautiful."

Smoke circled her still-trim waist with both arms and spoke over one shoulder, into her ear. "I'd buy you diamonds if you had anywhere to wear them."

"Oh, pooh, I already have diamonds." Sally looked around in eager appreciation. "Do you really think . . . that we can afford one of these?"

"We never go somewhere often enough to make it practical. And I, for one, don't find that unappealing," Smoke teased.

"Stick-in-the-mud!" Sally challenged.

The door to the observation platform at the rear opened suddenly. It caught Smoke and Sally in their intimate embrace. A gangly young man stood in the opening. He awkwardly held an alligator-skin gladstone bag.

"Excuse me" he said, in a somewhat squeaky voice. "I think you have the wrong car."

Smoke released Sally. "Maybe it's you who are in the wrong place," he challenged.

The boy stood his ground. "This is Colonel Joshua Drew's private car. I'm his son-in-law, his *new* son-in-law. I—we—we're on our honeymoon."

This was something be had not been advised about in advance. Smoke drew a deep-breath and removed his Montana Peak Stetson. He studied the callow young man and wondered how the colonel had ever consented to allow his younger and most precious daughter to marry such a one. Had the invitation to use the private car been in error? Smoke removed the tickets from his inside coat pocket, accidentally revealing the cartridge belt and the butt of his gunfighter-rigged crossdraw .45.

Immediately the youthful newlywed washed pale white and dropped the bag. He clutched at the arm of the girl who now stood beside him. "Watch Out, Priss," he bleated. "This ruffian has a gun."

Priscilla Drew looked beyond her husband's agitated face and her efforts at recollection moved fluidly across her face. "Why, I know you," she addressed Smoke. "You're Mr. Jensen. You worked for my father. You laid the course for the D & R G through the high passes of the Rockies."

"That's correct. But I don't recall you, Miss—er—Mrs. . . ."

A light trill of laughter came up a long, graceful throat and bubbled on pretty lips. "Small wonder, Mr. Jensen. I was only a child at the time."

Not much more now, Smoke thought to himself. He produced a smile, along with a memory. "The one who loved horses more than locomotives, am I right? That lovely blond hair gives you away. You wore it in sausage curls then, too, didn't you?"

Priscilla. absolutely glowed. "Oooh, I would have just *died* of ecstasy if I had known you noticed me then." She turned to her husband and said, "Thomas, it skipped my mind, what with everything that went on before and after our wedding. Daddy did say that we would be sharing the car with a good friend of his and his wife. This must be

them. Mr. Smoke Jensen, my husband, Thomas Henning."
Then she added with glowing pride, "I'm Mrs. Henning
now."

"How do you do?" Thomas Henning responded stiffly, his
eyes still fixed on Smoke's waistline, where had he seen
the cross-draw gun.

"Fine, thank you. I was about to show you our tickets and
travel itinerary. Your father is most generous, Mrs. Henning.
We have use of the car all the way to Boston."

"It's like him," Thomas Henning said poutishly. "Send
along a chaperone on our honeymoon."

"May I present my wife, Sally Reynolds Jensen," Smoke
finished the introductions, ignoring the petulance of
Thomas.

At mention of Sally's family name, Thomas cocked an
eyebrow. Now that he had calmed somewhat, his voice held
the distinct flavor of an eastern accent. "Would that be the
New Hampshire Reynoldses? Banking, the stock market, di-
versified investments?"

"The same," Sally informed him, fighting to suppress a
throaty chuckle.

"Well, I must say, I had no idea that these rough-edged
westerners even knew anyone from the distinguished families, let alone that one had married into a family so—so ac-
ceptable as the Reynoldses."

That torqued Smoke Jensen's jaw as very little else could.
"I think you have it wrong, boy. Sally married me; I didn't
marry into any family."

"Please, Thomas, don't be such a snob. You've had a problem with that since you came to Denver," Priscilla chided.

"But, he's—he's so—common."

"Thomas!" Priscilla cried, embarrassed for herself as
well as him. "One doesn't talk to people out here like that."

"Not unless one is prepared to back it up," Smoke prodded.

Thomas paled again and his upper lip trembled. "I'm not
armed. I abhor firearms."

"Which is what is keeping you alive right now," Smoke

growled, his dander fully aroused. Then, when he saw the sickly expression that washed over Thomas's face, he uttered a sound somewhere between a shout and a bark of laughter. "Come on, folks, this is rapidly going nowhere. Relax, Mr. Henning. Sally always tells me my bark is worse than my bite. Since we're going to be together in this car for . . . how long?"

"We're leaving the train at Kansas City, to take a riverboat to New Orleans," Priscilla informed Smoke.

Smoke turned to Sally. "That's where we should be going, instead on to the East Coast," he advised in an I-told-you-so tone. He continued his offer of peace. "Since we're going to be together in this car for at least three days, we might as well make peace and get along as well as we can."

"Call me Priss."

"I'm Sally." The two women smiled.

Uncomfortably, Thomas Henning extended his hand. "Thomas, if you please."

"Smoke," the most famous gunfighter in the penny dreadfuls responded.

"Aaaall abooooard!" the conductor cried from outside.

"Do you have more luggage?" Sally asked.

"Jenkins has taken care of it," Priscilla replied. "It should be in our compartment."

As though summoned by name, the butler, Jenkins, appeared from the door to one compartment. "Miss Priscilla, Mr. Thomas, I have taken the liberty of giving you the second compartment. That way there will be no one to either side of you." He actually blushed at the implication of his words. "Mr. Jensen? Yours will be the one at this end, Number Four."

"Thank you, Jenkins," Priscilla said, with all the polished casualness of those accustomed to dealing with servants. "If you will excuse us, we will go change to something more suitable for travel," she told Smoke and Sally.

Jenkins cleared his throat. "There will be champagne and hors d'oeuvres to celebrate the occasion in the parlor section in one hour."

"That . . ." Priscilla and Thomas exchanged glances. "Will be fine."

"Needn't hurry on our account," Smoke offered in an amused tone.

One long and two shorts shrilled from the steam whistle of the locomotive to announce departure. The great driver wheels spun until trickles of sand gave proper traction. Then the space widened between cars as they stretched to the limit of their couplers. Another long and three shorts celebrated the entire chain of cars getting under way.

Smoke and Sally entered their compartment and found it as opulent as the rest of the car. Wood-paneled walls with plush red-flocked wallpaper interspersed gave a rich glow to the room. All of the brasswork had been highly polished. A double set of facing seats would fold down into one bed, the other an overhead, swing-away model. Sally examined them and grinned impishly up at her husband.

"I wonder how the newlyweds will handle this arrangement?" she asked mischievously.

Smoke made a great show of offended sensibilities, eastern style. "You shock me. I never dreamed you could harbor such nasty thoughts," he teased, then added, "For that matter, how are we going to get around it?"

"We'll manage," Sally told him saucily.

Once the train had slowly rolled through the heart of Denver and beyond its suburbs, it was literally all downhill to Ellsworth. The journey across the rolling prairie would take the rest of the day and much of the next afternoon to complete. Although named the Daylight Express, numerous water and coaling stops would eat into the time on the 396-mile journey. Also, there would be passenger stops at Limon and Stratton in Colorado, and at Goodland and Fort Hays in Kansas.

With that thought in mind, Smoke and Sally Jensen returned to the parlor section of the private car shortly before the hour had passed. Before the happy couple put in an appearance, the conductor entered the car and came to Smoke.

"Mr. Jensen, ye'll pardon me for being blunt, sir. As it is, I happened to notice ye had borded the train armed. Sure an' that's a comfort to me," he added.

Smoke made a puzzled frown. "Why's that?"

"Because I'm travelin' armed this trip, also. The name's Liam Quincannon, and though 'tis true I work for the Santa Fe, Colonel Drew had a quick word with me when we made arrangements for his car to be placed on the Daylight. The good colonel asked that I keep a protective eye on his daughter, ya see?"

Smoke saw only too well. He began to suspect that Colonel Drew's generosity in offering them his private car, and then installing the newlyweds, might be tempered by a desire to have further protection for his dearest daughter. The old man had spoiled her outrageously whenever she had visited the railhead during construction. Fine with him, Smoke decided, so long as everything went well. Somehow, though, Smoke Jensen had the gut feeling that something would come along to see that it did not go so well.

5

Dutifully the happy couple showed up some twenty minutes late for the postnuptial celebration, obviously laid on the behest of Colonel Drew. They wore smirking, guilty expressions that clearly telegraphed how, besides changing clothing, they had spent the time since disappearing into their compartment. They sipped champagne, munched on small, heart-shaped sandwiches, carved a miniature of their wedding cake and passed out pieces to Smoke and Sally, and then, in a rush of egalitarianism, included a spluttering Jenkins, the cook, Lee Fong, and his helper.

John Reynolds would not have approved, Smoke Jensen thought amusedly over that. Following a chatty half hour, the bemused pair withdrew to their compartment once more. Smoke and Sally saw little of them from then on. When a tinkling silver bell announced a light supper at six o'clock that evening, Sally and Smoke ate alone. Another sounding of the bell by Jenkins at nine for dinner brought the lovebirds forth, both looking decidedly more weary than the rocking, swaying journey could account for.

They ate sparingly of excellent pheasant and boiled potatoes, and departed early. Smoke turned an amused visage on Sally. "I gather they have found a way," he opined.

"So shall we, dear; so shall we," Sally promised.

* * *

Despite Smoke Jensen's misgivings, everything went well through the night. Not until the train rattled down the track, well into Kansas, did the morning sunlight reveal a condition that warranted quick action by Walk Bigalow, the engineer.

A section of track had been ripped up and used with cross-ties to form a barricade. It could mean only one thing, Walt Bigalow thought: a train robbery. Hostile Indians had long been cleared from this part of Kansas. Fort Hays had been dwindling into the small town of plain Hays, Kansas. Yet he could use the cavalry now. He quickly pulled back the throttle, swung the reverse bar to the proper position, and hoped for the best.

Huge drivers squealed and threw out showers of sparks. All along the train, startled crewmen leaped to the large wheels of the brake controls for the cars. Last to be jolted by the emergency stop was the private car in which Smoke and Sally Jensen, Thomas and Priscilla Henning partook of a late breakfast. Coffee sloshed over the gold-filled rims of delicate china cups and stained the linen tablecloth. Thomas nearly impaled his cheek with a fork.

"What in heaven's name?" he blurted.

"Something on the tracks," Sally suggested.

Smoke cut his eyes to the window opposite his place at the table. "From what I can see, it's a two-legged some-thing," he stated tightly, as he came to his boots and started toward the passageway that led past the compartments and kitchen. Sally sent an understanding look after him, then rose in a composed manner.

"Come, Priss, I think it is wise if you and Thomas go to your compartment. Lock the door after you."

"Why? What is it, Sally?" Priscilla asked, suddenly alarmed.

"Perhaps nothing, but Smoke isn't often mistaken. It could be trouble."

It was Thomas rather than Priscilla who paled. "What sort of trouble?"

"Train robbers," Sally answered him simply, not one to mince words at this point.

Smoke stepped onto the vestibule at the same time as Liam Quincannon. The worried expression on the conductor's face made Smoke's question unnecessary. Quincannon's words confirmed it.

"Sure, I'm in a devil of a spot. I've me duty to the passengers and the railroad, but there's . . ." He nodded toward the private car.

"We'll take care of them first, reassure them," Smoke suggested.

"Foine thinkin', bucko," Quincannon responded. Under tension, his accent had thickened noticeably.

Inside the car, Smoke and Liam walked along the passageway until they came upon Sally. So far, she had failed to convince the Hennings to take quick action to disappear. She turned a worried gaze on Smoke.

"We're going to have to do something about breaking up this robbery," Smoke stated flatly. "I suggest you two lock yourselves in your compartment and pull down the window blind," he told Thomas.

"I've tried to get them to hurry and do that, Smoke," Sally answered in the tense silence that followed Smoke's instructions.

"If ye'll not use good sense, then I must stay to protect the colonel's daughter," Liam Quincannon insisted.

Sally delved into her pearl-studded clutch purse. "It's all right. I can do that. I have my Colt Lightning."

Thomas's eyes went wide as he stared at the compact, parrot-bill grips of the .38 revolver. A typical eastern establishment socialite, he twisted his face into an expression of extreme revulsion. "I thought I had made it clear. I despise nasty firearms."

With a wicked grin, Sally advised him, "If you won't use one, then I suppose I can protect you, too."

"Get them into their room quickly, Sally. We're going to

go cause some grief for those train robbers," Smoke informed her.

Once on the vestibule again, Smoke gave a satisfied nod when he heard Sally lock the door behind them. "I'd say we ought to cut down the odds some at first," Smoke suggested. "You take the off-side, I'll cover this one."

Smoke and Liam took the door opposite the side of the train where the robbers sat their mounts in silent contemplation. Well-seasoned to the job of looting trains, their leader, Buck Waldron, knew the advantage to be gained by making their intended victims sweat a while. Oblivious to resistance in the form of Smoke Jensen and the conductor, Waldron watched with steely gray eyes over the bandana that served as a mask while the passengers grew more agitated.

"I'll head for the cab. They always put one or two in there to watch the engineer," Quincannon offered.

"Good idea. I'll take to the top of the cars."

"You could be trapped there, Mr. Jensen."

"Smoke to you, Liam. I don't think so. I'll have the advantage of surprise, and try to keep it."

Liam's eyes widened and he drew a deep, hasty breath. "Saints above. Yer *Smoke* Jensen, the gunfighter an' mountain man?"

"Some have called me by those names," Smoke admitted, one foot on the first rung of the iron ladder. "We'll talk about it later. I'll give you time to reach the locomotive. Then don't shoot anyone until I open up. Better chance they won't know you've taken out their men that way."

"Yer a crafty one, I'll say that," Quincannon responded as he started along the right of way, bent below the thick layer of ballast that would mask his movements.

Smoke climbed to the roof of the Pullman next to Drew's private car. Belly down on the catwalk, he edged forward and then to his right, off the boards. When he neared the edge, he raised his head slightly to take in the scene below. Smoke immediately saw half a dozen of the masked hold-up men. None looked upward, for which he was thankful. Colt already in hand and cocked, Smoke poked the seven-inch barrel forward and sighted in.

Three fast rounds cleared as many unsuspecting men from their saddles. Uncertain as to from where the shots had come, the survivors looked around in confusion. One said he had heard shots from the cab, another swore they came from between the cars. Then one caught a glimpse of a streamer of powder smoke above the roofline of the coach.

"Up there!" he shouted.

Immediately three sixguns barked nearly as one. It did them no good. Smoke Jensen had been on the move the moment the last bullet left the muzzle of his .45 Colt. The slugs whizzed far over his head as he hugged the off side of the car, below the catwalk. He hand-walked his way back to his starting place, climbed down, and went to the ground in the direction Liam had taken.

A quick glance forward gave him sight of an all-clear signal from Liam Quincannon in the cab. Smoke went beyond the point of his first encounter with the bandits and crawled under a car, his action hidden behind the wheels of the rear truck. Smoke took a quick peek beyond one shiny steel disc. Fine place he'd picked, he thought sourly.

The trio he had left unharmed had been joined by five more. They spread out almost on top of him. Before any of them could notice him, a loud blast signaled the forced entry of the express car. That drew the attention of all the hard cases forward.

Smoke swiftly seized the advantage of that. His Peacemaker barked twice more and a pair of robbers crumpled over the necks of their mounts. Again Smoke disappeared before being spotted. Curses came from the remaining six. Seated with his back against the ballast gravel, Smoke reloaded his .45 while he reviewed the positions of his enemy.

Six across the track from him. He'd counted seven more in a cluster near the chair cars. Ten, perhaps a dozen, had gathered outside the express car before the blast. Nothing for it, Smoke summed up, but to keep taking the fight to them.

He eased his way along the grade to put himself between the two rearmost groups.

When next he popped out, he fired two rounds to left and right, then dodged behind the leading truck of the second Pullman. Hot, soft lead smashed into steel, to howl off in misshapen ricochets. Smoke holstered his Peacemaker and pulled the older .45 Colt Frontier from the holster high on his left. This time he chose to climb and add to the confusion of the bandits.

On top of the rear chair car, Smoke wriggled on his belly to the near edge and looked down on a group of empty saddles, the reins of the horses that wore them held by a single outlaw. A sharp report from the cab reached Smoke's ears a moment after the man jerked in his saddle, stiffened, and fell.

Eight pair of reins flew from his hands as he hit the ground. Smoke immediately fired two rounds over the heads of the nervous horses and set them off at a fast run. A shout of alarm, followed by heartfelt curses, brought most of the outlaws at a trot to find their mounts racing away across the prairie.

Although he had easy targets, Smoke held his fire. So did Liam, he noted with satisfaction. It took only a second for the bandits to grasp the situation. Grumbling, they chased after their hastily departing horses. Smoke Jensen climbed from the rooftop and started toward the express car. Liam showed himself in the doorway to the cab and swung onto the rungs that gave access to the ground.

He joined Smoke outside the combination mail and strongbox car. Voices came from inside. "See what the hell that's all about," one demanded.

"Buck's out there somewhere," another protested. "He can take care of whatever it is."

"I said for you to look. Now, do it."

A masked man appeared in the blast-shredded doorway. He looked forward, then to the rear, and finally downward. His eyes widened, showing a lot of white when he peered into the muzzle of the .45 Frontier in Smoke Jensen's hand. Smoke spoke softly.

"Climb down."

"Huh? I cain't do that."

"I'll blow you back through the car," Smoke promised. "Awh, hell . . ." Foolhardy courage replaced the wise caution with which the man had operated so far. "Hey, Travis, there's a couple of . . ." Smoke Jensen's bullet put a period to the sentence before the robber had intended.

Answering fire ripped from inside the express car.

Nothing had gone right on this job from the beginning, Buck Waldron thought, as he led the way out of the last chair car and into the vestibule between it and the first Pullman. So far they had taken only a hundred or so in cash and some trinkets. If Travis didn't hit a bonanza in the express car, they might as well have stayed in Hays and gotten drunk.

"Okay, Dorne, you go through there. Watch for some fool playin' hero," Buck ordered.

Dorne entered the sleeping car ahead of his boss, a fat Smith American .44 in his left hand. A woman shrieked a moment before the quartet of bandits heard the fusillade from the express car far forward. Buck Waldron spat a curse and shook his head.

"We'll have to take care of that later. First we pluck these fine folks of what they have." To a portly gentleman whose face had turned an apoplectic red, "Dump it in the bag. Watch, rings, then your pocketbook. We even accept small change, so be generous."

"I'll see you hang first," the outraged citizen grunted.

He complied, nevertheless, when Buck Waldron shoved the muzzle of his .45 Colt into the expanse of belly, an inch above the thick gold chain that retained his watch. Waldron glowered menace at him.

"Watch first, remember?"

Swiftly the gang stripped the passengers of their valuables. When they reached the back of the car, Dorne opened the door and stepped onto the vestibule. A frightened face jerked back from the window in the portal to the second Pullman. At Dorne's side, Rucker laughed sneeringly.

"Like a bunch of chickens with a fox in the roost," Rucker observed. "Want to bet they're already diggin' out their cash an' goodies?"

"Naw," Dorne replied scornfully. "They can't believe this is happening. Not to them at least."

Whoever had been watching for them had at least presence of mind enough to throw the bolt. Two .44 slugs from Dorne's Smith and Wesson weakened the metal sheath around the deadbolt enough to allow them to shoulder open the door. Two women screeched in this car, and three small children huddled together, large tears running silently down their cheeks.

When Dorne reached out and chucked a boy of seven or eight under the chin, the lad began to whimper. "Here, now," Dorne said gruffly, unsettled by the situation. "Big boys like you don't cry, let alone make noises like a baby. Lady," he added to the horrified woman who comforted the youngster, both arms draped over his shoulders, hugging him close, "don't be doin' that; it'll make a sissy out of him."

"How dare you!" she exploded in outrage.

Dorne winked at her. "Because I'm the one with the gun."

"Empty out," Buck Waldron commanded. "We accept everything. Watches, then rings and ladies' brooches, then you gentlemen contribute your pocketbooks. Don't stint on the change in your coin purses, either."

Slowly the outlaws worked their way down the aisle, totally unaware of what awaited them in the private car behind this one.

Quickly as it had begun, the rattle of gunfire from the express car ended. Powder smoke streamed out over the upper lip of the shattered door and formed a gray billow. Smoke Jensen approached cautiously. Behind him, Liam Quincannon faced outward, watchful for the return of any of the robbers out chasing their horses.

Smoke gave him a swift glance, then edged up to one side of the splintered door, which hung downward to the ballast. With colt leading the way, Smoke poked his head around the side. At once the sharp report of a Peacemaker bounced off the inner walls. Poor shot, Smoke considered, as the slug went wild a foot above his head. Smoke answered in kind.

"My God, I'm hit, Travis," a voice rewarded Smoke's accuracy.

"Shut up and keep down," Travis growled back.

"How many of 'em is out there?" another bandit asked.

"I don't know," Travis said shortly.

"Enough," Smoke Jensen provided in a jaunty tone.

"You a railroad detective?" Travis demanded.

"Nope. Only a passenger," Smoke told him.

"This ain't yer money. Why you doin' the Santa Fe any favors?"

"I got bored back in that private car. Thought I'd mix in and put some zest in my life."

"Who are you, anyway?" Travis queried.

"Name's Jensen. Smoke Jensen."

"Oh, sweet Jesus," Travis moaned. "I don't need this. I surely don't need to face off with Smoke—by God—Jensen."

"You can always leave. Without the take from the safe, of course."

"Jensen, you still packin' a badge?"

"I am."

"Won't do you any good here in Kansas," Travis goaded, hoping he was right.

He was wrong. "Deputy United States Marshal," Smoke informed him. "I reckon it works here as good as in Colorado."

"Aw, hell, Jensen. We're good as goners as it is. Might as well come out."

"You do that. I'll be waiting," Smoke invited.

Travis motioned to the two unwounded men with him that he wanted them ready. They nodded silently, unseen by Smoke Jensen. Then Travis rose from behind the mail sorting frame and rushed the door, six-gun blazing.

Smoke Jensen shot him in the hip. Travis spun, stumbled, then swung back from his waist and fired at Smoke. A second round punched into the exposed belly of Travis. He doubled over as his underlings rushed past.

From behind Smoke came the roar of Quincannon's revolver. One of the attacking outlaws cried out and pitched through the opening. He landed on his head. Smoke could hear the dry stick crack of the bones in the wounded man's neck. The other loomed over him and a bullet cut a hot wind past Smoke's head a moment before he returned fire.

An expression of sheer surprise lighted the face of the man Smoke shot. He remained upright, made a desperate effort to recock his Colt, and then keeled over to one side and out of sight in the express car.

"I ain't armed," came a cry from the man Smoke had wounded earlier. "I'm comin' out. I'll crawl on my belly."

"Good enough," Smoke advised him. "Make it slow." He turned to Liam Quincannon. "We'll secure this one and head for the train. You can be sure there's a few of them looting the passengers."

"Right ye are, Smoke." Quincannon swung around at the rumble of fast hooves, his expression washing to one of gloomy resignation. "B'God, they're some of 'em comin' back."

6

Six of the Waldron gang had recovered their horses and now rode at a gallop back to the train. Laying along the necks of their mounts, they fired shots at the strangers who stood outside the express car. They risked no harm to any of their own, for one of the men they shot at wore the uniform of a conductor for the Atchison, Topeka, and Santa Fe railroad.

A spurt of smoke came from the weapon in the conductor's hand and one horse let out a wild whinny when the slug cut through the tip of its ear. The bullet did greater harm to the rider as it entered the top of his shoulder and splintered the collarbone. Pink froth formed on his lips as the damage it had done took effect.

Before they had closed half the distance, he sagged and fell from his mount, one lung filled with blood. The other five reined up short when the other intruder opened up. Three rounds from Smoke Jensen emptied three saddles. A single bandit remained when Liam Quincannon took aim on the hapless man's chest. Wisely he threw up his hands, sixgun held between thumb and forefinger.

Behind him, one of the wounded came to his knees and threw a shot at the big hombre in the expensive suit coat. His slug snapped the hat from Smoke Jensen's head. It didn't effect his aim any, which his assailant found out a split second later as hot liquid fire exploded in his chest. The lights went out for him and he died without ever knowing who had shot him.

"We had better find out where the rest are on the train," Smoke prodded, as he reloaded his .45 Frontier.

"Right ye are, Smoke. I'll tell the engineer to put her in reverse once we get aboard. That should give us a hair's edge on them spalpeen bastids."

Laughing, Smoke Jensen trotted along the stalled cars toward the last in line. Liam soon joined him and the chuffiing engine hissed to life. The drivers spun as Smoke mounted the steps to the last Pullman. Liam Quincannon came behind and paused long enough to give the hand signal to go to full reverse.

Space between cars compressed as the twenty-eight-ton locomotive began to overcome inertia. Wheels turned smoothly in the tracks and slowly the train rolled backward. Inside the Pullman, anxious faces greeted them with new apprehension.

"We've already been robbed," a pinch-faced woman accused. "We've nothing more to give you." Then she saw Liam Quincannon over Smoke Jensen's shoulder and her jaw sagged. "Oh, I'm so sorry. I thought, we thought, you were more of them."

"They went there," a small boy announced, a finger pointed to the rear door.

"Hush, Billy," his mother scolded. "We don't want any more trouble."

Smoke Jensen cut his eyes over his shoulder. "What do you think, Liam?"

"No sense in blunderin' right into them, I says."

"Agreed. I think I'll take to the rooftops again. You back me up from the vestibule once it's cleared."

"Denver and Rio Grande." Buck Waldron read into the initials inscribed above the door of the private car. "Well, boys, I wonder if that old fart himself is in here."

"I thought *this* was the Santa Fe," Rucker remarked doubtfully.

"It is. They're haulin' ol' Colonel Drew along as a courtesy," Waldron explained. "If that's so, we can make us a passel more money selling his carcass back to his railroad."

"Door's locked," Dorne announced. "Should I shoot it off?"

"No. Rich folks are more careful of their hides. Might be we can talk 'em into openin' it for us," Buck Waldron suggested.

Fitting action to his pronouncement, Waldron stepped forward and banged on the glass of the door. "Open up in there!" he bellowed. "You hear me? Open up right now!"

Inside, a thoroughly demoralized Thomas Henning wrung his hands and stared along the passageway toward the front of the car. The walls of the compartments and kitchen partly obscured the glass panel. He could not be certain how many outlaws had clustered there. All he knew for sure was that they were in desperate trouble. Nervously he slid his green gaze over onto the woman he now had doubts was indeed related to John Reynolds.

How could she lower herself enough even to touch a gun, let alone carry one in her purse? His ingrained loathing for any weapons blinded him to the fact that their present circumstances might well account for it. Why, any civilized person would simply give the brutes what they wanted and let them be on their way.

"God damn it, open this door!" Waldron roared.

Thomas Henning turned in agitation. "Well, what do you propose to do?" he asked of Sally Jensen.

"Exactly what Smoke said to do. We stay here, safe behind that door," Sally answered calmly. "Although it is too late for you to lock yourselves in your compartment. They'd see you going there and it wouldn't buy us anything."

"Then I think the reasonable thing to do is open up and let them in before they get any angrier," Thomas offered primly.

"Thomas, I don't know how it's done where you come from," Sally began patiently. "But out here, when a person lies down and rolls on his back, he's likely to be kicked in the belly."

Blanching, Thomas swallowed hard. "That's crudely put, but colorful. What has it to do with our present situation?"

"Everything," Sally snapped, her patience exhausted.

Right then the car gave a lurch and began to roll backward. From the vestibule came another furious shout. "Open up or we'll kill everyone in there."

Priscilla clutched at her husband's arm, which she noticed had developed a marked tremble. Her lips took on the shape of her disillusionment. She cut her eyes to Sally Jensen. "Do they mean it?"

"Possibly," Sally answered curtly. "All the more reason we delay them as long as possible. It wasn't any outlaw started up the train. Smoke will be here soon," she advised confidently.

"It won't do us any good," Thomas blurted in an anguished wail. He broke free of his wife and all but trotted along the passageway toward the door. Sally started after him, then held back. Maybe she should shoot the little coward . . . One look at the stricken face of Priscilla Henning disabused her of that idea.

"Come on, Priss. We have some planning to do, and some playacting."

In the parlor section of the private car, Sally explained what she intended while she hid her Colt Lightning between the cushions of a plush loveseat. Only seconds later, a jumble of voices overrode the frightened bleat of Thomas Henning. Five hard-faced, scowling outlaws advanced along the narrow corridor toward where the women waited. The one in the lead roughly shoved Thomas along ahead of himself.

"We—ell, what do we have here?" the big burly, barrel-chested thug pushing Thomas drawled when they entered the parlor area and took in the two lovely women.

"Who are you?" Sally Jensen demanded coldly.

"More to the point, sister, who are you?" Buck Waldron asked through a leer.

"Why, I'm . . . Sally, Miss Priscilla's maid."

Astonishingly, Waldron touched fingertips to the brim of his hat in polite acknowledgment. "Please to make your acquaintance, Sally." His eyes narrowed. "Who's Miss Priscilla?"

"She . . ." Sally began, to be cut off by Priscilla.

"That's all right, Sally. I can answer for myself. I am Priscilla Henning. That's my husband you were shoving around, you lout." For the first, time since he had betrayed them by opening the door, Priscilla got a look at Thomas. His hair was mussed and his eyes were wild. A thin line of blood ran down from a split lip. "What have you done to him?" she demanded hotly.

Waldron produced a wicked chuckle. "We didn't like the way he took his sweet time opening the door. So Lovell here gave him a lesson in manners."

"You brute!" Priscilla screeched, and made to rake Waldron's face with her long nails.

"No, Miss Priscilla," Sally cautioned firmly. "It would only get you hurt also."

"You've got some smarts, Miss Sally," Waldron offered.

While Priscilla Henning recovered her demeanor, Sally bored hot blue eyes into Waldron. "You still haven't told us your names. With those masks on, we don't know a thing about you."

Rucker and Dorne snickered. "That's the idea, Sally-gal," Rucker said, as though informing her of something she did not know.

"Don't see any harm in it, boys," Waldron proclaimed. "M'name's Buck Waldron. This is part of my gang. We rob trains for a living."

"How odd," Priscilla gave him. "Why do you rob trains?"

Buck Waldron shrugged. "Because they're where the money is."

Wincing at his atrocious grammar, Priscilla attempted to

ignore the lewd stares of the other four. Sally Jensen tried again to bait Buck Waldron.

"I'm sure it takes men of abounding courage to menace two helpless young women."

Buck scratched behind one ear. "Sally, you don't talk like a maid. You sound more like someone used to giving a maid orders."

Sally lowered her eyes and backed off. She had gone too far, she realized. "I suppose that after a number of years listening to my mistress's orders, I've taken some of her ways of speaking."

"There's somethin' rotten about people who have servants," Waldron declared in a rare philosophical moment. "Enough of this." He dismissed their testy confrontation. "Tell us where the valuables are kept and we'll help ourselves."

"There's nothing, really," Sally said, as she moved casually to the loveseat where she had concealed the .38 Colt.

"People like your 'mistress'"—Waldron sneered the word Sally had used—"don't travel without a lot of fussy stuff. That much I know. So, Sally-gal, be real good and tell us."

Sally held her breath as she sank into the cushion. She sighed it out before answering, indicating her surrender. "Anything you might want can be found in their compartment."

"Sally!" Priscilla cried in alarm at her newfound friend's betrayal.

"Number Four," Sally concluded, without a blink of an eye.

Silently, Sally prayed that Priscilla would not let relief flood over her face and give away the ruse. Surely, now that the train ran backward, Smoke would be here soon, she told herself. She tensed herself, primed for the right moment to bring her Lightning into play.

"Dorne, go get it," Waldron commanded.

"I—ah—I got somethin' else in mind, Buck. Here's a tasty young thing just beggin' to be loved proper. Stands to reason this sorry excuse of a husband can't satisfy her."

"And you figure you can?" Waldron taunted.

"I *know* I can," Dorne riposted hotly. "Gimme a chance and I'll prove it."

Buck Waldron considered that a moment. "Lovell, go fetch the jewels and cash. Go ahead, Dorne, have your try."

"No!" Thomas Henning shouted suddenly, the by-play between the robbers registering on his dulled mind at last. He leaped to his feet and rushed at the one called Dorne.

Grinning, Dorne waited until the slightly built Thomas closed in to a suitable distance. Then he unloaded a hard-knuckled right uppercut that came out of the cellar. It closed Thomas's rage-distorted mouth with a loud clop. The handsome young fashion plate stopped his charge in mid-stride as his head snapped back and his longish light brown hair swayed alarmingly. His green eyes rolled up in their sockets. A terrified scream came from Priscilla.

Thomas uttered a soft sigh and did a pratfall on the floor of the coach. Dorne turned away from him and started for Priscilla. Rucker left his place beside the bar and kicked Thomas in the chest to knock him flat. He twisted the waxed ends of his mustache on the face he revealed by removing his bandana and started in Sally's direction.

"I think I'll try a sample of sweet little Sally here," he advised through a leer.

Smoke Jensen heard a terrified wail from inside the car on which he lay. Cautiously he worked his way to the dome of the skylight and peered inside. He saw the unconscious form of Thomas Henning stretched out below. Beyond, he observed the head and shoulders of a man nearly as big as himself, his back turned toward Smoke. Faintly, he heard soft, whimpering sounds rising from a point out of sight.

Then he caught sight of Sally's dress and legs on the small loveseat near a window on the right side. That decided him. Smoke moved with all the speed he could and still remain silent. When he reached the proper position, he hooked his boot toes over a protruding grab-iron and lowered himself head first, arms in the lead.

Smoke popped into view, upside down, in the window nearest Sally. One man stood apart from the others in the room, his back to Smoke. The set of his shoulders indicated he waited impatiently for someone to appear out of the passageway. Smoke rotated his head and focused on two more hard cases who bent over the whimpering young Priscilla Henning. One of them fondled a breast, while the other pawed her body in obvious lust.

Then Sally saw Smoke. With effort, she kept a straight face, but winked to acknowledge him. A man started toward Sally and wiped a bandana off his face. Immediately Smoke pulled himself out of sight. He used powerful muscles developed over years of hard, demanding labor to handwalk back up the side of the car. When he was able, he grabbed onto a protrusion and pushed himself upright.

Swaying precariously, Smoke Jensen righted himself and got his boots under him. Stealthily he hastened to the place of his next planned appearance.

Rucker stepped over the prostrate form of Thomas Henning and advanced on Sally. Banning joined him and had snatched her left forearm when a shadow filled the largely glassed portion of the door to the observation platform. He looked up with a startled expression when it slammed open.

"Let go!" Smoke Jensen commanded with the voice of doom.

In the same second, Sally Jensen yanked her hand from the space between the cushion and the arm of the loveseat. She took quick aim with the .38 Colt Lightning and squeezed the double, action trigger. The Long Colt cartridge, far superior to the .38 Smith and Wesson, held plenty of punch for the 142-grain, round-nosed slug that splatted into Rucker's chest and punched through his heart.

At the sound of the shot, Buck Waldron spun around in

time to see his most trusted gun hawk bend forward as though making a courtly bow to the attractive woman beyond him. He saw the powder smoke rising between the two a moment before Banning reacted.

Smoke Jensen had not anticipated the shot from Sally at that particular point, though he did accurately gauge who would be first to recover. His own .45 Colt sounded loudly in the confined space of the parlor. Banning jolted from the impact, but continued to raise his six-gun. He got off a round that burned a painful swath along the outside point of Smoke's shoulder.

He still tried to cock his weapon when Smoke Jensen sent him off to join Rucker with a swift, sure safety shot right between the eyes. Recocking, he pivoted and put a round through the elbow of a slow-moving Dorne, who had turned from his lewd fondling of Priscilla Henning.

Dorne howled and his shotgun went flying. Buck Waldron blinked at the incredible speed and accuracy and belatedly made his move.

His hand halted its downward thrust when Sally Jensen swung the muzzle of her deadly Lightning to cover him. "Uh-uh," she grunted tersely.

Smoke Jensen had advanced two steps into the car by then and put another round into Dorne's belly as the robber went for a holdout gun in the small of his back. Reflex powered Dorne's legs as he did a backward leap that cleared the chair on which Priscilla sat. She let out a squeal of alarm.

With the odds rapidly diminishing, Smoke centered his muzzle on Miller, the other outlaw who sought to have his way with the bride. Priscilla's eyes widened as she took in the deadly steel glint in Smoke's eyes. She raised a hand as though to intercede for her attacker. At the same moment, Miller made a desperate try for his Colt.

Hot lead spat from the muzzle of Smoke's .45. It pinwheeled the tough, rangey bandit, who absorbed the impact with a grunt and a blink. He hauled his iron clear of leather and fired in haste. His slug dug a hole in the flooring, two inches from Thomas Henning's head.

Quickly Miller adjusted his aim as Smoke Jensen shot him again. For some reason it grew unusually dark for mid-morning. Miller felt overwhelmingly tired; he wanted to find a place for a nice snooze. To those watching, he sagged, reeled three steps, and dropped to his knees. Smoke turned his attention back to Buck Waldron.

In a crazed moment of desperation, Waldron tried his luck anyway. He cleared leather and swung his upper body at the hips to line up on Smoke Jensen, who had cast a quick glance over one shoulder at the vanquished Miller. The hammer came back noisily and Buck Waldron produced a nasty leer of triumph.

7

Sally's second shot took Waldron in the upper flare of his hip bone. He howled in agony and completed his draw. Sally shot again and missed. Then Smoke's Peacemaker boomed a third time.

Buck Waldron's .45 made a dull thud when it hit the Oriental carpeting of the parlor section. Eyes wide; the pupils already rolling upward, he swayed on his feet, an expression of curious disbelief on his face as he idly reached up to cover the hole in his chest.

Incredibly, Miller summoned reserves in the elapsed time to try for Smoke Jensen's back, now turned toward him. Another loud roar came from the door to the observation platform. Liam Quincannon stood, spread-legged, in the doorframe and cocked his weapon again, in case of need. He had none he saw as his slug struck Miller's upper lip, directly under his nose; and hastened him off to whatever eternity held for his likes.

"What the hell!" Lovell blurted, as he exited from the compartment shared by Smoke and Sally, his arms full of baubles.

He dropped them at once, as Buck Waldron sank to his knees. Never a slouch at hauling out iron, Lovell managed to clear leather and have his weapon pointed in the general direction of Smoke Jensen when Smoke blew the last thoughts out of Lovell's mind with a .45 bullet that shattered the back of the outlaw's skull and exited with a stream of gore. Dying, Lovell triggered a round that popped a neat hole in the skylight dome before he fell, face-first, on the floor.

"I could have handled it," Sally spoke with a mock pout.

"Of course you could, darling," Smoke answered dryly.

Thomas Henning had regained consciousness in time to stare groggily as Smoke Jensen finished off Lovell. His dry-throated reaction came across gummy lips. "My lord, that's barbaric, it's . . . inhuman. How could you know the man didn't intend to surrender?"

Smoke Jensen regarded him like a specimen from under a rock. "If he did, he picked a hell of a strange way to go about it."

Then Thomas saw the still-smoking revolver in Sally's hand. "You didn't . . . use that, did you?" he gulped in horror.

Sally nodded affirmatively. "Killed one, wounded another," she tallied her score.

Thomas Henning swallowed with difficulty and looked around him at the corpses and the welter of blood, bone, and tissue. "I think . . . I'm going . . . to be sick," he gulped out as he struggled to rise. His face ashen, he made an unsteady course through the parlor section and out onto the observation platform, where he bent over the safety rail and offered up his breakfast.

Liam Quincannon looked uncertainly from the young man he'd been paid handsomely to protect to Smoke Jensen. Smoke nodded to the eastern dandy, who continued to void the contents of his gut.

"No stomach for a fight, I'd say," Smoke observed.

Sally groaned and Liam eyed him with twinkling amusement. "Me mither told me never to trust a man who made bad puns."

"What did she say about men who made *good* puns?" Smoke asked, enjoying the exchange as tension eased out of him.

"Ah, the sainted dear," Liam exclaimed. "She said never to trust them, either."

He and Smoke began to laugh, to be interrupted by hysterical sobs from Priscilla Henning, who still sat between the corpses of the two men who had been molesting her. Smoke Jensen started her way when Thomas Henning recovered himself and brushed past him with a petulent snarl.

"Don't touch her, you depraved animal."

New anger kindled in Smoke's deep chest. This yellow-bellied punk had more than his share of nerve when the shooting was over. "Well, pardon the hell out of me, asshole," Smoke sent after him.

Typical of his mouthy ilk, Thomas cringed, then ignored him. "I'm right here, darling. Let me help you out of this . . . this charnel house."

"Don't touch me, you spineless poltroon!" Priscilla wailed, her voice roughened by disgust, rather than the horror of her experience.

"But, dear one . . ." Thomas implored, as he recoiled in shock.

"If you had been man enough to accept a gun and fight like you should, Sally and I would never had been subjected to such degrading attentions."

"But . . . but, you know how I *hate* those terribly wicked things," Thomas offered ineffectually in a whine. "A truly civilized man is above the use of such animalistic means of settling disputes."

Scorn darkened Priscilla's tearstained face. "Sure as God made billy goats, it wasn't your high-blown ideals that saved me from a fate worse than death. It was Smoke Jensen and his 'terribly wicked' guns." She glanced at Sally, who had risen, her .38 Lightning still in hand. "And, of course, Sally and that cute little gun of hers."

Cute? Smoke thought he'd been caught in a flashback. Did every woman think like Sally about that lady's hand-cannon? He cut his eyes to his wife, who smirked like a cream-fed pussycat. Priscilla, it seemed, had only begun to warm to her topic.

Arctic ice filled her tone and her reddened eyes. "You've shown me a side of you I never suspected. Frankly, Thomas, I'm shocked and disappointed."

Wounded, Thomas made a poor choice of means to plead his case. "How can you say that? Surely you cannot advocate such wanton taking of human life? Surely those men . . . *these* men," he corrected with a weak wave at the sprawled bodies, "could have been reasoned into surrender."

Priscilla laughed at him, a harsh, bitter note. "There's not a one of them that would have meekly given up. What were Smoke and Sally to have done? Stand there babbling sweet reason to them while these sons of bitches gunned them down?"

Thomas turned an even paler shade of white. Scandalized, he blurted, *"Priscilla!* In all the time I've known you, I've never heard you use such coarse language. A legacy from your father, no doubt."

"Yes, I got it from my father. Also my shooting skills," Priscilla snapped.

Thomas appeared ready to swoon. He put a delicate hand to the area of his heart. "I can't imagine you putting your hand on one of those obscene instruments of violence."

"You can be sure that I did. And enjoyed it to the fullest. I was five when my father taught me to shoot. Mother had died the winter before and he was pushing the D & R G south toward Pueblo. He took me along. That summer I learned to ride and to shoot a gun. That year, and the next seven, were the happiest of my life."

Shocked to the depths of his most tender sensibilities, Thomas collapsed, rubber-kneed, into the nearest chair. "What have I done? I can't accept that I've married a gun-slinger. Mother—Father—they'll never understand."

Something snapped in Priscilla. Her detestation of this husband who had become a stranger turned to pitying contempt. "They won't have to," she said softly, her voice vibrant with regret at her sudden decision. "I thought I knew you. I find I do not. Thomas, no matter how much this pains me, how much it might hurt you, I am entirely serious about this. I want an annulment."

Thomas groaned wretchedly. "Please, not that. Think of your future, your reputation, if not of mine."

Priscilla studied on that for a while. Her expression lost its harshness and a sublime serenity eased the taut lines around her eyes and mouth. At last she came to her feet, head cocked to one side.

"Frankly, Thomas, I don't really give a damn."

At first, Smoke Jensen had listened to her tirade with a sense of embarrassment. When she waxed most eloquent in her defense of western custom, he began to smile. Her arrival at this unexpected conclusion set off chuckles. After Priscilla departed in haughty isolation, he laughed even louder, until the tears began to roll. For her part, Sally looked at him as though he had lost his mind, then hurried off to commiserate with Priscilla.

Liam Quincannon turned away from the meeting of crewmen and spoke to Smoke Jensen. "We have a portable key. With it we can send for a track crew to replace the ties and rails. It will take some time, I fear. The nearest gandy dancers are at the division point in Fort Hays. We'll also have to report the robbery attempt."

Smoke frowned about that. "I'd be obliged if you kept my name out of it."

"Why? Yer a famous man as it is. Another victory over the bad ones can't possibly do you any harm."

"On the contrary," Smoke countered. "It will attract unwanted attention." He considered the realities of the situation and grunted in resignation. "You'll do what you must, but I would appreciate being kept out of it."

"Devil take it, man, the law will have to know who is

responsible for saving the passengers and the express car contents. An' that was you."

"Who shot the hard cases in the cab and got the train rolling again?"

Liam grinned. "Ye have me there. I'll see what I can do."

An hour went by after Liam climbed the nearest telegraph pole, during which time the bodies of the outlaws had been removed to the express car, before a shrill hoot came from a work engine on the opposite side of the breech. The 0-4-0 locomotive rapidly grew in size and detail. A whoop of encouragement came from the train crew as the three flatcars behind the locomotive ground to a halt and two dozen burly track layers scrambled off.

Within half an hour the barricade had been broken up. The old rails were discarded, along with about a third of the ties. Muscles bulging, teams of two hefted new, creosote-fragrant wooden beams and laid them in place. Others stood by with shovels to fill around the base of each with coarse gravel. When finally the long, gleaming strips of steel rail were lowered in place by a hand-operated crane, the fish-plates bolted to them, and the spike setters pounded the last giant nail into the last tie, all hands turned to raising the ballast level to the original.

Three short shrieks of the work engine whistle signaled its backward departure to the nearest siding, where it would get off the main line to let the express flash past. Although the repair procedure held little interest for Smoke Jensen, he had absorbed himself in it, rather than keep company with the moping Thomas Henning. When the passenger train got under way, he returned to the private car to find a much revived Thomas seated in the dining room, industriously polishing off a generous portion of meatloaf. To Smoke, the crusty brown slices smelled suspiciously of lamb, a meat he generally avoided.

Thomas looked up and interrupted his chewing. "Lee Fong tells me this is antelope. I've never had it before. Actually it's quite delicious."

Smoke wondered if Thomas was trying over-hard to compensate for his wife's earlier outburst, or had he actually managed to forget the tongue-lashing? Smoke sniffed the air again. "I thought at first it might be lamb. Now I can tell that it's goat."

"What?" Thomas's expression of gastronomic pleasure altered subtly to one of incredulous alarm.

"Antelope are in the goat family. They're sort of overgrown, wild goats." Smoke took secret pleasure in the shift in Thomas's features that betrayed the images of revulsion that must be dancing in the young fop's head. "But then, deer are also related, and every classy restaurant back East features medallions of venison. I think I'll find Sally and we'll join you."

"Th—there's plenty," Thomas invited in a sickly mutter.

Once past the sidetracked work train, the express took slightly less than an hour, at full throttle, to reach Fort Hays. Smoke Jensen experienced the familiar unease even before he saw the swarm of gawkers, local journalists, and a tight knot of lawmen who waited on the platform. Someone had wasted no time in passing the word about the robbery attempt.

It wouldn't be the first time some politically ambitious sheriff leaked information to the newspapers in order to get his name on the front page, Smoke reasoned resignedly. Perhaps Liam Quincannon had kept his name out of it as promised. Or the private car of Colonel Drew of the D & R G would serve as a bather between them and the inquiries of the scribblers and law alike.

Smoke's hopes were dashed when a deputy U. S. Marshal, the sheriff, and two of his deputies became the first to open the safety chain and step onto the observation platform. They entered the car full of urgency, then removed their hats in deference to the two ladies.

"We understand that one of the passengers in this car was instrumental in foiling the robbery," the marshal began peremptorily.

Smoke sighed and quickly cut his eyes to Sally, imploring

her to remain silent. He rose from his chair. "I'm the man you are looking for."

"And who might you be?" the sheriff pushed in.

"My name's Smoke Jensen."

Jaws dropped among the deputies. The sheriff's face rivaled a beet and he spluttered as he spoke. "By God, what's to say you didn't engineer this whole robbery? I know you, Jensen," he hastened on. "Know all about your outlaw connections, gunfighter ways, and so on."

"No, you don't Sheriff." Smoke answered the old accusations tiredly. "What you 'know' you got from reading dime novels and some spurious wanted posters put out by my enemies. And even if the bullshit—er, excuse me, ladies—was true, do you think I would plan a train robbery and bring along a newlywed couple and my own wife?" He made a curt gesture with one big, square-palmed hand to include Sally and the Hennings.

Pasting a sneer on fleshy lips to go with his words, the sheriff replied, "I wouldn't put it past you."

"Let me handle this, Alf," the marshal put in. "I think some introductions are in order. I'm Deputy Marshal Dale Walker, from the U.S. Marshal's office in Dodge. This is Sheriff Alf Carter of Ellis County." He gave Smoke a "now it's your turn" look.

"May I present Mr. and Mrs. Thomas Henning. Priscilla Henning is the daughter of Colonel Drew of the Denver and Rio Grande Railroad. And this is my wife, Sally. This is the colonel's car, which he put at our disposal for a journey east. The Hennings are starting out on their honeymoon."

Sheepishness replaced the skepticism on the face of Sheriff Carter. Logic belatedly told him that robber baron he might be, but Colonel Drew did not associate with people who held up trains, even as a pastime. And he didn't lend that sort his private car. Still, he could not back down too easily. It would make him look bad.

"If you don't mind," Carter cut in, "we'll have to verify that with Colonel Drew."

Priscilla came out of her chair. If Thomas showed tendencies to be timid, she had enough boldness for them both. "How dare you, you provincial buffoon! *I* certainly mind, and so will my father, if you are stupid enough to disturb him for something as inconsequential as this."

Face flushed even darker, Sheriff Carter made a spluttering disavowal and beat a hasty path for the door, trailed by his deputies. Marshal Dale Walker made apologies for the local law and then led Smoke Jensen through a carefully detailed description of the robbery attempt. When it had ended, he roused himself from a comfortable wing chair and shook Smoke's hand.

"Somehow I feel I've met a piece of history. I doubt the other passengers are aware how fortunate they were that you happened to be on the train. Now," Walker went on in a changed tone, as he nodded toward the crowd that had grown on the rear platform, "I'm afraid I must leave you to the tender mercies of the local press. I'll have a talk with the conductor—Liam Quincannon, you said?"

"Yes. He did more than his share in breaking it up," Smoke added his compliment to the fiery Irishman.

"I'm sure he did," Walker agreed, and excused himself again.

He had shouldered his way only through the first line of journalists when the tide broke and they spilled into the parlor section of the car. Their pencils poised to scribble on notepads, they vied to outshout each other with a cascade of questions.

"Where are the bodies?"

"How many did you kill, Smoke?"

"Did they have their way with you ladies?" one oily-haired scribbler asked with a nasty, anticipatory leer.

"Get your mind out of the gutter and your butt off this train," Sally Jensen barked, surprised at the crudeness of her words and their delivery.

"Say, Sister . . ." the smutmonger drawled, then blinked at the bulge in her purse that outlined the cylinder and barrel

of her Colt Lightning. That convinced him it would be wise
to ignore her. He turned to Priscilla. "What about you? Did
those outlaws manage to defile you?"

His sneering innuendo struck some heretofore unsus-
pected chord in Thomas Henning. He rose and spoke in icy
fury. "If you don't do as the lady said, I'll kick your butt so
hard you'll be wearing your asshole for a fur collar."

"Thomas? *Tommy?*" Priscilla spoke wonderingly to her
husband.

"Excuse yourself and go to our room, dear. I'll show this
guttersnipe out," Thomas replied to her.

Smoke Jensen couldn't quite believe it. Thomas Henning
had sniveled and whimpered in the presence of real danger, but
right now he had stood up for his wife's honor as any man
would. Maybe the sand was there, all right, only covered by too
many layers of eastern-upbringing mud. His own temper inflamed by the insensitivity and pushiness of the press, Smoke
turned a hot, gray gaze on the small, aggressive reporter who
shoved his cigar-chomping face up close to Smoke's chest.

"You're the notorious Smoke Jensen, right? How many does
this make? Four, five hundred innocent men you've killed?"

Smoke Jensen took him by the front of his soiled, once-
white shirt and lifted him clear of the floor. When they came
face-to-face, he spoke in a low, menacing rumble. "Listen,
you little pile of dog crap, I've never killed an innocent man.
That's for starters." The diminutive journalist gulped and
tried to sputter a clever retort. Smoke cut him off. "Further,
I don't keep records. I quit counting after the fourth one. If
I'm such a big, bad hombre, you'd be wise to keep a hard
rein on that snotty tongue of yours so you don't get it ripped
out by the roots. I can give you a shot-by-shot account of the
fight down the line today, if that's what you want."

Rapidly nodding in nervous jerks, the offensive reporter
bit through his cigar. It left a small gray-black smudge on his
shirtfront as it fell and bounced to the bare floorboards. Smoke
released him and he made swift, fussy adjustments to his coat.

"That would be quite satisfactory—er—Mr. Jensen."

"Well," Smoke began. "I shot the first one between the eyes, blew most of his brains out the back of his head. They sprayed everywhere," he added with a wicked twinkle in his eyes.

For the next three minutes he invented the most chilling, gory details be could imagine. It had the desired effect. First one, then another of the offensive journalists gave in to their more tender sensibilities. By the time he launched into a graphic description of how the outlaws in the express car met their end, three more with weak stomachs had scurried away. With the departure of the last, Smoke laughed uproariously. Sally looked at him with real concern.

"Smoke, do you know what you've done? They'll print every word you said, along with self-righteous condemnation of such 'barbarity.'"

"To hell with them. Let them print whatever they want. They would anyway, even if I'd refused to tell them a thing. Only theirs would be a lot bloodier than mine.

"I hope all this won't take much longer," Smoke changed the subject. "I'm eager to get to Kansas City, so we can part company with our lovebirds."

"I . . . wonder . . ." Sally began. "Perhaps they will patch it up before then. Thomas did something a while ago that offered promise."

"I know, I saw it. Will you do your best to make it happen? Because, barring another train robbery, that's the only problem we'll have from now on."

Smoke Jensen could not have been more wrong.

8

Thick, red velvet drapes protected diners in the Cattle-
men's Club wing of Chicago's Livestock Exchange from the
prying eyes of the hoi-polloi outside. At a small, round table
in a turretlike section of the eatery, Phineas Lathrop sat with
Arnold Cabbott. Lathrop scanned the pages of the *Chicago
Tribune*. After he'd made a cursory reading of the headline
story, another item caught his attention. He read it carefully,
a frown growing with each line. Their waiter brought a refill
of their drinks and left silently, well accustomed to the vag-
aries and relaxed attitudes of these moguls of the livestock
trade. When Lathrop finished the article, he slammed the
paper onto the table with enough violence to spill bourbon
from both glasses.

"Damn that man!" he exploded.

Heads turned at several nearby tables and Arnold Cabbott
leaned forward to urge a more discreet demeanor. "What we
don't need is to draw attention to ourselves. I gather something in the paper upset you?" he added, then sipped from
his old-fashioned.

"'Upset' is a mild term for what I feel," Lathrop snapped
back.

"The man you refer to is, no doubt, Smoke Jensen?" Cabbott prompted.

"Precisely, Arnold. The *Tribune* is full of his latest exploits."

Arnold Cabbott smiled. "If he's up to his old ways again in Colorado, it should make it easier for Tanner, right?"

"No. Jensen is on the move. I don't know where, but he's headed east. He was on a train that some gang led by a Buck Waldron tried to rob. I say 'tried' because Smoke Jensen took a hand. In fact, he took every trick from then on. The paper claims he killed twenty-three single-handedly. I'd believe ten; he's done that before. The point is, Tanner is doing us no good out in Colorado. I'm going to telegraph him and tell him to forget Jensen. He's to go back to helping Buford Early intimidate holdouts over Utah way."

"What are you going to do about Smoke Jensen?" Arnold asked.

"For the time being, nothing. According to the report in the paper, he'll be here in two days. We're scheduled to leave for New York tonight. If Middleton hadn't made it appear so vital, we could stay and handle it ourselves. If only I knew where Jensen was headed."

Food was brought. Uncharacteristically, Phineas Lathrop paid it little attention. When they had eaten their fill, Lathrop downed a last glass of wine and rose from the table. "Take care of this, will you, Arnold? I'll go along and telegraph Tanner. I'm also sending one to Sean O'Boyle. Perhaps his presence will have a calming effect on Victor Middleton."

Cabbott raised an eyebrow. "Is he needed so early?"

"If we expect to accomplish our goals on time, he is. If for no other reason than that he and his bully-boys can intimidate Middleton and his New York crowd into cooperation. Take your time, finish off. It's all quite good, only that thinking about Smoke Jensen has spoiled my appetite."

Lathrop stopped in the small telegraph office attached to the stockyard sales office. He sent off a terse demand that Wade Tanner quit chasing shadows and do something productive by helping Buford Early. Then he addressed an even shorter message to Sean O'Boyle. It contained a single line: "Meet us in New York with some of your men when our train arrives Grand Central Station, three days from now, at one P.M."

With those matters accomplished, Phineas Lathrop departed for their hotel to pack his luggage and be ready to catch the New York Central Daylight at five that evening. All the while, the news about Smoke Jensen kept nagging him.

After the circus in Hays, Smoke Jensen calmed down enough to enjoy the trip somewhat. Beyond Salina, Kansas, on the long run to Topeka and Kansas City, Sally spent patient, though tedious, hours in the Henning compartment talking earnestly with Priscilla. Thomas Henning had moved into the first cubicle, exiled by his estranged wife. For reasons Smoke could not understand, Sally took it on herself to reconcile the unhappy couple.

The first Smoke knew of her progress came when Sally emerged one night for a late supper. She had a soft smile on her face, rather than a downturned mouth and the vertical furrow between her brows. After Jenkins had served them and retired, Smoke gained more assurance from the way Sally dug into her pan-fried catfish. Always a hearty eater, Sally had an appetite this night that brought a smile to his lips.

"I gather you are gaining ground," he remarked offhandedly.

Sally chewed and swallowed a forkful of potatoes and onions and washed it down with a sip of water. "A little," she replied sparingly. "They're such a nice couple, Smoke. It would be a shame if Priss persists in her intentions."

Smoke stopped eating. "She is serious about leaving him?"

Sally considered her words a moment. "Not so much as at first. But she's stubborn, and quite used to having her way."

"Can she get their marriage dissolved?" Smoke asked.

He had never had occasion to learn about such proceedings. With Sally, their vows had meant they'd be together forever.

"I'm not certain," Sally answered candidly. "Although, with enough money and influence . . . and her father certainly has that, it can be arranged." She looked at him pointedly. "Have you spoken to Thomas about it?"

"Not really. I'm afraid we don't have a lot in common," her husband answered.

"Of course you do. You're both men," Sally retorted archly.

"We'll have to leave the persuading up to you. Maybe time will work it out."

Beyond Topeka, Smoke had reason to recall that conversation. A smirking Sally led Priscilla Henning out of the compartment to sit beside Thomas at the dinner table. The young bride hardly spoke, but she did respond to an effort on his part to make amends.

"I behaved wretchedly toward you," he began tentatively.

Sally cut her eyes to Smoke, her expression one of questioning. Smoke shrugged and sliced another morsel of the medium-rare chateaubriand on his plate. Priss wore a face of surprise.

"I should never have said the things I did," Thomas offered.

"If you—if you believe something, you should stand up for your beliefs," Priscilla responded.

Anguish cut across the worried face of Thomas. "Well, you see . . . I'm not entirely sure I do believe all that. I'm not certain I wasn't just parroting things I learned at home, and at Harvard."

Oh, Lord, Harvard, Smoke thought. *Spare us that.* Thomas correctly read the expression on the big gunfighter's face.

"They have some professors there who are opposed to this entire westward movement. There's a poem they like to quote, it starts, 'Lo! The noble redman.'"

Smoke made a face of disgust. "I've heard it."

"They say you westerners are destroying the land, the

animals, the last noble savage race. And that it is the fault of guns that it is happening."

Smoke Jensen blinked, then blurted without thinking, "Do you think we should go back to using spears and stone clubs?"

"That's not the point. They contend that we don't belong out here," Thomas answered painfully.

"*They* don't belong out here, that's one thing for certain," Smoke declared flatly "Nor their ideas."

"That's silly, Thomas," Priscilla prodded her husband.

"Yes, yes it is. At least I'm beginning to think so." To Smoke, he offered, "We owe you our lives. Priss was right. if it hadn't been for you and your guns . . ." Thomas shrugged and raised his hands plams up in surrender.

"I think there's some hope here." Sally pronounced her judgment.

Later that night, the young couple patched up their quarrel on the observation platform. Thomas moved back into the second compartment. And Smoke and Sally Jensen had a delightful night, doing terribly naughty things in the lower bunk of their room.

Thomas and Priscilla Henning left the train at Kansas City for a stern wheeler bound down the Missouri to the Mississippi and New Orleans. Arm in arm, they strolled down the depot platform and paused for only a moment to wave a farewell to Smoke and Sally Jensen. Priscilla gazed adoringly up at her husband as the steam whistle shrilled and the train pulled out, headed across Missouri and on north to Chicago.

"That ended nicely, I thought," Sally remarked to Smoke, as they stood on the observation platform later that night.

A full moon lit the prairie and cast silver light on her face as Smoke bent to kiss her gently on one cheek. "And now we have the car all to ourselves," he murmured.

Sally gave him an expression of mock disapproval. "Is that all you can say?"

"Not at all. Henning has a lot of changing to do if he's going to last with that girl. They are a nice couple," Smoke declared, then started to add more when Sally cut him off.

"I'm glad to hear you say that. Do you really mind so much making this visit to my family?"

"No, not really."

"You're resigned to it, is that it?"

"Sally, let's not get started on that. Think about something else."

"All right, I will." Her famous smile bloomed and her voice grew wistful as she opened a new topic. "I've never seen anyone so proud as punch over where he slept as Bobby."

Smoke nodded. "He figured he's made it through growing up to be able to sleep in the bunkhouse with the other hands. I thought the little nipper would bust when I told him. Then, when the avalanche knocked the building off its foundation, he looked so glum when I had him stay in his old room those five nights."

"Surely he realized it took time to arrange rollers and enough teams to pull the bunkhouse back in its place? It was his room in the house, or sleep outside under a tree with the other hands."

Smoke's indulgent chuckle stirred something deep in Sally's breast. "Bobby would have preferred the ground, I'm sure. He got over it quickly enough, though, when he learned he would not be going to school for the three weeks we'll be gone."

Sally produced a fleeting frown of concentration. "You're really fond of the boy, aren't you?"

"I am. He reminds me of our brood when they were his age," Smoke admitted.

"You never told me how it came to be that he wound up with you on the way to Mexico that time."

Smoke sighed. "It's not a nice story, Sal. I'd rather not go into it."

"Oh, please. Bobby never speaks of it, either. At least, nothing past that you saved his life."

Smoke shrugged and cut his eyes away from her lovely, moon-whitened face, uncomfortable at the recounting. "I saved him from a beating. I'm not sure I saved his life."

"How did that come about?"

"I killed his stepfather," Smoke said dully.

Sally's eyes went round and wide. "However did that happen?"

"When I came upon them, the stepfather had beaten Bobby's pony to its knees," Smoke began. In a lifeless voice, he recounted the confrontation with Rupe Connors, their fight, and how Connors had come at him with a pitchfork. "I heard him running across the corral, but Bobby's shout of alarm helped me move in time. I shot him. Then I told him my name. He died knowing for the first time in his life that he had made a big mistake."

"That's awful," Sally declared. She had thought nothing of the outlaw she had killed only two days ago, yet this unvarnished tale touched her deeply as that never could.

Smoke nodded and held her closer. "You know the rest. Bobby has no family and could not stay there alone. After a few encounters with some rockheads along the way, I sent him to you. There's something else I didn't tell you: Connors pounded on Bobby as savagely as he did that pony from the day he married the boy's mother. He also beat her so badly she died of it. For a man who abused helpless women, children, and animals, he got what he deserved."

"Yes . . . I suppose he did," Sally answered simply. "What a terrible life the boy has led. I'm so grateful I had the parents I did. It shaped the way I look at raising children. And I'm so glad you had Preacher to bring you up to be the man you are. Our children never knew how bleak life could be." She sighed, flashed a winsome smile, and changed the subject. "Ever since that shootout in Keene, my father has thought the world of you."

"I suspected that. And I hope John Reynolds hasn't turned out the whole town as a welcoming committee."

"Father is quite enthusiastic about this visit," Sally replied cautiously. "I know he gets carried away sometimes, but he's promised me that everything will be done quietly this time. Only . . . he did say something about having something planned for you."

Smoke laughed softly and kissed the top of Sally's head. "I'm afraid to ask what it might be."

"We'll find out soon enough," Sally replied vaguely, her mind already on the wonderful night that lay ahead, with them making love in the moonlight while the train rocked them gently.

Tall, stately maples and leafy American elms lined the streets of Keene, New Hampshire. Their shade fell in dappled patterns on the wide, trellis-edged porch and white clapboard front of the two-story house that belonged to John Reynolds. Inside the far-from-modest dwelling, the senior Reynolds, his son, Walter, and his son-in-law, Chris, sat at a table in the spacious dining room.

John Reynolds looked up from his study of a handbill just presented to him by an inkstained printer's helper. He nodded and passed it to Walter. "I think these will do nicely. Tell Silas he can begin printing them right away. Make it a thousand copies."

"Yes, sir," the adenoidal youth squeaked.

"'The New England Lecture Society proudly presents the *Mountain Man Philosopher of the Rockies,*'" Walter read aloud. "It sounds mighty impressive, Father. But do you think there will be enough interest to fill a hall?"

"Was there any interest the first and only time Smoke Jensen visited Keene?" John Reynolds challenged.

"How do you know he'll go along with it, sir?" Chris asked, still deferring to his father-in-law, although he was himself the father of four Reynolds grandchildren.

John smiled a soft, knowing smile. "I have an ace in the hole."

"Sally," Chris responded immediately, with a chuckle.

"Precisely. If anyone can get Smoke Jensen to take to the lecture circuit, she can. He's a wealthy man in his own right now, and no longer has need to undertake those hair-raising adventures of his. Thank God."

"Amen to that," Walter added. "Even though you stood side-by-side with him against those ruffians who invaded Keene, I know your heart wasn't in it."

John Reynolds gave his son an odd expression. "To say it like Smoke put it, I wouldn't be alive now if my heart wasn't in it. I actually enjoyed my short opportunity to employ western justice."

"Oh, dear," Chris let slip out. "What—what did the firm say?"

John Reynolds grinned broadly. "Don't you remember? Old Hargroves called me a barbarian. The younger partners actually envied me. Hargroves came around, though, about a year ago, just before he died. Said he'd begun to think lately that we could use some of that western—ah—'creative law enforcement' back here. Particularly down in Boston and New York." He snorted. "Enough of that. I want you two to go down to the newspaper office and see that the first of those flyers are put up here in Keene before the ink is dry."

After the younger men had departed, Abigale Reynolds joined her husband. Her cultured voice remained soft as she gently probed John about his plans for the lectures. When he admitted to her that Smoke knew nothing about the proposed grand tour of New England, her words took on a more chiding tone.

"Perhaps Smoke Jensen will not be too happy about this when he does learn?" she suggested.

"Well, now, Abigale," John huffed, "he'll simply have to accommodate himself to it. After all, he's a man of the world, traveled, and well educated, albeit not in formal institutions. Why, he himself informed me of that 'University of the Rockies' that the mountain men had for themselves. That's what gave me the idea. And it will do Smoke some good. Get some exposure to the people who have been reading those dreadful dime novels about him.

"This way he can dispel some of those myths that have grown up," John concluded. "Besides, the grandchildren will be coming home from Europe this summer, and they won't want to be trailed about by the wild tales of their father."

Abigale's lips compressed. "Louis Arthur is too much like his father already," she spoke her harshest criticism of one of her beloved Sally's children.

"At least he doesn't go around wearing a brace of pistols," John defended his favorite grandson.

"No," Abigale agreed. "Not around here, or in London. And certainly not *two* of them. But I've heard stories of what goes on when he visits that ranch of theirs. Absolutely bloodcurdling."

"No doubt," John said shortly, anxious to get off this subject. "It's hard to realize Sally will be here in only three more days."

"Yes. I can hardly wait. I do hope I'll be strong enough to cook all her favorite dishes."

"You'll do fine, Mother. Only, don't overdo," John cautioned.

"I sincerely pray that Smoke does not," an uneasy Abigale Reynolds replied to her husband, the last bullet-riddled visit still fresh in her mind after so many years.

9

West of Chicago, the Santa Fe KC Limited train, to which the private car had been attached, took Smoke and Sally Jensen into a dark and stormy night. With a suddeness rarely seen outside the High Lonesome, huge billows of black clouds roiled up and snuffed out the stars. For a while the still full moon tried valiantly to pierce the stygian cloak, a pale nimbus in the thinner portions of the gathering storm.

When a chill wind whipped around the corner of the observation platform, Sally shivered and drew a shawl close to her shoulders. "Why don't we go in?" Smoke suggested.

"There's certainly no more moonlight to make us romantic," Sally agreed. "I smell rain in the air."

"You're more western every day, Sal," Smoke said with a chuckle. "I think Jenkins left out that custard pie from supper," he hinted.

Sally had never seen her caged lion husband so relaxed. There had always been a tenseness about him, as though the next turn in the road, or the next tree, might reveal someone waiting to menace him. Tonight he seemed almost like her father.

A graduate of the law school at Harvard, John Reynolds had married early in his career. Sally remembered him always as a kindly, easygoing man who literally worshipped the canon of law and the image of blind justice. He had raised his children that way as well. Her experiences in the West had long since disabused her of her father's naïveté, yet she cherished his sweet, self-imposed blindness to the real evil in the world.

Not even when the brute violence of reality invaded his home in the form of Rex Davidson, Bothwell, Raycroft, and Brute Pitman did it remain in his consciousness for long. He had simply become another man for a while, a western man, with a gun in his hand, and later he admitted to enjoying immensely the long, bloody hours of fighting that followed. It made him "feel really alive," as he put it. Smiling to herself, she followed Smoke inside.

Poking in the icebox, Smoke found the pie and cut himself a large slab. A quick glance at Sally put him to carving a second, smaller piece. They stood in the narrow, cramped kitchen, eating their pilfered desert in grinning silence, enjoying the closeness of the moment. Without warning, a flash of actinic light washed through the darkened room.

Ear-splitting thunder came right on top. Smoke Jensen had a retinal imprint of a telegraph pole wreathed in flames. A sudden drumming on the metal roof above them announced the rain. Streaks of wetness blurred the view out the window. More lightning crackled and flickered, though not so close. Through it all, Smoke Jensen leaned calmly on the small-scale butcher's block and contentedly munched bites of the custard pie. At last, Sally could bear it no longer.

"I know that after all these years I shouldn't feel this way. But those damned storms terrify me."

"Long as you are not out in it, there's no way it can harm you," Smoke told her levelly.

"What if lightning strikes this car?" Sally asked, her unease mounting.

"If you're holdin' onto something metal that's attached to the car, you'd get fried like a thin-cut steak."

Sally made a ghastly expression. "My dear, you certainly have a colorful way of putting things."

"Thank you," Smoke answered dryly.

Without warning, the brakes slammed on suddenly. By the time the effect reached the private car, it propelled the remaining half of Smoke's pie off the plate to splatter on the wall next to Sally's head. The blob of custard on the tip of her nose did nothing to heighten her allure. Smoke followed his pie a split second later. He dropped the plate, which shattered into a hundred pieces, and caught himself with both hands.

Sally rebounded off the cook stove and rubbed at the painful line, across her abdomen made by the retaining rail, much like those used on shipboard. Her eyes went wide. "What is it?"

"I'll go see," Smoke told her. "I doubt it is another robbery."

"I should hope not," Sally sent after him, as he left the kitchen and started to the door to the vestibule.

Paul Drummond, the conductor on the Santa Fe KC Limited, peered forward in the poorly illuminated gloom to what had caused the engineer to throw on the brakes. Water ran at an undetermined depth over the bridge ahead. Slashing sheets of drops caused the light from the headlamp to waver and give off untrustworthy images. Drummond held a hand over the bill of his cap to shield his eyes from the horizontally driven rain. The wind that whipped them kept him from hearing the approach of the big man from the private car until he was right upon the conductor.

"What is it?" Smoke Jensen asked above the howl of the storm.

"Illinois River's out of its banks and over the bridge," Drunimond answered.

"Can we cross it?"

"I doubt it." Paul Drummond looked up at the cab where Casey O'Banyon, the engineer, and his fireman were sheltered from the tempest. "Ho! Casey! Can we get over that?"

"I don't know, Paul. We'll have to have trackwalkers go out ahead and see," came the reply. Steam hissed noisily from the relief valves on the huge cylinders.

"I'll get them on it right away. We've got a schedule to keep, and we sure don't want to have a cornfield meet with ol' Number Nine."

Smoke Jensen had been around railroad men long enough to know that a "cornfield meet" meant a head-on between two locomotives on the main line. He touched Drummond lightly on one shoulder. "Can you telegraph ahead to hold the other train at the next station?"

Drummond looked at the broad shoulders, recalled the powerful muscles bulging in the arms of the man. He occupied the private car of the president of the D & R G, so no doubt he knew something about railroading. "We can try. Line's out to the west. Lightning took out a couple of poles. I've got my portable key." Then curiosity pushed him to ask the question he had wanted to ask since the private car had been put on his train. "Are you an official with the D & R G?"

"No. Used to work for them. I'm ranching now. Horses," Smoke told him.

Drummond absorbed that, not entirely satisfied, and noted the streams of rainwater coursing down the big man's slicker. We're not doing ourselves any good standing here getting wet. I'll get a couple of brakemen on walking the trestle."

"Fine. I'll go back and reassure my wife." Smoke Jensen turned and walked away along the train.

Sally wanted to accompany him. It took a while before he convinced her to stay dry in the comfortable coach. Jenkins, Smoke noted, had awakened Lee Fong, who had started to prepare a huge pot of coffee. That would be for the crew, Smoke knew. Colonel Drew made a practice of looking out for the men loyal to him and his line.

When Smoke reached the front of the locomotive again, the engineer had dismounted from his cab and stood alongside Paul Drummond. Two half-inch ropes extended from the cowcatcher into the tunnel of light from the headlamp. At the far end, a pair of crewmen sloshed along in the swiftly moving chocolate water of the flooded river.

It was obvious to Smoke that the storm had not come upon them; rather, they had run into a huge weather front that had stalled out and continued to dump inches of rain on already sodden ground. The resultant runoff had created flash floods, not only here, but no doubt in many other places. With luck, the bridges would hold up. One of the brakemen turned and waved a lantern, signaling that the track was clear to that point.

He took another step and was suddenly swept off his feet. His partner did a crazy dance in an attempt to remain on the unstable platform of a railroad tie and reach for the other. The lantern winked out as the swift current rolled the fallen man over a second time. A wild yell, barely heard above the tumult of the storm, came from the upright crewman a moment before he lost his tenuous hold and the raging stream claimed him.

He rolled and thrashed in the water as it swept him toward the edge of the trestle. Thoroughly sodden, his partner lay against an upright of the siderail. In mounting panic, the newly doused man made frantic grabs for the crossbar of the safety barrier as he neared it. Their mistake, Smoke grasped instantly, had been in not securing themselves to the ropes they payed out as they advanced. Several of the remaining crew gathered beside Smoke Jensen. One pointed and spoke excitedly.

"Look, Luke and Barney can barely hold on. That water's fierce."

"Which ones of you will go out and bring them back?" Drummond asked.

No one answered. Uncomfortable glances passed among the train crew. Smoke Jensen made a quick assessment of the situation. If someone didn't act fast, both men would be swept down the raging river.

"I'll go, if you can get me another rope," he volunteered. Drummond gave him an odd look. "It ain't your problem, Mr. Jensen," he informed Smoke.

"I don't see it that way," Smoke snapped. "If you want a reason, say I don't want to stay out here all night in that flood water. Who knows how high it will get?"

Drummond nodded. "You've got a point." Quickly he issued orders.

Once he had the rope secured to the cowcatcher, Smoke fastened the other end around his waist. Without a backward glance, he waded out into the swirling water. Ahead of him he saw the dark outline of a small tree trunk racing along the frothy surface. Smaller flotsam spun in eddies, some of which collected against the straining bodies of the half-drowned crewmen.

Water surged around Smoke's waist when he felt the footing under him change from ballast gravel to the wooden beams of the trestle platform. A strong undertow tugged at his boots. About a third of the way out onto the bridge, the first of the brakemen, Barney, clung frantically to the siderail. Smoke plunged through the torrent toward him.

Slippery footing made for slow going. Smoke had to accurately gauge the distance from one tie to the other. Even with perfect pacing, each step proved hazardous. The current provided one benefit, he noted: with each advance, the pushing, sucking water forced him closer to the edge and the man he sought to rescue.

If only he could time it so that the sideward movement matched the forward and eased him in position where he wanted to be. He took another carefully calculated step and peered into the fuzzy gloom at the extreme edge of the headlamp beam.

White-faced, Barney clung to the railing and glanced anxiously toward the approaching figure. He broke off repeatedly to try to see into the dark upstream and judge his chances. A sudden bellow of pain came when a submurged hunk of waterlogged tree limb slammed into his ribs. Then, to his overwhelming relief, the rescuer towered over him.

"I brought your rope. Hold on while I tie it around you," Smoke Jensen told him.

With that accomplished, Smoke started out for the other man, some thirty feet beyond. Startled that the man who had come to save him now abandoned him, the first brakeman yelled after him, "What are you doing? Come back and get me out of this."

Smoke held up the loose end of the second rope. "I have to tie this around your partner, then I'll be back."

"A lot could happen in that time, mister." Sudden horror enveloped the battered, weary Barney. "For God's sake, don't leave me behind!"

Tension had drained Smoke of any patience. "Stop the damned whimpering and get ahold of yourself, man." His hot retort served well to spur the sodden man to renewed effort at survival.

One more step . . . two . . . three, four . . . the rapid current plucked at Smoke's clothing with invisible fingers. Fifteen feet more and he would be there. Ahead of him, the man's head disappeared under the rising flood. Smoke rushed a stride and nearly lost his footing.

While Smoke teetered precariously, Luke's nearly bald pate reappeared. Luke spluttered furiously and choked up a gout of water. "Help me. For God's sake, help!" he bellowed.

"Hang on. Be there in a second," Smoke called back.

From beyond the diffuse cone of light, Smoke heard a loud crack as a large branch struck the trestle. A moment later, in midstride, he felt the whole structure shudder from the impact of something against the pilings that supported the bridge platform. Barney and Luke both howled in alarm. Only inches separated Smoke from the brakeman pinned to the 4 x 4 post by the rushing water. One more step.

Smoke reached out and wound the sodden shirtfront in thick, strong fingers. Fighting the current, Smoke hoisted Luke to his feet. "Hold on to the rail," he instructed.

"Don't have to tell me twice," the walleyed Luke spluttered. His knuckles whitened from his grip on the crossrail.

In less than a minute, Smoke fitted the rope around a thick waist and tied firm knots. "Can you walk?" he asked over the roar of the water.

"My legs are numb, but I can move them," Luke told him.

"Good. I don't think I can carry you against the current. Let's go."

"Ca—can't you take Barney first?" Luke asked nervously.

"And fight my way back out here again?" Smoke snapped a rhetorical question.

Luke shrugged and made his first tentative step away from the false security of the safety rail. He swayed like a drunken man in the surge of brown water. Smoke steadied him and they made slow progress back toward the edge of the flood. A moment later, when the slack in the line was noticed, two stout crewmen began to haul on it steadily. Another pair began to tug on Luke's rope. It helped, Smoke noted at once.

He signaled for a pause when he reached Barney. "Hold tight, I'll be back when I have your partner on solid ground."

"If you don't mind, I'd like to come with you now," Barney said with quiet urgency.

"Not enough men to haul on your line and ours, too." Smoke rejected the idea. "You'd only get swept off your feet again."

Smoke started off at once. The water had risen to his chest now, over a part of the track that should be in a shallower condition. No sign of a cresting, he thought with growing concern. A few more steps should see them off the trestle. Smoke sensed the fury of the flood draining his stamina. Would he be able to go back for the other brakeman? He'd see when he got this one to safety; he dismissed the worry.

Gravel gave under the sole of his boot. What should have been reassuring only concerned him more. The water level had not yet dropped. He felt less surge from the current, though, which helped. Beside him, Luke made more confident strides. Ten feet closer to the cowcatcher of the locomotive and the swirling surface dropped dramatically to mid-stomach, then to his waist, and then was knee-deep. Smoke breathed easily for the first time since he'd come forward to see the river racing over the trestle.

"One more to go," Smoke told Drummond as he and Luke stumbled into the welcome of warm, dry blankets.

"You can't go out there again," Drummond protested. "We can pull him in from here."

"And risk drowning him?" Smoke retorted. "Give me a minute to catch up, and I'll head back."

"A little nip of brandy to warm you?" Drummond suggested.

"That would help," Smoke allowed. He took the offered flask and drank deeply. Then, without another word, he stood and strode off into the rampaging torrent.

Smoke returned in half the time. Barney had fared better than Luke in his tumble toward the oblivion of the trestle side. He struck out with as confident a stride as allowed by the current. Once free of the cloying danger of the flood, he sluffed off the rope around his waist and moved with alacrity toward the waiting comfort.

"Mr. Jensen, we've decided to wait until the water goes down below the trestle," Casey O'Banyon, the engineer, informed Smoke as he walked up from the last rescue effort. "No way we can tell the conditions out there until we can see them."

"Good idea," Smoke agreed. His two perilous outings on the swaying bridge had changed his mind about hurrying on. "Might be wise to back up a little. That flood hasn't crested as yet."

O'Banyon's eyes widened. "Then there's more danger?"

"A whole lot, the way I see it," Smoke informed him grimly.

* * *

Sheriff Monte Carson looked up irritably from the wanted poster on his desk in the Big Rock sheriff's office. "Now gawdamnit, Victor. It ain't against the law for someone to make you an offer on yer spread. Thing is, you don't have to sell if you don't want to."

"I suppose you told the others that, too," Victor Mitchem complained.

Monte stroked both sides of his walrus mustache with a crooked finger. "Yep. The Smiths, the Evanses, Xavier. Gomez, an' Gil Norton. All of them who've come so far. Any idea who this Early is fronting for?"

Mitchem shook his head in a negative gesture. "None. He won't tell us. But I ask you, Monte, is it legal to ask to buy a man's land with half a dozen gun hawks glaring death-in-a-minute at you all the while?"

"Now, that puts a different light on it," Monte said, after considering it a moment. "Did any of them make a direct threat?"

"No. Not in so many words. Early said I would be sore-pressed if I refused the offer."

"What'd you tell him?" Monte probed.

"To go to hell, what do you think?" Victor snapped. "I tell you, you ought to look into this, Monte."

"I will. I surely will. Damn, I wish Smoke weren't gone clear th' hell back east. You have any idea this Early paid a call on the Sugarloaf?"

"Said they'd already done a deal. That's why Smoke's gone, he told me."

"That's bullshit, Victor," Monte snapped, his eyes narrowing. "You know Smoke'd never sell the Sugarloaf. Where can I find Early and his hard cases?"

"Don't know. They come and go. Last I heard, they were off to Rabbit Ears Pass and Steamboat Springs way." Victor's face clouded with suppressed anger. "They'll be back, you can be sure. Told me I could count on it."

After Victor departed, Monte asked three other angry, obviously disturbed ranchers to hold up a while in his office.

He had something to do that couldn't wait. Alone on the street, not quite sure where he was headed, Monte Carson considered all he had learned in the past three days. Smoke should be made aware of this, that much was obvious. Only Monte didn't know where to contact Smoke right then. All he had was a destination: Smoke's father-in-law's house. Well, it looked important enough; he'd better wire New Hampshire.

10

The same morning that brought Monte Carson his problems in Big Rock saw the flood waters of the Illinois River greatly receded. Once more, brakemen served as track-walkers ahead of the big 0-4-0 American Locomotive Works funnel-stack loco. They took along sledgehammers and tested rails and fish plates with solid whacks. Halfway across the trestle, both men showed considerable agitation and shouted back to those watching from the west end of the bridge.

"Not so good," Casey O'Banyon summed up for Smoke Jensen. "They've found a dozen cross-members broken and two pilings smashed out of place."

"Will the trestle carry the load?" Smoke asked.

"It should, if there's not a lot more damage," O'Banyon opined, then he frowned. It wouldn't go well for him if this important man, friend of the Denver and Rio Grande, were to plunge to his death in a still restless river. "Though I recommend against it."

Smoke considered that a moment. "We've had enough delays as it is. I say so far as the track isn't warped out of line, we should give it a try. If I may, I'd like to take the throttle until we cross over."

O'Banyon didn't like it, yet he saw a way out of dilemma. "I'm sure we can arrange that. In fact, I'm ready to get under way. A little weight on this end of the trestle should tell them what shape the rest is in. Climb aboard."

Smoke Jensen swung up into the high cab of the huge locomotive and settled himself comfortably, spraddle-legged, on the corrugated steel plates of the floor in the position occupied by the engineer. O'Banyon pointed out controls with which Smoke was already familiar. Satisfied that his pupil knew the rudiments, he gave a curt nod.

"Sure an' I'll lose me job for this." He sighed heavily. "But best be gettin' underway."

Smoke grabbed the wooden handle of the steam whistle and drew down on the chain connected to the valve. Raw steam gushed through the brass pipe and erupted out of the whistle, located between the steam dome and sandbox.

With the brake off and the throttle engaged, the drivers spun and then dug in. Slowly the big 4-6-0 edged forward. Gradually the speed increased. Smoke gave a glance to O'Banyon, who sat on the fold-down seat on the left side of the cab. The engineer gave a nod and Smoke pulled on the whistle chain again.

Immediately the trackwalkers cleared the trestle on the far side. That accomplished, Smoke smoothly increased toward full throttle. Creaks and groans came from the stressed timbers of the trestle as the big loco rolled its pilot trucks onto the western edge. The fireman set to work shoveling more coal into the firebox. Smoke Jensen leaned out the right-hand window and gazed over the land. The view was terrific. For all the flatness of this land, the high banks of the Illinois River made a plains version of the spectacular gorges of Smoke's beloved High Lonesome.

Flood waters had receded to a point midway down the sheer bluffs formed in ancient times when melt water from glaciers had caused the river to run brim full all the time. Smoke looked directly forward in time to see a nervous sway of the cowcatcher as the pilot truck delivered the first of six drivers onto the bridge. Two more crewmen used the grab-irons at the rear of the cowcatcher to swing aboard and moved slowly back to the cab on the catwalks above the spinning drivers of the locomotive. They increased their pace as the traction improved and the forward third of the American Locomotive Works 4-6-0 left solid ground for the tenuous security of the trestle.

"Didja feel her settle when the pilot truck rolled out on the bridge?" O'Banyon asked cheerfully.

Smoke nodded and spoke over the hellfire roar coming from the firebox. "I hadn't expected something like that so soon."

"Oh, she settles in even at the best of times. Folks ridin' back there never feel it. First-timers in the cab tend to get set to jackrabbit out the door," O'Banyon added with a chuckle.

With the entire weight of the locomotive and tender on the trestle, the creaking and groaning grew loud enough to be heard over the chuff of the pistons and constant noise of the boiler fire. The swaying increased also as the baggage and express car joined the power plant. Smoke had to admit to a certain undefined uneasiness.

Then he recognized it. He was risking not only his own life, but that of his beloved Sally. If the bridge collapsed with all the cars on it, none of them would survive. Visions of Sally perishing in the torrent that raced below them made Smoke regret pushing for the attempt to cross. More of the train eeled onto the trestle. At a nod from O'Banyon, Smoke gave the locomotive full throttle.

Near objects began to blur as the train gained speed. The bridge popped and groaned when the pilot truck rolled onto the weakened center span. They passed the midpoint with a frantic, nerve-straining sway when the last car, the one in which Sally must be fretting over the risk, rolled onto the bridge. O'Banyon broke off his distant stare to the front and produced a relieved smile.

"The hard part's taken care of. Now all we need to do is reach the far side."

Smoke Jensen forced the grim expression off his face. "You make it sound damned easy. I've faced six armed men in a gunfight with fewer butterflies in my gut."

"B'God, yer *that* Jensen right? Smoke Jensen?" O'Banyon blurted. "I thought there was something familiar about you."

Smoke had to smile. He had long since become accustomed to his notoriety. People whom he'd never met kept coming up to him and speaking with the familiarity of old friends. After all the years he had put between him and his youthful exploits, he wanted to believe it had died down.

"I admit to it," Smoke allowed.

"Well, I'll be damned. Sure an' it's a great pleasure to make your acquaintance, Smoke Jensen. My grandsons will never believe you rode in the cab with me."

Smoke made no reply. He had his hands full with the speeding locomotive. Right then, the trestle began to shake like a palsied man. Smoke tried to urge more speed out of the laboring engine. He signaled the fireman to put on more coal. The frightened man shook his head and pointed to the steam pressure gauge. Smoke cut his eyes to the white dial. The needle hovered near to the red danger area.

"Do it anyway, damn it," he shouted over the tumult of the speeding locomotive.

A quick glance at O'Banyon showed Smoke that the situation had worsened decidedly. The gamecock engineer occupied himself intently with fervent prayer. One by one the cars rattled over the endangered span. At last the signal telegraph over the boiler waggled to indicate the last car had passed the area of greatest risk. Paul Drummond knew his job and did it well, Smoke Jensen thought gratefully. Already Smoke sensed a slight incline as the locomotive raced toward the eastern bank of the rampaging Illinois River. They flashed past the abutments of the trestle. Only a little way to go now.

"Yer doin' it, bucko, yer doin' it!" O'Banyon shouted exuberantly.

Smoke Jensen leaned far out the window of the cab, ignoring the rush of air and puffs of steam past his head, and looked back. Only the private car of the D & R G remained on the last span of the bridge when the middle gave away with a mighty creak and a loud crash of collapsing pilings. Cross-braces shot into the air in all directions. Smoke kept the throttle open until the entire train cleared the doomed trestle.

Then he hauled back on the control and eased them to a stop. The trackwalkers ran to catch up with the train as it rolled past them. The rumble of collapsing bridge chased them. Casey O'Banyon looked with wild eyes at the spume and shattered wood that fountained upward.

"Jesus, Mary, and Joseph, I'll lose me job for this, certain sure."

"No, you won't, O'Banyon. We made it, and that's what counts. Besides, I'll be glad to square things through Colonel Drew."

O'Banyon looked embarrassed for a moment, then beamed as he flashed a smile and offered Smoke his hand. "Sure an' yer every bit the fine gentleman I believed ye to be, Smoke Jensen."

"I take that as a damned generous compliment, O'Banyon. Now, I had better let you have your train back. We're due in Chicago in a short while."

Not yet called the Windy City, Chicago sprawled on the shore of Lake Michigan, a metropolis large enough to win the immediate dislike of Smoke Jensen. These huge, urban centers, which had begun to develop over the past few years, represented for him everything bad about the direction the country had taken of late. The plains tribes, and even most of the eastern, "civilized" Indians, had long ago learned the lessons of close living.

They found it impossible, as all people eventually did, to

keep large masses of people living in close proximity peacefully month after month and year after year. Not without an all-powerful central authority that strangled individual freedom and responsibility. When the tribes had grown in population to the point that they could no longer be governed by a single chief, or group of chiefs, units would break off along family lines, with representatives of several clans forming separate bands, to live elsewhere, away from the main body.

It worked well for them, Smoke reasoned. Why couldn't his own people understand and benefit from that? They made the change of trains in the New York Central yards and departed with only a window's view of the crowded conditions of the working class and most of the smaller merchants. Once clear of the suburban clutter of single houses, Smoke asked Jenkins for champagne.

"We're celebrating," he informed Sally.

"What is there to celebrate, outside of not being destroyed in that river?"

"Oh, there's that, too. I want us to celebrate escaping from Chicago without being drowned in all those people."

A tiny vertical frown creased Sally's brow. "Smoke, you promised," she began.

"I can't help it," he responded, cutting her off. "But I will keep my promise not to let it get to me when we reach your family."

Sally brightened at that. "Just think, in another two days, we'll be in Keene. I certainly hope Father and Mother haven't gone to too much trouble."

Smoke produced a rueful grin. "You can be sure they have."

Chris appeared in the study of his father-in-law's home in Keene, New Hampshire, shortly after the latest issue of the *Keene Guardian* came out. Eyes wide with shock, he waved the newspaper before him as he addressed John Reynolds.

"I thought you said Smoke Jensen had mellowed, Father Reynolds," Chris's voice broke over the words.

"He has. Sally assured me of that," John Reynolds said past his thinning gray mustache.

"Then take a look at this." Chris shoved the newspaper forward.

John Reynolds took the *Guardian* and quickly found the source of Christopher's agitation. Bold, black headlines spelled out the latest of Smoke Jensen's encounters with the forces of lawlessness.

NOTORIOUS SMOKE JENSEN GUNS DOWN WALDRON GANG!

Beneath it, couched in the typically florid prose of eastern yellow journalism, the article gave a colorful, if inaccurate, account of the train robbery in which the Waldron gang had met their end. Near its conclusion came a paragraph that caused icy fingers to clutch the heart of John Reynolds:

No stranger to our fair city, Smoke Jensen is expected to return within a matter of days. He is scheduled to participate in the late spring lecture tour of the New England Lecture Society, speaking as the 'Mountain Man Philosopher of the Rockies.' After the bloodbath he brought to Keene on his first visit, the *Guardian* wonders if he should not be heralded as the Philosopher of the Colt .45.

"And here, see what the Boston *Globe* has to say," Chris urged, revealing another newspaper.

Frowning, John Reynolds set his eyes to absorbing the inflammatory expostulations of the Boston reporter. It certainly seemed to him that someone had set his cap for Smoke Jensen. John wondered how the most mercurial of his sons-in-law would react to this.

Probably with a shrug. No doubt Smoke Jensen had seen worse over the years. "Doesn't appear as though they are set to offer him the key to the city."

Chris threw his hands in the air in a gesture of hopelessness. "This is terrible publicity, and at the worst possible time. It will simply ruin our tour."

"Nonsense," John thundered. As an attorney, he had long ago been made privy to the secrets of public opinion. "What we are doing is promoting an entertainment. And among entertainers, there's no such thing as bad publicity. The more people who see these articles, the better for us. They'll pack the halls, sellout crowds, standing room only. They'll each and every one want to get as close to this 'dangerous' man as possible. If only for an hour, they'll want to feel that they have shared his adventures. Although, I daresay, the *Guardian* could have been a bit less censorious. After all, he *is* married to a daughter of Keene, and he's my son-in-law."

Somewhat calmed, Chris considered what John had said. It made sense of a sort, he granted. If only Smoke Jensen could be kept in a peaceful mood while here, it all might go well after all. "I suppose all we can do is hope for the best," he offered lamely.

"In the case of Smoke Jensen, 'the best' can be positively awful," John Reynolds recalled from experience.

Coarse, black hair, topped by a derby of matching color set at a rakish angle, formed a forelock that just came short of being bangs. The oily strands hung over a low forehead, creased by a perpetual scowl. Beady obsidian eyes sparkled with a shrewdness that spoke of a hard life, lived in the gutters and cruel streets of Boston. They studied the expensively and immacuately dressed man across the rude table in the low tavern on Beal Street in Boston, Massachusetts.

Phineas Lathrop had contacted Sean O'Boyle earlier in

the day at the offices of the Brotherhood of Stevedores and Longshoremen on Congress Street. Labor unions as yet were far from universally accepted, even among the mass of blue-collar workers along the Atlantic seaboard. Due to the wildcat strike called by O'Boyle and his puppet union officials, a cordon had been erected a block from the headquarters in all directions.

Manned by tough Boston policemen, it kept everyone away, including the rank-and-file of the union. Perhaps, Phineas Lathrop had considered, that was for the best. Militant anti-unionists had been known to toss dynamite bombs through the windows of union offices. Granted, most had been in retaliation for bombs thrown by the more aggressive of union thugs, but once having chosen a position, one had to maintain the perspective of that stand. The implied risk notwithstanding, Lathrop would have preferred to hold this meeting at the musty hall, rather than here.

Even in his most profligate days, Phineas Lathrop would have eschewed association with the likes of Sean O'Boyle. Yet he now found himself drinking a brandy of questionable origin, across the table from O'Boyle, in one of the grimmest dives he had ever encountered. O'Boyle had met him in New York, as ordered, a decision Lathrop had immediately begun to regret. Intrigue and empire building made for strange bedfellows, Lathrop decided. His mood changed, though, when O'Boyle handed him a creased, grease-stained handbill.

"Like I tole' you, Mr. Lathrop, they're plastered up all over town," Sean O'Boyle confided, in what for him came closest to a deferential tone.

Phineas Lathrop glanced up from the flyer he held in his flawlessly manicured hands. "How delightfully ironic!" he exclaimed to O'Boyle's startled expression. "Here I am, devoting hundreds of man-hours to seeking out our Mr. Jensen, and he obligingly hands himself over to us, complete with advance publicity."

"Yer—ah—yer really pleased, Mr. Lathrop?" O'Boyle asked doubtfully.

"Why, certainly, Mr. O'Boyle. In fact, I am going to place the entire matter of disposing of Smoke Jensen in your capable hands. Right here in Boston is the ideal place to terminate his interference in our plans. How fitting that the ultimate westerner should meet his end on a rat-infested dock in a teeming eastern city."

11

Colonel Drew's private car created quite a stir when it rolled into the depot in Keene, New Hampshire, at the rear of the New England Zephyr. The glittering brass brightwork rivaled even the opulent steam yachts of the wealthy New Englanders. The fact that it brought the notorious Smoke Jensen to town added to the excitement. Troops of small boys materialized out of nowhere and formed gaggles of giggling, wriggling gawkers along the platform edge. They shrilled enthusiastic information and pointed with grubby fingers at the first sign of movement from within.

More restrained, their parents and other adults in Keene held back under the shade of the roof overhang. It didn't prevent them from gaping every bit as much as the tykes when the lovely Sally Reynolds Jensen and her legendary husband, Smoke Jensen, appeared on the observation platform, light carpetbags in hand.

"I shall arrange for your luggage to be transported to the Reynolds manse, Mr. Jensen," Jenkins advised from the doorway.

"Thank you, Jenkins. You have arranged a place to bunk down?" Smoke responded.

"We shall be quite comfortable here, sir," Jenkins replied stiffly.

"I'd think you'd want to get off this rattlin' wreck for a while," Smoke observed.

A fleeting ghost of a smile creased Jenkins' lips. "A stationary bed would be pleasant for a change," he wistfully admitted.

"Done, then. The best hotel in town. For you, Lee Fong, and his helper," Smoke concluded abruptly.

Jenkins hastened to decline. "We really should keep close to the car, sir. There's no telling what mischief might get afoot if it were abandoned."

"Cow plop! Lock it up when you leave. Nothing will go wrong in Keene, New Hampshire."

"Very well, sir," Jenkins acquiesced. To himself, he muttered, "Nothing will go wrong with Smoke Jensen around."

Right then, Sally spotted her mother in the crowd. She waved energetically and dismounted from the platform. Both women rushed into each other's arms.

"Oh, my dear, dear girl," Abigale, trilled as she embraced Sally.

"I've missed you, Mother, terribly," Sally offered dutifully. "And Father, too," she added, as John Reynolds approached.

After a powerful hug, John Reynolds spoke over his daughter's shoulder to Smoke Jensen. "Come along, you two, the carriage is outside the depot."

Smoke Jensen had to endure the stultifying heaviness of a traditional New England boiled dinner before retiring to the room John Reynolds used as a study for cigars and brandy. John used a delicate, gold-filled scissor to cut the tip of his Havana cigar, while Smoke bit off the end of his. Both men puffed them to life with the aid of sulfurous lucifers, took deep drags, and exhaled.

John poured brandy and they sipped appreciatively before he sprang his latest enterprise on his son-in-law. With an elegant flourish, he presented Smoke with a copy of the handbill. Smoke read only half a dozen words, then looked up in consternation.

"Pardon me, John, but what in the hell is this? 'Mountain Man Philosopher of the Rockies'?" he quoted.

John Reynolds ran long, lawyer-soft fingers through his leonine mane of white hair. "That's you, Smoke."

"Not by a damned sight," Smoke snapped. "I'll not be turned into some sort of—of performing bear."

"That's not it at all. The—the cream of society will attend these lectures. And you'll have an opportunity to explain the way of life in the West. Is there anyone better qualified?" he added flatteringly.

"No."

"That's what I thought," Reynolds stated with satisfaction.

"No means that I'm rejecting the idea out of hand. I'm not a damned speechmaker. I'm plainspoken, direct. Hell, John, I'd wind up insulting the audience before I'd said ten words."

Their voices had risen enough that it attracted Robert and Chris to the open doorway of the study. Their stricken expressions showed how clearly agitated they were by Smoke's vehement opposition. Smoke cut his eyes from them to John Reynolds.

"I honestly thought you'd be pleased by this," the elder Reynolds offered by way of explanation. "Or at least encouraged by this opportunity to cast the light of truth on the miasma of those terrible dime novels."

That, at last, struck a responsive note for Smoke Jensen. "You've a point there. But I think you'll find that whatever audience is drawn to such a lecture comes with the expectation of tales of bloodshed and derring-do."

John Reynolds produced a wry smile. "It wouldn't hurt to give them a little of that, too, would it?" He sighed and nodded toward the flyer. "Besides, we've booked the lecture into several theaters and lecture halls. These are up all over New England and as far south as New York City. After all, you'd be joining a long list of notable persons who have made lecture tours. Even the famous Irish playwright Oscar Wilde did the tour circuit. Not only here in the East, but out West, too."

"That was different," Smoke snapped. "Oscar Wilde was a twit."

"No," John persisted. "He was a wit, a playwright, and an essayist. A man of many talents. At least consider it, Smoke," he pleaded his case. "It would be a shame to have generated all this interest . . . ah, most of those who have contracted for the tour report sellouts for each performance . . . only to have to cancel."

"I—we," Smoke amended, when he glanced up to see Sally in the doorway with her brother and brother-in-law. "Don't need the money."

"The honoraria won't be that large," John Reynolds offered.

"Damn it, John, that's all the more reason I'd look foolish accepting them," Smoke growled.

"You could donate them to charity," Sally suggested through a smile. "Like the Boston Shelter for Orphans. Think what that would do for your desperado image. 'Notorious Gunman Contributes Lecture Fees to Provide a Dry Roof and Full Bellies for Poor Children,'" she quoted an imaginary headline.

Smoke Jensen cut his eyes to his wife, his face wrapped in disbelief. "You're in favor of this, Sal?"

Sally entered the room, small fists on hips. "As a matter of fact, yes, I am. I think it's a wonderful opportunity for you. Please, tell Father that you will at least think about it."

Rarely able to deny Sally anything, Smoke Jensen drew a deep breath and turned away from her cool, level blue gaze. "All right, John. I'll give it some consideration. How soon will I have to be ready for the first one?"

Sensing victory, although with less satisfaction than he might expect, John Reynolds smiled winningly and patted Smoke Jensen on one shoulder. "Fine, fine. The first appearance is right here in Keene, on the evening of the eleventh."

"That's . . . only three days," Smoke said miserably.

* * *

Later, when they were at last alone, Sally came to Smoke, where he stood gazing out over the back lawn of the Reynolds home. She lightly touched fingers to his cheek and gently pressed her full, still firm, bosom against his arm.

"Seriously, dear, it could do you a world of good, this lecture tour Father has designed."

Horseshit! Smoke thought angrily, then cut off his hot flow of negatives. "I can't see it worth a damn, Sal," he stated calmly.

"Think about it, dear. I can see it now. What a deliciously funny joke it will be on these stuffy easterners when the notorious gunfighter Smoke Jensen appears in front of them, dressed in white tie and tails, six-guns slung around his waist. The women will swoon and the men will get apoplexy."

"And I'll tell them about wrestlin' a bear and havin' the critter insist on best two falls out of three? Maybe mention the time I outran a whole band of Arapaho warriors, barefoot and buck naked?"

"When did you do that, dear?" Sally asked, familiar with nearly all of his past adventures.

"I didn't," Smoke informed her with a smirk, as he got into her mood. "They were the ones without moccasins and clothes. I stole them all and burned them."

"Perhaps you shouldn't relate that one. The good people of Keene would be scandalized," Sally suggested seriously. "Honestly, I think you should try it. At least here in Keene."

For all her ability to tame him, Smoke Jensen wasn't yet ready for bridle and bit. "The big-city newspapers would get ahold of it and make me into some kind of circus performer."

"Ooh?" Sally drawled. "Since when has your dignity been so important?"

"It's not that. Only that . . . I'd feel I was being used."

"What's wrong with that . . . if it's for a good cause? I meant what I said about giving what you earn to charity. You never know when you might be in need of a little goodwill."

Smoke grimaced. "From easterners? Fat chance of that."

Sally stood her ground. "Father's taken a lot on himself for this," she began, to be cut off by Smoke.

"Funny, but I don't have a whole hell of a lot of sympathy for him. He could have at least consulted me first."

"To be told no at the outset?" Sally demanded, a nascent sob lurking at the back of her voice.

Smoke Jensen read it correctly. As usual, his beloved Sally had cooled his anger and replaced it with a humorous view of the affair. He could not bear hurting her. He turned her to him with big hands and brushed lightly across her long, dark tresses.

"Does it mean so much to you, Sal?" Her tiny nod tugged at his heart. He caressed her long, graceful neck and down her arched back. Sighing, he relented. "All right. I'll do it. Mind, I'm only agreeing to do it one damned time, to see what it's like. And for you."

Wise in the ways of her man, Sally Jensen decided she would have to be satisfied with that . . . for now.

". . . Now, if you want to talk about the true philosopher of the Rockies, there's only one name to turn to," Smoke Jensen said to his rapt audience about midway through his first stumbling attempt at public speaking.

"I'm talking about the kindest, smartest, wisest two-legged critter that ever forked a horse or trapped a beaver. He was also the meanest, most ornery, toughest, wildest, most downright livingest man in the High Lonesome."

"How could he be the kindest and the meanest, the wisest and the wildest?" a voice shouted from the back of the hall.

"Well, now, I was fixin' to tell you that."

Smoke had surprised himself at how easily he had slipped back into the patois of the mountain men. He had started with a straight delivery, to be answered by a barrage of foot-shuffling, coughing, program-rattling, and whispering. When he let the round tones of his polished delivery slide into the crusty-edged twang of those redoubtable pioneers of the fur trade, utter silence descended on the town hall in Keene, New Hampshire.

Here, as Smoke had predicted, was what they'd come for. From that moment, Smoke held his audience in the palm of his hand. Now came the time to squeeze a little. "His name was Preacher. He had a first handle, Arthur, and one of my sons is named after him. But ev'ryone called him Preacher. He raised me from about the age of fourteen. Taught me how to hunt and trap, how to skin and cure beaver, deer, and elk hides, make a buffalo robe, or trade for one with the Indians and keep the edge.

"Preacher was also one of the founders of the University of the Shining Mountains—what you folks call the University of the Rockies. He made me read Milton, and Shakespeare, Sir Walter Scott, even Pliny and Plato."

"Oh, sure," another heckler chimed in. "If you know Shakespeare, how did General Canidius describe Cleopatra to the other Roman officers in *Anthony and Cleopatra?*"

Smoke thought a moment. "'Age cannot wither, nor custom stale her infinite variety. Other women cloy the appetites they feed, whilst she makes hungry where most she satisfies.' Will that do?" he ended, with a growl of challenge in his voice. "Now, Preacher was a real learned man . . ." And so it went on.

Following the questioning period, John Reynolds led his family back to the house, where the servants had laid out a late-night supper of cold cuts, cold fried chicken, cheeses, and champagne. John declared the lecture an overwhelming success. Over the rim of his hoisted glass, he cut his eyes to Smoke Jensen.

"You were marvelous. I've never seen so many gaping mouths in one place at the same time. You have to go on, do more, do them all."

"I'm not so sure, John. I don't know how to handle those big mouths, run by small minds, except with my fists or a sixgun."

Portly John Reynolds considered that for a moment. "Well, now, we can't have that—not on stage, at least. Your next appearance is for this Saturday, in Concord."

Smoke produced a fleeting smile. "There's a town not far from here called Lynchville. I'm glad it isn't scheduled for there," he quipped.

"Then you'll do it?" Sally asked from his side. "Don't appear I have a hell of a lot of choice. Not with my wife and my father-in-law conspiring against me."

Smoke Jensen knew Concord would be a disaster from the moment he peeked through a spy-hole in the asbestos main curtain and got a look at the audience. Just behind the rows of seats that John Reynolds told him were properly called the orchestra, occupied by the state capital's prominent citizens, came three files of rough, hard-faced men with mean eyes and smoldering temperments. He knew damn well they had come to poke fun. Half of them looked piss-pants drunk, or well on the way to being there.

After the scrawny, overdressed twit who was host sponsor in Concord made the introduction, and Smoke walked out on stage to a podium arranged in the center with a pitcher and glass of water at the ready, he heard the titter of youthful laughter. Belatedly a spatter of applause broke out. Hell of a way to start out, he grumbled silently.

Kerosene footlights flickered in front of the rostrum, and washed the faces of those beyond into an amorphous mass. Sally, whose education had included several courses in public speaking, had impressed upon her husband that he should find several people in the audience and make eye contact alternately with them, so that each individual felt he spoke directly to them.

How in hell was he supposed to do that? Smoke fumed, under his breath. Smoke raised one arm to signal silence and launched into his prepared portion of the program.

"Thank you for your warm reception. You came tonight to

hear from the Mountain Man Philosopher of the Rockies. Actually, what I'm going to do is tell you about the man who deserves that title. His name was Preacher. He was, to quote Shakespeare, 'made of sterner stuff.' Preacher never remembered how old he was when he went to the Shining Mountains. He did recall that he celebrated what he thought was his twelfth birthday in the camp of Beau Jacques and Curly Parnell, washing down half-raw elk steaks and cold biscuit with the most poisonous homemade whiskey that ever crossed his lips.

"You have all heard the expression 'a man among men.' Preacher was *the* man among men. Was he a failed man of the cloth, as some have claimed? No, but he was on the closest, most intimate terms with the Almighty. Was he a renegade schoolmaster?" Smoke produced a rueful look. "Not likely. Although he taught me every thing I knew until long after I'd reached my majority. And that was a lot."

Smoke went on to list the subjects and authors he had mastered under the rough tutelage of Preacher. He spoke of the Indian troubles in the sixties, and how Preacher had maintained a tenuous peace among the tribes of northern Colorado and the white Indian haters of Chivington's ilk. In glowing terms, he brought his listeners along to the point where Preacher came into his life. In conclusion, he touched on the subject of the handbill that had been circulated.

"Preacher helped create what this broadside calls the University of the Rockies." Smoke paused and tried to peer through the brightness at the audience. "To those who made use of it, it was called the University of the Shining Mountains. By the time I came into the High Lonesome, it had already been disbanded, along with the fur trade, for some thirty years. But its spirit remained, and its goal of enlightenment among the wanderers of that far place had been kept alive."

"What about those twenty-eight men you killed on the way here?" one of the bully-boys in the center of the auditorium demanded.

"It wasn't twenty-eight, it was more like seventeen. And the conductor on the train accounted for some six of those."

Gasps of shock and surprise flitted through the crowd. Men who deserved a fair trial and a chance to rehabilitate themselves," came the challenge.

"Nope. They were murderers and thieves, bent on killing anyone who got in their way and determined to rob even children and have their way with the women passengers. They got what they had coming to them."

A distraught mutter rippled through the audience. Smoke gauged it and cut off the protests short of a roar of outrage. "I've nothing more to say on that. If it offends any of you, then I suggest you're in the wrong place. Instead, let me tell you what it's like wakin' up in the mornin' in the High Lonesome. The rich, bitey scent of pine makes your nose tingle. Then there's the powerful aroma of coffee brewin' on a wood fire. Fatback never smelt better sizzlin' in a pan, than out there . . ." He had them again. At the end of the lecture, enthusiastic applause almost turned into pandemonium.

Smoke, Sally, and her parents were leaving the building by a side entrance when a scuffle broke out in the aisle above them. Three men burst through the ushers and two policemen who tried to contain them and rushed directly at Smoke Jensen. Faces flaming, they mouthed obscenities and threats. The blade of a knife glinted in the yellow lamplight.

A pig-faced lout in the lead cursed foully as he neared and swung his knife, only to arrest his action abruptly when he found himself sucking on the muzzle end of the barrel of Smoke Jensen's .45 Colt. Sweat broke out in large beads on his forehead, and blood from a broken-off tooth trickled from the corner of his mouth. His bushy brows waggled in agitation at his precarious position.

Smoke's other hand plucked the thin-bladed filleting knife from paralyzed fingers and he snapped it against the nearest marble column. His icy gray gaze swept over the trio. "Fun's fun, boys, but I don't think you want to wear your friend's brains home to show to your wives. Join the others who are leaving and we'll forget all about this."

They beat a hasty retreat. At John Reynolds's direction, the knife-wielder was taken off to jail by the police. Outside in the carriage, Stewart Buffington, the host, broke a tight silence.

"A lamentable incident."

"It won't happen again, I assure you," John Reynolds quickly added.

"What now?" Sally Jensen asked, concerned for her husband and wondering what he must be thinking.

Smoke Jensen still retained the buzz of excitement that had come from feeling a tooth break as he jammed the muzzle of his six-gun in the thug's mouth. "It's on to Boston, I'd say. I'm beginning to enjoy this," he answered them, to their mutual consternation.

12

"He's on his way to Boston," Sean O'Boyle stated tightly when he arrived in Phineas Lathrop's New York office.

"Boston? Why is he on his way to Boston? Smoke Jensen was supposed to be dead by now, not on his way to Boston."

Sean O'Boyle had long ago noted that when his boss got excited about something, he tended to repeat himself a lot. He tried to direct that agitation elsewhere by giving a rough shove forward to the man he had in tow. "Better ask him, Mr. Lathrop. He's the one was supposed to knife Jensen."

Lathrop turned his malevolent gaze on the hapless man with the puffed, bruised lips. "I never saw anyone move so fast," the Boston longshoreman lisped. "I'd just got my knife out an' he shoved the barrel of his shootin' iron in my mouth. Broke off a tooth, too."

Contempt blazed in the burnished walnut eyes of Phineas Lathrop. "I've heard it all now. Smoke Jensen is the most notorious gunfighter in all the West, and you go after him with a knife. It's a wonder he didn't blow what little brains you have out the back of your head." He rounded his anger on O'Boyle again. "Is this the best you have? Is this the result I can expect when next you go after Jensen on your home ground?"

"Oh, no, sir. We'll get him, right enough. He'll not leave Boston alive."

Fleshy lips twisted in a sneer, Phineas Lathrop responded hotly. "I certainly hope so. For your sake, Mr. O'Boyle. We have only three weeks to tie up the land we want, and Smoke Jensen is not going to stand in the way. He must be eliminated," Lathrop continued, "or everything is lost. How do you think this is going to look to my New York associates in the boardroom over there?"

"They'll not be likin' it, I'm thinkin'," O'Boyle answered with low-toned sullenness.

"You're damned right on that. You are to take your men to Boston at once. There is a new plan to implement at once. Arnold Cabbott will fill you in. Oh, and take this bumbling incompetent out somewhere and finish what Smoke Jensen failed to accomplish."

O'Boyle's man paled and began to tremble. "You can't do that. Please, Mr. Lathrop—I ain't done anything that deserves bein' killed for."

Lathrop eyed him like some form of vermin. "You failed Mr. O'Boyle and you failed me. That's more than enough, I'd say. I expect to hear of results on Jensen within two days," he shot at O'Boyle as the pair exited.

Phineas Lathrop took a deep breath and ran long, soft spatulate fingers across his high brow in an effort to steady himself and rid his mind of the encounter just completed. After another deep inhalation, he walked toward the tall double doors to the boardroom. When he opened them and stepped quietly inside, Lathrop interrupted a trio of hushed conversations.

"Gentlemen, I must report a slight setback in clearing the way to obtain the land in Colorado. As we speak, it is being taken care of. Nothing to concern yourselves about."

Simon Asher looked up, his moon face flushed slightly, and peered at Lathrop through wire-rimmed half-glasses. "Then the payment of our share of this enterprise will be set back accordingly."

"Come now, Abe, there's no call for that," Lathrop all but begged.

"We believe there is. No sense in throwing good money after bad." Asher quoted the old saw in a tone of virtuousness.

"No, there isn't," Lathrop put iron back in his words. "There is also no reason for further delay. We need that money in place now. All of the others have committed right on schedule. Only you six gentlemen are holding back. Perhaps you could not raise the sum agreed upon? Your assets are not liquid enough to take out such an amount?"

"Certainly not," Asher blustered. "Any one of us could write a bank draft for the entire figure right now."

Lathrop's eyes glittered with determination. "Then I suggest one of you do so. You are either in or you are out, all the way out."

"You were going to take care of the major obstacle." Victor Middleton reminded Lathrop of his failures so far.

"It *is* being taken care of. Smoke Jensen will not leave Boston as owner of the Sugarloaf, or he won't leave there alive."

Reluctantly, Abe Asher reached for his checkbook. The others did the same.

More preperformance noise came from this audience than from previous ones. Their low chatter ran in waves across the auditorium, every third one a bit louder than the other two. All except for a section occupied by some thirty tough-looking dock wallopers, dressed quite unsuitably in formal attire. They remained motionless, glowering at the main curtain, lips in grim, straight lines. Smoke Jensen studied them from a peephole in the stiff material and didn't like what he saw.

"This was a fool's errand from the start," he muttered to Sally, who stood at his side, prior to retiring to her seat in the audience.

"Now, dear, Bostonians can't be any harder an audience than you've encountered before."

"Take a look at those thugs in the monkey suits. I've a hundred dollars says they aren't here for cultural enlightenment."

"We'll have to wait and see, won't we?" Sally returned sweetly, as she saw the master of ceremonies headed their way. "Give them hell, dear," she added, as she started off.

The introduction went without incident and Smoke Jensen walked out onto the stage to a polite scatter of applause. Contrary to Sally's description of Smoke in white tie and tails, he had chosen for this appearance to wear a more conservatively cut western-style suit, with a low-crown fawn Stetson. The long, tasseled leather pull-straps of his boots slapped rhythmically with his steps. He paused at the lectern and cleared his throat.

Immediately a raucous call came from the midst of the thirty-some longshoremen. "Where's yer greasy, smoked leather britches?"

"Yeah. You ain't no mountain man. You look like a sissy-boy from New York City."

Smoke cleared his throat again and tried to fix a smile on his lips. "Funny you should mention New York City. I've only been there once before. I'll be ending my tour there, in a week," he addressed the ruffians. Then he launched into his prepared lecture, to which he added a prickly barb. "Unlike some I could mention, the mountain men were not ignorant louts, bent on the butchery of beaver and Indians alike. Many were well-educated men. One of those was the legendary Preacher."

"Weren't no Bible-thumpers trappin' fur and killin' Cheyenne and Arapaho," one heckler retorted.

Smoke fought back his rising temper. "Quite right. You know, you are a lot more perceptive than I thought you might be. Let me tell you about the man who taught me everything I know about the High Lonesome part of the Shining Mountains. Preacher was everything to me. He had a way . . ." Once launched, Smoke's informative talk flowed around and over a steady stream of heckling.

He hadn't time for their nonsense and he made it known from the outset. Near the end, the insults grew more pointed and personal. Smoke bit back the urge to climb down off the stage and deliver a set of lumps to each of the burly men who had interrupted his talk. When he wound down to his conclusion, Smoke added a new summation.

"So, if I rate as a mountain man philosopher, then I play a poor second-place Plato to Preacher's excellent Socrates."

"Who're them fellers? Never heard of them before," one out-of-place stevedore bellowed through a guffaw.

"I don't imagine you have," Smoke said in an aside.

"They come from your Shinin' Mountains?" the heckler pressed.

"No. They were from Greece, and they died more than two thousand years ago."

Laughter showed Smoke he had most of the audience with him. Warmed by it, he ignored the distractions. "This is the open-forum portion of the program. Does anyone have a question?"

Smoke pointedly overlooked the noisy gathering directly in front of him and took questions for half an hour. At a quarter to ten that evening, he thanked his audience and left the stage. In the tiny dressing room allotted to him, Smoke changed into clothes he found more comfortable than the high, stiff collar and stifling cravat his stage appearances demanded. With his brace of sixguns securely belted into place, he left to meet Sally and her parents, who would be waiting in a coach at the stage door.

Instead of his inlaws and his wife, Smoke Jensen opened the metal-strapped door to find an angry throng of some fifteen of his detractors from inside. Not the least pleased with this turn of events, Smoke quickly sought to identify the leader of this impromptu mob. He had little trouble doing so.

A cocky bantam rooster of a man stepped out from the front rank, his swagger accented by his small size. He pointed an accusing finger at Smoke Jensen and spoke with a voice laden with the lilt of the Emerald Isle.

"Ye're a fraud. Ye're nah mar a mountain man than me Aunt Nettie."

"Who are you?" Smoke demanded, making no effort to hide his contempt.

"Seamas Quern, that's who. These friends o' mine have come to watch me give ye a right proper whippin', bucko. So make yerself ready."

To Quern's consternation, Smoke Jensen laughed at him. A deep, full, uproarious peal of mirth filled the narrow alleyway. Smoke controlled it after a moment and pointed a big, thick finger at Quern.

"Did you bring only your fists to a gunfight?" Smoke asked incredulously. "Another fool tried that a few nights ago, with a knife. He wound up sucking on the muzzle of my Peacemaker. He and his friends departed right fast. And not a shot was fired."

"Yer a gawdamned coward to hide behind your guns, I say. If you'd but take 'em off and fight like a man, we'd soon see who wars the better."

Smoke slowly sized up the runty agitator and produced a wan smile. "Where I come from, we don't allow anyone to pile shit that high. Even if we did, it couldn't get that job done," he added, as he reached for the buckle of his cartridge belt.

"B'God, yer all wind, Smoke Jensen," Seamas Quern bellowed, and launched himself at him.

Smoke stood his ground, his cartridge belt in his left hand, and batted Quern aside with his right arm. Then, cat quick, he swiftly rapped the hard knuckles of his right fist into the foreheads of two longshoremen who circled to move in on his blind side. One howled in rage and pain and the other did an abrupt pratfall in the litter of the alley. Smoke had time to sling his holstered six-guns over the wrought-iron railing of the short flight of steps to the stage door before Seamas came at him again.

He was joined by another pair of bully-boys. The trio closed on Smoke and Quern sent a blur of lefts and rights in the direction of Smoke's head. Smoke parried them with only stinging damage to his thick forearms. Quern worked himself too far inside and Smoke belted him with a round-house left that staggered the little man.

A dark object made blurred motion in the dimly lighted passageway and Smoke made out the fat end of a cudgel. His attacker swung again, aiming to break Smoke's left forearm. Smoke took a step back and when the stevedore made his follow-through and opened himself, Smoke kicked him in the balls.

A thin, shrill, porcine squeal came from the twisted lips of the injured man. He staggered knock-kneed to one side, the club still in his hands. Smoke pressed his advantage by a step inward and a solid smack to the jaw of the no-longer-dangerous man. The breathy squeak ended, the eyes of the club's owner rolled upward, displaying a lot of white, and he sank to his knees.

An instant later, while Smoke lined up a coup de grace on the downed bully, Quern grabbed at the back of Smoke's shirt and yanked him away. Smoke pivoted on one bootheel and planted the other solidly on Quern's kneecap. A howl of anguish rose to echo off the tall brick buildings. Another of O'Boyle's union thugs moved in on Smoke at an oblique angle.

He dived forward to wrap his arms around Smoke's middle. Off balance, Smoke tottered sideways into a whistling fist from out of the shadows. Callused knuckles of a longshoreman ripped skin below Smoke's left eye and bright lights went off in his head.

"Get 'im, boys!" Seamas Quern shouted through his fog of pain. "Make him pay."

Smoke set himself for yet another attack. It didn't take long to get there. Two men, swinging soft leather pouches above their heads, charged him. One of the birdshot-filled coshes whistled past his ear and slammed painfully on the top of his right shoulder. Smoke grabbed the wrist of his assailant and ducked low, pivoting out from under, and yanked downward. His knee came up at the same time and a loud, dry-stick snap sounded when he broke the man's arm.

Screaming, the assailant staggered blindly away down the

alley. Well accustomed to brawls, the others didn't slacken their attack on Smoke Jensen. Smoke met them readily, one and sometimes two at a time. His big fists smeared a nose across the fat face of an enemy nearly as big as himself. Smoke caught another with a hard right to the heart that dropped the dock worker to his knees where a pistonlike drive of Smoke's left leg took him out of the action for good.

"Shoot him!" Seamas Quern shouted. "For God's sake, shoot."

A burly longshoreman came up with a revolver that looked ridiculously small in his huge, hairy fist. He swung the muzzle in Smoke's direction, then froze at the loud clicks of a hammer being drawn back. From beyond his intended victim came a voice hard and deadly, yet touched with a cultured tone.

"Drop it, or I'll send you to hell."

John Reynolds' timely intervention bought Smoke Jensen the time he needed to reach his own pair of heavy Colt revolvers. "What kept you?" Smoke said over his shoulder, as he unlimbered a much-used .45 Peacemaker.

"Some of these wharf rats had the entrance to the alley blocked. I—ah—convinced them to let me through."

Smoke quickly and roughly searched those street thugs still on their feet and disarmed them. "I didn't know you carried a gun, John," Smoke remarked, while he went about his task.

"I haven't, not since Rex Davidson paid a call on Keene. Though after what has been going on, I decided it might be advisable here in Boston."

"Good thinking. I owe you one, John."

"Think nothing of it. Do you have any idea why these louts attacked you?"

Smoke didn't answer at once. Instead, he addressed a harsh command to the battered longshoremen. "Those of you who can, gather up your friends and get the hell out of here." As they grumblingly complied, Smoke spoke to his father-in-law. "I figure it was a bit too much whiskey. Friend

Barleycorn tends to give some men an exaggerated sense of their own strength."

"We'll turn them over to the police?" John Reynolds asked.

Smoke studied the bruised faces, bloody noses, and split lips, and answered quietly, "No. I think they've learned a damned important lesson. Besides, the police ask too many questions and that tussle whipped up my appetite. I'm hungry enough to eat the back half of a skunk."

Smoke Jensen breakfasted with Sally early the next morning. Well accustomed to the ways of the West, Sally put away a substantial portion of ham, fried potatoes, and three eggs, along with biscuits and jam. She gently patted the corners of her mouth with a linen napkin, then rose from the table in a sunny alcove of their hotel suite.

"You have a matinee this afternoon, Smoke. I'm going shopping. I'll see you at the theater this evening."

"Women and their shopping," Smoke grumped good-naturedly. "In that amount of time, you could buy up all of Boston."

"That's unfair. I have to come back here with my purchases, and change for the lecture tonight. After all, Beacon Hill is some distance from the commercial district."

"Is your mother going with you?" Smoke asked casually.

"No. She's not feeling well. Perhaps after lunch."

"Sally, you know I don't like you going around alone in a big city," Smoke admonished gently. "There are too many things that can happen. And if they did, how would anyone know to get in touch with me?"

"You worry too much," Sally said lightly. "After all, I'll have my friend Sam Colt along."

Smoke frowned. "I was thinking of runaway horses or a beer wagon accident."

"Oh. Well, I'll stay far away from the middle of the streets. Don't you worry. Nothing can happen to me."

With that, Sally draped a knit shawl over her graceful shoulders, fitted a small, stylish hat into place, and departed. A knock sounded a minute later. Thinking it to be Sally returned for some forgotten item, Smoke answered it readily. He opened the portal to reveal a young man in his early twenties, slightly built, with a pigeon breast and boyishly eager expression.

"Mr. Smoke Jensen?" he asked in a tenor rush. "Oliver Johnson, the *Boston Herald*. If you have a few minutes, I'd like an interview with you."

"I was just finishing breakfast," Smoke began, framing a refusal.

"That's all right. I've already eaten, but I could use a cup of coffee," Johnson rattled off, as he pushed past Smoke and entered the suite. He paused suddenly and turned full about. "This is quite the most opulent hotel room I've ever been in."

Smoke couldn't understand why his face colored while he explained, "My father-in-law made our travel arrangements." Then, accepting the inevitable, he gestured to a chair. "What is it you wanted to ask me?"

Oliver Johnson produced a small notepad and a stub of pencil. He wet the lead with thin lips and poised the point over the paper. "Is it true you've killed more than four hundred men?"

"No," Smoke answered forcefully, then amended his denial. "That is, I'm not sure. I don't keep score."

Johnson cut his eyes to Smoke with a sly expression. "No notches on the old six-shooter, eh? I thought every hired killer in the West cut notches for his victims in the grips of his revolver?"

At the best of times, Smoke Jensen had little use for representatives of the press. By Smoke's lights, this proper, typically dressed Bostonian was quickly wearing thin a tentative welcome. In three short sentences, he had proved himself to be a typical reporter, rude and pushy. Memories of other eager young men over the years directed Smoke to give Johnson more than an even break.

"Let's get one thing straight. I am not, and never have been, a hired killer."

"Yes, but . . ." Johnson interrupted, to be silenced by the faint hint of violence in those hard, gray eyes and an up-raised hand.

"I have killed men in self-defense, or in protecting my property or that of others. I have killed outlaws stupid enough not to surrender to me or to other lawmen. But I have never been paid money for the purpose of taking another human life. To me, the only justifiable circumstances for that is being a soldier, during time of war."

Johnson seized on that. "Did you serve the Union cause, sir?"

"No," Smoke answered shortly. "Nor the Confederate, for that matter. That's why I can tell you I've never taken money to kill another person."

"That's . . . quite surprising. I understand your wife is traveling with you. What does she think of your exploits?"

Smoke's hard gaze bore into the eyes of the impetuous reporter. "We've remained married long enough to raise five children to adulthood. I think that speaks for her outlook."

"Seriously, she must have some strong feelings about the subject," Johnson pressed.

"I'm sure she does. We rarely discuss them. But, I can tell you one thing—you're getting entirely too damn nosy. I'll answer any reasonable questions about myself, but keep my wife the hell out of it."

Johnson blinked and cleared his throat. "Agreed. I—ah—understand you were engaged in a bloody uprising down in Mexico not long ago."

"You've done your research rather thoroughly," Smoke stated, sincerely impressed by this eager youth's knowledge. "It was hardly what you could call an uprising. In fact, the opposite. Two old friends prevailed on me to help them put down an uprising by a bandit leader that threatened to take over the central region of their country. I obliged them."

"And those gentlemen were Esteban Carbone and Miguel Martine?" Johnson prompted.

"The same. We go back a long ways," Smoke filled in.

"But they are notorious gunmen," Johnson blurted.

Smoke Jensen smiled without mirth. "Some say that applies to me, too." Johnson's unexpected reaction to the mild rebuke prodded Smoke into an explanation. "Both had retired several years before. Both are large landowners in the state of Nayarit. They stood in the way of an hombre named Gustavo Carvajal, who called himself *El Rey del None*—the King of the North. Carvajal believed himself to be the reincarnation of Montezuma, the last Aztec emperor."

Oliver Johnson shook his head in wonder. Here was a story well worth telling. He only hoped he could keep Smoke Jensen talking long enough to get the whole piece down on paper. "Crazy as a loon," he opined.

"You could say that," Smoke answered dryly.

"Tell me more."

Relaxed under the shift in Johnson's attitude, Smoke did as he was bidden. They extended the interview until an hour before Smoke's matinee performance. Johnson departed after exacting a promise for another interview over a late-night supper. For some reason, Smoke looked forward to it.

13

Her hands filled with bulky packages, Sally Jensen paid no attention to three burly, dark men in blue cotton work shirts who trailed along in her wake down Tremont Street, on the east side of Boston Common. She had had her fill of shopping and now wanted to return to the hotel before Smoke left for his afternoon performance. She could have facilitated that by taking one of the many hansom cabs, but considered that a lot of bother with all her parcels. Instead, she decided on a shortcut through the park to Beacon Street and to Beacon Hill Road beyond.

Sturdy old elms, oaks, and maples provided a refreshing shade that cooled her as Sally walked along a gravel pathway. Children frolicked on the slopes of the hilly park, where in winter they would squeal with delight as their sleds followed the long runs to the small lake where older youths placidly skated on the ice.

Near the halfway mark, the three men increased their pace and rapidly closed with Sally. Two of them grabbed her by the arms and the third spoke hoarsely into her ear from behind. "Don't make a fuss, Mizus Jensen. Just come with us and do as I say."

Sally dropped a hatbox and made a grab for her brocaded purse. "Let go of me this instant," she demanded.

One of her captors stayed her hand. "We ain't out to rob you, Mizus. But you're gonna come with us, like it or not."

"Who are you? What do you want with me?" Sally blurted.

"It's yer husband we want, Smoke Jensen? We figger he'll come for you when you don't show up at the hotel."

Her anger and indignation were overridden by fear for Smoke's safety, and Sally ceased struggling. Her sharp mind worked quickly to devise some means of escape, or lacking that, to warn Smoke. The incidents in New Hampshire, and the previous night here in Boston, imprinted themselves on her consciousness. Someone out there was after her Smoke and she had to prevent them from succeeding.

Grim-faced, the men steered her toward a side exit of the common. Sally looked about her for some way of getting a message to Smoke. To her regret and frustration, she found none before the men whisked her into the rear of an enclosed wagon, some sort of furniture mover to judge, by the name on the side. Her packages were taken from her and her hands were firmly bound behind her back. Then they sat her unceremoniously on a quilted pad and the wagon started off.

Sean O'Boyle sidled through the Cambridge Street entrance of Fin O'Casey's on Charles Street at three that afternoon. A quick glance at the back bar told him that the spirits dispensed differed little from the Irish saloons that lined Atlantic Avenue and Commercial Street down by the docks. Only the prices indicated a better class of clientele. Even the soft glow of highly polished brass, the rich, dark wood paneling, and the plush velvet upholstery of comfortable chairs told him this place was at least two classes above his accustomed watering holes. He spotted Phineas Lathrop sitting with a friend on a shadowy corner banquette. He whipped the cloth cap from his thick thatch of black hair as he approached the table.

"A good afternoon to ye, gentlemen," he delivered with deference.

Phineas Lathrop and Arnold Cabbott looked up at their Boston henchman and did not reply. O'Boyle noted their mood and forced more affability than he felt into his beaming Irish face.

"Not to worry about our little project. Everything is at hand. Within the hour the—ah—package will be delivered to the warehouse on Pier Seven. By evening, the trail will be laid to the whereabouts of that lovely bit of goods. Smoke Jensen will be able to follow it easily."

"You're certain this time?" Lathrop growled.

"Positive. By midnight Smoke Jensen will be dead."

Patrons lined the rear wall of the lecture hall where Smoke Jensen would speak that night. Every seat had been filled by twenty minutes before the program was to begin. In contrast to his usual calm, calculated demeanor, Smoke paced the corridor outside the line of minute dressing rooms, a dark expression drawing together his heavy brows and turning down the corners of his mouth.

So far, Sally had yet to appear. He had not seen her since breakfast. He had at least expected to meet her for a light supper after the matinee. When she had failed to join him in the suite while he dressed, he had sent Robert and Walter Reynolds out looking for her. They reported negative results at the lecture hall two hours later. He told them to look harder, that he knew she had mentioned the shops along Tremont Street.

"She can't have disappeared," Smoke insisted. "Someone has to have seen something."

"It's been hours, Mr. Jensen," Robert protested. "A whole different sort of people will be along Tremont, and most of the shops closed."

"I don't like the idea of bringing in the police," Walter began.

"Nor do I," Smoke agreed. "Sally's a resourceful girl. If you look hard enough you'll find something that leads to where she's gone," he insisted.

By the conclusion of the lecture, Robert and Walter returned, excited by a discovery they had made. "We found two children playing with a woman's hat and hatbox on the common. It was the sort of thing Sally would like," Robert blurted to Smoke.

"What else did you find?" a worried Smoke asked.

"There were some scraps of paper, like from a parcel. They had blown some, but led to the north edge of the park. On Winter Street. That's where we lost sight of anything."

"You're sure nothing else could lead us to Sally?" Smoke queried urgently.

Both young men shook their heads in defeat. A commotion raised at the stage door as a small waif of about eleven squirmed past the doorman and bolted down the corridor toward Smoke and his brothers-in-law. He had a scrap of paper in one hand and a thatch of carroty hair that sprouted from under a cloth cap. He looked over the three men carefully and spoke to Smoke.

"You Smoke Jensen?"

"I am."

"This is for you." He thrust the paper toward Smoke and turned to run without even waiting for a tip.

Smoke took a quick glance at the first words of the folded note: "We've got your wife . . ." and went for the boy. He caught him in three long, fast strides.

"Who gave you this?" he demanded.

"Leggo!" the kid shouted as one word.

Inflamed by the implication in the note, Smoke lifted the lad off his brogues and shook him roughly. "Answer me. Who gave you this note?"

Eyes wide with fear, the boy screwed his full, curved lips into a pout. "It was just a man. A big one. Not like you, but thick through the shoulders and chest."

"Tell me more," Smoke demanded.

"Put me down, okay?" Feet on the floor again, he went on, "He had real black hair, short and curly. A mick face."

"What do you mean?"

"He looked like Irish to me."

Smoke studied the flaming hair, freckles, and cornflower blue eyes. The boy looked Irish enough to him. "Does this Irishman have a name?"

"No—I don't know. He didn't give me one."

"If you're holding something back, I'll drop your britches and blister your behind," Smoke threatened.

"You can't touch me. We got a Child Protective League in Boston."

These pint-sized hard cases learned all the angles at an early age, Smoke reflected. Forcing himself to stay calm, Smoke looked the boy over again. He didn't appear to be beyond redeeming. Smoke decided to try a little naked intimidation.

"I'm not from Boston," he stated nastily. "Where I come from, they still use razor straps and willow switches on smartass punks like you. So I reckon I can do anything with you that I want to. Don't you doubt that if you brought any of those do-gooder ladies around here to complain I'd give them a look at my forty-five Colt. They'd wet their bloomers and faint dead away. Better open up before I hurt you a little.

Not that Smoke Jensen would ever deliberately harm a child, a woman, or an animal. He'd skinned a knuckle on the jaws of more than one so-called man he'd caught in the act. Popped a few caps, too. The now-terrified messenger didn't know that.

"Honest, I don't know his name. I've seen him around, though."

"Where?"

"Places." Smoke glowered at him and he hurried to elaborate. "Like on the docks, outside the gin mills, that sort of place."

Smoke released his grip on the boy's shirt front. "All right.

You've saved yourself from a world of hurt. I want you to take me to the exact place where he gave you the message."

The kid shrugged. "It must be important."

"Believe me, it is," Smoke confided. He looked up to find Oliver Johnson from the *Herald* standing close by, notepad in hand, pencil skipping over the page.

"Just what's in that note?" Johnson inquired around the unlighted stub of a cigar in one corner of his mouth.

It occurred to Smoke that he had not read beyond the first four words. He delayed his answer to Johnson, opened the scrap of paper, and read the entire contents. "I don't know why I'm telling you this," he directed to the reporter. "It's from someone calling themselves the Defenders of Erin. It says that she'll be released unharmed if I do what they say."

"And what's that?" Johnson pressed.

"I'm to go to a place called Pier Seven, alone. To walk down the center of the pier to the far end. There's a building there, a warehouse. I'm to go inside."

Johnson looked up, frowned. "That's where O'Boyle and his anarchist union thugs hang out. Not a place you'd want to be going in the best of times. Certainly not at half past ten at night."

Recollections of the encounter the previous night flooded over Smoke Jensen. Could this be connected somehow? "What do you suggest?"

"Truth to tell, I'd say don't go. That's not what you're going to do, I can tell. I'll go with you."

Smoke started to refuse, then considered it to be wise to have someone along to scout the area who knew the lay of the land. "All right. If this is as dangerous as you suggest, it might be good if you knew how to use a gun."

Johnson produced a broad, youthful smile. "As it happens, I know a little about shooting. Nothing to match your skill, but satisfactory for around here."

After they left the lecture hall, Oliver Johnson hailed a passing hack. Once they had settled into the leather-upholstered seat of the use-worn surrey, Smoke spoke his thoughts aloud.

"Aren't they making this a little bit too easy for me?"

"That had occurred to me," Johnson agreed. "Those hoodlums don't often advertise their activities."

"Maybe we should approach the place from a different route."

"That makes sense. For at least one of us."

Johnson groped inside his suit coat and withdrew a small, compact revolver, a tilt-top Smith and Wesson .38. He made a quick glance at the blunt gray noses of the bullets in their chambers and dropped it into a side pocket. Then he nodded to Smoke Jensen.

"Do these wharf rats know what you look like?"

"We have to assume they do."

"The reason I asked is that I think you should be the one to come in from a different way," Johnson suggested. "We're of close to the same size. If we swap hats and coats, I can show up on the pier and probably get close enough in the dark before they notice the difference. The note did say to come alone, right?"

"You've got me there," Smoke allowed. "All right, we'll do it like that. Slipping around and surprisin' folks is something I used to do a lot of."

"I'll have the driver let you off on Atlantic Avenue. There's an alleyway that will lead to the blind side of that warehouse," Johnson advised.

A wicked anticipatory smile lighted the face of Smoke Jensen. "I like your way of doin' things. I only wish that I had changed out of these boots into moccasins. These leather boot heels are about as quiet as a cow in a briar patch. If it works and we catch them between us, I intend to make them the sorriest sons of bitches for miles around."

James Finnegan saw him first. A surrey hack stopped under a streetlamp that had been deliberately turned low. A tall man in a formal black evening coat and top hat climbed out, handed the fare to the driver, and turned toward the high wooden-slat gates that closed off access to the pier. Finnegan watched him search out the smaller human-sized portal that had been conveniently left unlocked. The cab rattled away down Adams Lane as the latch rattled and the silhouetted figure of Smoke Jensen entered.

"He's here," the sharper-sighted Finnegan informed his friends.

"Sure it's him?" Henny Duggan asked.

"Who the hell else would be comin' here this time o' night?" Finnegan shot back.

"Yeah. I see him," Brian Galagher verified. "He's alone like he's supposed to be."

"Unless there's a flyin' squad o' Boston's Finest waitin' down the dock," grumbled Liam O'Toile.

"Shut yer face," a fifth man grumbled. "He could hear you from there."

"Why don't we pop him right where he stands?" O'Tolle complained.

"Liam, ye couldn't hit the broad side of a barn from the inside with that pop gun yer packin'," Finnegan retorted. "There's six of us to make sure the job's done right. This here Jensen is a dangerous feller."

"That's why I say do it now," O'Tolle defended himself.

"Wrong," Finnegan responded in a harsh whisper. "We wait until he's close enough for you boys with the cargo hooks to snag him in the shoulders. That way, we who've got shooters along can empty them into him without any risk. Now hush up."

Smoke Jensen had scaled the secondary gate that barred entry to the pier on the back side of the warehouse. He stealthily approached the blind narrow end of the lofty, metal-clad wooden structure. There he found an iron ladder that led to the roof. He removed his boots and closed his mind to the discomfort climbing would bring to his feet.

Silently Smoke ascended and worked his way along a catwalk until he reached the far end. His gaze reached the black, oily water of the upper end of Boston Harbor, where it received the outpouring of the Charles River. He recalled from his reading of history that just across an inlet to the southeast was the spot where the Sons of Liberty had staged the Boston Tea Party. A fitting place for this night's work, Smoke thought wryly. A sibilant rustle of voices wafted up from below.

Smoke listened in on the discussion of tactics and glanced toward the street end of the warehouse in time to spot the approach of Oliver Johnson. He knew at once he occupied a disadvantageous position. Starlight picked out a duplicate of the ladder at the other end. Smoke eased himself along the steep pitch of the roof until he reached it.

Why had they built it this way, and not directly below the catwalk that topped the roof crown? Probably to keep anyone from easily jumping ship or boarding unwanted visitors, he decided, as he lowered himself down the rungs.

With three treads to go, Smoke Jensen saw movement from the corner of one eye. Two men materialized out of the deep shadows between large bales of some sort and made a dash toward Oliver Johnson, who had walked beyond their hiding place and had his back to them. Light from a fat, yellowish rising moon glinted off wicked, curved hooks held high to strike. Smoke set a foot on the next lower rung and held on with one hand while he hauled out his .45 Peacemaker.

A second later, the big .45 roared in the night, a long yellow-white tongue of flame spearing from the muzzle. Firing in the dark and from above had him at a disadvantage. The hot slug tore a ragged, agonizing trench across the upper portion of the nearest assailant's right shoulder. Howling, he let go of his longshoreman's hook and looked around for the source of the shot.

"Up there. On the side of the building," he yelled a second later, just as Smoke adjusted his aim and fired again.

This time the bullet smacked solidly into the chest of the other hook wielder. He let out a sharp, short cry and pitched face-first onto the rough, splintered planks of the dock. His boot toes drummed a sharp tattoo while Oliver Johnson hauled out his own six-gun. Smoke let go and dropped the rest of the way to the dock flooring. By that time, he saw Oliver Johnson had recovered from his shocked discovery of men lurking to kill him.

He had his revolver out of the coat pocket and aimed doubtfully toward a darkened doorway in the side of the warehouse. Three men came pouring out toward him, one with an even smaller revolver than Johnson's on the way to line up with the reporter's chest.

Johnson fired twice. One .38 slug caught an attacker in the thigh and spilled him onto the dock to squirm, crablike, away from the fray. Flickers of muzzle flame lit up the area before the door and Oliver Johnson spotted Smoke Jensen.

"Oh, shit, I think there's more of them than we expected," Johnson called to his resourceful partner.

14

Only when he realized his carefully worked-out plan had failed did Seamas Quern hasten to summon five of the longshoremen assigned to guard Sally Jensen. That would leave the wife of Smoke Jensen in the custody of Connor O'Fallon and Sean O'Boyle.

Both men had been drinking heavily, celebrating the anticipated demise of Sally's husband. That provided Sally with an opportunity to learn something of what lay behind these attacks on Smoke and her. Throughout her ordeal, Sally kept her wits about her. She had no longer resisted her captors after being trundled into the furniture van. Once at the warehouse, she'd remained silent and out of the way.

When the drinking started, Sally noted, her wardens tended toward ignoring her presence. They spoke freely about their role in the dock strike and in the plans of someone named Lathrop. By the time the ambush went awry, O'Boyle and O'Fallon completely lacked the judgment to guard their tongues.

"Wha' th'hell does Lathrop want this Smoke Jensen dead for, anyway?" O'Fallon asked, after a long pull on a bottle of Irish whiskey.

O'Boyle gave an owlish stare and accepted the bottle. "It's all part of a grand plan, it is. What got us into it is, a boyo workin' for Mr. Lathrop didn't do his job right. Both th' Jensens' was to die in an avalanche, they was."

O'Fallon paled. "Good Lord, any man who can walk away from tons of snow is more than I want to cross knuckles with."

O'Boyle winked at him. "Don't ye worry, lad. This ruckus'll be over in a few minutes an' the door will be wide open."

O'Fallon belched whiskey fumes. "What door, damn it, Sean?"

Horrified by the revelation O'Boyle had made, Sally rallied her spirits and grew coldly determined to survive her captivity and see them all brought to justice. All she had to do was bide her time. Smoke would be here.

"Why, the door to the entire west, bucko," O'Boyle stated grandly, after another swig from the bottle, the liquor adding to his own importance in the scheme and loosening his tongue even more. "Ye know yerself that the big-time fixers, and most of the boys on the dodge on the East Coast, have come to the same conclusion that Mr. Lathrop has, don't ye? The police are gettin' too much power. Now they've made it against the law for a man to carry a gun in near every city— not even honest folk are safe from their oppression, they're not. Once Smoke Jensen is taken care of, our Irish gangs and others of the brotherhood will be ready to pull out of here and head west."

"When's all this to happen?"

"We're supposed to go soon's Jensen is taken care of, we are. Mr. Lathrop and two of his partners, Middleton and Asher, are to leave from New York City before the end of the week and join up with twenty men, handpicked by me, in some place called Dodge City, they are. Think of it, bucko! We'll all be rich as an English lord, we will."

"A pox on those damned English lords," O'Fallon growled. "They had me Pap strung up, they did."

"Ah, did they now? 'Tis a cryin' shame."

"That's true, it is. Only, what makes Smoke Jensen so important he has to be killed?"

O'Boyle winked roguishly. "Now, that's something in itself, it is. Seems this Jensen is some sort of leader among the folks out there in Colorado. They look up to him, they do. Alone, they say, he's a power to deal with, he is. If he led the locals against us, we'd be in a bad position. Lathrop figures they could run us clear the hell an' gone outta there. There's lots of land out there in those mountains, there is. More than a hunnerd an' fifty miles on a side, Lathrop told me. He wants to make his headquarters at the ranch owned by Jensen, the Sugarloaf, he does. With Jensen gone, it's all ours for the takin'."

That's when Seamas Quern burst in with the news that the ambush had failed. "B'God, he's done for three of the boys in the twinklin' of an eye."

O'Boyle recovered enough of his senses to blink blearily and wave a hand at the others in the room. "You boys go along and give Seamas a hand." After they left, he bent toward O'Fallon and spoke in a conspiratorial manner. "There's another reason Lathrop wants Smoke Jensen to die."

"Oh? An' what would that be?" O'Fallon asked.

Speaking in a hushed tone, O'Boyle replied, "Though I don't have the whole of it, I gather there's bad blood betwixt the two of them. Lathrop has this half-brother who ran afoul of Jensen some while back. He had sort of a little empire goin', much like what Lathrop wants to do, only a lot smaller. He crossed Smoke Jensen and paid the price. Jensen killed him."

O'Fallon considered that a moment. "It's said Jensen's killed a lot of men. Any idea which one it might've been?"

"Oh, I've the name, right enough. Phineas Lathrop's half-brother was named Rex Davidson."

Mention of the name sent a chill through Sally's heart.

* * *

Five more men came in a rush from the doorway behind
Smoke Jensen. They had remained out of sight in the bowels
of the warehouse during the initial attempt to ambush the
mountain man gunfighter. Now they spread out and closed
on Smoke and Oliver. Three held longshoremen's hooks.
Moonlight flashed off the keen edges of the long, slim
knives in the hands of the other two. At Oliver Johnson's exclamation, Smoke Jensen turned to face them.

Smoke's first inclination was to holster his Colt and take
them on a more even standing. Then Seamas Quern joined
his last upright fighters and Smoke saw the revolver in his
hand. That decided his course of action. Only ten feet separated Smoke from the reinforcements, with more like thirty
between him and Quern. Smoke snapped a fast round at
Quern as one of the stevedores lunged at him with a wicked
hook.

Hot outrage ripped through Seamas Quern's side and he
cried out in pain. He dropped to the planking of the dock as
Smoke Jensen backpeddled and brought his .45 Colt up to
parry a swishing question mark of death in the hand of the
nearest assailant. Metal screeched as the two objects met.
Seamas felt a lightheaded dizziness sweep over him and he
slowly edged himself away from the developing fight.

Smoke Jensen jammed hard knuckles into the ribcage of
his attacker. The longshoreman grunted and gave a twist of
his hook that tore the Peacemaker out of Smoke's right hand.
Although everyone agreed that there was no backdown in
Smoke Jensen, he did make a tactical retreat to regain balance and fill his hand with his other six-gun. Incorrectly
sensing weakness, the hard-faced dock worker pushed his
slim advantage.

A bad mistake, he soon learned, when the tip of his
weapon snagged the front of Smoke Jensen's coat and bit on
through to the shirt. An instant later, fire literally blasted into
his gut as Smoke triggered another shot. Hot gases, burning
flecks of powder, and of course a 240-grain lead slug blew
through the hole that had been made in his belly. A vicious

yank downward on the hook ripped apart Smoke's clothing and left a thin red line on his chest.

It turned out to be the final act of a dying man. His eyes rolled up and the stevedore gave a terrible shudder, then fell into Smoke's arms. Lacking any sympathy for the would-be murderer, and intent on maintaining a whole skin, Smoke dropped him at once. He turned to find the others attacking Oliver Johnson.

"Behind you, Ollie," Smoke barked, as he raised the Colt into action again.

Oliver Johnson did something Smoke Jensen would never have imagined could work: he raised his gun arm and bent it backward over his shoulder. The small .38 barked loudly and a hole appeared under the nose of his assailant. Smoke's .45 blasted a fraction of a second later.

His bullet found a home in tender flesh, which ended the career of a budding dockside thug. "Thanks, I needed that," Oliver Johnson called out cheerily.

His jovial manner, coupled with Smoke Jensen's deadly efficiency, put the survivors to flight. Smoke started at once for the door to the warehouse. "If Sally is here, we'll find her," he promised. He didn't even notice the missing Seamas O'Boyle.

Seamas O'Boyle had crawled through the doorway into the warehouse and took long, painful seconds to pull himself upright. He staggered as he hurried to the small office cubicle where his boss held the woman captive. The long, oily locks of his jet-black hair hung in dirty disarray. He had a wild-eyed appearance when he burst through the door and confronted Sean O'Boyle.

"Well? Is it over, then?" O'Boyle asked, eyes glassy from drink.

"Yeah. Only, not like you'd expected, it ain't. They're all down. Every man jack of them. That Smoke Jensen is a terror. An' there was two of them."

O'Boyle blanched. He didn't think for even a second about using Sally Jensen as a hostage. "We've gotta get out of here, we do," he blurted, coming unsteadily to his feet.

"There's a back way," Connor O'Fallon suggested.

"Damn it, man, don't you think I know that?" O'Boyle snapped.

"We had best be takin' it, we had."

"What about the woman?" Seamas Quern asked.

"Leave her. She'd only slow us down."

"Yer the boss, Sean," Quern allowed.

Quickly the trio left the office. Only they didn't move quite fast enough. Their leather brogues made loud, clicking sounds on the hard oak planks of the warehouse floor. From the direction of the quayside door they heard a sharp exclamation.

"There they go, Smoke."

Twin muzzle blooms winked in the darkened building. A bullet cracked past uncomfortably close to the ear of Sean O'Boyle. It did a great lot toward sobering him. He turned to run backward while he emptied the five shots in his diminutive .32 Smith and Wesson. Fired by a booze-soaked, frightened man, the small lead pellets struck at random, without doing harm.

Smoke Jensen fired again, to be rewarded by a startled cry when the .45 slug tore a gouge in Sean O'Boyle's right ear. Smoke and Oliver began to run now, guided by the dim yellow glow of a lamp in the office. Smoke ignored the fleeing felons. Only one goal directed him.

He had to know the whereabouts of Sally. Would he find her still alive in that office? Anger and anxiety distracted him from the idea of apprehending the culprits. Chances were, he could find them later. First, he had to locate Sally and free her.

In his haste to depart, Sean O'Boyle had roughly shoved the castored chair to which Sally Jensen had been tied out of the way, into the shadows, between two tall, wooden file cabinets. After the principal conspirators had hastily departed, Sally sat in apprehension as she heard gunshots and shouts from outside. Running footsteps faded in her ears, to be replaced by the clump of fast-moving boots approaching. Only which belonged to whom?

Suddenly the door flew open and a broad-shouldered figure dived inside, its progress led by the muzzle of a .45 Colt. The force of the entry dislodged the coal-oil lamp from the desk. It fell to the floor and smashed, the wick drowned to darkness in a flood of kerosene. Her heart surged in her chest. It had to be her beloved Smoke. A moment later she had confirmation as his familiar profile rose in silhouette above a desk, head swiveling to let his eyes take in the entire room.

With her lips sealed by a bandage made of a man's shirt-tail and sticking plaster, Sally had no means of calling out to her husband. Her hands had been tied to the arms of the chair and her feet bound together. She thought frantically of some means of letting him know where she was. When it came to her in a flash of embarrassed enlightenment, she cursed herself silently for not seeing it at first. All she had to do was kick one of the file cabinets.

Sally's initial thumps had a muffled quality. Her captors had removed her shoes. Well, damn it, she thought, and let go a stronger kick. A sharp pain shot up her legs from her toes, although she was much different today from the eastern tenderfoot who had married the handsome mountain man so long ago.

"Sally? Is that you?" Smoke's deep, familiar voice demanded.

"Ummf! Mugguh! Aaaugh!" Sally tried to respond through her gag.

Smoke came to her in a rush. He bent and swiftly cut through the bonds that restrained her hands, then knelt to slice the heavy cord that secured her ankles. Then he rose again and put gentle fingers to the sides of her mouth.

"This is going to smart some," he advised her.

Then he edged the corner of the sticking plaster away from her skin, peeled back enough to get a good grasp, and yanked with a swift, sure movement. Sally yelped at the insult to her skin, then sprang into Smoke's arms. Her legs would not hold her and her fingers had gone numb long ago. She clung, though, while Smoke hugged her back.

"You could have taken that nasty thing out of my mouth first," she made mock complaint. "At least that way I could have told you my arms and legs were numb."

"It's all right, Sal. You're safe now," Smoke told her, as he nuzzled her graceful neck.

"I may be, but you're not," Sally snapped back, more in her normal mode.

"Those who could ran away," Smoke rejected her worry.

"That's not what I mean." Quickly Sally recounted what the inebriated Sean O'Boyle had said about Phineas Lathrop and his grand design on the High Lonesome. "That terrible man O'Boyle said Lathrop plans to make his headquarters at the Sugarloaf," she wound down. "To do that, he knew he had to have you killed. In fact, that avalanche was planned to kill us both."

"His men have tried a couple of times since, and failed. I don't imagine we'll see Mr. O'Boyle again."

"There's more, Smoke, honey. Lathrop is related to someone who came very near to killing you. He's half-brother to Rex Davidson, and considers this a personal affair between you and him."

Smoke looked at her hard, trying to read her expression in the dimness of the office. "I'll worry about that later. Now, let's get you out of here."

None of the trio who fled the warehouse could be called coward. Sean O'Boyle had grown up on the wharfs and docks of Boston, a scrapper and hard-nose almost from birth. His widowed mother and an uncle had brought him there from County Cork, after his father had been killed in one of the uprisings. He'd never lost his brogue nor his old country manner of speech. Neither had Connor O'Fallon, who had come to America with one of his older brothers, a priest, and had immediately gone wild. He and Sean O'Boyle had fought back-to-back as boys, carving out a place for themselves among the other waifs of Boston's waterfront.

Early on they had attracted a follower in the form of Seamas Quern. Seamas was some four years younger, the son of a waterfront whore and a visiting Irish sailor. He had been on his own since he was old enough to walk and feed himself. By the age of thirteen, he'd led one wing of Sean O'Boyle's mob of street hustlers, pickpockets, and sneak-thieves. As they grew older, their crimes became more serious and more violent. All three had killed grown men before they'd reached their fifteenth birthdays.

When, at 18, most Irish lads of recent immigration looked toward the Army Recruiting Office for a means out of the squalor of the East Coast tenement neighborhoods, Sean O'Boyle and those of his gang, which now numbered close to fifty, turned to the piers to improve their standard of living. They did that by stealing from the ships, from the docks, and out of the warehouses where they worked. All three had served time in Railford by the time they reached the majority. They had also accumulated considerable wealth by their standards.

It was along about then that first Rex Davidson, then his half-brother, Phineas Lathrop, took Sean O'Boyle as a protégé. The relationship had not been one made in heaven. Even so, O'Boyle now sat at the head of a union of 350 longshoremen and stevedores, nearly half of whom were hardened criminals.

With a little coaching from Lathrop, O'Boyle and his thugs steadily bled the ship owners, shipping companies, warehouse owners, and merchants of Boston for a healthy share of the profits. These added costs brought on by the pil-

lage naturally had to be passed on to customers on everything brought into Boston by ship.

Sale of the pilfered merchandise—sometimes items as
large as whole cargo pallets of lumber—contributed signif-
icantly to the coffers of Phineas Lathrop and had financed
the initial stages of his western dream of an empire of crime.
Only two flaws marred Lathrop's grand design.

First, so accustomed were Phineas Lathrop and his partners, associates, and henchmen to the manner of "doing
business" in the East—everyone seemed to have his hand
out and could be counted on to look the other way when the
palm was properly crossed with silver—that they could not
see that things were done differently in the West. Not even
when they were presented with deadly evidence of it.

The second flaw was Smoke Jensen. Determined to carry
out their assigned task of eliminating the famous gunfighter,
the three hard cases set out to locate more of their men.
Three blocks from the warehouse, they came upon fifteen of
O'Boyle's bully-boys.

"Go on to Seventh Street," O'Boyle commanded. He
added a description of Smoke and Sally Jensen, and Seamas
Quern contributed details on Oliver Johnson. "Seamas, you
go back with them," he added, much to Quern's disappointment. "I want ye to make sure not a one of them leaves there
alive," O'Boyle concluded ominously.

15

While they made a hasty exit from the warehouse, Smoke Jensen introduced Sally to Oliver Johnson. He immediately became "Ollie" to her. They had only rounded the shoreward end of the building when sixteen burly longshoremen appeared inside the gate.

"There they are!" a voice shouted. "Let's get 'em, boys."

Smoke Jensen made an immediate estimate of the situation. "Back to the warehouse. We'll have a better chance there.

Sally Jensen found she could not run fast enough to keep up with Ollie Johnson. Smoke slowed his pace to keep beside her. A bullet sped by them, well off target, followed by the crack of a small-caliber revolver.

"These easterners are the lousiest shots I've ever seen," Smoke observed to Oliver.

"Not much opportunity for practice in the big cities," the reporter informed Smoke.

"I can see that," Smoke agreed, as they banged through a narrow doorway. "But I'd think they could go out in the country and improve their skill."

"Most of that bunch would be lost a mile away from the Charles River. Besides, do you seriously want them to be better marksmen?"

Smoke laughed. "You have me there."

He called for a stop to check the loads in their weapons. Smoke had retrieved his primary .45 and reloaded before they set off. Now he tended to the iron in its cross-draw rig. Oliver Johnson frowned as he groped in a pocket for loose cartridges.

"Damn, I didn't count on a protracted gunfight," the *Boston Herald* staffer complained to himself.

"Does that thing chamber thirty-eight Long Colt, Ollie?" Sally asked sweetly. "I have half a box in my purse."

Ollie gave her a startled look in the twilight dimness of the warehouse. "No, damn it. It's a Smith." He groped again in his coat pocket. "I have enough rounds for two reloads, Smoke," he announced.

"I'm not much better off. I'm glad you have your Lightning along, Sal. How is it they didn't take it off you?"

"Never knew I had it. They might be a pack of hardened criminals, but being easterners, they wouldn't think of a lady carrying a gun."

Oliver Johnson gaped openly at Sally Jensen. A loud banging and muffled curses announced the arrival of the fresh pack of thugs at the door. Smoke had had the presence of mind to slide the bar before they'd delved into the darkness of the warehouse.

"That won't hold them long," Smoke announced. "I suggest we find places among these stacks of cargo and make them come to us. Sally, dear, it might be better if you took up a place above, on that catwalk."

"Think I've forgotten how to hit what I shoot at?" she asked testily.

"No, damn it, I only want you out of the way of any danger."

Sally produced a hint of a pout. "I've handled worse bastards than this pack," she snapped.

"You're our back-up, all right?" Smoke barked back at her.

She scurried off to the cast-iron stairway at the other side of the building. Oliver Johnson found a convenient hiding place atop a mound of tarpaulin-covered machine parts. Smoke Jensen surveyed the positions, made careful note of where Sally hunkered down behind a concealing plank on the catwalk, then faded into the mounds of unidentified items.

With a bang, the door slammed open. Five men spilled inside. Another quintet followed, while the remaining longshoremen spread out to secure all exits. The first set moved directly to the center of the warehouse. Their voices echoed in the high-ceilinged structure as they gave directions to the others.

"Someone check the office." Sally recognized the voice of Seamas Quern.

"Make sure you cover every way out of here."

"Spread out and start looking down the aisles."

"How are we supposed to see?"

"There's light enough. Your eyes will get used to it in a little while."

"Maybe you will, but I don't thi—*unnng!*" A meaty smack preceded the abrupt end of his remarks.

"What the hell?" Quern blurted. "Where are you, Joe? Are you all right?"

Not by a long shot, Oliver Johnson thought, as he hefted the long, wooden leverage handle of a chain come-along. Silently he moved to the far side of the pallet and peered into the gloom for another target. One appeared, two aisles over, only to suddenly disappear as a big, brawny arm whipped out and yanked the uneasy stevedore off his feet. A soft thud, of revolver barrel meeting skull, followed. Johnson grinned tightly. Smoke Jensen was adding to the score.

"Nobody in the office," a distant voice advised. Then, a second later, "There's one of them."

A knife swished through the air and made a musical hum when it stuck in a wooden crate three inches from the throat of Smoke Jensen. The front of the office washed yellow-white in muzzle bloom and the slug from Smoke's Colt drilled a hole dead-center in the knife-thrower's chest. He catapulted backward and crashed through the glass of the office window, dead before he hit the floor.

Low-light vision had not returned to the eyes of Oliver Johnson when two longshoremen rushed to the place where their companion had had a fatal encounter with Smoke Jensen. Smoke saw them, though, and moved in on cat feet. Both dockyard thugs leaned inside the cubicle to stare at their dead friend. Smoke bent low and snatched the ankles of one, then heaved and dumped him on his head in the office.

"Wha' th' . . ." jolted from the other a moment before Smoke Jensen's big left fist connected under the hinge of his jaw and sent him spilling into darkness.

His partner had recovered enough to come to his knees. He swung a vicious blow with a cargo hook that swished past the point of Smoke's shoulder and buried the tip in the wooden partition to the office. Smoke made a backhand swing with his Colt and caught his assailant in the temple. Bone made a crackling sound and the man uttered a breathy gurgle before he fell over backward. That made three more down. Smoke moved off into the darkness. He well knew he would have to hunt for the others.

Brian Galagher could be considered one of the brighter of O'Boyle's gang of wharf rats. After he had regained consciousness outside the warehouse, he had crawled away to find more of his brothers in crime. He soon found six of them and informed them of how their ambush had been turned into a trap by Smoke Jensen. They, in turn, had been pressed into returning by Sean O'Boyle and Connor O'Fallon. Now, separated from the commanding presence of O'Boyle, Brian let his brains dictate his actions.

"I got me somethin' figured out," he advised the two thugs with him. "We can see everything a whole lot better from up there." Galagher pointed to the catwalk.

"Jeez, yer right, Brian," a not-too-savvy dock walloper whispered back.

"What say we go up there and have a look around?" Brian Galagher winced as Smoke Jensen blasted the knife-throwing longshoreman into eternity. "Might be we'd stand a better chance of staying out of the line of fire, too," he opined.

"What if one of them is up there?" the timid dolt asked.

"Don't think they had time. What's to worry about? There's just two men and a girl."

"Two men who kicked shit out of a dozen of our boys," his nervous companion reminded Brian.

Brian grabbed the reluctant one's shirtfront and jerked him close. "I'm one of those they kicked the shit out of, re-member?" he hissed. "And I'm not afraid of them. Come with me."

Galagher started up the wooden treads of the iron stair-case. Hesitantly, the others followed. At the top, Galagher turned to his left and skirted along the catwalk. Behind him, the others did likewise. He had only turned the corner at the far end when he came upon a delicious bonus. The young woman brought to the warehouse as a captive sat near the barrier and peered over one thick plank.

"Well, look what we have here," Brian Galagher smirked aloud. For all his higher intelligence, Galagher had one ter-rible flaw. The sight of a helpless woman completely at his mercy caused him to abandon reason and be led by his gonads. Now he approached Sally Jensen, one hand groping at his crotch in what he considered a suggestive manner. "You have something for me, pretty thing?"

"I sure do," Sally answered sweetly, and drilled him through the heart with a smooth draw and pull-through of her double-action .38 Colt Lightning.

"Jesus! Oh, God, she's got a gun!" the uneasy thug bleated, as he beat a hasty retreat.

Although stunned, the remaining hard case noted an omission on the part of the gun-wielding woman. When she swung the muzzle toward him, he advanced on her, sneering. "You forgot to cock it, sweetie. And I'm gonna take it away from you before you can."

Sally squeezed through the double-action trigger and shot him in the kneecap. "I don't need to. It's double-action, asshole."

Her victim didn't hear her reply; he lay, hunched up and howling, on the grid flooring of the catwalk. Would these vermin ever learn to take them seriously? Sally wondered. Then she thought of the effect this incident could have on Smoke. She would have to sacrifice safety to reassure him, and she quickly abandoned caution.

"It's all right, Smoke. I shot two, one ran away," she called out, then swiftly moved a long distance from where she had fired her weapon.

This was all going to hell right before his eyes. Connor O'Fallon cut his eyes to Seamas Quern. What the hell? They'd both taken a drubbing from this Smoke Jensen. He could see no good reason for being killed by the big, hard-faced gunfighter. Quern seemed to read his thoughts. He flashed a nervous grin. Quern replied and jerked his head in the direction of the door through which they had entered. Grinning broadly now, Connor O'Fallon nodded in assent.

Both started toward their agreed goal when a high shriek, which cut off in a hair-raising gurgle, froze them in place.

"What the hell?" O'Fallon asked rhetorically.

"They got another of the boys," Quern suggested.

"Aw, shit. Let's get out of here."

"I sort of figured we were about to do that, I did," Quern answered.

"What about the rest?"

"Best let them know what we have in mind, Connor."

"Aye, Seamas. Though it's not in me blood to tuck me tail and run."

Two flashes and sharp reports punctuated Seamas Quern's

timely reply. "Ye've a strong desire to wait for that to come get yer?"

Connor O'Fallon rose and called to his men, "All right, boys, we're pullin' out. We're leavin', ye hear, Mr. Smoke Jensen? Don't be for shootin' us in the back, don't ye," he urged, as the search broke off in fits and starts.

With shuffling shoes, the longshoremen began to withdraw to the safety of the out of doors. O'Fallon had nearly reached the doorway when a deep voice set the air to ringing.

"What says you won't lie for us outside?"

Exasperation colored O'Fallon's words. "Devil take ye, man. We've had enough taste of yer sneakin' Injun ways, we have. We'll not be doin' ye any more harm."

"Besides," Seamas Quern whispered up close to Connor O'Fallon's ear, "we can get at them some other time. Like out west, eh?"

Not entirely convinced of the truthfulness of the one he had heard called Seamas, Smoke Jensen and Oliver Johnson made a thorough search of the warehouse floor before relaxing their guard. They came together at the foot of the catwalk stairs. Smoke glanced upward.

"They're gone, Sal. Come on down," he called out.

Three minutes later, Sally Jensen joined them. "Why did they leave?" she asked with sincerity.

Smoke considered that a moment, and noted the signs of strain etched into her face. "They must have decided they were outnumbered," he remarked dryly.

Oliver Johnson began to laugh first, joined quickly by Smoke as a titter welled up to Sally's full, sensuous lips. She had never looked better to Smoke. All of the reasons why he loved her came forth during their moment of gratifying release. When their merriment dwindled, Sally looked worriedly toward her husband.

"Do you think it's safe to go outside?" she asked.

"We'll give it a while," Smoke suggested. "Now, tell me everything that happened since I saw you last at breakfast."

Quickly, Sally related her day. She could see how the account of her abduction angered Smoke. She went on, giving as much detail as possible about her ride through Boston to the dockyards. For all the lack of adequate light, Smoke noticed with amusement, Oliver Johnson made copious notes on his small pad. When she concluded, Smoke commented on the reporter's dedication.

"You have visions of filling the front page, I take it?"

Shadow concealed Johnson's blush of pride. "That I do. I already have the headline drafted. 'SMOKE JENSEN FOILS KIDNAPPING GANG, HERALD REPORTER WITNESS TO DERRING-DO.' How's that?"

Smoke chuckled. "You journalists are all alike. Even those with enough sand to fight with more than a pen."

"I'll take that as a compliment," Oliver said lightly.

"Smoke, I've been thinking," Sally interrupted.

"What's that?"

"I told you about the one called Sean and his friend, Connor, getting drunk and talking about Phineas Lathrop and his relationship to Rex Davidson. Sean also said Lathrop was on his way to New York to round up thirty or more hoodlums to take west with him. Are you going to go after him?"

It took no time at all for Smoke Jensen to make up his mind. "Looks like the lecture tour has to be cut short. I'll take the first train tomorrow for New York."

"I'm going with you," Sally announced.

"No, you're not," Smoke stated flatly. "You'll go on back to Keene with your father and brothers."

"Smoke!" Sally exclaimed, exasperated.

"No argument. I'm going after Lathrop and his partners. That's what's important. I don't want to be worried about your safety, or to have to rescue you from kidnappers again. I mean it, Sal. You're to go back to New Hampshire."

"What if you can't find them in New York?" she tried another ploy.

"Then I'll be headed after them until I do catch up."

Sally's stubborn streak exerted itself. "The Sugarloaf is my home, too. I'll not be left behind if you head off for the High Lonesome."

Smoke weighed that a moment. "No, of course you won't. You'll have to join me in New York or take the private car on the next train out."

"It would be easier if I came along from the start."

"No, Sally."

Familiar with Smoke's bullheadedness, Sally had to admit to herself that he was determined. "All right, Smoke. I'll do it that way," she resigned herself, though she was unwilling to admit it would be his way.

"You can't keep me from going," Oliver Johnson stated.

"Still hungry for a story?" Smoke asked him, as the trio started for the door nearest to the street end of the warehouse.

"Well, yes, that, too. But the fighting has been sort of exciting so far. I'd like to get another taste, if possible."

"Reporters," Smoke Jensen summed up with a snort.

On his first visit to New York City, Smoke Jensen had been fascinated by Central Park. Up until the War Between the States, sheep had grazed here, he had been told. It had been "improved" with the addition of benches, a bandshell, seats around a large pond where ice skaters gathered in winter, and gravel paths laid out. Fashionable houses had been erected on the streets facing the park and oil street-lamps placed along the pathways. A riding stable and its attendant school had been under construction when Smoke had come to the park on that trip.

On the train down from Boston, Oliver Johnson had informed Smoke Jensen that the Central Park Riding Academy had become quite popular. Smoke could not imagine why riding had become so fashionable, even though many of the horses he bred had been sold to the East. From what he recalled, walking provided the most common means of going from one place to another. Public transportation, in the form of horse-drawn trollies and the newly formed Electric Railway System, took care of most of the rest.

Smoke dismissed contemplation of this aspect of the mysterious East and concentrated on their main purpose in coming to the big city. When they arrived in Grand Central Station, the first destination was the files of the *New York Ledger,* one of the leading dailies. There, they found vague references in the financial section to the offices of Middleton and Asher, but no references to Phineas Lathrop.

Not unexpectedly, when they located the office complex, on the fifth floor of a marble-faced building on Wall Street, Smoke and Oliver found the premises closed and apparently vacated.

"What now?" Oliver asked.

"I can track a man across bare rock, if I have to," Smoke admitted. "But I don't know the first damned thing about finding someone in a town this size."

With an expression that asked for eager compliance, Oliver suggested, "The thing to do is find a nearby saloon, a gentleman's bar, as a matter of fact. We can put out the word and see what we learn."

Smoke gave him a warm smile. "By damn, that's exactly what I'd do in any western town. Go to a saloon and let it be known who I wanted to find. Don't seem things are all that different, anyhow."

After a visit to a third gentleman's bar, with an obligatory drink in each, Smoke called a halt to their inquiries for the day. "Now we let the word get around. By tomorrow we should hear something."

"Where to now?" Oliver asked, longing for another shot of rye and a beer at yet a fourth spirits emporium.

"How about Central Park? I must have sold fifty horses to

the riding school there. I'd sort of like to see what's been done with them."

Oliver Johnson readily agreed and suggested they take the horse trolley north on Broadway and Park Avenue to 106th Street and walk the two blocks to the entrance nearest the stables. Smoke considered that a good idea, particularly since they were at about the southernmost tip of Manhattan Island, with Central Park more than a hundred blocks north. On the trip, Smoke soon discovered that little had changed since his first visit. And that reminded him of why he had such an immense dislike for easterners.

Bony and droop-headed, the nag that pulled the wheeled conveyance along its street-level tracks showed signs of mal-treatment along with extreme age and exhaustion. A small, hot coal of anger grew in Smoke's middle while the driver shouted and liberally applied the lash to the tired beast. Smoke's anger had almost burst into flame by the time they reached the 106th Street stop.

His fury fanned into full blaze the moment they entered the compound around the stables and riding school. A small man with a cruel, narrow face struck furiously at a hand-some bay with a riding crop that sported an excessively long leather lash.

"You'll not try to bite me again, you miserable, stupid animal," his high, thin, porcine voice raged.

Clearly visible in the white blaze on the forehead of the horse were dark lines of other, recently healed wounds. Smoke Jensen's face darkened and he started forward, his outrage over such blatant abuse fueling the anger he already felt. His slate-gray eyes had turned to Arctic ice. Belatedly, Oliver Johnson realized that the life of the man abusing his horse now hung by a very narrow thread.

16

Blood had welled up in a deep cut by the time Smoke
Jensen reached the disagreeable little man. As Smoke closed
on him, he raised the crop for another slash.

"Yes, I'll show you, you miserable beast."

In the next instant, thick, powerful fingers closed in iron
bands around the wrist behind the upraised hand. "No, you
won't," Smoke Jensen growled close in the ear of the furious horse owner.

Increasing pressure turned the hand cherry red. Its owner
yelped and directed his fury against the big man who had in-
terfered. "Get your hands off me!" he bleated, although he
had intended it to come out in an angry roar.

Darker red, now, the hand began to swell and throb. "It's
only one hand. If I'd wanted to use two, it would be to break
your goddamned neck."

Purple now, the captive appendage opened and released
the quirt. Frantic with pain and fear, the man screeched
through his misery. "Help! Someone help me! Anderson,
Norton, come here at once!"

Aware the riding crop no longer represented a danger,
Smoke Jensen spun the little man around and gave him a
solid backhand slap with his huge left paw. "Don't ever hurt
that animal again," Smoke said with deadly finality.

He gave the helpless man a hard shove that sent him sprawling into a high pile of used straw and fresh horse manure. Then Smoke turned and walked away as though nothing at all had happened.

In the small office of the academy, Smoke met the man who had so far been only a name on a letter. He seemed genuinely pleased to meet Smoke Jensen and they talked of the horses purchased over the years. Some had been sold outright to wealthy clients, as gifts for wives or children. Others still walked the tree-lined trails of the park. A few, who had grown older, had been sold to the New York Transit System.

That last rankled, when Smoke thought of the savage treatment rendered to the draft animals he had seen so far. What the manager told him next averted any outburst.

"There's one I keep back. He's reserved for some special, very skilled riders. Sort of an outlaw."

"I never sell outlaws," Smoke contradicted.

Looking embarrassed, the manager spoke with his eyes averted. "He became one, though. Really, it might be said it was in part my fault. I allowed our Mr. Armbrewster to take him out several days in a row. That was before Mr. Armbrewster purchased a horse of his own. I'm afraid Mr. Armbrewster maltreated the animal. We never knew until we had a chance to observe how he dealt with his personal mount. Then it became clear."

"This Armbrewster," Smoke began, after several moments' thought. "Is he short, with a pinched-up face and a horse's ass attitude?"

Oliver Johnson, who stood at Smoke Jensen's side, chuckled.

"That—ah—describes him fairly well. Why do you ask?"

"I've met him. Only a short while ago."

"Oh? Under what circumstances, Mr. Jensen?"

"He was beating his horse. I rearranged his outlook on the considerate treatment of animals. You shouldn't have any more complaints about how he cares for his mount. If he backslides, though, just mention my name to him."

"I—ah—see. And . . . thank you from everyone at the academy."

"You're welcome," Smoke responded. "Now, I think I'd like to have your outlaw saddled. If I'm here a few days, maybe I can turn him around for you."

"That's most generous of you, Mr. Jensen. I appreciate it, you can be sure. I'll see that he's brought up at once."

Out on the bridle path some twenty minutes later, Oliver Johnson found out what all first-timers learned about riding horseback. His thighs started to ache, and he strongly believed he had endured irreversible damage to his crotch. He endured it, though, in order to point out the ambitious building projects, endowed by such wealthy men as Grandville Dodge and the grandson of John Jacob Astor.

"Astor got rich on the fur trade, as I'm sure you know," Oliver pointed out.

"He was rich before he started the American Fur Company," Smoke responded. "Though from what people say back here, he was generous with what he had."

Three men blocked the path ahead. Two of them moved aside as Smoke and Ollie approached, and muttered polite greetings. The third, a stout, heavily muscled individual with a shock of coarse, black hair, did a double-take, his face tightening as Smoke rode past.

Ollie Johnson started also and then put a blank mask on his face. Once beyond the trio, he spoke softly to Smoke. "Believe me, I'm not imagining things. We just rode past Phineas Lathrop and Victor Middleton. The one with them who looks like a stevedore, is one. That's Sean O'Boyle, the cause of your recent troubles."

"B'God, let's go get them," Smoke exploded.

"They're bound to have more men close by," Johnson cautioned. "Just because they're dressed in fancy riding habits doesn't mean Lathrop and Middleton are any less thugs than O'Boyle." He looked around uncomfortably. "It's too isolated here."

Smoke smiled at that. "Which makes me like it all the more. I mean to get them off my back for good and all."

With that, Smoke Jensen wheeled his horse and gigged it to a trot. Certain of the folly of this course, Oliver Johnson hurried to catch up. When he joined Smoke, his face mirrored his misery.

"I—I didn't bring my gun along," Oliver admitted. "I have a spare," Smoke informed him, and handed over the .45 Colt he carried high on the left side.

When they rounded a curve in the sylvan trail, Smoke discovered that their quarry had disappeared. He sprinted ahead to a break in the trees that lined the bridle path. There he paused only a second while he took in the broad backs of the men he sought as they fogged across the grassy meadow that sloped down toward the large man-made lake.

"They recognized me, that's for sure," he declared, a moment before an agitated shout came from the trail behind them.

"Damn! That's Smoke Jensen."

Smoke shot them a quick glance and saw four men in the process of trying to mount horses with which they were definitely unfamiliar. He touched blunt spurs to his fractious mount and sped off after Lathrop and the others, ignoring the threat from behind. Oliver Johnson joined him.

It took the better part of two minutes for Johnson's slower mount to close up on Smoke's frisky stallion. Picnickers on the meadow scattered as the horses ridden by Lathrop, Middleton, and O'Boyle bore down on them. They shouted their indignation and shook angry fists as Smoke and Oliver followed. Unfamiliar with the terrain, Smoke was unable to anticipate the destination of the fleeing partners in crime so as to cut them off. He and Oliver came within shooting range, but caution whispered in Smoke's mind that so far they had no justifiable reason to shoot anyone. At least, not as the New York police would see it.

Their quarry entered another clump of trees and faded

from sight. Thirty yards separated them from Lathrop, and it proved to be their undoing. By the time Smoke Jensen entered the grove of ash, he found three chest-heaving horses and not a sign of the men they sought.

"Split up and we'll circle these trees," Smoke suggested to Oliver.

Conscious of the four men behind them, Smoke made a hurried search and had to concede that Lathrop and company had gotten cleanly away. He turned back to the inept horsemen who only now had reached the edge of the copse. One of the Boston hard cases saw him coming and made the mistake of pulling a small revolver from under his coat.

Smoke Jensen reacted with blinding speed. The big .45 Colt filled his hand in an eyeblink and bucked comfortably in response to his twitching trigger finger. Hot lead sped to the target and cleared the man from his saddle. Without regard for their comrade, the remaining three fled with all the speed they could muster from their rented horses.

Implacably, Smoke came after them. One of the longshoremen showed even less aptitude than his companions. He drummed heels into unresponsive flanks and shouted uselessly.

"Giddy-up! Giddy-up!"

His mount turned a big, doubt-filled brown eye to him and ambled at its chosen gait. Desperate now, the dockyard thug slapped an open palm on the animal's rump. Ahead he could see his friends streaking away toward the safety of public streets. Behind he saw Smoke Jensen looming closer.

Riding western style, albeit in an English saddle, Smoke leaned forward and far to the right, one arm extended. He clubbed the laggard off the top of his mount, sped on past, and made a quick shout over his shoulder.

"Take care of that one, Ollie, I'll get the others."

Smoke Jensen swept past a woman who shook a parasol at the backs of the fleeing men and mouthed some of the foulest oaths Smoke had ever heard from a woman. And that included the madam of a certain bordello in Deadwood City, Dakota Territory. She increased the stridency and heat of her blast as

Smoke flashed over the mound on which she stood, clots of dirt flying from the shod hooves of his laboring mount.

The strength of the animal impressed Smoke. Then he recalled that the stables had ordered a stallion in order to improve the bloodlines of their existing stock. Most riding academies preferred geldings or mares. For the moment, he was grateful for their desire to upgrade, particularly when the powerful horse brought him within two lengths of the men he chased by the time they reached the walking path that bordered the meadow.

Gauging the distance, Smoke freed his boots from the stirrups and launched himself at the trailing hard case. His widespread arms slammed into the ribcage of his target and snapped closed with enough force to drive the air from the thug's lungs. When they hit the ground, Smoke heard the ribs under him crack.

A quick grasp of the situation encouraged the partner of the fallen man. He reined sharply, dismounted unsteadily, and lumbered toward the prone pair. New York sunlight glinted off the keen edge of the knife in his hand. At the last moment, he bent slightly, arm upraised to drive the blade into Smoke Jensen's back, between the ribs, and into Smoke's heart.

Sensing the danger, Smoke did a snap roll sideways and snaked the .45 Colt from his holster. Unable to check himself, the villain continued the plunge, to drive the fine tip of his knife into the chest of his friend. Smoke Jensen shot him a second later.

Smoke's quick action saved the life of the longshoreman he had hurled off his horse. The impact of the big 240-grain bullet stayed the motion of the blade artist's hand a moment, and reflex threw him backward in reaction to the intense pain. As the man fell, Smoke came to his feet with fluid motion.

Gasping, the man who had nearly been stabbed considered Smoke accusingly. "You broke my ribs. All of them, I think."

"I also saved your life," Smoke told him indifferently.

Oliver Johnson, who had dismounted, prodded his prisoner along as he approached. He sized up the situation in a moment. "Two for two, that's not bad," he said cheerfully. "Old Abner Doubleday would say you were batting five hundred." Oliver lost his jocularity as he gazed at the prostrate men. "Some of O'Boyle's union trash. What do we do now?"

"Return the horses and then pay another visit to the office of Victor Middleton."

Their trip to Wall Street proved nearly as fruitless as the previous one. A stout, matronly woman who claimed the title of Office Manageress greeted Smoke Jensen and Oliver Johnson icily after Smoke's intimidating size and harsh growl had frightened a male secretary into summoning the Valkyrie of the financial district.

"Mr. Middleton is not presently in and is not expected for some time," her haughty tones informed them.

"I saw Mr. Middleton with a Mr. Lathrop less than two hours ago in Central Park," Smoke Jensen pressed.

"Yes?" she countered with frigid rejection, not believing it.

"Indeed," Oliver Johnson added. "Both of them, and five unsavory associates."

His description of O'Boyle and company thawed her some, coinciding with hers as it did. "I do believe you are correct. There was some talk of acquainting a number of his lesser employees with the intricacies of horseback riding. For the life of me, I do not understand why they delayed so long. Both Mr. Middleton and Mr. Lathrop should already be boarding the train west."

"Where in the West?" Smoke probed.

"I'm not at liberty to disclose such information," came the newly frosted reply.

"You could reveal your knowledge to the police instead," Smoke suggested.

"The . . . po—*lice?*" she stammered.

"Just so. Exactly where is Phineas Lathrop headed?"

She studied the hard face and determined set of the jaw of Smoke Jensen and moderated her stand. "Who might you be, that I should tell you these things?"

"My name is Smoke Jensen."

She paled. She had seen the name recently in the newspapers. Some sort of notorious shootist from out west. She had also heard mention of Smoke Jensen, though not the context, in conversations in Mr. Middleton's private office. Could it be he might have some connection to the western enterprise of Mr. Middleton and Lathrop?

"Mr. Lathrop, Mr. Cabbott, and Mr. Middleton are taking the train to Denver; that's in Colorado."

"Yes, I know," Smoke responded, with a twitch of amusement.

"They are taking along some thirty of, if I must say so, the most disreputable gentlemen from here in New York that I have ever seen. Another twenty like individuals, from Boston, I believe, are to learn to ride and follow on tomorrow's train."

"Thank you, you've been most helpful," Smoke turned on the charm. Outside in the hall, he smacked a hard fist into an open palm. "Damn it! Sally said they had their sights on the Sugarloaf. Looks like she was right; they want to grab all of the High Lonesome. I have to get back there. But first, I need to let Sally know what is happening. I'd also like to know who else Lathrop is partnered with and dry up any help they might send."

"That last part is easy," Oliver Johnson assured him. "You take care of letting your wife know. I'll go at it through some newspaper friends. The best way, I think, is to ask about Middleton's connections."

By afternoon, the newspapers in New York City had gotten ahold of the police report on the chase and shootout in Central Park. The first to rush it into print, a tabloid called the *New York Eagle,* put out a single page, the front bearing their masthead and screaming headlines, the back covered by advertising. They hadn't even gotten the facts correct. They identified Smoke Jensen as "a Mr. Smoking Johnson, most likely a gentlemen from the colored section of town," and stated that a dozen innocent bystanders had been trampled by horses.

Smoke Jensen purchased a copy from a tough-faced ten-year-old who hawked the scandal sheet on a street corner. The purple prose and alarmist tone of the article left him unimpressed with the quality of journalism in the big city, and slightly uneasy over the "lock-your-windows-and-barricade-the-doors" advice to readers. Out West, Smoke knew, the editorial slant would be more like: "If the sheriff can't do anything about it, then maybe a vigilance committee is in order." Smoke wasn't certain which treatment bothered him more.

After an interesting hour with the police, from which he had extricated himself and Oliver Johnson by showing the precinct captain his U.S. Marshal's badge, Smoke and the journalist paid their call on Lathrop's office, and then Smoke wired Sally regarding the need for a speedy return to the High Lonesome. Again he urged her to remain with her parents.

An efficient and well-maintained telegraph system brought Sally's reply by early evening. She and the D & R G private car would arrive late the next day at Grand Central Station. She spent the extra money to add her clincher to the argument she anticipated from Smoke. There was no reason, she said, for him to suffer in an uncomfortable chair car or Pullman that would get him there no sooner. Which left Smoke Jensen with nothing to do but wait, and fume at his wife's stubbornness.

17

Over breakfast, Smoke Jensen glowered at the bold, black headlines of the *New York Sun*. "CRAZED FRONTIERS-MAN LOOSE IN CENTRAL PARK," it declared.

At least the *Sun* had done some research and had his name right. The article went on to decry how "the notorious Smoke Jensen, gunfighter and mountain man, went on a rampage in Boston, ruthlessly murdering innocent dock workers and leaving a trail of widows and orphans behind. Only yesterday," it continued, "Smoke Jensen raised havoc in Central Park. Two men were left dead, and four more seriously injured. What the *Sun* does not understand is why the police questioned and then released this dangerous hired killer."

"What a lot of crap," Smoke snorted, as he laid down the paper. His full lips curled with contempt. "Typical yellow journalism."

"Hey!" Oliver Johnson erupted. "I thought it was a well-written article. By far it's the best of the lot."

"Present company excepted, Ollie," Smoke advised with a shrug. He reflected once more on how much he had come to like this brash young reporter. "You've proved your worth more than once."

Oliver Johnson tilted his head to one side, a forkful of

ham and fried potatoes halfway to his mouth. "You're too kind, Smoke." He continued by explaining, "I don't mean that to sound sarcastic. I'm serious. You've opened some doors for me. So, what I'm wondering is, what do we do now?"

"I haven't any choice but to wait for Sally. I don't see there's much for you to do."

"Of course there is. I could use some help looking into the background on Middleton, Asher, and company. Then, I suppose I should pick up a few things for the trip."

"What trip?" Smoke asked, certain he knew the answer.

"Out west, naturally." Oliver raised a hand to forestall the flood of objection he anticipated from Smoke. "I'm sitting on the story of the decade, if not the century, and there's no way I'm going to be kept out of it."

Smoke's slate-gray eyes darkened. "Ollie, you said yourself that Middleton and Asher are the key to this. You can handle that better from right here. No need running off to the Colorado mountains."

"No, the story is you, Smoke. Where you go, I go. At least, until I have the whole account of this. Think of it, 'Conquest in the Name of a Criminal Empire,' or make that; 'Smoke Jensen Conquers Criminal Empire, Ends Reign of Terror in Far West.' How about that?"

"Too long, Ollie." Smoke wanted nothing to do with it, especially getting his name attached to such folderol.

"Then how about, 'Smoke Jensen Ends Reign of Terror in Rockies?' You like that?"

Smoke shook his head, partly in exasperation, and responded in a low, steady voice. "First, there has to be a reign of terror in the mountains, and second, I have to end it. You're getting ahead of yourself, Ollie."

"Maybe so, but there is a story here, and I want to be the one to write it. And I promise, no yellow journalism. Deal?"

Smoke studied him a long while, then sighed. "These men we heard about are dangerous. Being out of their element could likely make them more so."

"You know I can shoot, take care of myself, right? Well, then, I rest my case."

This fiery young newspaper man had a point, Smoke had to admit. It might not be a bad idea to have along someone who knew the facts from the start. At least, as much as he knew about it himself. "All right. You're coming along."

"I thought so."

A telegram arrived late that morning on the desk of Thaddeus Foley, City Editor of the *New York Eagle*. It lay there until Foley returned from a liquid lunch at O'Dwyer's on Lexington Avenue. Foley slit the yellow envelope with a slim silver letter opener. Inside the standard form bore the date and time of the transmission, the source and address of the recipient. Below it was a terse message: "CONGRATULATIONS X DOING A FINE JOB X KEEP UP THE PRESSURE ON JENSEN X" and signed, "LATHROP."

Foley smiled whitely and thought again of the fat sheaf of hundred-dollar notes he had received early that morning by messenger and put away in his private, personal safe. So long as that kept coming, he would see that Smoke Jensen remained the most hated man in New York.

For all the inevitability of it, Smoke Jensen remained grumpy about Sally accompanying himself and Ollie Johnson up until the time Colonel Drew's private car was attached to the rear of the New York Central's Daylight Express. Then, with Sally in his arms, he lost all attempts at gruffness.

"I missed you," Sally informed her husband.

"I—ah—felt empty without you," Smoke confirmed his own displeasure at their being apart.

Half an hour later, packed to overflowing in all but the last car, the train pulled out. There would be stops only at Philadelphia, Pittsburgh, Cincinnati, and finally Chicago.

They would arrive in the Windy City shortly after dawn the next day. That would put them three days behind Lathrop and his New York City hoodlums, and two days behind O'Boyle and his union gangsters from Boston. Not the hottest of trails he had followed, Smoke allowed. But, with the information they had squeezed out of Victor Middleton's office manager, he had the destination of the enemy, which would save a passel of time.

"You have some interesting and impressive friends, Smoke," Ollie Johnson interrupted Smoke's reflections.

"Yes, well, it goes with the trail you ride," Smoke said, presenting Ollie with one of those "mysteries" of western speech.

"What do we do when we reach Chicago?"

Smoke looked hard at Ollie, recalling again that the young man had never been east of Worcester or south of New York City. "We change to the Santa Fe and make the run to Denver."

"And after that?"

Smoke smiled, a wide, white band in sun-browned cheeks. "I hope you've taken a liking to horseback riding. We'll be doing a lot of it."

Wade Tanner sat his horse in the dooryard of the head-quarters of Rancho Puesta del Sol. He and ten others held smoking sixguns on the surviving ten *vaqueros* and the owner, Ramon Sandoval.

There had been Sandovals in Colorado since the coming of the Spanish. Ramon shook with outrage at the humiliation handed him by these *cabrónes* in their flour-sack hoods and bedsheets. If they had not run out of ammunition, they would have made these *bastardos* suffer. These *gringos* would have learned what it meant to make war on a descendant of the *conquistadores*.

"Waall, what do we do with these greasers, Wade?"

Wade Tanner studied on it a moment. "Same's we did with

them white folks a ways back. Th' man said, 'If they don't sell, deal with the widows.'"

Five Colts barked and as many Mexican ranch hands fell without a sound. Three of them twitched for a while, then went still. The survivors made the sign of the cross with solemn movements. Two knelt.

"Santa Maria, madre de Dios, orar por nostros pecadores . . ."

A harsh roar of sixguns drowned out their prayer.

"That takes care of all but Sane—yore Sandoval," Wade observed with a chuckle. "Got any prayin' to do, best get to it. Or . . . you can still sell this place to Mr. Early."

"¡Vaya a! infierno, pinché ladrón!"

Tanner's face turned stony under his hood. "I know what them words mean. It ain't gonna be me goes to hell." The heavy .45 Colt bucked in his hand.

A hot slug smacked into Ramon Sandoval and spun him sideways, so that Tanner's second round took him in the temple. The already dead rancher dropped in a heap and quivered as his wounds pumped out his life's blood.

"An' I'll have you know I ain't no *little thief,*" Tanner growled, as he turned away and led his men toward the next ranch to be visited.

Flames crackled in the barn. Long, orange columns of sparks shot from the open door to the haymow. *Damn it,* Buford Early thought, *that will lower the property value. And if those sparks set something else off, it will be even worse.* Stray bullets had shattered a kerosene lantern and set the place ablaze.

"You men, watch those other buildings. Don't let the fire spread." To his satisfaction, Early saw that his order had been obeyed without question.

It had not always been that way. Until a short time ago, when Buford Early had shot a ranch hand and saved the life of Wade Tanner, he had been viewed with contempt by the hard-faced killers who followed the man Phineas Lathrop had put in charge. Tonight they had come closer to Smoke Jensen's Sugarloaf ranch than ever before. Too bad about the barn, Early mused, as he watched the hooded raiders spread out with wet blankets and buckets of water to extinguish any sparks that lighted on the bunkhouse and tool sheds. Still others hunted around the barnyard for stray hands who had not as yet been run off. Early sighed with satisfaction.

"Mr. Tanner, it appears we have added another jewel to Mr. Lathrop's crown." Remembering his earlier humiliation at Smoke Jensen's ranch, he added, "I can't wait until we take over the Sugarloaf."

Considerable complaining had gone on all the way from New York City to Dodge City, Kansas. None of the former longshoremen in the O'Boyle gang liked the idea of Dodge being the end of the line for them. When Phineas Lathrop appeared on the loading platform, he soon heard about it from Sean O'Boyle and Eamon Finnegan.

"Sure an' the train would get us to Denver a lot faster," Eamon Finnegan protested.

Lathrop had forgotten how big Finnegan was. His broad, thick shoulders bulged the cloth coat he wore over a flannel shirt. A shock of black hair hung over his brow. Finnegan had one flaw, which Lathrop had taken note of at their first meeting. The black Irish bruiser had the florid complexion and ruddy, broken-vesseled nose of a heavy drinker. Only in his late twenties and already caught up in the "Irish disease," Lathrop thought uneasily. Such a man could quickly go unstable.

"Your introduction to horseback riding in Central Park was entirely too short," Lathrop snapped at the two leaders of the Boston gang.

"Half me boys is still saddle-sore from that encounter, Mr. Lathrop," Sean O'Boyle complained. "It's sheer foolishness makin' a man ride astride a horse when there's this perfectly good train to take us on, it is."

"Nonsense. Riding to Denver will toughen you up for what is ahead." Accustomed to having his way, Phineas Lathrop made it clear he brooked no differences of opinion among his underlings.

O'Boyle looked again at the line of heavy western saddles, the leather pouches behind the cantle bulging with camp gear and boxes of ammunition. "We'll be hampered with such overloads, we will," he objected.

Lathrop's chin rose pugnaciously. "*You* won't be carrying the load, Mr. O'Boyle; the horses will. Now, get your men organized and take these saddles to the livery down the street. Your mounts have been selected."

Chafed by long hours of inactivity, Smoke Jensen opted to walk the three blocks from the New York Central station in Chicago to that of the A T & S F. Their private car would be shifted through the common railyard. A block down the Street, he, Sally, and Oliver came upon five loungers who looked every bit the part of saddle tramps, to Smoke's practiced eyes.

One in particular eyed Smoke closely. After their party had passed, that one spoke up, confirming Smoke's suspicion that trouble was about to catch up to him again. "That's him, I tell you. Seed it in the paper this mornin'."

"Naw," another rejected the idea. "He wouldn't be walkin' around like that."

"I'll prove it to you," the young man pressed, as he came up from the bench on which he had been slouched. "Hey, you, mister. Smoke Jensen," he called after the three strollers.

"Ollie, take Sally across the street and go on to the depot."

"There's five of them, Smoke," Oliver protested.

"I know. That's why I want Sally safely out of the way. Now, go on." He turned to face the challenger. "You got that one right. I'm Smoke Jensen. Do I know you?"

"No. But the whole country's soon gonna know me as the man who shot Smoke Jensen."

"There's no call for that. Back off while you still can."

"Can't do that," said the youth. "Y'see, we're fixin' to earn us a free ride out to where the big action is. Word has it a ramrodder named Wade Tanner's hirin' all the guns he can get. There's a special bonus for whoever spots and guns down Smoke Jensen. That's the free ride I tole you about."

While the young prodder had run his mouth, Smoke had let his right hand lower to his holster and slide the safety thong off the hammer of his .45 Colt. Now he shook his head, almost sadly.

"You're not good enough to even come close. Give it up, boy, before you get yourself and your friends hurt."

At Smoke's pronouncement, the five spread out across the sidewalk and into the street. Smoke didn't like any part of this. They were so young, and calling him out like this was so senseless. One of the youths dropped into an exaggerated crouch and continued to walk, crablike, further into the street. Smoke could almost laugh at the image it created. Obviously all these boys had ever learned about gunfighting had come from the pages of dime novels.

"I'll ask you nicely one last time. Forget about this and walk away. That way none of you will get hurt."

"You're the one's gonna be hurt, gunfighter," the aggressive one snarled.

Then he made a terrible mistake. He went for his gun.

Smoke Jensen's Peacemaker cleared leather before the youth had his fingers closed around the butt-grip of an old .44 Colt Frontier model. Smoke aimed to disable the revolver. His slug entered the young man's thigh at the mid-point and deflected to exit on the right side, smashing itself against the holster. The kid cried out and fell to his left knee. Fearful of the speed they had just witnessed, yet goaded by their friend's shout of pain, the other four went for their guns.

"Aw, shit!" one groaned, as he realized he had not slipped

the safety thong off his iron. He tugged uselessly at it while he watched the black hole in the muzzle of Smoke Jensen's .45 center on his belly. Suddenly he wanted no part of this. He raised both hands in surrender and stepped off in a direction away from the developing fight.

Smoke let him go. The other three had unlimbered their weapons and now fired wildly, their bullets cracking through air to both sides of Smoke Jensen. Smoke put a hot round in the shoulder of the nearest shooter, who tried inexpertly to do a border shift. Pain caused him to jerk uncontrollably and he missed his catch. His revolver fell solidly on the hard-packed dirt street and discharged. The bullet cracked and whined off the marble facing of a bank across the street where Smoke stood.

That left two, Smoke kept mental score. One of them had presence of mind to extend his gunhand to arm's length and try to take aim. His hand shook so badly he could not line up on Smoke's chest. Smoke ignored him momentarily to take care of the other would-be gunfighter.

Still in his crab-walk crouch, the snarling youth fired with his right shoulder sloped downward, which placed him off balance. The slug cut high, past the front brim of Smoke's hat. It broke a window on the second floor of the bank and a woman's scream of alarm came a second later. Eyes wide, the shooter indexed the cylinder again.

No time for fancy work, Smoke admitted to himself. He brought the Colt to bear and loosed a .45 lead pellet that took his assailant in the gut, a fist's depth below the sternum. Eyes bugged, the youthful thug did a pratfall and tried feebly to raise his suddenly heavy six-gun.

A soft sigh left his lips and he toppled over his gunhand as shock brought on unconsciousness. By that time, the mouthy one had revived enough to retrieve his .44 Frontier and make use of it lefthanded. He got a .45 caliber hole in his shoulder for his troubles. The shaky one recovered enough to be a threat. Instead of gunning him down without pity, Smoke Jensen stepped in on the scared youth and knocked the menacing gunhand away, then brought the barrel of his Peacemaker down on the center line of the kid's forehead.

His eyes crossed and he fell with a soft groan. "God damn you, Smoke Jensen!" the instigator shouted, white froth spraying from thin lips.

"You've got two holes in you, boy, and one of your friends is dead. Back down or I put the next bullet between your runnin' lights."

Tears filled the pale blue eyes and the young gunhand sat sobbing in a spreading pool of his own blood. By then, two guards from the bank and a policeman had reached the scene. The encounter with the police ended abruptly when Smoke showed his badge and explained that the five had jumped him, and that he had a train to catch.

"You can reach me through the sheriff's office in Big Rock, Colorado. Monte Carson is the sheriff." With that final advice, Smoke Jensen walked away from the gape-mouthed policeman, on the final leg of his search for Phineas Lathrop.

18

"I'm tellin' ye, Mr. Lathrop, sure an' we're goin' crazy out here, we are," Sean O'Boyle complained to Phineas Lathrop on the third night stop on the trail from Dodge City to Denver. "It's too quiet. Nothin' but birds singin', it is, an' bugs buzzin' around. An' at night, saints preserve us, it's them spooky wolves howlin'."

"They're coyotes," Phineas Lathrop snapped.

"Whatever. It's got us all wore thin. We need somethin' to do."

"Such as what?" Lathrop asked coldly.

"Well, me an' some of the boys have been thinkin' on that. We saw that stagecoach yesterday. And we read about stage holdups in them books about the West. Connor O'Fallon an' I sort of thought it might be somethin' to while away our time, we did, if we was to rob one of those coaches."

Lathrop didn't like that in the least. "Just the two of you?"

"No, sir. We're not daft, man. Paedrik Boyne an' Seamas Quern have a hankerin' to join in. Sure four of us could take one man with a little bitty shotgun."

"Don't be too sure." Something troubled him about this, yet Lathrop found himself hard put to express his discomfort. "Those shotgun guards are tough men. Wells-Fargo doesn't hire eastern dandies to protect their strongboxes."

O'Boyle's black Irish temper flared. "Are ye callin' us boys 'dandies,' Mr. Lathrop?"

"Oh, no—no, of course not."

"I should think not, now you got us decked out all a-bristle with firearms. When the stage folk get a look at that, they'll see reason, right enough, they will."

"I could order you not to." Then Lathrop saw their side of it. The prairie could be mighty lonesome for someone not used to it, the mountains more so. Perhaps it would be good to get some of the men blooded to how things are done out here. "But this time I won't. Take the men you've picked, and go rob your stage. There will be one coming back around ten o'clock in the morning. Mr. Finnegan and I will continue on with the others. You can catch up at night camp."

Force of habit directed the tug at his forelock that O'Boyle gave to Lathrop. "Thank ye, sir. An' we'll be sharin' fair as fair."

Rattling along on the high driver's seat of the Concord Coach, behind a matched team of powerful-rumped bays, Walt Tilton could sense through the reins that the off-wheeler had started to slacken, let the others pull the load. The gelding ran just fast enough to keep up, but not put strain on the harness.

"C'mon, you lazy sod. Jaspar, put your shoulders into it," he shouted over the grind of the steel-tired wheels. A quick touch of churning hindquarter with the whip brought the animal into tandem effort with its partner.

"How'd you always know?" Slim Granger, the express guard, asked.

"I've been driving these rigs for nigh onto twenty years now," Walt informed him. "After a while you get a feel for what the teams are doin'. It's sort of like you knowin' when to put hands on that scattergun of yourn."

Slim shook his head. "That's plain instinct. It's like I can sense trouble before it happens." Slim's hands found the barrel of the L. C. Smith 10-gauge as he spoke and raised the weapon to the ready, thumb on the right-hand hammer. "Like right now."

"You funnin' me?" Walt asked.

"Nope." Slim had gone white around his full lips. His mustache wriggled like a live thing. He nodded ahead along the high road.

Four men in long white linen dusters appeared suddenly from behind tall brush. Each held a weapon in an awkward fashion, as though ill trained in its use. The one to left center rose in his stirrups and pointed the muzzle of his six-gun skyward.

"Stand and deliver!" he shouted, after the shot barked from his Colt.

Walt Tilton didn't even slow the stage. As the other highwaymen brought their guns into ready positions from beside Walt, Slim let go one barrel of the ten-gauge. The double-aught buckshot column quickly flashed across space to turn the face of Paedrik Boyne into a wet, red smear. His arms flew into the air and he flopped off his horse into the dust stirred by the nervous animal's hooves.

Three .33-caliber pellets from the second barrel punched painfully into the left shoulder of Connor O'Fallon. Howling a pain-filled curse, O'Fallon awkwardly turned his mount away and put spurs to the flanks. At once the horse dug in and set off at a pounding sprint. O'Fallon bounded and swayed in the saddle like a bag of flour. Smoke still poured from the muzzles of the double-barrel when Slim opened the latch and fished out two long brass cartridges.

Fresh ones quickly took their place and Slim bit at his lip as the speed at which the attack had come on them forced him to snap shut the action. The big ten-gauge roared again and another of the highwaymen spurred away, shrieking in pain and outrage. Only one unharmed man stood in the way of the careening coach.

"God damn it, you said this would be easy," Seamas Quern screamed over his shoulder as he made hasty retreat.

Sean O'Boyle glowered after him and then turned back to fire on the driver, heedless of the danger that created. The .38 S & W bullet from his long-barreled Ivor Johnson tilt-top revolver splintered wood from the seat between the legs of Walt Tilton. Both hands tending the reins, Tilton could not return fire. He relied on Slim for that.

With the range closed to only a few feet, Slim believed he could not miss. To his utter surprise, he did. Beside him, Walt began to haul on the reins and slow the coach. "That's the last one. Let's get him and take him on to Dodge."

Alone now, Sean O'Boyle decided against a final attempt to rob the stage. As the vehicle slowed, he made a fast move in the opposite direction. Once well out of range, he slowed and looked back while the guard and driver picked up the dead Paedrik Boyne and an unhorsed Seamas Quern.

"Somehow, bucko, I've a feelin' Mr. Lathrop is not going to be pleased with this, he's not," O'Boyle said aloud, as he raced in the wake of Connor O'Fallon.

When the Denver-bound train carrying Smoke and Sally Jensen arrived in Ellsworth, the town was abuzz with the latest novelty in outlawry. The Dodge City newspaper carried a detailed account. Smoke read it carefully, but did not display the amusement it generated in others.

"I'll give you one guess as to who these 'funny-talking dudes' are who tried to rob the stage and got caught," Smoke remarked to Oliver.

Oliver Johnson nodded agreement. "Some of Lathrop's New York or Boston thugs. What do you suppose went wrong?"

"I don't know, but it's worth finding out."

"We're going to Dodge City, Smoke?" Sally asked.

"You're going on to Denver, where I want you to take a

room at the Brown Palace. Oliver will go with you. I'm thinking of a short detour through Dodge City."

Eastern cynicism colored Oliver's words. "Do you think you'll learn anything worth the time to go there?"

"Considering that they hang a man for just about any offense out here, yes, I expect some cooperation."

Subdued, Oliver nodded thoughtfully. "Our eastern gangs have a strong bond of loyalty."

Smoke cocked an eyebrow, cut his eyes to Oliver's deadpan expression. "You sound almost proud. The way I see it, the sight of some new three-quarter-inch hemp rope, with thirteen wraps to the knot, will loosen the most loyal tongue."

Sally came to him in the wing chair of the parlor section of the private car. She put a hand on Smoke's arm. "Smoke does real well in getting information from people who don't want to talk."

"Then you're going to Dodge City." Oliver made it a statement.

"Right," Smoke closed the topic.

Ford County Sheriff Pat McRaney greeted Smoke Jensen with a firm handshake. "A bit far from your bailiwick, Marshal."

"I am. But we have reason to believe these men were headed for Denver."

"Are they wanted for anything else?"

"I'm not sure, Pat. How many were there on the holdup?"

"Four. One's dead, two are wounded, one of them in jail, two got away."

"Only four? There should have been a lot more than that."

"Oh, they came through here, a whole lot of them. Got off a train from back East and took horses out of town, headed west. All of them talked peculiar. The first batch seemed to talk through their noses."

"First batch?"

"Oh, yes. They had an overnight for the City of Denver. Kept to themselves, didn't get into any trouble. A rough lookin' lot, though."

Smoke thought about that. "What about the gang your prisoner came in with?"

Pat McRaney scratched his balding head. "Most sounded Irish. There were some who talked real flat. You know what I mean? Sort of, 'fawht in a cawdbwaad cawton.' Ever hear of anything like that?"

"Boston. That's the way people from Boston sometimes talk," Smoke informed the lawman.

"Hmmm. I see. Or then again, I don't see. What are a lot of single rough-lookin' fellers headed to Denver for?"

"Maybe to work in the mines, but I doubt it," Smoke offered.

"D'you want to talk to the prisoner?"

"That's what I came here for," Smoke said, rising. "I shouldn't be long."

"Take your time," McRaney offered generously.

Once in the cell, Smoke Jensen looked over a crestfallen, pain-wracked Seamas Quern. "I know you," the mountain man charged. "You were in the warehouse with my wife."

"Don't know what yer talkin' about, lad," Quern evaded.

"I'm Smoke Jensen. Does that refresh your memory?"

Quern blanched. His jaw sagged and his lower lip began to tremble. Agitated beyond the agony in his wounds, he jumped up and grabbed desperately at the bars. "Jailer! Hey, Jailer, help me. I'm being murdered!"

Smoke grabbed Quern by the shoulder, spun him around. "The turnkey's developed a hearing problem. There's just you and me in here, Quern."

"How'd you know my name?"

"I got it from the sheriff. You *are* Seamas Quern, aren't you? You're in Sean O'Boyle's gang of dockyard thugs? What are you doing headed toward Denver?"

Quern turned surly again. "You know so goddamned much, you answer your questions."

Smoke hit him in the gut, where it would not show, hard enough, though, to double over the cocky longshoreman. "Did you know they still consider stagecoach robbery a hanging offense out here?"

Gagging, gasping for air, Seamas Quern looked up at the hard face of Smoke Jensen. His eyes watered and he worked full lips to form low, breathy words. "Th-that's not true, is it?"

There hadn't been anyone hanged for a stage robbery that didn't include a killing since the territories had become states, yet Smoke recognized that running a bluff would work with this dock rat from Boston. He nodded wordlessly.

"Oh, Jesus. I—I never counted on a rope around me neck, I didn't. Is there . . . isn't there any way . . . anything I can do to get the judge to go easy on me?"

"You can try cooperating. Tell me what I want to know and I'll put in a good word for you. What you and your guttersnipe friends didn't know is that I am a deputy U.S. Marshal. My word can carry a lot of weight with the courts."

From that point on, it went a lot easier than even Smoke Jensen had anticipated. Within half an hour, he had learned everything Seamas Quern knew or had guessed about Phineas Lathrop's operation and his eventual goal. Sally had not been misled by the danger to herself, and Ollie had been right in labeling it a criminal empire.

With nearly fifty men to swell his ranks, Lathrop had every possibility of achieving his purpose. Smoke Jensen chafed at the delay of the train to Denver. He saw Lathrop as the greatest threat ever to the High Lonesome. And only he could do something about it.

Phineas Lathrop cut a sour gaze around his dingy surroundings. He had been forced into hiding out at this third-rate fleabag hotel in Denver by the unbelievable stupidity of Sean O'Boyle. How could anyone be so stupid, so inept? The foiled stage robbery had left them with one man alive and in custody. How much Seamas Quern knew of his actual plans, Lathrop had no way of knowing. The anger that had smoldered ever since flashed to new flame as he considered it.

When O'Boyle and his wounded henchman O'Fallon caught up to the column, Lathrop had personally administered a savage beating as object lesson to O'Boyle and anyone else who might have delusions that criminal activity on the frontier was no different than back east. Fools! They had been damned fools, and gotten one man killed and two others wounded, one of them locked away in jail.

Victor Middleton interrupted his dismal thoughts. "Let's get out of this disgusting pigsty and get some fresh air, something to eat, a good, stiff drink."

"All right," Phineas Lathrop agreed. "We have to be careful, though. We don't know what that lout Quern has told the law."

"To hell with him. He may have bled to death by the time he got to Dodge City. Here in Denver, we're simply honest businessmen, going about our affairs like anyone else."

"That's why we're living in this rat's nest," Lathrop grumbled. Yet his spirits rose somewhat on a promising thought.

His ignominious station in life would be a short one, Phineas consoled himself. Already his imported gunmen from the East had dispersed to carry out the land grab necessary to spell triumph for him and his associates. Even if Smoke Jensen came directly back to Colorado, he would arrive too late to prevent their enterprise from a successful conclusion. By the time Jensen could organize any sort of resistance, all of the northwest corner of Colorado would belong to their consortium. He could not lose!

Smoke Jensen caught up with his wife and the *Boston Globe* reporter at the Brown Palace in Denver late the next day. They had a late, sumptuous dinner, stayed the night, and caught the early-morning milk train to Big Rock. Monte

Carson had been alerted by telegraph and met the trio of weary travelers on the depot platform. Immediately Smoke noted a changed, charged atmosphere about the people waiting for the return run to Denver.

Particularly among those who knew him. The women shielded their faces with fans or gloved hands; some of the men deliberately turned their backs on him. When the luggage had been unloaded from the baggage car, Monte led the way to his office. There he glowered his suspicion at Oliver Johnson. He addressed his remarks to Smoke Jensen.

"'Pears you got some influential people riled at you, Smoke. Some of those eastern reporters have been filing stories with the papers in Denver, Pueblo, Dodge City, Saint Louie, near everywhere west of the Mississippi, I'd reckon. They ain't sayin' nice things 'bout you, either."

"We got enough of that back there, Monte."

Monte's eyes narrowed even more, a dark glitter sparking out from lowered lids. "That's why I can't work out why 'n hell you brung one along with you, Smoke."

"Ollie's okay, Monte. He filed five favorable stories. Three of them even got published."

"Ain't hardly a fart in a cyclone, Smoke. For every good word he wrote about you, there's a hundred bad ones . . . and they *all* got in print."

"Is that why I noticed a coolness from my good neighbors at the depot?" Smoke asked, his concern growing.

"You could say that. Seems they forgot real quick that out here we judge a man by how tall he walks and how much sand he's got, not by what some East Coast asshole writes about him . . . er, sorry, ma'am," Monte added, for Sally's benefit.

"Oh, that's quite all right, Monte. I agree with you entirely," Sally replied, without even a hint of a blush.

Smoke broke in to change the subject to that of his greatest concern: "Have there been a lot of strangers showing up around town lately? Pale faces, with arms and shoulders too big for the rest of them, say?"

Monte Carson's brow wrinkled. "There's . . . been a few. Can't rightly place what's oddest about them. You're right about some of them's shape. Heck, they've got wrists the size of some men's biceps."

"Longshoremen," Smoke explained, convinced now of the imminent danger to the people of his beloved High Lonesome. "Dock workers from Boston and New York City. When they're working at their regular jobs, they wrestle around bales of cargo all day that it would take you and me both to move. Let me guess—the ones from New York arrived first, right?"

"Yes. Only, they didn't hang around town long. Looked sorry as hell to be on a horse's back, but they grained and rested their mounts overnight and took off to the northwest. You ask me, they'd have been happier walkin'."

"Don't underestimate them, Sheriff. They're dangerous," Oliver Johnson contributed.

"How's that? Oh, they had plenty of shootin' irons along, but the experiences of a lifetime tell me they didn't have too much idea of how best to use them."

"Ollie's right, Monte," Smoke took up the narrative. He explained what had happened in Boston and New York, of the bungled stage robbery outside Dodge City, and some of what he had learned of the eastern criminal network from Oliver Johnson. Monte shook his head more than once during the recitation.

"So what yer sayin' is that these boys could be a real threat to folks hereabouts? Well, there's been some unsavory deals struck, I can tell you that. Folks won't talk about it much. Seem real scared. But they sold their places anyhow and left the area."

"I'm liking this even less," Smoke growled.

Monte rose, crossed to the potbellied stove in the corner by his desk, and poured four cups of coffee. "Now that you're back, Smoke, I suppose there's nothing for it but you an' me go out and find these eastern hard cases of yours."

"That's my idea exactly. But first, I'd fight a whole litter of wildcats for some of your coffee," Smoke spoke with rekindled enthusiasm.

Looking wounded, Oliver Johnson entered his protest. "You're not leaving me out."

Smoke's cool, level gaze cut to the young reporter. "No. I wouldn't dream of it. As soon as we get Sally back to the Sugarloaf, the three of us are going out and kick hell out of Lathrop's hooligans."

19

Thin tendrils of smoke rose from the tree-shrouded clearing ahead. Off to the right, a pair of redheaded woodpeckers made Gatling gun rat-a-tats on the grizzled bark of a tall, old pine. Lowering the brass-bound field glasses from his eyes, Smoke Jensen nodded and pointed ahead to their quarry's night camp, already laid out at not quite four-thirty in the afternoon. Typical eastern dudes, tenderfeet, he thought scornfully.

He, Monte Carson, and Oliver Johnson had left the deep valley that sheltered the Sugarloaf two days earlier, by way of Vail Pass. Monte had taken the customary frontier way of legitimizing the reporter's presence by deputizing him. They angled along the Arapaho Pike trail north and westward. The three lawmen had found immediate evidence of the presence of Lathrop's henchmen.

A burned-out barn and vacant house told them a clear story. Similar, apparently abandoned properties added to their store of knowledge. They had encountered their first living resisters at twilight the previous night. Monte Carson went forward to talk with the crusty, hard-bitten rancher in his dooryard, faintly illuminated by the spill from a single, low-burning coal-oil lamp inside the cabin. Smoke's name came up in the course of their conversation.

"Smoke Jensen's gone plumb crazy back East," the gnarled, bent old man stated as fact. "Even if he was out here, he'd as like line up with them that's givin' me grief, least that's what the papers say."

Monte laughed. "Howard, how long's it been since you saw a newspaper?"

Howard Daley frowned. "Saw one last week, when me and the mizus went for supplies. All about yer friend Jensen killing helpless women and chillun in some park in New York City."

"He's your friend, too, Howard. At least, he used to be."

Daley took Monte's gentle chiding in stride. "Used to be is the right of it. Got no truck with someone'd harm a woman or chile."

Smoke Jensen chose that moment to walk into the yellow shaft of lamplight. "Howard, I'd never kill a woman or a kid, unless they were tryin' to kill me. And you know that."

"Love o' God, it's *you,* Smoke Jensen." Suspicion colored Daley's next words. "You come to run me off, too?"

"No such thing. How's your ammunition holdin' out?" Smoke asked in his slow, deep drawl. "And we could use a place to rest our mounts, fix some supper."

Smoke's offer of replenishing his ammunition won over the mercurial rancher. Daley stepped toward Smoke with his hand outstretched to offer his apology. "Gotta say I'm sorry for them harsh words I laid on Monte, here. I shoulda knowed better. I *do* know better. I'm right shamed, Smoke."

"No offense, Howard. If you've the need, we can leave off a couple of boxes of forty-fours for that Winchester of yours. We have plenty along."

Daley cut his eyes between Smoke and Monte. "You up to trackin' down them that wants to run us out?"

"Something like that."

"Then you're as welcome as the first rains of spring. C'mon in. The mizus has got some pie set back. There's venison stew, greens, and cornbread. You can doss down in the barn, if it's right by you."

"Couldn't have better. And thanks to you," Smoke accepted the generous change of heart magnanimously.

They had eaten a good breakfast before riding out from the Daley spread that morning. Now the faint odor of boiling coffee and cooking meat tormented Oliver Johnson's belly and reminded Smoke and Monte of their own lack of solid food for the rest of the day.

"That's our first bunch," Smoke stated softly. "What say we go down and relieve them of supper?"

Eleven of the eastern gangsters, their rumps tender and their thighs aching from saddle-soreness, gathered around three cook fires. Two of them already picked disinterestedly at plates of food, their appetites numbed by discomfort. The first any of them knew of their troubles came from the distant rumble of many hooves.

At least to them it sounded like a lot. Three men suddenly appeared, from as many directions, over a rise in the grassy meadow where they had made camp. Three ex-longshoremen, thinking it might be more of their kind, came upright from their efforts to fill tin plates. They looked hard at the swiftly approaching riders and decided too late that these were unwelcome guests. One of them shouted an alarm and reached clumsily for the sixgun strapped around his waist.

Smoke Jensen had wisely decided that arming Oliver Johnson with a shotgun would provide the best chance of the reporter hitting something. Especially when firing from horseback. The big Greener ten-gauge roared off to Smoke's left and ten of the 15 OO buckshot pellets struck the chest of an outlaw who had dropped his supper and gone for his gun.

Lifted off the ground, the novice gunman fell backward into the fire pit. So massive was the shock dealt him by the .33-caliber lead balls that he did not even scream from contact with the flames and glowing coals. His companions at the nearby fire jumped aside.

That spoiled Smoke's first shot, which cracked past and punched a hole in the blue granite coffeepot on the gridiron over the second pit. Scalding brown liquid splashed onto four slow-reacting New York hoodlums. Skin blistered in an instant, they shrieked their pain. All thought of resistance vanished as they ripped at sodden clothing in an attempt to end the agony.

Smoke cut his eyes to the right in time to see Monte Carson lever three fast rounds through his Winchester repeater, which spooked half a dozen horses, improperly tied off to a picket line. A flicker of an approving smile raised the corner of Smoke's mouth. Immediately he sighted in on a barrel-chested stevedore who stood in his path, a rifle raised to his left shoulder.

Time slowed to a crawl by Smoke's perception as the rifle discharged and the thug's shoulder rippled from excessive recoil. *Must not have held the butt tightly enough,* Smoke thought fleetingly. *That feller isn't going to hit what he aimed at.*

A sudden hot stinging along the outer surface of Smoke's upper left arm told him that the shooter had more control than he'd thought. The big Peacemaker in Smoke's hand bucked, and at less than ten yards, delivered a lead messenger to the New York crook. A dark hole appeared between bushy eyebrows and then disappeared as the rest of the head disintegrated in a crimson shower. Smoke, back astride Dandy, flashed on past the corpse.

"Over this way," Oliver Johnson shouted. "Some of them are getting away."

Eddie Meeks didn't know how he'd let himself in for this "going west" thing. He hated horses, empty land where a guy could see forever without a sign of a building. Manhattan was his town. Why in hell had he ever left there? And this dockyard trash with him. The sons of bitches let three lousy guys put them on the run.

He was running, too, wasn't he? Hell, yes. It made sense. Whoever these lunatics on the horses were, they knew how to shoot. Over his shoulder, Eddie saw one bearing down on him now. His eyes locked on the twin black circles of a shotgun muzzle. Fear sweat popped out on Eddie's forehead and he found he could not take his eyes off that terrible weapon.

Still racing through the knee-high grass, Eddie felt his left boot make contact with a hidden rock and he went ass-over-ears in a dusty sprawl. Quick as he could, he came to one knee. Shaken, he raised empty hands over his head.

"Don't shoot," he yelled. "Oh, Jesus, *don't shoot me!*"

Ollie Johnson reined up in a fog of flying clods. After a precarious moment, he steadied the Greener on the chest of the frightened hard case. He looped the reins over the saddle horn and took a soft leather sap from his left-hand coat pocket. Smiling in a rictus of an adrenaline high, he bent toward Eddie Meeks and smacked him solidly on the temple.

"One less," Oliver muttered, as he started off after another fleeing enemy.

Still thinking in terms of their experience with the law in the East, the newly created gun hands made a show of resistance, then most quickly surrendered. Only three of the eleven died in the brief fight, with two wounded. When the last who had fled were brought to the meadow, Smoke Jensen made a quick evaluation.

"We can't drag this garbage along with us. We'd get nothing done but guarding them. Ollie, you can find your way back to Howard Daley's ranch without trouble, can't you?"

"Sure. You want me to go for help?"

"No. I want you to escort the prisoners to there, stay overnight, then get Daley's help taking them on in to Big Rock. Then I want you to go on to the Sugarloaf, keep an eye on Sally."

Oliver's face printed his disappointment. "Trying to get rid of me again?"

"Not at all. I have something for you to do," Smoke told him. "I'll send along a note to my foreman. I want Linc to arm the hands, put a round-the-clock watch on the ranch. The note will also tell him to send Sam Waters, Harb Yates, and Zeke Tucker with you, to make a sweep south and west, to close off any escape route for the rest of these polecats. That badge Monte gave you gives you the authority to deputize them. Once everyone is in place and we have their backs against the mountains, the roundup should be easy."

Oliver Johnson gusted out the breath he had been holding and nodded, then gestured toward the simmering pots that had not been disturbed. "What say, the first thing we fill our bellies?"

Smoke chuckled. "Spoken like a true frontiersman."

Early the next morning, Smoke Jensen and Monte Carson happened upon a dozen of the neophytes. It hadn't been difficult. The greenhorns had blundered around making enough noise to drive away all the game for five miles around, and had it been a few years earlier, gotten their hair lifted by the Arapaho. One actually managed to ride his horse into a tree. If the weapons they carried in great quantity had not packed so much potential death and destruction, it would have been laughable.

Their ineptitude allowed Smoke and Monte to remain out of their sight or ken as the babes in the woods thrashed their way by the canny frontier marshal and Preacher-trained gunfighter. Once the tenderfeet had gone out of earshot of any but themselves, Smoke revealed his hastily assembled plan to Monte.

"I'll go in among them tonight, well after dark. My bet is, they won't even have night riders out guarding the camp."

Monte spat a stream of red-brown tobacco juice. "Won't take that bet. I reckon yore right."

"I figure a few cut cinch straps, a couple of them hog-tied, and such will give those boys something more to worry about."

Monte chuckled. "Smoke, you could glide in there and slit all their throats while they slept, yet you always open yer dance with these shenanigans."

"Way I figure, not all of them are killers. Most, in fact, are only overgrown spoiled brats with guns in their hands. They find out there's someone around who's meaner, tougher, and smarter than they are, they'll light out sure enough. Better that way. I don't enjoy taking a man's life," Smoke added, in a rare flash of introspection.

Smoke and Monte gnawed cold biscuits and strips of jerky while the bunglers stumbled through the pines and Douglas fir forest that blanketed the swollen bosom of the mountains. They ate more while the flatlanders roasted a deer haunch over a poorly made, smoky fire.

"Hope they like the taste of pine resin with their meat," Monte observed jokingly. "When you headin' out?"

"Let them all get to sleep."

The two lawmen sat in silence after that, listening to the distant sounds of the easterners as they dwindled into quiet. A sliver of moon added only slightly to the frosted starlight that shimmered down on the grassy clearing where the out-landers had settled for the night. Then, with a soft runt and a light hand on Monte's shoulder, Smoke faded into the darkness on foot.

Smoke Jensen found his first candidate within five hundred yards of where Monte waited. For whatever reason, the man had wandered off from the others to sleep alone. Smoke crouched beside him for two long minutes before ensuring a long, deep slumber by the application of the barrel of his .45 Colt to the greenhorn's head.

Quickly he trussed up the unconscious object lesson with a piggin' string and the victim's belt. A dirty sock and a strip of the man's shirt served for a gag. Smiling to himself, Smoke Jensen took all the weapons with him as he moved away into the dim light of the stars. He found two restless souls further in toward the camp. Unable to sleep, they had come away from those who could to talk about their lives in the East. Smoke positioned himself and called to them in a hushed whisper.

"Pssst! Over here."

"Who's that?" one asked in mild alarm.

"Luke."

"Oh. Sure, you're one of the Seventh Avenue gang, right?"

"Right. Come here," Smoke coaxed.

"You go," the talkative one urged his companion.

"No, you go."

"You're closer. You go."

"Don't take all night," Smoke hastened them along. "Both of you come here."

Grumbling under their breath, both young hoodlums got to their boots and headed toward the sound of his voice. The first to reach the place found the muzzle of a revolver stuffed in his ear.

"Quiet now. No sudden noises," Smoke suggested. Quickly he relieved them of their sidearms. "Do you know the way out of here?" To their shaken heads, he added, pointing south, "It's that way. I suggest you start walking and don't look back. It's about ten miles to the nearest ranch. You should make it about daylight. From there, it'll be easy for you to find the nearest train and get the hell back to New York."

"Who do you think you are?" the lippy one demanded.

"Smoke Jensen."

His name had the desired effect. "Oh, shit! H-h-how'd you get up on us like that?" the youth with lesser bravado asked.

"These mountains have been my home since I was younger than you. I'm not going to let some street scum take them from me. I'll put it in the simplest terms, so you can understand it. You leave . . . or you die."

"We're gone. We're already out of here," the nervous one gasped out.

"Dennis," his braver companion protested. He left rather rapidly with his friend a moment later when he heard the loud clicks of a Colt's hammer being pulled back and remembered the muzzle of that gun still pressed into his ear.

Nick diMenfi didn't like being out in these woods alone. No matter what that English bastard Lathrop said, there were wild Indians on the loose around here; he knew it. Hadn't he read it a hundred times in those books by Ned Buntline? Nick's family had immigrated from their home in Menfi, Sicily, when his father was a young man with a new bride. Their name had been Struviato, but that had been too much for the immigration guy, his father had laughingly recounted at hundreds of family gatherings. So, this English-speaking guy had listed him as Hubert diMenfi and his wife as Carla.

As the fourth of seven sons born to Humberdo and Carlotta, Nicolo diMenfi had grown up fast and tough in some of the roughest streets in New York City. With big, wise brown eyes, he had watched the old Sicilian dons squeeze money from the shop owners, whores, and street gangs that had just naturally begun to form among the young Italian, Jewish, and Irish boys in the mixed neighborhood.

At eight, Nick had joined the junior auxiliary of the Tony Frescotti Family. He graduated to the exalted position of a runner for policy slips at age 13. He knew which cops on the beat were on the pad, which sergeants, lieutenants, and even captains received the discreet small white envelopes each Sunday afternoon in Tony Frescotti's restaurant, where they all went with their families to a table-groaning feast.

Proudly, Nick made his bones with the Frescotti family at 17, when he knifed to death a sneaky mick gunsel who was lining up on Don Tony Frescotti from a dark doorway of the brownstone in which the diMenfi family lived. He had been hidden out for three weeks by one of Frescotti's underbosses. Then, in a windowless room, with walls draped in black, and illuminated only by two candles on a kind of altar, he had sworn by Saint Ann to live by the knife and the gun and to die by the knife and the gun. His finger had been pricked and he had signed the compact with his blood.

Word on the streets had it that a new force of Irish from Boston and New York was forming, for some unknown reason, and it bothered the families of New York City. Although warring among themselves, they joined at a sit-down to mutually agree to do something about this. At the recommendation of Don Tony Frescotti, Nick had been given the task of getting inside this outfit and learning all he could.

Which is what had brought him out to this godforsaken country in the first place. And, oh, how he hated it. No cobblestone streets, no brick sidewalks. And no buildings. Nick saw himself as one of his family's best soldiers. What was he doin' lost in the trees?

A slight rustling of leaves attracted his attention. Curious, his streetwise instincts aroused, Nick pulled the .32 Smith & Wesson from his coat pocket and walked through the leaves and fallen branches with less-than-satisfactory silence. In the dim starlight he noticed a bush that swayed and rattled wildly. Nick braced himself and raised his revolver to eye level.

"Okay, come out of there, smart-ass," Nick challenged, in proper street-hood style.

The bush only vibrated with greater violence. Nick jumped to one side and quickly rounded the suspected area. There he found two of the Irish gang hanging upside down from an alder limb over the bush. They were tied and gagged and flexed their bodies from the hips in a desperate attempt to attract attention.

Nick hastened to their side. "Jeez, what happened to you two?" he asked in a low whisper.

"I did," an equally soft reply came from behind Nick.

"What th' fu—" Nick began, as he whirled and came face-to-face with the biggest, broadest man he had ever seen. Starlight gleamed off the barrel of a huge .45 Colt revolver lined on Nick's chest. "Who th' hell are you?" he managed to croak.

"I'm your worst nightmare. But I answer to Smoke Jensen."

"Oooh . . . shit," Nick breathed out slowly. Something told him he was going to die in this lonesome place, far from his Brooklyn neighborhood.

20

"If you want to stay alive," the man called Smoke Jensen told the Black Hand kid from Brooklyn, "do as I say."

Quick of wit, as well as with a knife or gun, Nick diMenfi swiftly evaluated the situation. "Yeah—yeah, sure. What do you want?"

"Mr. Jensen. What do you want, Mr. Jensen?" Smoke taunted.

"'What do you want, Mr. Jensen?'"

"I've already told you that. You can begin by handing me that toy in your fist, before you hurt yourself."

Pride in being a button man for the Frescotti mob momentarily flared. "I know how to handle a gun."

"I was thinking of what a mess a forty-five slug would make of your chest."

"You wouldn't dare shoot. You don't have a chance if you do. There's fifteen of us out here, all with guns," Nick continued in defiance.

"Wrong. You and three others are all that's left who aren't tied up or otherwise disposed of," Smoke Jensen gave him the bitter news.

"What's . . . 'otherwise disposed of'?" Nick queried, as he numbly handed over his revolver. He held a dread that he knew the answer before he heard it.

"Three of them gave me some trouble. They're dead. Five of them saw the light. They're on the way home. You'd be wise to make the same choice."

"Naw, I think I'll stay. Free my buddies and hunt your ass down."

"Talk about not having a chance!" Smoke hissed at him. His patience had worn to the thinnest. "Listen, you little guttersnipe, how do you think I managed to move around and through all of you, fix the wagon of eleven, and not make a sound? I can guarantee that after tonight, not a one of you New York trash that stays in the High Lonesome is going to leave here other than in chains or dead."

Nick diMenfi had fixed on one phrase. "Jeez, you got that right. This is the lonesomest place I've ever been."

"No one will even find your grave."

Nervously, Nick cut his eyes to the pair thrashing in the bush, then back to Smoke Jensen. "Okay, you made me a believer. I'm on my way back to Mulberry Street. See ya around, Mr. Jensen."

"You'd better hope you don't," Smoke growled at the departing young gangster.

Smoke Jensen had picked his spot well. Monte Carson, on the other side of the trail, waved to show he had gotten into position. They had trailed this small band for half of the next morning, then swung wide to get ahead of them. The narrow, unnamed pass in the Medicine Bow range of the Rockies didn't allow for much deviation. Unless these flatlanders turned back, they could go nowhere else but into the ambush.

He would need two well-placed shots, in rapid succession, to activate the key to that ambush. Smoke had planned a diversion that would effectively seal off any retreat. Nestled down behind a fallen forest giant, the barrel of his Winchester .45-70-500 Express rifle resting across the trunk, Smoke sighted in on the knot that held the weighted gunnysack in place. The trill of a wood warbler, produced by Monte Carson, alerted Smoke to the appearance of the first two members of the gang. Smoke broke his sight picture a moment to study the approaching eastern hard cases.

Two hats—derbies of course—appeared over the drop in the trail. Under them were heads with outlandish hairstyles, the eyes locked straight ahead, ignoring the terrain to either side. The nodding heads of the mounts showed next. The birdcalls continued numbering the enemy party as they came on. Smoke returned his attention to sighting in on the knot.

When the spurious birdsong ended, Smoke took a final deep breath, let out half, and squeezed the trigger of his rifle. The Winchester bucked against his shoulder and he swiftly cycled the lever action to chamber another cartridge. His second round severed the rope that held their diversion out of sight among the branches of the alder.

When the huge hornet's nest cracked open on the trail, an angry roar rose in the morning quiet as the winged insects swarmed out to seek vengeance on whoever had disturbed them. They quickly found the greenhorn gunmen, who had reacted to the twin rapid shots by halting and looking around themselves in confusion.

"What th—ow! Ouch! Get 'em off me, get 'em off!" Toby Yellen shrieked, as a dozen angry hornets descended on his exposed flesh and repeatedly sank their venom-dripping stingers into his face and arms.

Yellen began slapping at the vicious insects, his reins forgotten. When others of the swarm settled their rage on the horse, it exploded into a frenzy. Lashing out with impotent hind hooves, it jolted and bounced until its gyrations dislodged Toby Yellen. He sprawled in the dirt, mercifully spared the attention of the hornets, though his right shoulder had been dislocated and his left collarbone cracked.

From his position on the far side, Monte Carson put a bullet through the shoulder of one eastern thug who had drawn his six-gun. Smoke Jensen took the hat off another with his Winchester. Acting as one, the five intruders who remained mounted jumped their horses forward in an attempt to escape the gunfire and the hornets.

Smoke led them as they approached his position so that his slug cracked past inches in front of the face of the man in the lead. He reined in so violently that his mount went to its rear haunches. That spilled the inexperienced rider out of his saddle. They'd had enough time to change their outlook, Smoke considered.

He stood up, Winchester covering them, and sealed their fate. "Rein up and put your hands in the air." The four who were still mounted did as told. "All right, slowly," Smoke commanded. "Drop all your weapons. Every one, or you die right here."

Monte Carson appeared from his concealed position and ambled down the slope toward the roadway. He appeared relaxed. But to his practiced eye, Smoke could see that Monte efficiently covered the more distant pair that faced him. When the lawman reached a spot where the greenhorns could see him, they began to obey by shucking their assortment of arms.

When that had been completed, Smoke admonished them to turn around and ride like hell out of the high country, all the way back to where they'd come from. Grumbling like the self-centered brats they were, they complied, speeded along by several shots over their heads. They paused only long enough to retrieve Toby Yellen, and skirted widely around the still disturbed hornets. After the last disappeared down the trail, Monte turned to Smoke.

"They'll go right back to Lathrop."

"I expect them to, Monte. I'd like to see his face when they tell him what happened." Smoke grew serious and a furrow formed between his full brows. "I'd like to see his face. It galls me not to know what my enemy looks like."

"You'll get that chance soon, I reckon."

Smoke Jensen began gathering up the discarded firearms and knives. "No, this chasing could go on forever. What I need is a way to smoke out Lathrop and his partners." He paused, considering his options. "I think the thing to do is go back to the Sugarloaf. Then let it get around that I'm there, ready for a showdown."

Wade Tanner found Phineas Lathrop and Victor Middleton seated in a sunny area of the city park. The thin, cool air of Denver apparently didn't agree with them, he reckoned. They had their noses buried in pages of the Denver *Sentinel,* and continued to read for a couple of minutes, ignoring him. Recalling the information he had for them assuaged the anger building in Tanner.

At last, when he could contain it no longer, Tanner interrupted. "Mr. Lathrop. It's something important."

Phineas Lathrop looked up with an expression of boredom painted on his sardonic features. "What is, Tanner?"

"I got the word on Smoke Jensen. He's holed up on that ranch of his, the Sugarloaf. What's goin' around is, he's makin' a fort of the place. Says he'll lock horns with anyone who tries to move in on the place."

Lathrop considered it frowningly, his fleshy lips working as though forming words. "He needs a lesson in cooperation," he said at last.

"Now, Phin, I'd advise against that. Never attack a man in his position of strength."

"That how you got so far in the business world, Victor?"

Victor Middleton ignored the barb behind the thrust. "As a matter of fact, yes. Far enough that you came to me for financing, remember?"

"Let's cut this crap," Lathrop snapped hotly. "So far, it's one against one. We'll decide what to do after we talk with Arney Cabbott."

At eleven that morning, Lathrop, Middleton, and Cabbott gathered around a table piled high with juicy roasted pork, potatoes, and applesauce in a small eatery on Pike Street. Fuming, Wade Tanner waited outside while his stomach rumbled.

They attacked the food first. Then, over coffee, they discussed alternatives based on Tanner's intelligence. Middleton remained adamant. Cabbott swayed in his direction at first, then abstained from agreeing with either of his partners.

"We're back to one-to-one," Lathrop summed up. "In which case, I'm going ahead. Get Tanner in here, and we'll send him to round up all of our guns. We're going to take this fight to Smoke Jensen."

Newly dug rifle pits dotted the sloping meadows of the Sugarloaf. They had been positioned to guard all approaches to the ranch, their flanks protected by trees or boulders. Their zigzag arrangement also allowed a covered route from one to the other, so that as few as three men could blanket the area with gunfire. Smoke Jensen looked on them approvingly from where he stood before his gathered hands. Their soft conversation ended when he raised a gloved hand.

"You've done a fine job, but there's more to do. I'll leave the rest, sandbags along the inside walls of the bunkhouse, filling water barrels, and of course, tending the stock to Linc and the day crew. Four of you will come with me. I'm going to set up some nasty surprises for whoever takes our invitation to the dance."

Enthusiastic, meaningful nods went among the hands as they broke up the meeting to attend to their tasks. Smoke went to the four men he had selected, Dandy walking obediently at his side. He swung into the saddle, a signal for the four to do the same, and nodded for them to move out.

Smoke's first stop was half a mile inside the ranch property, on the main road to Big Rock. When the men had dismounted, he issued his instructions.

"We're going to dig a pit here, clear across the road. I want it at least five feet deep." Smoke lamented inside over the image of the horses that would suffer because of this. Then he drew a pickax from the latigo ties on the skirt of his saddle, stripped off his shirt, and joined his men in their labors.

When the pit had been completed to Smoke's satisfaction, he studied the area a while. "We'll have to carry away the dirt. Then cut saplings to cover the pit with a light framework. The tarps you brought along go over that, then enough dirt to make the trail look normal."

Fists on hips, Hank Bowers studied it. "Gosh, that's a nasty thing, Mr. Jensen."

"Wait until you see what I'm going to do while you get rid of the dirt."

Smoke set about selecting wrist-thick limbs of several nearby pines. These he cut with an ax and drove into the bottom and leading side of the gravelike excavation. Then he shaped the protruding ends into fine points. Bowers swallowed hard when he returned from the last load of rocks and soil.

After the narrow roadway had been restored to normal, Smoke led the way to the west, where a logged-off section on the mountainside allowed easy passage for anyone invading the ranch. There he pointed to the new growth above.

"Cut saplings from up there and bring them down here. Once we get them like I want them, we'll form them into big caltrops with rawhide strips."

By noontime, ranks of star-shaped obstacles extended between tall stumps, closing off all access but a straight line that provided a clear field of fire from the rifle pits beyond. With a nod of satisfaction, Smoke Jensen pulled off his thin leather gloves and delved into his saddlebag for whatever treasures Sally had sent along for his nooning. He wasn't disappointed. A fat ham sandwich on freshly baked bread was rounded out with a boiled egg and cold beans, and she had even included a slab of apricot pie.

Attended to by Cynthia Patterson and the bunkhouse cook, the others fared equally well. They settled down to eat. Between bites, Hank Bowers asked about the afternoon's plans.

"The high pass is what bothers me," Smoke informed the

hands, referring to the seven-thousand-foot pass behind Sugarloaf Mountain. "If we hurry up with our noonin', we can ride there in time to rig some deadfalls and swing traps."

"Are you expectin' an army?" Bowers asked.

"At least fifty men." The flat tone of Smoke's voice convinced the wrangler.

"Think they'll all come the same way?"

"No, Hank. Not even an eastern dandy is that stupid. I expect this Lathrop to split his force in half, at least, and come at us from several directions at once."

Bowers shook his head in sad wonder. "It's gonna be one hell of a fight."

His words stuck with Smoke Jensen through the rest of the day. By the time they returned to the ranch, a hair short of twilight, they had worked their way deep into his conscience. After tending to their horses, Smoke walked with his hands to the bunkhouse, where a line had formed for evening chow.

"Listen up, men," Smoke addressed his crews. "This ain't your fight. You've no reason to risk your lives in it. I've provoked a powerful man, with a lot of guns backing him, so I've no call to expect you to take extraordinary chances. What I'm getting at is, you're free to go. Ride on out, with no prejudice. You'll remain on the payroll and will be welcome back when the battle's over."

Buttermilk Simms, the cook, screwed up his pink cherub's lips and spat a stream of tobacco juice. "If you ride for the brand, you fight for the brand," he summed up everyone's feelings on the subject.

"Damned right," a chorus of voices answered.

"I'd be growin' myself a beard if I ran out on you," Linc Patterson drawled. "Couldn't look myself in the mirror t'shave."

Smoke still had a large lump of uneasy conscience to calm down. "Five of us could hold the place against all the men Lathrop could throw at us. Three would do in a pinch."

"Ain't gonna be that way, Mr. Jensen," Hank Bowers

offered. "I seed what we done today. I reckon the next few days are gonna be full of makin' more dirty surprises for them eastern so-called gunfighters. I aim to be in on that. An' I want to see what those things do to them."

"You know how I feel. You men didn't sign on to be gunfighters. Hell, I'll bet that half of you can't find your butt with a bullfiddle, let alone hit what you shoot at."

"That ain't fair!" half a dozen shouted back. Hank Bowers explained their pique. "We may not be up to standin' in the middle of the street, trading slugs with five or six randy sons, but we can, by God, hit what we aim at. You done seen to that, Mr. Jensen."

Trapped by his own penchant for excellence, Smoke could only chuckle. "Thanks for the reminder, Hank. And for the duration of this fandango, you can all call me Smoke."

"All right, Smoke," Hank bantered back. "An' another thing . . . there ain't a man jack of us can't outshoot them New York queers."

A rousing cheer signaled general agreement with those sentiments. A warm glow spread through the chest of Smoke Jensen. These were men to ride the river with. They all had sand, and plenty of it. He raised both hands for quiet.

"We're going to make certain that Lathrop's hard cases come to grief any way they choose to come at us. First thing after supper, Linc and I will be passing out boxes of extra ammunition to each of you. You'll wear your sidearms at all times and keep a rifle or shotgun close at hand. I'll have a watch list drawn up and posted by nine o'clock tonight."

"I thought you'd already have one," Linc Patterson said with a wink.

Smoke Jensen made a mock expression of hurt feelings. "I had to know who'd be here first. But from here on out, we've got only one thing to do: bring a world of grief to Phineas Lathrop."

21

Fifty-three men left Georgetown, Colorado, at the northern base of Gray's Peak and rode north through Berthold Pass, on the way to Big Rock. Phineas Lathrop took the lead. He had been told that they had more than a day and a half ride to the small town, nestled in the folds of the Rockies. Almost at once the flatlanders began to complain.

Everywhere they went, the terrain seemed to be up or down. The steep trails put a strain on them that few had ever experienced. By the time they reached their first goal, all of the eastern crime elite agreed that what they needed were a long soak in a hot tub, a soft bed, and a real chair to sit in.

So many hard-faced strangers banded together and riding into the small town roused a lot of curiosity, and more fear, in the residents of Big Rock. Monte Carson stood on the stoop of the sheriff's office and watched the cavalcade walk their mounts silently down the main drag. When the last had gone out of sight, he reached down a hand and put it on the spindly shoulder of the Seegers boy, who stood at his side.

"Jamie, I don't reckon those fellers would suspect a tadpole like yerself of carryin' a message to Smoke Jensen. Are you up to it?"

Red-haired and freckled, Jamie Seegers turned his big, brown eyes up to the sheriff. "Yes, sir. What is it?"

"You take yer pony and skirt around them hard cases, ride lickety-split for the Sugarloaf. Mind, you stop before you get half a mile inside the gate. If I know Smoke, there'll be someone on watch. And you might run into something unpleasant on your own. Tell Smoke that they're on their way, Lathrop's bunch. Tell him, too, that as soon as I can put together a posse, we'll be on the way to pick up the leavin's. Can you remember all that, boy?"

"Oh, yes, sir. I'll go tell my Paw, then get right on my way."

"You leave that to me. It's important you get to Smoke Jensen well before those bushwhackers do."

Smoke Jensen found Bobby Harris exactly where Sally had told him the boy would be. Bobby sat on a large stump behind the sprawling house that had started as a simple log cabin, his feet dangling, hunched over with elbows on thighs, his chin in the palm of his upturned right hand. He had shoved his lower lip out in a pink pout. Smoke strolled up and rounded the stump to face the boy.

"I hear you're vexed about something."

Bobby looked up at Smoke and telegraphed his misery from cobalt eyes. "You should know."

"Sorry. I don't. What is it, Bobby?"

"Don't want to talk about it."

"Come on, son, tell me. If you don't talk things out once in a while, they just fester inside."

"It's done festered, all right," Bobby agreed. "I—I—ah—" He began stumblingly, took a deep breath and tried again. "I ain't no use to the Sugarloaf anymore."

"Meaning you're no use to me?" Smoke probed.

"If that's the way you feel."

"C'mon, Bobby, you can't hide behind an attitude."

Suddenly large tears welled in Bobby's eyes. He gulped and swallowed and fought them back. "I *know* I can't be any use to you. You cut me out of this fight that's comin' up. I do a man's job, I can fight like a man, too."

"Bobby, you *can't* fight like a man. For all of your abilities with horses, you're still an eleven-year-old boy. I care a good deal for you. I want you to be safe. So does Sally."

The pout grew larger, until Bobby exploded. "You said the other hands could stay and fight when they brought up that they could hit what they shoot at. Well . . . I can hit what I shoot at, too."

"Damn it all, I don't want you killed. Is that too awful to accept?"

For all the misery on the face of Smoke Jensen, Bobby refused to melt even a little. "Go away. I don't want to talk anymore."

Exasperated beyond all patience, suspecting that he was somehow to blame for his failure, Smoke Jensen turned away. He'd crossed only half the distance to the house when his keen hearing picked up the wretched sound of the deep sobs that wracked the small boy's shoulders. Inside the house, he recounted his lack of progress with Bobby to Sally.

She exerted her usual sensibility in such matters. "Don't worry, dear. I'll talk to Bobby and help him see this is for his own good."

Smoke threw up his hands. "Did we have the same problems with our own?" he asked unhappily.

Help came to Smoke Jensen shortly before midnight, in the form of a skinny redheaded kid. Little Jamie Seegers, escorted by one of the hands, arrived with his message from Monte Carson. Once he had delivered the sheriff's terse words, he stood in wonder, staring around the living room, which had once been the entire interior of the Jensen home.

"It's late," Smoke observed. "If that army of war hawks wasn't right on your heels, I'd say you should stay the night. As it is, we've got to get you out of here." The boy appeared startled. Smoke noticed that he was unarmed, unusual for anyone traveling at night in the High Lonesome. "Do you have a gun, boy?"

"No, sir. My paw won't let me."

"That's a stupid attitude," Smoke said musingly to himself. "With Lathrop's men on the loose here, it isn't safe for you to go around unarmed." Smoke continued thinking out loud. "If I could spare one of the hands . . . wait a minute!" he barked a second later.

Smoke strode to the split logs set into the inner face of an outside wall to form the staircase to the second floor. There he paused to tell Jamie that he would be right back. Upstairs, ducking his head under the low ceiling, Smoke went to Bobby's room. He rapped sharply before opening the door.

Bobby sat on the end of his bed in the unlighted room, staring out at the darkness beyond. Smoke crossed to him. He put a hand on the boy's shoulder and Bobby squirmed away. *He'll sing a different tune in a minute,* Smoke thought.

"Bobby, do you have your six-gun cleaned, oiled, and loaded?"

Excitement bloomed on the youngster's face. "Then you've changed your mind?"

"Sort of. There's an important thing that needs doing. I think you're the right one to handle it. Downstairs is a boy who brought me a message from Monte Carson. With Lathrop's gang swarming around the place anytime now, he can't get back home safely by himself. He's unarmed and needs someone to escort him back to Big Rock. I think you're the one to do that. Are you game?"

"Am I!" Bobby squeaked. "I'll get dressed right away."

"You'll have to take the high pass and go the long way around. I'll have Sally pack enough food. Take your carbine along, and I think a shotgun for Jamie Seegers."

"Jamie! I know him from school. His Pop's dumb; won't let Jamie learn to shoot."

Smoke Jensen hid his grin. "Don't speak ill of your elders, Bobby. Though in this case, the truth is, I agree with you. That's why I think a scattergun is best. Now, hurry along and we'll get you on the way."

Downstairs Smoke crossed to Sally's side. He spoke more to her than to Jamie Seegers. "I think we've got the problem solved. Bobby Harris will be going with you, Jamie. You'll take the high pass and circle down to Big Rock. Should be there by late afternoon tomorrow."

"Oh, Smoke, you've done it again," Sally praised him, with a light laugh.

"Just takin' care of loose ends, ma'am. Now, fix them enough vittles to last. They're growin' boys, remember."

"What are you going to be doing?"

Smoke smiled at Sally. "I've changed my mind about sitting here and waiting. I'm going to take a dozen hands out and give Phineas Lathrop a headache."

At first, Phineas Lathrop thought some idiots were taking potshots at squirrels and woodpeckers. Dawn had just put a pink haze across the steep grade their horses pulled into, the stretch of road that marked the last five miles to the Sugarloaf. Sharp cries of alarm and a sudden increase in the volume of fire changed his mind. He slowed the heavy-chested mount he straddled and swiveled in the saddle.

Darkness still shrouded the trail behind. From it he marked the yellow-orange winks of muzzle blast. He counted five . . . no, seven points from which fire was directed into the rear of his column. It had to be Smoke Jensen. How in hell could he have found out so soon?

Frantically he pointed to the source of attack. "Up there, in those rocks."

Return fire proved to be of no avail. Lathrop's inexpert gunmen chipped a lot of granite and sprayed lead high over the heads of the Sugarloaf hands. Mounted men, twirling loops and covered by riflemen, charged the rear. The lassos settled around the arms and shoulders of three New Yorkers.

A trio of quick dallies and sharp turns, and the hoodlums went flying. They landed hard.

In the next instant, they were slithering through the grass, away from their companions. Out of sight of the column of thugs, hardhanded wranglers deprived them of their weapons, boots, trousers, and shirts. A few punches convinced them to head back in the direction from which they had come.

Then, quickly as it had come, the attack broke off. Only echoes of the flurry of gunshots remained in the narrow defile between high mountains. Driven beyond his customary reserve, Phineas Lathrop could only pound an impotent fist on his saddle horn and bellow his displeasure.

"God damn you, Smoke Jensen!"

None of which bothered Smoke Jensen. He had heard it all before—many times.

Another plan had developed in Smoke's head on the way to attack Lathrop in the rear. He now led his men, none of whom had received a scratch, on a wide run around the approaching column. Smoke had been surprised to learn that Lathrop had not been battle-wise enough to divide his large force and assault the ranch from several directions at once. Perhaps, he decided, unwilling to underestimate his opponent, Lathrop's lack of unfamiliarity with the terrain had caused this mistake. Whatever the case, Smoke Jensen determined to make use of the error to the detriment of the would-be empire builder.

Phineas Lathrop had barely managed to regain his composure and reorganize his column of eastern guns when Smoke Jensen and his twelve ranch hands struck at them from the front. Caught by surprise and confused as to who this could be, Lathrop bellowed to his men to resist with all they had. His hat went flying as a bullet punched through the crown.

Two more popped through the widespread sides of his coat.

That sent Lathrop out of the saddle to sprawl in the thorny underbrush. At once, panic ensued. Wade Tanner assumed command and tried to rally the demoralized gangsters.

"The boss is down!" one of them shouted. "Let's get outta here."

"No! Hold on. We outnumber them," Tanner urged.

Gradually, his determination and appeal to reason reached a few, who also turned back to take wildly inaccurate shots at the Sugarloaf hands. A yelp of pain showed one of the greenhorns to be a better shot than most. Another Sugarloaf rider threw up his hands and tumbled from his saddle. A friend swiftly swung from his saddle to scoop up the dead wrangler. With a wild whinny, a wounded horse set off out of control of its rider. Then a shouted command ended the encounter.

Swiftly as they had descended on the flatlanders, the mountain-wise wranglers set off at a fast run toward the distant ranch. Tanner was quick to seize upon it.

"Mount up. Get after them. Run them to the ground," he commanded.

Numbly the products of the New York tenements and Boston docks began to comply. Then the rage- and pain-hollowed voice of Phineas Lathrop came from the chaparral to the side of the trail. "Someone get me out of here."

Wade Tanner hurried to do just that. When a rumpled, leaf-bedecked Phineas Lathrop rose out of the spiny brambles, he looked furiously off in the direction Smoke Jensen had taken.

Both fists shook over his head as he wailed, "Smoke Jensen . . . *you baaaastaaard!"*

Smoke Jensen and his hands led the waterfront hoodlums off on a merry chase—one at least that the men of the Sugarloaf enjoyed a lot. Not the same could be said for those who followed. From a vantage point above a box canyon into which the unwitting eastern garbage had been led, Smoke studied their antics.

"Any bets as to how long before they realize the only way out is back the way they came?"

"Not me, Smoke."

Smoke gave Zeke Tucker a fleeting smile. "What about you boys? Zeke's not takin' a chance."

"Count me out," Sam Waters declined. "Where to now, Boss?"

"We'll pick up the main body and lead them right to the Sugarloaf . . . over the west slope."

Delighted smiles lighted the faces of the Sugarloaf riders. They well knew what waited for the invaders. Less than twenty minutes later, they got the chance to lead the unsuspecting greenhorns into the deadly lane of fire established by Smoke Jensen.

At first, the Lathrop gang gave off excited hollos, like eastern foxhunters, when they sighted their former tormenters. They raced along eagerly, drawing closer as the grassy incline increased. Boston soft *A*s vied with nasal New York twangs as they cursed when the quarry disappeared over the crest of the rise.

Then they topped the ridge and found their way blocked by large, star-shaped wooden obstructions, their outward-pointed arms sharpened to wicked points. They closed up to thunder through a pair of gaps formed by three stumps. Beyond, they jinked to the left to negotiate another such opening. Their pace slowed, while that of those familiar with the layout remained steady.

Distance widened between pursuers and pursued. More angry curses rose among the flatlanders as they imagined these easy targets escaping them. It all worked the way Smoke Jensen had expected. The hard-riding mass of gunmen advanced at best possible speed, unaware that they were being channeled into an increasingly narrow passage.

Surprise registered on the faces of those in the lead when the fleeing ranch hands reined in and dismounted halfway up another slope, twin to the one down which they rumbled. Concealed rifle pits suddenly took on life and the meadow blossomed with spurts of gray-white powder smoke.

Only then did the oncoming hard cases realize that they had heedlessly ridden deep into accurate rifle range. Three men left their saddles, one with a terrible yell of pain. A second later, another New Yorker pitched to the side and fell under the hooves of the horses behind.

All at once it became too much for the city-bred gunfighters. Too unnerved to press the attack on Smoke Jensen's ranch, they halted their headlong advance and milled in confusion for precious seconds, while the marksmen of the Sugarloaf picked off four more of their number.

In the middle of their fear-numbed debate, Smoke Jensen and three men took to their saddles again and rode off, bold as brass, taunting Phineas Lathrop to come to some solid decision. Deep in his heart, Lathrop had to admit to being as demoralized as his followers. He felt helpless, out of his element, and unable to direct the conditions of battle to his liking. He also knew Wade Tanner to be frontier-wise and capable.

Regretfully, he directed a turnabout and started away from the Sugarloaf. Once beyond the ridge, safely out of range and sight of the dead shots they had faced, Lathrop halted his mob. He directed his first remarks to them, in order to keep them from turning it into a total rout.

"We're pulling back for the time being. There's too many of them. I want Eamon Finnegan and two men to keep a watch on this approach. I wasn't even aware of it, I'll admit. Now we know, and we'll find a way to take advantage of it. Now, Wade, I want you to take six men and go after Smoke Jensen. If he's taken out of the action permanently, those gunmen he's hired won't have any reason to stay here and protect the ranch. Who'll pay them?"

Wade Tanner produced a tight grin and a slight nod. Out here, he knew, men who had signed on to ride for the brand stood by it, many times even after the owner had been killed.

Range wars had taught him that. Also that fighting to protect a man's holdings, often won by long, hard battles against Indians, weather, and other land-hungry men, was a lot different from squabbles over defending this neighborhood or that back East.

Yet he found himself in the same situation. Wade Tanner had signed on to back Phineas Lathrop and his partners. Grudgingly he saw the necessity of his answer.

"Right away, Boss." He named off those he wanted to accompany him and rode out.

After Tanner's departure, Lathrop revealed his next stratagem to his uneasy men. "For the time being, I want you to break up into groups of eight or nine and go out and terrorize this whole countryside. We can draw Smoke Jensen out that way, get him where we can kill him. And . . . we have another advantage in such a tactic. With a little help from a friendly newspaper editor in Denver, the blame for your rampage will fall on Smoke Jensen."

22

Over the next few days, the Sugarloaf knew relative peace. Not so the surrounding countryside. Smoke Jensen soon found himself busy protecting his neighbors from Phineas Lathrop's predators. Since by the time news could be relayed to the Sugarloaf it would be too late, watching over the beleaguered ranchers of the northwestern corner of Colorado kept Smoke constantly in the saddle. Half a dozen of his hands rode his circuit counterclockwise to his schedule. It kept everyone busy trying to counteract the outrages directed by Phineas Lathrop. Like the situation Smoke Jensen had stumbled into only a minute ago some twenty-five miles west of the Sugarloaf.

Smoke had come upon trail signs of eight horses, each with a moderate burden, ridden fast toward the location of a ranch owned by Cyrus Hammer. Cyrus and Smoke had been friends for years. The portly, gray-haired Hammer had been in the High Lonesome nearly as long as Smoke. Now it looked like Cyrus Hammer had become the next target of Lathrop's terror. Although saddle-weary, Smoke picked up Dandy's pace.

He was still half a mile off when he heard the first flat reports of gunshots and saw the initial white puff of smoke rise. In these thick stands of resinous pines and firs, any fire could quickly get out of hand. Smoke eased Dandy into a rolling gallop.

Smoke burst into the clearing with a six-gun in each hand, his reins looped around the saddle horn. Two hard cases had Cyrus's foreman on the ground, savagely beating him. One of them looked up in time to die with the terrible knowledge that Smoke Jensen had found them. His partner soon joined him. Smoke pivoted from the hips and lined up his .45 Colt on yet another of the hoodlums.

Not surprising to Smoke, the New Yorker threw up his hands and ran. Smoke hastened him along with a bullet that clipped cloth from the shoulder of a linen duster. The other five outlaws had spread out behind any sort of cover they could find and exchanged shots with Cyrus Hammer and his wife. Smoke's sudden arrival instantly disrupted their strategy.

Two of them made the mistake of turning to confront this threat. Smoke Jensen put a slug through the fleshy part of one man's thigh. Howling, the former Boston longshoreman dropped his weight on his right knee and gamely tried to bring the .45 Colt into line with Smoke's chest. He found the weapon unwieldy at the best of times. Yet he managed to get off a round that cut a path uncomfortably close to Smoke Jensen's right side.

Smoke righted the situation with a shot that shattered the gunsel's breastbone and showered his lungs with bone fragments. Dandy flashed past the dying man, guided by the knees of Smoke Jensen. Dandy's broad chest smashed into the head and shoulders of the amateur gunman as Smoke rode him down.

A rifle roared in a shuttered window and another of the outlaws flopped face-first in the barnyard. Smoke Jensen turned his attention to the others, who remained out of the line of sight of Cyrus Hammer. It appeared that they had had all they wanted of this encounter. Dragging their wounded friends with them, they scurried for their horses, tied off to a corral post.

Smoke Jensen sped them on their way with a few close

rounds to remind them of their desire to leave. Then he holstered his off-hand six-gun and set to reload the other Peacemaker. While he did, he reflected on what a fitting name the Colt people had come up with. Things were definitely a lot more peaceful around the Hammer ranch after the proper application of the big .45.

Cyrus Hammer came from the house as Smoke started to fill the chambers of his other revolver. "You got here just in time. Of all the things, those son of bitches set fire to the *outhouse*. A couple of my hands got it out before any more harm was done. Light a spell, Smoke Jensen, looks like you could use an hour or two's rest and a good meal."

"I'm obliged."

"No, sir, it's us who's obliged. You know, Maw an' me was positive it couldn't be you attackin' the ranches hereabout."

"What are you talking about, Cyrus?"

"You ain't read the Denver papers, Smoke?"

"Not lately. I've—ah—had my hands full."

Cyrus chuckled at Smoke's dry humor, then explained. "The paper's been full of stories claimin' that you're behind these burnin's and such. Says you want to take over every inch of ground for the Sugarloaf." Cyrus paused and thought a moment. "Never can believe what they put in some of them papers."

"I'm glad to have you on my side, Cyrus. I only hope there's more with the good sense to see that. If not," Smoke summed up, "I could be in for some real hard times."

Over those past few days, Wade Tanner and his six men had been following Smoke Jensen by a distance of half a day. Try as he might, Tanner could not close the gap. At least, not until Smoke accepted the hospitality of the Hammers.

From the far side of the cleared meadow where the Hammer ranch headquarters had been established, Wade Tanner watched Smoke Jensen's broad back blend in with the dark forest of pines. Quickly he sorted out what should be done.

"This ranch is on Mr. Lathrop's list of those to be raided. Looks like Smoke Jensen runned off the boys that was supposed to do it. That was him, over on the far side." Tanner's eyes narrowed. "I'm gonna fix his wagon this time for sure. Rucker, I want you to come with me. The rest of you boys, wait here until we come back. Then we'll take care of this place, too."

In order to avoid detection, Tanner and Rucker skirted around the ranch, screened by the trees. Back on the trail, they rode hard to make up for lost time. Even so, they blundered upon Smoke quite unexpectedly.

Late evening put Smoke Jensen in a solitary camp under a large rock overhang that provided shelter from the elements. Clouds had gathered during the afternoon and a light rain began to fall around 4:30. The storm backed up against the higher peaks of the Rockies and stalled out. Drizzle plagued Smoke as he continued on his rounds. At last, soaked to the skin, he had spied the cavelike rock formation and rode off the trace to inspect it.

He found it had been used for a shelter before. A stack of small, dry limbs rested against the back wall of the granite lean-to, and near it, a fire pit. Smoke removed the saddle and wiped down Dandy, then started a fire. When it blazed to his satisfaction, he stripped bare and arranged his sodden clothing to dry. Smoke stood on the back side of the fire, buck naked, to dry his body.

He had only begun to dress in clean, dry clothes when he heard the clop of approaching hooves and the low grumbling of two voices. Tense and suspicious, Smoke left off putting on a shirt and instead strapped on his cartridge belt. His use-worn weapons settled comfortably into place. Quickly he shielded the low blaze with a ground cloth. But his action had not come quickly enough.

"Wade! Up there!" a voice called out down the trail.

Silence followed. Slowly, Smoke Jensen regained his

night vision. Although sundown remained a good hour off, heavy clouds had blackened the sky, making it seem like midnight. Smoke strained his hearing to detect the least sound from the darkness beyond his shelter. When it came, it bore with it almost fatal results for Smoke Jensen.

A darker shape on the trail directly below the overhang resolved itself into the form of a man. The figure had arms upraised as though holding a rifle. The moment he saw the yellow-orange muzzle bloom, Smoke dropped to the pine needle–strewn floor of the shelter. A slug cracked through the space formerly occupied by his chest and shattered into a hundred fragments against the back wall.

Smoke Jensen immediately rolled to his right and unshucked his right-hand .45 Colt. He sighted in on the unseen killer and waited. When another muzzle blast illuminated the shoulders and head of the assassin, Smoke triggered a round. A pain-filled wail choked off abruptly after the bullet had ripped through the side of the assailant's throat. Sudden light flooded the platform on which he lay.

Already rolling away from his own muzzle bloom, Smoke Jensen continued to spin on the ground, eyes closed, until he reached the outer darkness. The dying man's slug had cut the rope on one side of the shielding ground cloth and let free the brightness of Smoke's fire. Stupid to have built it, he thought now, although he had been convinced he was alone on this mountainside.

"Smoke Jensen," came a voice out of the down-trail darkness. "You ain't goin' anywhere from here, Jensen. You done kilt my partner. That was sneaky. But . . . you ain't got a chance of gettin' away. So why don't you come out of there and face me like a man?"

Smoke reckoned he might be a little thick about some things, but he sure wasn't stupid. Go out there? Without knowing how many waited for him? He wisely kept silent and cautiously eased himself downward, over the rain-wet pine needles. Again the voice taunted him.

"C'mon, Jensen. Be a man. I got it. I'll make it easy for

you. I'll come up into the edge of that firelight. I know enough about you to know you'll not shoot me if I don't have an iron in my hands. So that's what I'm gonna do. I'll leave my rifle behind, an' come forward with my six-gun in leather. No tricks, I promise."

Smoke held his silence while the seconds ticked off. Then, slowly, he made out the figure of a big man, wearing a tall-crowned Montana Peak Stetson. When the stranger entered the reflected glow of Smoke's fire, the seasoned gunfighter saw his features more clearly.

An angular face with a large nose, rabbity teeth, and slicked-back black hair seemed to ripple from the effect of flickering flames. It made him look like a rodent. Thin wisps of mustache twitched in a ratlike manner. Dark eyes that could be ebony in color cut from side to side, measuring his surroundings.

"What say, Jensen? Ain't you man enough to face me?" Tanner turned one way, then the next. "You tryin' to sneak away in the dark? This storm's gettin' over with. I reckon I'll have th' best part of an hour to track you down if you rabbit on me."

Cursing himself for a fool for allowing this big mouth to goad him into showing himself, yet unwilling, to gun down a man with empty hands, Smoke Jensen inched the last few feet down onto the trail, then came to his boots. When he walked into the light, it startled Wade Tanner, who jerked as though he had touched a hot stove.

What Tanner saw was enough to shake any man. Scars. From the round, puckered pink spots of gunshot wounds to the thin white lines of knife slashes, stab wounds, and tomahawk gouges, Smoke Jensen's bare torso was a terrain map of aged damage. Wade Tanner swallowed hard and lost the initiative of speaking first.

"What's your name?" Smoke asked.

"Why do you want to know?"

"I sometimes like to know the names of the men I kill."

That didn't set well at all. "I—I'm Wade Tanner. And, I'm about to become the man who gunned down Smoke Jensen."

"There's a lot of others who have said the same thing. Only you can't hear it from them anymore."

Tanner raised his left hand, pointed to Smoke's bare chest. "You've got pine needles on yer chest."

Far too wise to fall for that stunt and glance down, Smoke kept his eyes fixed on Tanner's gun hand. "You want to open the dance?"

"Goddamn, I do!" Tanner's voice cracked with tension and fear.

For all of the outlaw gang leader's prowess, his squinty eyes widened in alarm and terrible comprehension when he saw the blur of movement made by Smoke Jensen. His right-hand Smith American .44 had barely begun to move up and out of his holster when Smoke's .45 Peacemaker slid clear of leather and leveled on Tanner's middle. Tanner's mouth formed an "oh" of surprise as fire and smoke spat from the nearly half-inch muzzle pointed at his gut.

An invisible fist smacked hotly into Wade Tanner's middle. It doubled him over as he discharged his first round, still in the pocket, which ripped down his thigh and calf, a quarter-inch under the skin. Suddenly nerveless fingers released the heavy Smith & Wesson, which thudded to the ground.

Immobilized, Tanner sank to his knees. Blood poured from the leg wound. Desperately, he tried to focus on Smoke Jensen. His vision blurred as he studied on the muzzle that seemed to take forever to rise for another shot. Then Wade Tanner remembered he had a second .44 Smith American and drew it.

Smoke Jensen shot him again, a fist-depth below the sternum. Knocked backward, Wade Tanner shot high. The bullet cracked past Smoke's right ear and popped a hole through the brim of his hat. With a dying man's desperation, Wade Tanner fired again. Better aimed, this bullet gouged a trough through Smoke Jensen's shoulder point.

It felt like liquid fire. Although he had been shot and stabbed, and even been on the receiving end of a tomahawk many times before, Smoke Jensen had never exactly got used to being wounded. He certainly didn't take it for granted and pass it off as nothing important. A bullet gouge hurt like hell. More than a through-and-through wound, Smoke believed. Accordingly, he made sure his next round shattered the gun hand of Wade Tanner.

Tanner's last shred of loyalty washed away by the pain, his only thoughts were of buying his life. He raised his blood-dripping hand toward Smoke Jensen and spoke imploringly. "Wh—what do I gotta do for you not to kill me?"

"Stop trying to kill me, you damned fool," Smoke advised him.

"All right, all right. I ain't much good for that now, anyway."

"And answer some questions."

Wade Tanner blinked at this. "What do you want to know, Jensen?"

"Where can I find Phineas Lathrop?"

Tanner nodded knowingly. It figured. "You're goin' after Lathrop, huh?"

"I reckon to put a stop to his harebrained scheme," Smoke allowed.

Pain narrowed Tanner's eyes. "He's got near sixty men to go through first."

A fleeting smile curved the corners of Smoke Jensen's mouth. "Not anymore."

New waves of agony sapped Tanner's confidence along with the last of his strength. "He—Lathrop—was holed up in some rat den hotel in Denver along with this fancy New Yorker, Victor Middleton. Lathrop rode with us for a few days. Then, when you an' your hands made those eastern dudes turn tail an' run, Lathrop went back to Denver. He's lickin' his wounds in some fancy mansion Middleton found for them somewhere in Denver."

By that time, Wade Tanner had worked his left hand

behind his back to where he could wrap his long, spatulate fingers around the small bird-head grip of a Henderson & Richards .38 tilt-top that he carried for a backup. He waited for an incautious moment when Smoke Jensen would look away. When it came, he whipped the small five-shot revolver around and fired at point-blank range.

Tanner's trigger work came a fraction of a second too late. Always the fastest, Smoke Jensen sensed the furtive actions in time to spring to one side and squeeze off his .45 Colt. Tanner's slug cracked past Smoke's head a fraction of a second after Smoke's bullet gave Tanner a third eye and ended his life of corruption and evil.

"Never could abide a sneak," Smoke told the cooling corpse at his feet.

He also saw that chasing after Lathrop's underlings would not get the job done. So, Smoke Jensen headed back to the rendezvous point where he would gather his hands, send them to the Sugarloaf, and then go on himself to Denver to hunt down Phineas Lathrop and his partners. He wondered how, if possible, he could keep Oliver Johnson from accompanying him.

Once again, that problem did not resolve itself to the liking of Smoke Jensen. When he and his hands returned to the Sugarloaf, and fresh men sent out to keep the pressure on Lathrop's outlaw legion, Smoke announced his intention to go after the would-be empire builder.

"I'm coming with you," Oliver Johnson announced simply.

"No. I think it would be better if you stayed here."

"Remember when I told you that *you* are my story? Nothing's changed that."

Reluctantly, Smoke Jensen admitted to himself that he stood little chance of stopping the reporter. Together, the two men packed what they would need and set off to take the train from Big Rock. What Smoke regretted most was missing out on two or three nights of tender reacquaintance with his beloved Sally.

When he and Ollie got to Denver, all thoughts of blissful romance had disappeared. Not willing to waste time in a fruitless search of every "mansion" in Denver, Smoke Jensen prevailed on his friendship with Silas Greene at the Denver Livestock Exchange. If that failed to produce results, he knew he could rely on Captain Pat Patterson of the Denver Police.

Silas Greene responded to the question of a Victor Middleton making a recent purchase of a mansion with a long silence. His full lips pursed and relaxed as he ran through his copious knowledge of the aristocracy of Denver. At last he made a wet smacking sound and sighed heavily.

"I'm not sure he's your man, mind, but the only recent purchase of a comfortable house was made by a man calling himself Virgil Medford. The names are similar, but it's not the one you're looking for."

"Perhaps too similar," Smoke opined. "Same initials. Could it be Victor Middleton has a monogrammed gladstone, or some such item he can't part with, and needed to keep that V.M. in his new name? It's worth a try if nothing else develops. Where's the place this Medford took over?"

"It's the old Hampstead house, up on Gold Hill."

"Thank you, Silas. I owe you one."

Chuckling, Silas Greene rose to see his visitors out. "You owe me more than one, Smoke Jensen."

Smoke's visit to Pat Patterson proved to be even more fruitful. When Smoke stated his purpose, Patterson hardly hesitated before he announced, "Virgil Medford, alias Victor Middleton, bought the Hampstead mansion on Gold Hill only last week. I think he's the one you want, isn't he, Smoke?"

Smoke gave him a nod. "From what I heard elsewhere, yes. But I did want to make sure before I went barging in there."

"Now, wait a minute. If he's wanted for something, it's up

to the law to bring him in." Patterson's portly frame fairly jiggled with agitation and the anticipation of some action involving gun smoke.

"I don't think there's anything the law can prove Middleton has done illegally. Besides, there's someone else I'm after. Name of Phineas Lathrop. He's supposed to be hiding out with Middleton."

"Well, then, we've got harboring a criminal," Patterson offered.

"Again, there's so far only my word against Lathrop's. If I can flush him out, though, I think I can get him to talk."

Pat Patterson considered that. "Yes, Smoke, you do have your ways . . . Injun ways. Sounds dangerous enough. I'd like to send along a couple of my best—to sorta plug any escape holes. I'll come along, too."

23

Three rough-edged characters lounged around the small stone gatehouse that commanded the large, wrought-iron barriers which denied access to the average person to a wide, graveled drive at the Hampstead house. They aroused themselves with alacrity at the approach of four men in a light carriage, followed by a dark blue Denver PD paddy wagon.

"You folks have an appointment?" one of them growled, when the buggy turned in and stopped at the closed gate.

"We don't need an appointment," Captain Patterson answered. "Captain Patterson, Denver Police, and U.S. Marshal Jensen."

"Jee—zus, Smoke Jensen," one of the other thugs spoke in awed tones.

"Are you going to open that gate?" Patterson made it a demand.

"Not without the say-so from Mr. Mid—er—Mr. Medford, we ain't."

"Oh, I think you are," Smoke declared, rising.

His .45 Colt appeared in his hand as though by magic. Before its presence had registered on the four gunhands, it belched smoke and flame, and a loud spang sounded as the slug smashed into the lock case at the center of the double-hung portals. Another quick round finished the work and the wrought-iron barrier swung slightly inward.

"Drive on," Smoke told the policeman who sat to his right in the driver's seat.

Another officer had stepped down from the paddywagon and come forward now to widen the gap. Smoke Jensen kept his eyes and the muzzle of his .45 Peacemaker on the stunned guards. The black bristle crests on the headstalls of a pair of matched dapple gray's bobbed up and down as the carriage gained speed. The paddywagon rumbled behind and the dismounted policeman did a grab-iron mount like a railroad switchman as the rear lurched past where he stood.

"Now the thing to do is reach the house ahead of the news of our arrival," Ollie Johnson remarked.

"I think the element of surprise has already been lost," Pat Patterson observed dryly.

"There'll be more of the sort we left at the gate around the house," Smoke cautioned.

Ollie Johnson's pigeon breast swelled as he reached into his coat for the Smith .38 he carried. "I don't think we'll get past them by just shooting up a gate."

Smoke Jensen had not reholstered his Colt. "I reckon not, Ollie."

"There's two of them now," Captain Patterson pointed out.

Two hard cases rushed toward the approaching vehicles. One reached for the holstered Merwin and Hulbert .44 at his hip while the other shook an extended index finger at the buggy. "This is private property. Get out at once."

"Denver Police. Put your hands in the air and stay out of our way."

"Damn lawmen!" the man with the Merwin and Hulbert snarled, as he hauled his six-gun from leather.

Smoke Jensen shot him in the shoulder. His companion immediately skidded to a stop and raised his hands. The buggy rolled on by. The officers in the patrol wagon would tend to both of the guards. Another thug appeared in the opening made by tall double doors at the front of the mansion. He quickly popped back inside and slammed the thick oak portals closed. When the two police vehicles came to a stop under a portico, lawmen jumped out of the rear of the van and ran to encircle the main building.

Shooting started almost at once. Smoke Jensen, Ollie Johnson, and Captain Pat Patterson headed directly for the door, which Smoke assumed to be locked and probably barred. Smoke's suspicion proved true. The thick panels failed to yield to the turn of the brass handle. Smoke stepped back a pace and fired three rounds into the shiny plate of the lock. Still the door failed to yield.

"Let me," Pat Patterson offered as he snatched the ten-gauge Purdy from the hands of Ollie Johnson.

The stoutly built lawman gave it both barrels. Then he and Smoke hit the opposing doors with their shoulders. The impact hurt like hell, Smoke had to admit, especially on his slightly wounded side. It had the desired effect, though. A crack and groan preceded the inward movement of the big portals.

Smoke Jensen let his .45 Colt lead the way inside. Two Lathrop gunmen made the mistake of trying to block their way. Smoke and Patterson fired as one. Both thugs went down moaning over their wounds. Smoke holstered his nearly empty sixgun and drew the other .45 Colt from the left side.

"People are just like rats," Pat Patterson suggested. "They sense danger and they tend to go up." He nodded toward an elegant, curving staircase that led to the balcony that surrounded the grand entrance hall, and beyond to the second floor.

"I'm way ahead of you," Smoke tossed over his shoulder, as he headed for the bottom tread.

Two men popped up over a balcony railing and fired wildly. They perforated plaster and raised a fog of whitish dust for their efforts. Smoke Jensen shot one of them in the hip and Ollie dusted the other with fifteen pellets of OO buckshot. Screaming, the outlaw dropped his weapon and thrashed on the floor.

They met no further resistance from the railed half-floor and continued on to the second level. At the head of the stairs they paused a moment to orient themselves. Using hand signals, Smoke Jensen silently dispatched Captain Patterson along one hallway and Ollie down another, and he took the third wing of the mansion. He didn't need to go far to encounter trouble.

"Jensen!" a man shouted triumphantly behind Smoke.

Smoke hit the floor before the hard case's bullet left the muzzle of his six-gun. The wily mountain man did a forward roll and came up facing his back-shooting assailant. The big .45 Colt in Smoke's hand barked and the gunman doubled over the tremendous pain in his gut. Smoke's safety shot sent the man on his way to eternity. Doors banged open behind the big gunfighter.

"Shit, not again," Smoke complained to the empty hallway, as he dived full-length to put the corpse between him and his enemy.

His maneuver saved Smoke's life when, a second later, three slugs plunked into the dead man he used as a shield. Smoke spotted the nearest gunny and dropped him with a solid round to the chest. He shifted aim and took a gape-mouthed thug in a shoulder. Another bullet cracked past his head as Smoke lined up on the third former longshoreman.

Such blind good luck unnerved the Boston bully. "Oh, God, no. Don't kill me, Jensen."

"Lay it down. Now! Then shuck your cartridge belt and boots, drop your drawers around your ankles."

"Awh, hell, man. I'll look stupid like that."

"You'll look dead if you don't."

"All right—all right!" Quickly he obeyed.

Smoke Jensen came forward and hog-tied the man with his trouser belt, cartridge and holster rig, and his woolen pants. Then he set off after the elusive Phineas Lathrop.

* * *

The overconfident Victor Middleton had been first to hear the muffled gunshots at the gate. His poise quickly slipped and he was the first to urge that the conspirators make use of the unique escape route afforded by the Hampstead house. Arnold Cabbott and Abe Asher immediately agreed. Strangely enough, the taste of western-style fighting given him by Smoke Jensen had aroused a fierce combativeness in Phineas Lathrop. He proposed that they stay and shoot it out with the invaders.

"Fine, fine, that's what we pay those louts out there to do," a flustered Victor Middleton reminded him. "They can delay whoever is on the way here, while we get away. Abe and I didn't put up all that money to see it fly away from behind bars . . . or used to buy a fancy funeral."

Lathrop considered that last and gave a curt nod. "Lead the way," he stated in resignation.

Their route led to the door to the cellar stairs. Each of the conspirators took a pre-prepared set of saddlebags from wooden pegs fitted into the stone walls. With Victor Middleton at the point, they proceeded to the narrow wall at the far end. There, a cleverly concealed section of the stonework swung inward at a touch.

Beyond the hidden access, the trio lighted brass carbide gas lamps and placed the miner's helmets that held them on their heads. Only then did Middleton swing shut the secret door. Their lamps made eerie shadows dance on the damp stone walls. Victor Middleton directed them to the top of a flight of stairs.

Steep and rickety, the steps gave access to a stope that formed part of an old, abandoned gold mine. It honeycombed the domed hill on which the Hampstead house had been built. The stope angled sharply to a lower level, where Phineas Lathrop found them to be in a long, seemingly endless tunnel. Blaze marks, made of a swatch of whitewash, gave them the key to the maze.

"I—ah—I—" Phineas Lathrop began tentatively, after the

first hundred yards. For all his discomfort, he loathed revealing his fear of close, dark places to his partners.

"Just keep moving; we'll be out of here in no time," Victor Middleton assured him.

With the second floor cleaned out, and no sign of Lathrop and company, it left Smoke Jensen with a puzzle: had they run out the back before the police could get in place? That was a possibility worth looking into. To that end, he led Captain Patterson and Ollie Johnson downstairs and out through the large, well-equipped kitchen. The officers guarding the back gave negative shakes of their heads.

"No, sir, Marshal Jensen. No one came out after we got here. An' you can see, the ground is clear in all directions for a good three hundred yards. They'd have had to fly to get shut of that."

"What about those stables?"

"A horse in every stall, Marshal," the second policeman answered Smoke. "We done checked."

"Then, how could they . . . unless Lathrop and his partners weren't here when we came calling?" Smoke broke off his speculations and headed back inside the mansion. "We've overlooked something. What makes this place so special?"

Captain Patterson came forward. "Wendal Hampstead was a partner in the Galconda Mining Company. At one time they had five mines operating here and in Alder Gulch. Made literally tons of money. When the Rainbow played out, Hampstead bought this land and had the house built. Nothin' unusual in that."

Smoke Jensen considered a moment. "How's that again?"

"I said there's nothin' unusual about land goin' cheap when the mine under it runs dry."

"The Rainbow was a mine? I thought you were talking about Hampstead's personal fortunes changing."

"Oh, no. Er, yes. The Rainbow's what gave the name to

Gold Hill. It bored into about every inch of this hill not needed to keep the shafts and tunnels in shape. It's dang near hollow."

Smoke cut cold, gray eyes to the police captain. "Is there any possibility that Hampstead drilled a connection through to that mine?"

Understanding dawned for Pat Patterson and his eyes went wide and round. "By damn, I think you're right. He always bragged about having the world's largest wine cellar."

"Then let's find it," Smoke commanded.

It took the efforts of all three, plus those of a couple of burly policemen, to locate the hidden entrance to the Rainbow mine. That gave Phineas Lathrop and his partners a full hour head start, a condition that would soon come to haunt Smoke Jensen.

Lathrop and his three principal partners now became the fugitives. On the run constantly after leaving the far side of the mini-mountain that housed the Rainbow mine, they constantly felt the pressure brought to bear by Smoke Jensen. Deprived of the advice of Wade Tanner, whose death they assumed, they did little to hide their trail.

It led due northwest through the Rockies. On the way, they gathered what men Chance Lovell and Ed Miller had to offer. The latter two had taken over for their dead boss, Wade Tanner. Gradually the lost babes in the woods, led by Sean O'Boyle and Eddie Meeks, began to straggle across their path. On their second day out, Phineas Lathrop had cause to be thankful for their presence.

Like a wraith, Smoke Jensen appeared out of a low ground fog that blanketed their night camp. Although it was well after sunup, that bright orb had yet to burn through. One instant Phineas Lathrop saw Smoke Jensen, and the next he did not. Then all hell broke loose as dynamite sticks sailed into camp, their passage marked by arcs of sputtering sparks.

"Get down!" Sean O'Boyle barked. Then he amended, "No, get out!"

The powerful explosives began to detonate. Numbed, shaken, and confused, the eastern outlaws staggered about blindly. Dirt became a deadly weapon as the blast effect hurled pebbles and clods about at high speed. A piece took an eye out of a young punk from New York. Two of O'Boyle's Irish longshoremen howled in pain as sharp-edged pebbles slashed into their legs. Their horses panicked.

Shrieking in a demented state of fear, the poor beasts broke free of their picket line and added to the befuddlement of the gang by racing one way and another in random disarray. Following up quickly on the last explosion, Smoke sent a spray of bullets into the unnerved mass of men.

"God damn you, Smoke Jensen!" Sean O'Boyle screamed. "This ain't fair, it's not."

Over the subsiding pandemonium, O'Boyle could later swear he heard only soft laughter answering him.

After two more days of trying to impede Lathrop's progress, Smoke concluded that the trail seemed to be leading somewhere specific. All efforts to drive them in another direction had failed. Trouble was, Smoke couldn't put his finger on the destination. He found himself out of dynamite and low on ammunition, so Smoke decided to break off contact for a short while and resupply.

By his reckoning, the small town of Hurley, Wyoming, lay not five miles off the indicated course taken by Lathrop and the remainder of his eastern gang. Smoke rode there with expectations of a hot bath, ample fresh supplies, and a stove-cooked meal, and then the chance to ride back after the band of despoilers. Unfortunately, his high hopes were doomed to disappointment.

Smoke got his bath at the Hurley barbershop, left off his list to be filled at the general mercantile, and sent a telegram to points along the back trail, addressed to Monte Carson.

Then he headed for the only saloon, to wash away the trail dust and powder residue. He entered the barroom in his usual cautious manner, the leather safety thong slipped off both his six-guns, and a casual, though penetrating, glance to all corners of the room.

He strode to the bar on his left and ordered a beer. The moment Smoke entered, he noted one probable trouble spot. Seated in the far corner, by a painted-over window, their backs to the wall, were three young men, obviously drifters, who paid no more attention to the locals than to his entrance. When Smoke turned away to pick up his foam-capped schooner, the trio got their heads together in a swift, yet furtive move.

Their whispers rustled like leaves in Smoke's keen hearing. The one in the middle produced a flyer and showed it smugly to his companions. His voice rose above their earlier, muted conversation.

"I tell ya, it's him."

"Naw," the youth on his right objected. "What t'hell would he be doin' up here?"

"I don't know, an' I don't care. What I'm fixin' to do is collect this here re-ward offered by that Lathrop feller."

"Take it easy, Buck," his comrade to the left urged.

More than the blustery war talk, mention of Lathrop's name advised Smoke that he had become the topic of conversation. It put him on that fine, keen edge that one feels when about to make the choice between flight and fight. Chances were, Smoke told himself, that he could talk them out of anything deadly. But then, he'd told himself that a hundred times before. He kept his eyes fixed on the back bar and waited for things to develop.

It didn't take long.

Chair legs scraped on the bare plank floor and the lanky Buck came to his boots. His husky "You boys spread out" had no need for amplification.

Smoke Jensen sighed and set himself. He spoke without turning. "That would be a terrible mistake."

Confused, Buck blurted, "Say what?"

"Thinking that you can take me. A very bad error, my friend."

"I ain't your friend, damn it!"

"You put that so delicately," Smoke said through a sneer, as he slowly lowered the half-full schooner of beer and turned around. "Just what sort of beef do you have with me?"

Confronted by the level, steely gaze of Smoke Jensen, Buck Singleton went suddenly icy. Cold, bony fingers strolled along his spine. With obvious effort, he stumbled through his half-prepared statement, intended to goad this stranger into a shoot-out.

"You don't know us, but we know you—of you, that is—an' seem' as—ah—how we can read, we figure on cashin' in on the re-ward offered on yer hide."

"And just who the hell do you think I am?"

"Smoke Jensen, that's who," a reemboldened Buck sneered.

"Well, boys, this is indeed not your lucky day. Because . . . *I am Smoke Jensen.*"

Five chairs, at as many tables, emptied at this ominous announcement. Prudent men scattered for the exits, front and rear. Those unable to reach these laudable goals shrank back against the walls, as far out of the line of fire as possible. One old coot gnawed on the age-yellowed ends of a once luxurious mustache and crouched behind the far end of the bar.

Those deadly words of verification electrified Buck Singleton into the worst and last error he ever committed. His long, slender fingers curled around the butt-grip of his hog leg and he hauled it out with what his sycophants always assured him was blinding speed. Speedy Buck Singleton didn't hold a candle to Smoke Jensen.

Buck's eyes began to bulge when he saw the muzzle of Smoke's .45 centered on his chest before the cylinder of his six-gun had cleared the left-hand leather pocket. As though in slow motion, Buck watched the hammer of Smoke's Colt drop. He witnessed only the slightest flash of flame and wisp of smoke before the 240-grain slug smashed light and life out of him.

Before Buck's body hit the floor, Smoke turned to the nearest of the dead drifter's companions. "You want yours now?"

"Aw, shit. No. Aw, shit, yes!" the frightened would-be gun hawk wailed as desperation forced him into the draw.

24

With the speed of a mountain man, Smoke Jensen dropped to one side a fraction of a second after the slug left his .45 Colt. His opponent discharged a round far too late. The foolish young man who sought to even the balance for his dead friend died himself as Smoke's bullet smashed through ribs and burst his heart.

"Oooh, Mother," he moaned, as he collapsed like a wet bag of oats.

Blood had sprayed everywhere from his mortal wound, including on the face and hands of the third youthful drifter. His eyes showing more white than iris, he staggered about in uneven circles, mumbling unintelligible words. He had his six-gun in hand, the barrel canted toward the floor. Only extreme personal danger, or the same to an innocent person, could drive Smoke Jensen to kill yet another. He stayed his third round until this mentally disconnected young man made his intentions clear.

Buck Singleton's last living friend recovered his senses sooner than Smoke Jensen expected him to. Face ashen, eyes wildly darting from object to object without clear focus, he seemed gradually to become aware of the weight of a six-gun in his hand. Moving with the lethargy of the aged, he raised his right thumb and ever so slowly eared back the hammer.

Head moving slothfully, he glanced down at the weapon he clutched. It draggingly dawned on him the use for which it was intended. Comprehension spread with molasses slowness across his blank features. A torpid grin stretched his thin lips. Suddenly the deceleration left him. The muzzle of the Smith .44 came up and steadied on the chest of Smoke Jensen.

"Don't do it, kid," Smoke warned.

"Noooo! Youuuu kiiillled Buuuuck!" the hapless youth shrieked, as he struggled to remember how to fire the gun.

By instinct, or perhaps belated design, he fired first. But Smoke Jensen no longer stood directly in front of the muzzle. The bullet cracked through empty space, converted the glass of Smoke's schooner into a thousand shards, and sent beer spraying all over the saloon. Meanwhile, Smoke spun in profile on one boot heel until he again faced the astonished drifter. An eye blink later, Smoke's slug took the boy at the point of his right shoulder, dislocated the joint, and caused excruciating pain.

Reflex sent the teenager's six-gun sailing toward the ceiling. Driven now by terror as much as rage, he pounced forward to fall on the Merwin and Hulbert dropped by his idol, Buck Singleton. Awkward with a left-hand hold, the wounded youth scrabbled to steady his pain- and terror-convulsed body long enough to finish off the object of his hate.

Smoke Jensen didn't give him that chance. Another round punched through the young saddle tramp's left lung and propelled him back against the table where he'd sat with two living friends only seconds before. His weight collapsed the spindly legs and he ended up spread across the green baize covering like a Christmas goose on a platter.

"Jesus, I didn't want to do that," Smoke spoke huskily to no one in particular.

"He didn't give you no choice, Mr.—ah—Mr. Jensen," the barkeep answered in an equally low, awed tone. "None of 'em did."

"I need a beer."

With a nod to the recumbent drifters, the bartender observed, "Some of them'll need a doctor."

"No. Just the undertaker."

The local law arrived five minutes later. Puffing to overcome the labor of his soft, doughy body, a cherub-faced man, with the whitest skin Smoke Jensen had ever seen on an outdoorsman, waddled through the batwings and stared with pink-rimmed eyes at the carnage in the corner. Wet lips, colored too dark a red, formed a rose-petal pout.

"All right, who's responsible for this?"

"He is," the apron informed the lawman. "Stranger in town. Matter of fact, they all are—er—were."

"This stranger have a name?"

The barman snickered as he offered, "Yep. Smoke Jensen."

Knees turned to India rubber, bowels to water, the overweight town marshal cut his gaze and gape to Smoke. He licked his scarlet lips with a quick flick of a long, thin tongue. *Holy Mother,* he thought wildly. *How do you go about arresting a living legend?* Then he spotted the four empty casings lined up on the bar beside Smoke's restored schooner.

"Three men, four rounds. That's mighty good shooting." Again the nervous lick of lips.

"Would have been three and three," Smoke responded. "I tried to give this one a break, only he wasn't havin' any of it. Wanted to be with his friends, I reckon."

"That's cold. Mighty cold." The pink-edged lids gave a reptilian blink.

"You want to see 'cold,' Marshal, I'll show you . . . aw, what the hell. Three fool kids who thought they were good with a gun are dead because of a coldhearted son of a bitch who offered an unauthorized bounty for my head."

Hurley's chief lawman narrowed his eyes. "What do you know about the law to say whether a reward is authorized?"

"I'm not wanted for anything, anywhere. Phineas Lathrop is a highbinder who's set on taking over a large chunk of

Colorado in the High Lonesome, and he doesn't care how many people get killed in the process. Also, I'm a Deputy U.S. Marshal."

"I've known other killers with a badge," the law said nastily.

"D'you think I'm cut of the same cloth?" Harshness gave a rasp to Smoke's voice.

Marshal Gib Brewster turned even paler, if that was possible. "You might be."

"I'll guarantee that I'm not. If that's not enough, send a wire down the line for Sheriff Monte Carson, from Big Rock, Colorado. He's following me up with a posse. He'll vouch for me."

"Maybe he will, maybe he won't. Meanwhile . . ." The marshal went for his six-gun, only to find himself staring at the muzzle of Smoke's. He swallowed hard and reached for his handcuffs instead. "Meanwhile, you'll sit out the answer in my jail."

Smoke shrugged, relaxed his grip, and reversed the Colt in his hand, offering it to the law dog. "I'm on Lathrop's trail, Marshal. Every day's delay I'll take a mite personal."

Flustered at how easily the notorious gunfighter had acquiesced, the marshal didn't even bother with the manacles. "Th' name's Gib Brewster. I'm marshal here, as you seem to know, Mr. Jensen. You just come along and I'll try to make your stay as short and comfortable as possible."

Deep lines etched into the face of Phineas Lathrop by worry eased and smoothed out as a beautiful smile spread on his face for the first time in five days. He cut his eyes to the informant who had brought him the splendid news.

"You're sure of this?"

"Yep. I was in the saloon when the shootin' started. Man said he was Smoke Jensen. The marshal took him off to jail until his story could be checked out."

"Did Jensen mention my name?"

"I don't know. First cap busted off, I dived for the door."

Lathrop mulled that over. "At least you're honest enough to admit that. Would it be any problem to get men close enough to that jail to—ah—visit the prisoner without anyone knowing?"

"Mr. Lathrop, you could march a brass band up to the back of that building any night. Marshal Brewster sleeps like a log. He ain't got a jailer. Handles ev'rything himself."

"Better and better." Lathrop paused, making quick plans. Then he asked his key question. "Why is it that you brought this to me?"

"I was in town the day you came ridin' through, too. I heard about your big gamble from some of the boys. I . . . well, I thought you might hire me on."

"Good man! And prudent, too. I can always use someone like you. Now, if you'll excuse me, I have some preparations to make."

After a brief, detailed conference with Banning and Dorne of the late Wade Tanner's crew, and O'Fallon and Killian of O'Boyle's gang, Lathrop wished them good luck and sent them on their way.

"Where are they going?" Victor Middleton asked testily. He wanted only to get on to the promised sanctuary.

"I sent them to deal with Smoke Jensen. There's nothing he can do from inside a jail cell. It'll be like shooting fish in a bathtub."

Unaccustomed to the wilderness, Connor O'Fallon and Brian Killian, who had won the toss and led the way to the back of the Hurley jail, were unaware that nature had built-in alarm systems. Their advance along the alley was preceded by a wave of sudden silence.

When the usual symphony of crickets and katydids went silent, Smoke Jensen became instantly alert. Conscious of possible danger close at hand, the big, rangy gunfighter flattened himself against the bars at a right angle to the small window, high up in the outside wall. He listened intently. In a scant second he received confirmation: the scuff of a boot heel in the darkness outside.

Moving soundlessly on stockinged feet, Smoke climbed onto the narrow bunk and peered through the tiny barred window. His eyes already adjusted to darkness, he quickly made out the figure of a man who made a clumsy attempt at moving silently toward the jail. Then he saw another, on the opposite side of the passageway. Beyond him, a moment later, he made out a third form.

More at home in the city, the nearer pair came forward in relative silence. Smoke watched them with cold amusement. When they reached the plastered-over stone wall, they paused, fists on hips, and stared upward at the black rectangle of the window. One whispered in the ear of the other, who shook his head.

Smoke figured that they knew that any attempt to climb the wall would make noise. Apparently that had been the subject of their conference. One of them turned and made a come-here gesture to the third skulker. That one seemed to melt into the shadows and advanced with the perfect quiet of a frontiersman. When he reached the two beneath the barred window, they put their heads together and discussed the situation.

With some agitation, and breathy complaint, the duo who had come first got to their knees and bent forward. The third man slipped off his spurs and climbed onto their backs. Smoke ducked back as the figure rose up the wall. A face appeared in the opening above Smoke. The barrel of a six-gun soon followed.

Acting with legendary speed, Smoke Jensen reached up with both hands and snatched the revolver out of the hands of his would-be assassin. He fisted the weapon with equal swiftness and fired point-blank into the man's face. He fell away without a sound.

Not so his companions. "Jeez, he done shot Dorne," one blurted.

"How'd he do that?"

"I don't know. But we gotta get out of here, fast."

Boot heels pounded on the hard-packed alley. Smoke Jensen raised himself and sighted in on the nearest retreating back. "Hold it right there," he shouted.

They were having none of that. Smoke fired and clipped Brian Killian high in the left shoulder. Suddenly another man appeared in the mouth of the alley with four horses. Stumbling, Killian reached his mount and painfully dragged himself into the saddle. Connor O'Fallon seemed to vault to the back of his animal.

"Where's Dorne?"

"He ain't comm'," O'Fallon informed Banning. "Let's get out of here. That damned Jensen's got a gun."

At the range of one block, Smoke held off any further gunplay. Behind him, the steel door to the cell block rattled and banged open. Pale white, Gib Brewster waddled down the corridor, his face working in agitation, emphasized by the flickering light of a coal-oil lamp.

"What the hell's goin' on in here? Where'd you get that gun? Who'd you shoot at?" The words spilled from his mouth in a rush.

"One at a time, Marshal. Say, I bet they call you Pearly."

"God damn you, Jensen. Answer my questions."

"First off, three men tried to kill me. I took the gun away from the one who climbed up to the window and shot him. Then I sent some lead along with the ones who ran off."

"I'll take that gun now. I thought we had an agreement."

"We did."

"Then answer me this: how do I know they didn't come to break you out of here?"

Smoke Jensen crossed to the inside bars and handed the six-gun to the lawman. He chuckled as he considered that question. "Tell me this, Pearly. Does it make sense to you that I'd shoot the men who came to help me?"

The logic of this deflated the bluster in Gib Brewster. "Well, I'll have to admit, it's not too reasonable. Now, you settle down while I go out and look into this."

"Marshal, I gave you that iron willingly enough. In light of maybe some other boys coming here to do me harm, what say you let me have it back?"

"Nope. Can't do that. Officially, you're a prisoner."

"Damn," Smoke muttered, after the lawman left to check the body.

Morning brought Smoke Jensen hard biscuits and gluey gravy. It also brought a telegram from Monte Carson. Gib Brewster looked almost disappointed when he came to Smoke Jensen's cell. He stared pointedly at the untouched breakfast. •

"Telegram came. Just like you said it would. 'I verify person you are holding as U.S. Marshal Smoke Jensen. He is in pursuit of Phineas Lathrop, Victor Middleton, Arnold Cabbott, and Abe Asher, along with a gang numbering some thirty-five men. They are wanted in Colorado for murder, arson, and numerous other crimes. Please give Marshal Jensen your fullest cooperation. I am bringing a posse on and will provide paperwork that didn't get done before Marshal Jensen went in pursuit of the gang. He is to wait there for me.' And it's signed, 'Monte Carson.' So, I guess I gotta let you out."

Keys jingled and the lock rattled. Pin hinges squeaked noisily as Brewster threw open the door. He continued to block Smoke's exit with his bulky body. Finally he drew long, spatulate, deathly pale fingers across his brow.

"Thing I can't figger is, how you gonna stop that many men?"

Smoke sighed heavily. "I can but try. Actually, Pearly, I'm glad there's a posse coming on behind me, should be less than a day from here. With Monte will be a young eastern reporter by the name of Ollie Johnson. When they get here, you tell them which way I went."

Brewster nodded affably. "I'll do that. I heard once that you took on twenty men, single-handed. That right?"

"No, Pearly, it was only sixteen."

"Damn it, Jensen, you stop callin' me Pearly."

"All right, Marshal Brewster. I'll thank you for my guns now."

"Gib's all right, twixt you an' me, Mr. Jensen," Brewster mumbled in embarrassment.

"Call me Smoke. Now, I do have to be going."

"Right enough. An' if you get back this away, you look me up, right?"

"Count on it, Gib."

Half an hour later, Smoke Jensen set off from the livery. Actually, Monte accompanying that posse bothered him. Monte was slowing down a bit, and Smoke didn't want his old friend to take the risks involved in tracking down Lathrop. So he wasted no time in departing Hurley. He had been given the direction taken by Lathrop's gang and set his course northward. Although he admitted he needed help to corral so many hard cases, he sort of hoped that the posse, with Ollie Johnson, would not catch up too soon. He had grown to like the fiery young journalist, and didn't enjoy the thought of anything happening to him, either.

Lathrop's trail led northward, then cut sharply west to the neighboring town of Burley, Wyoming. Smoke Jensen mused over the names of these two communities as he ambled Dandy down the main street. Saloons and barbershops being the best sources of information, Smoke rubbed his clean-shaven jaw and decided on the Gold Bucket Saloon.

"Yep. There's a method to our madness, I reckon you could say," a talkative bartender confided to Smoke, when asked about the similarity of names.

"I thought there might be, with the two towns only five miles apart."

"Well, now, we used to be one town. But political differences between the leading families turned to real rancor over some long-forgotten matter. Half the folks moved out, settled here."

"Let me guess the name of the original town," Smoke offered dryly. "Hurley-Burley."

A cackle of laughter assured him he had hit it right.

"Right on the nail head! He-he! We took half the folks, an' half the name, too."

"Original, to say the least," Smoke quipped.

The short, big-headed apron studied Smoke to detect any hint of sarcasm. Then, with eyes narrowed, he asked, "Hear there was a big shooting over Hurley way. Know anything about it?"

Smoke hesitated, eyes searching the faces of the other occupants, who had cut off their conversations at mention of the shoot-out. He avoided the direct gaze of the barkeep, sighed, and answered quietly, "Not much. What did you hear?"

"Some gunfighter came to town, or so they say. He was evidently on the prod and called out three youngsters from here in Burley. Killed them all."

Unable to allow such distortion to survive longer, Smoke contradicted the barman. "That isn't the way it happened."

"I say it is," a young voice came from behind Smoke.

"Well, it's not. The three of them called out someone they thought was a wanted man. They drew first. He happened to be better."

"I say you're a liar, mister. Who was this gunfighter who was supposed to be faster than Buck, and Larry, and Hal?"

"Smoke Jensen," Smoke said quietly.

"Horseshit! Smoke Jensen ain't nowhere near here. I say what we oughtta do is go over to Hurley and get justice done for our dead friends. What do you say, boys?" he asked three other young toughs like the ones who had forced Smoke to kill them.

During the entire exchange, the bartender had been cutting his eyes from the prodders to Smoke and back. He looked hard at the craggy jaw, calm demeanor, and cool gray eyes, then at the nervous twitches and tics of the half-grown saddle tramps. His brows suddenly knit, lids lowered to slits, as he spoke through pursed lips.

"I don't think you'll have to go over there, Harper."

"Oh, yeah? Why not, Doolie?"

"Because I think the man you're lookin' for is standin' right here."

The one he called Harper choked off another taunting challenge and gaped for a moment, digesting the meaning of Doolie's words. "No. Can't be. This is just a bag of wind with no brain behind it. He ain't no gunfighter. He's a nobody."

Bartender Doolie sidled to one end of the bar, eyes fixed on everyone involved. "Why don't you ask him his name?"

"Yeah. What is your name, Mister Mouth?"

"Smoke Jensen." Smoke's voice echoed in the deadly silent room.

Harper blinked, then paled. He worked his mouth but no sound came out. One of Harper's companions finally found his voice. "You really are Smoke Jensen?"

"I am."

"Well—ah—well, then, Mr. Jensen, I gotta apologize for my friend here. Ya see, Harper ain't got all his smarts. Puts his mouth in gear before his brain is engaged."

"You shut your mouth, Willie Lowe," Harper screamed. "I can apologize for myself." He took a deep breath and sighed it out, his eyes closed to summon calm. "I'm right sorry I doubted your word, Mr. Jensen. Uh—what—ah—what did them boys do?"

"Exactly what I said. They pushed and I pushed back. End of story."

"Yeah," a chagrined Harper agreed. "For them."

"It don't have to repeat itself," Smoke prompted.

"Right! You're absolutely right, Mr. Jensen. Matter of fact, we was just leavin'—right, boys?" Three heads nodded in unison. "Pleasure to meet you, Mr. Jensen. Have a good afternoon."

Smoke breathed deeply as the last one left the saloon. At least he had prevented a shoot-out this time.

25

Tall columns, with black bottoms and white anvil heads, climbed tens of thousands of feet into the azure sky to the northwest. Like scouts ahead of a military movement, long, roiling fingers of the gathering mass tumbled across the vast dome of blue. Smoke Jensen eyed the building storm with a wary eye. All hell could break loose at any time, he knew.

Although not as tempestuous as their brothers of the plains, these mountain thunderstorms could unleash enough violence to claim their relationship. So far, the leading edge of this jumble of cumulonimbus skirted diagonally across the trail Smoke followed. It didn't yet look dangerous enough to take his mind off the gnawing certainty that he knew the destination sought by Phineas Lathrop. The problem was, he couldn't put a name to it. A muted rumble of distant thunder brought his attention back to the building storm.

Fully a third of the horizon to the north and west now lay robed in green-tinged black. The clouds towered up and seemed to bend out over him. A huge, rain-bloated thunderhead glided over the sun. Eye-hurting in their brightness, silver shafts splintered outward around its edge as the solar orb tried to exercise dominance. This was getting serious, Smoke Jensen realized. He raised the collar of his sheepskin jacket as a jet of cold air squirted out of the forward wall of the tempest and rushed down the canyon where Smoke rode.

At once, Smoke began to look for someplace to take shelter. As a youth, he had traveled all of this country with Preacher. He knew of abandoned fur trappers' cabins, large rock overhangs, and an occasional cave. It was this latter he sought now. If he had reckoned his position right, a series of small caves dotted the canyon walls some short ways ahead.

The mutter of far-off thunder grew louder. Flashes of lightning could be seen in the overcast that spread toward him at an alarming rate. He touched blunt spurs to Dandy's flanks and urged more speed. The big roan stallion walled his eyes and twitched nervous ears. Smoke could physically sense the change in pressure.

Without warning, the sky split apart in the manner attributed to Judgment Day. A white bolt caved into half a dozen wicked forks with the sound of ripping sailcloth. The odor of ozone hung heavily long after the cannon blast of thunder rumbled away down the canyon. Dandy needed no more urging. The frightened animal set out at a fast lope. Smoke Jensen screwed the hat tighter onto his head, his eyes busy searching for any sign of the anticipated caves.

Large, fat drops, still bearing the chill of early spring, began to pelt Smoke's back and slap him in the face. They fell like balls of mercury attached to silver strings. The drops were reasonably far apart at first, then the downpour thickened and their size grew smaller. Visibility began to reduce for Smoke. If he didn't find a cave soon, he realized, he would be caught out in this tumult.

A freight train sound rushed at him from the left. Two minutes and half a mile sped by when Smoke thought he could make out a small, black dot against the buff and gray of the canyon wall. He drew nearer and located the narrow ledge that formed a path to the entrance of a cave. Quickly he reined in and dismounted. Already soaked to the skin, Smoke led his jittery mount up to the hoped-for shelter.

Smoke had to duck to enter, as did his horse. Once they

were beyond the low opening, the cave widened, the ceiling arched high above. Smoke ground-reined Dandy and used flint and steel, and a bit of treated thistledown, to light a candle he also took from his right-side saddlebag. With the limited glow of the wax taper, he searched his surroundings.

He soon discovered that he was not the first human occupant of the cavern. Powdery dry billets of wood lay in a natural crib. With a stick of that, and some kerosene from a tin flask in his gear, Smoke fashioned a torch. Its greater light revealed an astonishing scene. The walls, and part of the ceiling, were covered with petroglyphs, stick figures of animals and men, carved into the wall and crudely painted with natural dyes.

Darkness had protected them and they looked down on this modern intruder in all their original, vivid color. Smoke Jensen found himself gape-mouthed. Preacher had shown him examples carved in visible rock faces: men and the sun and animals that could have been elk, or even bison. The old mountain man had also spoken of such rare and beautiful examples of the art of ancient people who had lived in these caves long before the coming of the Spanish and other Europeans. Some said, Preacher went on, that they had been here before the coming of the Indians.

Smoke mulled over this scrap of information while he continued to examine the cave. He found some nonrepresentational designs also. Perhaps some sort of religious symbols, he speculated. Outside his shelter, the rain hissed and seethed down in a torrent. Smoke gathered wood for a fire. It would be utterly smokeless, he estimated, burn faster than hell, and keep him busy replenishing the fuel.

Once he had his blaze going, Smoke stripped to the buff and lay out his clothing to dry. Wisps of steam rose from coat, shirt, vest, and trousers as the rocks they lay upon heated up. Smoke made his way to the mouth of the cave. A careful study revealed why the entrance was too low.

Over the years, soil had collected in the roots of small trees. The network of intertwined tree roots had attracted more soil. At present, a huge pine dominated the overhead shelf. From slightly inside, Smoke could see the stone arch of the cave's natural mouth, partly buried in dirt, pebbles and roots. Once more it gave him pause to marvel at the intricacies of nature.

Breaking off his reflections, Smoke turned to his horse. "Well, Dandy, I reckon we could use a bit of something to eat."

Smoke filled a tin cup with water, added about a tablespoon of Arbuckle's Arabica, and set it on the fire, on a small trivet he unfolded from his camp gear. While it came to a boil, he put a double scoop of oats and cracked corn into a nosebag and fed Dandy. Then he returned to his coffee. The rich aroma made his stomach cramp. He broke out a smoked shank of deer meat and a couple of cold biscuits. That would have to do. For both of them.

While he ate, the fury of nature raged overhead. Rather than slacking off, the storm sent a second front sweeping down from Wyoming and dumped more rain into the canyon. When he completed his spartan meal, he retrieved a collapsible bucket he had set outside and gave Dandy a long drink. Nothing for it now but to make himself comfortable.

Darkness had replaced day with the coming of the storm and Smoke Jensen estimated it would remain until long after sundown. He unstrapped his bedroll and spread the blankets on the hard floor of the cavern. With his saddle as a pillow, Smoke leaned back, rolled a quirley, and puffed it to life. When the cigarette had burned down to his fingers, he extinguished it, put out the torch, and settled in for a long-needed solid sleep.

When the thunderstorm passed by, more water-laden clouds backed up against its rear and unloosed a steady downpour. The dim drum of raindrops lulled Smoke Jensen into so deep a slumber that he came only partway out of it at the sound of a loud crashing at the mouth of the cave. Only after he awakened with the first pale light of dawn did

Smoke find his path out of the cavern impeded by the large pine that had fallen during the night.

With both himself and his horse on the inside, he was going to have one dandy fine hell of a time getting out, Smoke Jensen pondered, as he stared at the obstruction. He pulled gloves from his hip pocket and slid long, thick fingers into the supple leather. Then he started to climb the rough bark of the downed pine.

A thick, resinous odor assailed his nostrils. It smelled fresh and clean. Quite a contrast to the mud-slicked surface he wriggled upon. The five-foot-thick trunk left space enough for light and air to enter the cave. It let Smoke get his head and arms through the opening. His shoulders hung up.

The harder he struggled, the more tightly he became wedged in the restrictive mouth of the cave. Anger fired determination for Smoke Jensen. He reversed his left arm and tried to reach past his shoulder to the big coffin-handled bowie knife at his side. No luck. With renewed patience, he began to pick and dig at the damp soil that denied him movement.

That, too, proved of no avail. The combined elements of his situation only fueled his burning humiliation when he heard an amused voice rise from below his line of sight, somewhere near the top of the up-ended tree.

"Well, dang me, am I witness to the raisin' of the dead?"

"Don't be such a jackass. Do something to help me," Smoke snapped. Then he paused, frowned. He knew that voice. "L'Lupe? Is that you?"

A cackle of laughter answered. "Sure's yer comin' back from the grave. Saay, don't I know that voice? Be you the growed-up version of the li'l boy brat what pestered me an' Preacher nigh unto death years ago?"

"I might be," Smoke bit off, his irritation growing.

"Smoke . . . Jensen. *De quoi s'agit-il?*" his accent

thickening with each word, L'Lupe climbed toward Smoke Jensen and the laughter began again. *"Puis-je vous être utile?"*

The French Smoke had picked up from this, and other old mountain men, came back slowly. "Hell, yes, you can be of assistance to me. Get me out of here."

L'Lupe—the Wolf—whose real name was Renard Douchant—continued to cackle while he studied Smoke's predicament from up close. An old friend of Preacher, L'Lupe had been ancient when young Smoke Jensen had first met him. He looked not a day older now. His hair, worn in a long, thick braid at the back of his head, seemed no grayer than during that initial encounter. Nor had his seamed, leathery face and bright blue eyes changed. The latter still twinkled with amusement at a world gone mad from under a jutting ridge furry with salt-and-pepper brows. L'Lupe had to be well into his seventies, or even eighties, yet he looked fifty.

And he carried himself like a man that age, Smoke observed, as Douchant stretched and bent to study the restricting material that held Smoke fast. He hemmed and hawed, squinted and rubbed his hairless, rock-square jaw. "You are fortunate, *mon ami.* I have a pick along. We can open the hole and pop you out like a grape from its skin, *ce n'est rien."*

"It may be nothing for you," Smoke grumbled, catching the buoyant mood of his old friend. "But I'm the one who's stuck here."

"Only for a moment, so take care to not excite yourself. Did not Preacher teach you patience?"

"Of course he did, but I have a horse in here which won't have any air to breathe before long."

"Aha! And I have two mules. The one I ride, and the one for the packs, *non?* With them we will pull this tree away in no time."

With that, L'Lupe popped out of Smoke's view. He was back in three minutes, during which Smoke continued to sweat and struggle to reach his knife. L'Lupe's bounding joviality grated on raw nerves while the energetic oldster toiled with pick and shovel to open the way for Smoke. At last he paused.

"This will take an ax."

"Oh, no," Smoke protested. "There'll be more meat than root in the path of that blade."

"Take—how you say?—your ease, *mon ami*. I mean to cut away from below, to let the bole drop lower. Then you can crawl out."

Twenty trying minutes later, Smoke Jensen sensed a loosening of pressure against his shoulders. Another solid *plock!* of the ax in L'Lupe's hands and the uprooted pine sank with a thud. Quickly, Smoke crawled his way to freedom. At once he took charge.

"Bring up your mules. I'm worried about my horse."

The jerry-rigged harness fitted the mules with an unlikely collection of odds and ends. Trailing from the leather portions, ropes led to the trunk of the pine, each secured around its girth. When Smoke Jensen and Renard Douchant had both inspected them and concluded their satisfaction, the old mountain man split the air with a shrill whistle between gapped teeth.

"Allons, mes amis, pull! Put your backs into it. Pull!"

Protesting vocally, the two powerful animals took up the slack, and leaned into their harness. Leather creaked and hemp rope hummed. The once tall, stately pine began to squeal in objection to the stress exerted on it.

Rocks and muddy rubble began to spill downhill. One of the mules, Biscuit, gave an impatient bray and set his haunches. An almost human groan came from the big animal and then a cascade of earth spilled out from below the fallen tree. The huge weight tottered on its exposed roots for a moment, then crashed downward, away from the cave.

L'Lupe clapped hands together and declared, "Well, that is done," before he bounded off after his pair of mules. When he returned, he found Smoke soothing Dandy at the bottom of the path to the cavern. L'Lupe wasted no time in satisfying his curiosity.

"Now, tell me, *mon ami*—what is it you are doing out here all alone?"

Smoke Jensen carefully laid out the threat to the High Lonesome posed by Phineas Lathrop and his gang. L'Lupe interrupted frequently with expressions of shock or outrage. His countenance darkened as each act of depredation unfolded. At last, clearly agitated, L'Lupe rose, dusted off his hands, and spoke in a quavering voice.

"This is monstrous, my friend Smoke. You say there are how many . . . thirty or forty? So, then, what you must do is keep on their track. And I? I shall go off and round up a little help."

Togwotee Pass, at over 9,000 feet, was one of the highest so far opened through the Rockies by man. From the summit, Phineas Lathrop studied the horizon in both directions. He nodded in apparent approval of his thoughts and summoned Sean O'Boyle with a crook of one finger.

"Yes, sir, Mr. Lathrop. An' what would it be ye'd be wantin' o' me and me boys?"

"I want you to select twelve of your best." Well aware of their abilities in this wild country, Lathrop could not keep the sarcasm out of his voice. "You are to stay here, erect a roadblock, and hold off Smoke Jensen."

"It's sure he's comin', then, is it?"

"You can count on it, Mr. O'Boyle. Not to worry, though. Given the narrowness of this pass, and a well-made barricade, I have every confidence that a baker's dozen of you can withstand any attack by one gunfighter, a broken-down old sheriff, and a green kid reporter."

"An' when would ye be expectin' this attack to happen?" Shrewdness glowed in O'Boyle's black eyes.

"Within a day, two at the most. So you had better get busy. And—ah—good luck."

O'Boyle's black glower told what he thought of that wish. He turned, nevertheless, and began to pick the men he wanted with him. He regretted he could not choose Eamon Finnegan. Eamon was the only one who could keep the rest in line. He settled for Connor O'Fallon, James Finnegan, Liam O'Tolle, Bryan Gallagher, and Henny Duggan among the first six he named off. He called them together and began to explain their assignment as the rest of the severely reduced column rode off to the west, toward Jackson's Hole.

Shortly after sundown, L'Lupe and three men of equal age glided silently up to the camp made by Smoke Jensen. From thirty feet out, the wily old mountain man called out to make their presence known.

"Hello, the camp."

"Hello, yourself," Smoke responded.

"Come on in, Reynard."

"How'd you know it was me?" L'Lupe asked, when he hunkered down beside Smoke Jensen and poured a cup of coffee.

"I heard you stumbling around out there."

"Sacre bleu! You lie; L'Lupe does not stumble around in the woods." They laughed together and then Douchant turned to the trio squatting across the fire. "Some friends from old times. They had nothing to do with their days, so I brought them along."

Smoke knew them and greeted all warmly. "Greener Jack, High Pockets, Lonesome Brown. Good of you to come."

"Hell, didn't take much thinking on," Lonesome Brown allowed. "'Pears to me to be the only fight around."

"Who is this Lathrop that L'Lupe was tellin' us about?" Greener Jack asked.

"He's from the East," Smoke began his explanation, to be interrupted by High Pockets, "It figgers." Smoke went on to detail what he knew of Lathrop's grandiose scheme, omitting the personal side to their conflict. When he concluded, the three reinforcements offered their allegiance in their own ways.

"Time's a-wastin', 'f you ask me," Greener Jack advised.

"They'll be gettin' close to Jackson's Hole. Lor' we had some high good times there a couple of years," Lonesome Brown recalled.

"Any idea where these bad hombres is headed?" High Pockets asked.

Smoke's high, smooth brow furrowed. "Now, that's been naggin' at me for some time. If I thought they knew anything about this country, I'd swear that Lathrop is trying to reach Yellowstone."

"The river, or that wild country with the water spouts they made into a na-tion-al park?" Lonesome Brown asked.

"Either . . . both. Thing is, I don't know if Lathrop knows about that country at all. Well, sunup comes early," Smoke concluded, as he poured the dregs of his coffee on the cook fire and rose to head for his bedroll. "I want us to be on the trail an hour before sunup."

"We'll be comin' up on Togwotee Pass in an hour," L'Lupe Douchant informed Smoke Jensen shortly after nine o'clock the next morning. "'Member that time them Blackfoot braves ambushed a company of fur trappers?"

That caused Smoke to reevaluate his estimate of L'Lupe's age. He had to be more than eighty. Which made him not an unusual man, but a remarkable one.

"Preacher told me about it. I wasn't even born then."

Each knew the incident L'Lupe had brought up and needed no discussion. With a wordless command, Smoke sent Greener Jack off with his two companions to approach the pass from a slightly different angle. No sense in taking unnecessary risks.

When their mounts leaned into the grade, Smoke grew even more cautious. He cut his eyes from side to side, took in every rock and bush, and the distant black smudge that marked stately firs. Supple aspen whispered to them as the steady breeze agitated their heart-shaped leaves.

L'Lupe's mule was blowing hard when they topped the crest and ambled down toward the summit of the pass. It lay in the bottom of a bowl-like basin, surrounded by steep, sharp peaks, much like the caldera of an ancient volcano. Smoke's keen eyes were first to spot a dark, irregular smudge across the trail. He pointed it out to L'Lupe.

Douchant studied it a moment and spat on the ground. "I do not believe the Blackfeet, they came back to life just for us."

"Nor do I. Reckon the best idea is to ride on down like we don't suspect anything."

For once, Smoke Jensen didn't have all that good an idea. He and L'Lupe found that out some three minutes later when a rifle bullet cracked past between them and a spurt of powder smoke rose from the log barricade.

26

"B'God, there he comes, bold as brass," Sean O'Boyle declared, as he studied the approaching riders. "Those of you who ain't seen him before, that's Smoke Jensen."

"Who's the old fart with him?" James Finnegan asked.

"Don't matter, it don't." A second later, O'Boyle let fly the first round in their encounter.

"Aw, you can't hit shit," Brian Gallagher derided Sean O'Boyle, when the bullet missed.

"Shut your mouth an' take yer best shot, wiseass." Sean continued to pout while he cycled the action of the unfamiliar Winchester.

"Don't look like we're scarin' 'em off any, it don't," Connor O'Fallon observed.

Half a dozen rifles barked in time. None of the eastern greenhorns hit what they'd aimed at. By then, Smoke Jensen had closed the range to under a hundred yards. Bent low over the neck of his stallion, Dandy, Smoke sighted along the barrel of his .45 Peacemaker and let fly a round. A risky shot at best, he knew, especially from the back of a cantering horse.

An instant later he turned his head to flash a smile of triumph to L'Lupe when a cry of pain rewarded his efforts.

* * *

Sean O'Boyle stared openmouthed at the wounded man beside him. "Mary an' all the saints, that man can shoot, he can."

"Better than any of us," Connor O'Fallon informed his boss.

"Aim more careful, damn it!"

Young James Finnegan stared at Sean O'Boyle. "They're gettin' too close for rifles, anyway."

"Then stand up. Use yer six-guns."

Reluctant to leave the security of the logs, they did so slowly. When the volume of fire increased to ten revolvers, it did cause Smoke and L'Lupe to swerve to one side. It also did another thing. It provided excellent targets for Greener Jack, High Pockets, and Lonesome Brown.

From a notch between two of the surrounding peaks, they each downed one of the eastern thugs. That sent those at the barricade in desperate dives to avoid a similar fate. It also allowed Smoke and L'Lupe to draw clear of the withering fire.

"Certainement they are not the Blackfeet," said L'Lupe dryly. "They were not stupid enough to tie themselves down behind *le rétranchement sans valeur."*

"That's more of a barricade than an entrenchment, worthless or otherwise, but I follow what you mean." Smoke changed the subject, "I wonder how long it will take them to realize we didn't fire those shots."

"I would say two or three times more should do it."

"You don't think too highly of these fellers," Smoke prompted.

"Au contraire. It is only that they are such terrible shots. Unreasonably terrible."

Smoke joined his laughter. "Shall we make another run at them?"

"Après vous." So saying, L'Lupe took the lead instead of Smoke.

* * *

"Far the love o' Jaazus, they're comin' back!" a young dockyard punk from Boston wailed, as Smoke Jensen and L'Lupe Douchant appeared over a swell in the basin.

Sean O'Boyle looked up from reloading his revolver to see the flared nostrils of a horse less than twenty feet away. He swiftly raised his .45 Colt and yanked on the hammer. All it got him was a sore thumb. The rear of a fresh cartridge protruded onto the loading gate ramp, which he had failed to close. Then pain and blackness exploded inside his head and he fell away.

"Hokka hey!" L'Lupe shouted exuberantly, as he recovered from the vicious butt-strike he had given the burly, black-haired Irishman.

Smoke Jensen shook his head in exasperation. Instead of killing the hoodlum, L'Lupe had counted coup. Smoke made up for the lapse by downing two in rapid succession. Long-range fire from the other mountain men began to rip into those manning the barrier.

It took little of this to break the spirit of two thugs. Sticking a cargo hook in the chest of a drunk sailor took little courage. A pitched battle against superlative shots was a far different thing. Especially ones who couldn't be seen. Where were these other bullets coming from?

The ex-longshoremen cut their eyes to each other, then to the menacing unknown beyond the barricade. "This ain't our kind o' fight, Paddy, it ain't," one spoke the thoughts of both.

"Aye, that's the right of it, it is."

"Then what are we doin' here?"

"I'm thinkin' the same thing, I am, Ryan."

"Then, Paddy, let's be far gettin' outta here an' visitin' our sainted mithers."

They broke and ran together. Paddy made it only ten yards when a fat slug from Greener Jack's .56 Sharps cut him down. Ryan sped on to where the horses had been tethered. The pound of his horse's hooves proved contagious to the others in the uneven fight. Several threw down their weapons and ran in panic to their mounts. Smoke Jensen fired two more shots, L'Lupe one, and the battle ended.

Inspecting the scene of carnage, Smoke Jensen gave little thought to the corpses. He called in the long-range shooters and soon they joined L'Lupe and himself. Smoke waved a hand at the fallen bodies.

"Look them over. See if there's any papers, something to indicate the leader, also where they're headed."

Smoke's huge frame swam fuzzily in the blurred eyesight of Sean O'Boyle. He had fortuitously regained consciousness without the usual moans, groans, or shiftings of his body that generally accompanied that condition. Now he fought to piece together just what in hell was going on. *Was he in hell?* The thought seared through O'Boyle's brain as he stared upward through slitted lids at the indistinct shape of the giant who towered over him. Sure an' the man had to be head an' shoulders above his own five-foot-seven, he did. *Could it be Old Nick himself?* Slowly, reality sifted out from confused myth. The giant had a name *Smoke Jensen.*

And Sean O'Boyle shuddered at the recognition. Grounded on what was, he gradually devised a plan. He recalled that he had been using a rifle when the world had turned upside down on him. His head had exploded in a shower of bright light and intense pain, then blackness. Now it throbbed and he felt a wet, stickiness oozing down from the crown. If he had used his rifle, that meant he still had a six-gun in its holster, and the small hideout pistol at the small of his back.

"Be clever now, Sean, boyo," he barely breathed out.

All he had to do was avoid the attention of the men searching the bodies of his fallen friends. He'd have to move slowly, ever so slowly. An inch at a time. Get to that heavy, awkward .45 at his hip and slide it free. Then, all unsuspecting, the end would come for Smoke Jensen.

* * *

Smoke Jensen had his back turned to Sean O'Boyle, whom he had belatedly recognized, believing the man still unconscious. When he heard the telltale clicks of a Colt, he quickly revised that assumption. Smoke had made a quarter-turn, and his .45 Peacemaker had already cleared leather, when a hot trail cut across his back, upward from near his left hip to his shoulder blade.

Good thing he had turned, Smoke Jensen thought giddily, or that slug would have got him in a kidney. Which would have ended an otherwise good life. He continued to pivot on one boot heel until he faced his assailant. Sean O'Boyle's eyes widened when he saw that his shot had not had the desired effect.

Desperately he tried to cock the hammer once more. Two bullets, in rapid order, destroyed his right shoulder joint and brought on more excruciating pain. Sean O'Boyle howled in release of his discomfort and dropped backward onto the ground. His blood stained the yellow earth a deep magenta. Smoke Jensen stepped closer as the others gathered around.

"Even a rattlesnake gives warning, O'Boyle," Smoke told him coldly.

"Ye know me, then?"

"Yes. From the lecture hall, and later, that warehouse in Boston. Ollie Johnson pointed you out to me in Central Park."

"Damned snoop reporters," growled O'Boyle. A new idea occurred to him. "Then ye'll be knowin' that I'm of some importance to Mr. Lathrop, an' 'twould be to yer advantage to keep me alive, it would."

While he spoke, Sean O'Boyle worked his undamaged left arm under his back. He fixed small, close-set, black eyes on Smoke's slate orbs and suppressed a shudder at the awful fate he saw reflected there. It took every ounce of his will to force Sean to continue with his intentions.

"The only advantage I see is to force you to talk, then finish you off," Smoke told him flatly.

"Ah, now, there's where yer wrong, ye are. Don't I jist know where it is the fancy Mr. Phineas Lathrop is headed? All the torture in the world won't get that from me lips. But . . . if I was to be treated for me wounds, all nice an' proper, then allowed to go me way in peace . . . well, bucko, that's a whole different proposition."

"Suppose I were to agree?"

"Mon ami, you've been hit. Come away and let us dress that wound," L'Lupe insisted.

O'Boyle rode over at the urging of L'Lupe. "Why, then, ye'd be richer by that knowledge an' I'd be on me way back to Boston, I would."

Smoke Jensen laughed soft and low. "It's not often I cut a deal with a piece of horseshit like you."

Pausing, Smoke considered how to phrase the rest. While he did, elation shot through Sean's aching body. Almost there. His fingertips brushed at the checked, black, hard rubber grips of the .32 Smith & Wesson.

A heavy sigh gusted from the barrel chest of Smoke Jensen. "But I am in a hurry and would like to know if I can bypass Lathrop and be waiting for him when he gets there. Go ahead. Tell me what you know and I'll see you are patched up and sent on your way."

He had it! Tightly gripped in his hand, the S & W .32 banished for the moment the awful pain that racked Sean O'Boyle's body. He forced a smile and spoke so lowly it forced Smoke Jensen closer.

"There's a place Lathrop spoke of, northwest of here, it is. It's called Yellow Stone."

O'Boyle's hideout slid free of his waistband. He edged it to his left side.

"You mean the Yellowstone? A river?" Smoke's excitement was electric.

"N-not a river, man, no it's not. It's some sort of park. A

place Lathrop said where hot water shot out of the ground. Can ye believe that, man?"

Muted laughter at such a preposterous idea covered the final movement as O'Boyle whipped the little revolver free. He fired two fast, desperate rounds. Smoke Jensen felt a pair of hard, painful punches to his belly, in the region of two crossed, thick leather belts and a heavy silver buckle. His own bullet came delayed only long enough for Sean O'Boyle to register utter surprise, before it crashed into the bridge of his nose and blew out the back of his head.

"Sacre Nom! He's shot you again," L'Lupe blurted, staring at Smoke's bent frame.

"Only a little bit. I think I'm all right." Smoke Jensen came painfully upright in a cloud of powder smoke and turned to a startled L'Lupe. "Our guess was right. Lathrop is headed for Yellowstone National Park. I'll leave a message for Monte and his posse. Then we have to ride hard and fast to outdistance that gang of vultures."

"Not you, my friend. Your back looks like he used a wooden plough to cut that furrow. At least I see no blood in the front."

"Lucky, I guess. Appears my belts stopped those little, underpowered slugs. I'll have a hell of a bruise, though. I'll let someone fix my back, then we're on the move."

Phineas Lathrop and his gang had been compelled to travel at a leisurely pace due to the number of wounded they had acquired along the way. That included those who had escaped from the disastrous ambush in Togwotee Pass. They had brought forward a horrendous tale of the prowess of the mountain men who had slaughtered their companions with cold detachment, and from impossible range. They, for certain, chafed at the delays, grumbled over the late-morning starts, and generally glanced fearfully over their shoulders for sign of pursuit.

They saw none, because with a destination in mind,

Smoke Jensen and his four associates could skirt wide of the trail taken by Lathrop and move a whole lot faster. That suited the rangy gunfighter. For all the physical discomfort he experienced, Smoke Jensen wanted an end to this land grab and to Phineas Lathrop. This had gone beyond mere arrest of a criminal genius.

Good men, and some women, too, had died as a result of Lathrop's mad desire to lay conquest to a vast portion of the High Lonesome. Smoke Jensen wanted Phineas Lathrop dead. He longed to see the photographs of Lathrop and his lead henchmen laid out in suits, arms crossed over dead chests, on the lids of hastily constructed wooden coffins that rested beside them.

He would have it, too, he swore to himself, as he, L'Lupe, and the other three thundered through tall ranks of ancient Douglas fir, north of Grand Teton, and only twenty miles from the heart of Yellowstone country. Along the way, Smoke Jensen kept looking for suitable locations to hole up and do battle. What continued to bother him was why Lathrop had made his goal the nation's first national park.

What could he hope to gain from that? Even though they knew for certain now that Lathrop intended all along to go to Yellowstone, it didn't make sense to Smoke. Not one for long ponderings on the unponderable, Smoke dismissed it as they neared the park entrance. There it suddenly came clear.

Smoke and his sidekicks rode past ranks of wagons, each with rows of seats and canvas shade covers, waiting for the daily flow of visitors. Clusters of crude cabins, the park people's mistaken idea of what fur trappers' cabins looked like, to house those who had come to see the marvels, dotted the partially denuded hillsides. Here and there, as they rode deeper into the park, they found tents, with ladies in long, high-necked dresses and parasols, men in shirtsleeves, mustaches waving in the breeze, and children, the boys barefoot and in short pants, gamboling in the meadows. A few fishermen plied the streams.

"Hostages," Smoke stated tightly. "He's got an idea he can come here, grab some innocent people, and bargain for his own safety and release."

"Par bleu, I think you are right, *mon ami."*

"Fits, with a skunk like this," Greener Jack agreed.

"I reckon he'll try to lose himself among the visitors at first." Smoke slowed the pace and glanced around. "That's what I'd do. Here's the only place those East Coast gangsters would not look out of place. They could spread out, board a train, and get away without anyone being suspicious."

"Oui. All too easily. So what shall we do, Smoke?"

"I hate to say it, but I think we should turn back, at least to the south entrance to the park, and wait for Monte and the posse. We need more men, more eyes, to pick out the wolves from the sheep."

Always persistent, Monte Carson pushed his men as hard as Smoke Jensen and the mountain men had traveled. After discovery of the message at Togwotee Pass, he had become an unflagging taskmaster. As a result, Smoke Jensen's wait proved a short one. He brought fresh news that energized Smoke as none other could.

"There's only one road in here from the south," the lawman reported unnecessarily. "An' Lathrop is on it. We plumb near run over the top of his gang when we cut west to come in here. Looks like he rode through Jackson's Hole on the way. Only makes sense."

"How far behind are they?" Smoke asked.

"Half a day at the speed they're movin'. We had to skirt wide to avoid contact, then cut a lick to get here well before them."

"Did you get a count?"

"Yep. Way I see it, we're 'bout equal in size now."

"Good work, Monte. That eye of yours don't miss a thing. I'm gonna wager everything on it. Any guess on what they are fixin' to do once they get here?"

"They've got to split up, Smoke. The way I see it, they don't want to upset the visitors. Or draw any attention to themselves. Thirty or so boys ridin' in a bunch tends to do that. Particular' to eastern dudes."

Smoke chuckled at that. "Same as I see it. So we have to put men on each of these smaller groups. No place for scare tactics. The dudes would panic at Indian drums in the night, or fellers skulkin' around in the dark. What I want is Lathrop. Cut off the head and the snake dies."

"Damn, but yer gettin' windier every year, Smoke. That's the most I've ever heard you say at one time."

A big grin answered Monte. Smoke turned to L'Lupe Douchant and his aging companions. "We'll consider they'll break into five groups for a start. Each of you take one. Monte an' I'll do the same. Monte, if you'll divide the posse into five groups, we can keep an eye on Lathrop a mite easier."

"Sure thing, Smoke."

"What about me?" Ollie Johnson asked.

Smoke considered a moment. "You'll come with me. You've hung in there pretty good, so far, Ollie. Be a shame for you to miss out on the end of this."

27

Wood smoke from the fifty or so campsites filtered through the thick stands of pine and fir. The trees further added to the tantalizing aroma with tangy resin. Pink dawn light permeated the little clearings where tents and cabins offered shelter to park visitors. By the time it had diffused through gold to day white, frying bacon and the savor of brewing coffee made a tempting medley of pleasant scents to the mountain men and volunteer lawmen in Monte Carson's posse.

Stomachs rumbled, and even Smoke Jensen allowed as how he could use something to fill his. Common sense, and years of experience, said to put something away when you could, so the gathering of lawmen, concealed by the trees and undergrowth left standing, set to preparing breakfast. Coffee came first for these hardened outdoorsmen, then fatback, beans, eggs obtained from the sutler's store next to park headquarters, and trail bread.

Smoke Jensen wiped the last of the yolk of three eggs, and some grease from his pan with a partly consumed wedge of the biscuitlike trail bread when the first of Lathrop's gunmen walked their horses into the park. For a moment they stood out, wary looks telegraphing their identities as desperados. Then, when the accents of voices around them rose, they made subtle shifts in expression and chatted among themselves in the same, or similar, dialects.

Before long, save for the vigilance of the hidden watchers, they would have disappeared into the throng of visitors. Three men set off from the posse to follow them. They reported back that the newcomers went directly to the depot and inquired about the earliest train out of Yellowstone to a destination where they could transfer to an eastbound.

"That won't be until near noon," the posse man reported to Smoke and Monte.

"Let them get settled in, then take them all at once," Smoke ordered the man. "Try not to have any gunplay. We don't want to tip our hand."

By the time the surrounding peaks echoed the shrill hoot of a steam whistle, which announced the day's shipment of gawkers and brave souls who had come to "rough it" out West, five more groups, numbering from three to seven, had been identified and men had been detailed to make the capture. It gave Smoke another idea.

He offered it to Monte and L'Lupe, whose opinions he respected. "To keep it as quiet as possible, why not let them board and, once the train pulls out, take them in the coaches? Less chance of some innocent bystanders being harmed that way."

L'Lupe wiped the back of one knuckle-gnarled hand over his lips. "That shines, youngster. The one we're after is this Lathrop, right?"

"Him, Middleton, Cabbott, and Asher, right enough." Smoke gave a nod to L'Lupe to go on.

"Ainsi, we reduce the strength of his supporters without arousing any suspicion. *Ensuite,* these marauders stand alone."

"Provided, L'Lupe, they do not board the first train out of here."

Douchant stared at Smoke and shrugged. "They are not here, so far. Already people are taking the train. It will leave in a few minutes. No, *mon ami,* they have something else in mind. And if I am not mistaken, it is to kill you before they leave."

Lathrop and his partners entered Yellowstone National Park with only seven bodyguards. Another party of fifteen had preceded them and set up fortifications in a part of the park that a map had shown to be easy to defend, and equally easy for Smoke Jensen and whoever accompanied him to find. Lathrop, much to the objections of Victor Middleton and Arnold Cabbott, made little effort to conceal his arrival.

Consequently, word got to Smoke Jensen within ten minutes of the arrival of Phineas Lathrop. By that time, the posse had been reduced by two-thirds. They had followed the New York and Boston thugs onto the train. The odds did not deter Smoke, who set off on Dandy to follow to wherever Lathrop led him.

It didn't take long for Smoke, Ollie, L'Lupe, and Monte to find whom they sought. As they were topping a rise, a shot cracked overhead, barely heard in the hiss and roar of the geysers that erupted around them. This was the Land of Spirit Smokes, as the original inhabitants had called it.

Subterranean sources heated basins at the water table to boiling and then to steam, which expanded rapidly and jetted to the surface to spew hundreds of feet into the air. It was a frightening land that trembled all the time and shot off its scalding fountains unpredictably to the Indians who lived nearby, who knew nothing of minutes or hours. A mysterious land, a sacred land.

Now, Phineas Lathrop and the remainder of his gang defiled it for their own murderous purposes. Smoke took placid note of the bullet even as he and his companions spread out and hunkered down on their horses. A cold, hard smile creased Smoke's lips. Those ahead, so confident of success, had no idea of what Smoke had in store for them.

Monte Carson had brought along with the posse eleven more cronies of Preacher and the youthful Smoke Jensen.

They had a noisy, boisterous, and profane reunion that shocked the visiting womenfolk, made nervous the men, and won the admiration and hearts of the small, young eastern boys, who had never heard such colorful swearing.

Over Smoke's not too enthusiastic objections, jugs were passed around, and then a general plan was laid out. The old lobos of the mountains would sidle along on the flanks of the trail that Smoke and L'Lupe followed, and deploy themselves to cause the most grief to the "hostiles" as they could when the time came. So Smoke judged it fine to play target at a safe distance in order to allow those keen-eyed, hard-bitten men to get in place, and also to count the number of guns they faced.

That part of the plan worked excellently. It was only when Phineas Lathrop decided to turn about and carry the fight to Smoke Jensen that things got hot and hairy.

Smoke Jensen watched the ragged charge of Lathrop's ragtag army with a sudden grim expression. "What'll you bet that Lathrop and his partners aren't in that bunch?"

"Do we wait to meet them?" L'Lupe replied in answer.

"No, leave that to what's left of the posse and our friends up there." Smoke nodded to the ridge that overlooked the trembling geyser basin.

Smoke Jensen turned aside, followed by L'Lupe Douchant, Monte Carson, and Ollie Johnson. Within minutes the sounds of a violent clash between the desperate eastern gunmen and the tough, gritty men of the posse rose in a growing din. Their goal, Smoke informed his companions, was a group of six mounted figures near the center of the steaming ground.

Their approach went unnoticed until too late to make an escape. Eruptions of three of the minor geysers helped mask their advance on Phineas Lathrop and his partners. The four corrupt financiers watched with interest while the accurate fire of the posse repulsed their underlings. Lathrop made an unheard comment to Middleton, which Smoke noted with interest. In a momentary flight of fancy, he wondered if they were laying bets on the outcome. A second later he dismissed such frivolity as it became apparent they had been observed.

"They know we're here," he observed laconically.

Surprised that Lathrop had kept only two bodyguards, the avengers spurred their mounts to a fast lope. Weapons at the ready since they had sighted the enemy, they held their fire and chose their targets well. Booming reports rolled by overhead and echoed off the thick ranks of pines to their right. The old-timers had opened up. Which meant that the outlaw charge had been broken.

Smoke Jensen spared no time to check it out. He focused on the figure of Phineas and veered Dandy to close on the man he wanted most. Lathrop seemed oblivious of this intense interest, choosing instead to look frantically about for some means of escape. To Smoke's left, Ollie Johnson tripped a round from his shotgun.

A column of OO buckshot cleared one of the bodyguards from his saddle. Copying the style of the mountain men, whom Ollie admired greatly, he whooped and yipped gleefully over his victory. His celebration cut off abruptly when Victor Middleton coolly shot him through the heart. Smoke Jensen blinked in surprise. At first he could not believe it.

Not Ollie. Not the game young reporter who had dared and endured so much. Smoke's shock put words in his mouth. "Why, that son of a bitch!"

Immediately he changed the focus of his charge. He veered to the right to face off with Middleton. The Winchester Express was too unwieldy to fire from horseback, and Smoke had tied it behind his saddle. The short-barreled Marlin carbine in his hands came to his shoulder and he triggered a round that tore through the crown of Middleton's hat.

While he cycled the action, Smoke reined in to take better aim. Victor Middleton lost the moment of shocked paralysis as the sight of the .44 Marlin centered on his breastbone. His eyes went wide and his mouth formed a startled "oh" as the light weapon gave an angry bark and blinding pain erupted in his chest.

While Victor Middleton swayed in the saddle, Smoke Jensen worked the action of the Marlin again and sent another speedy messenger of death toward the New York financial wizard. The blunt-nosed slug did terrible things to Middleton's liver. Sagging like a deflated hot-air balloon, Victor Middleton spilled from his saddle to fall under the nervous, prancing hooves of his horse.

Witnessing the sudden, violent death of his partner broke Phineas Lathrop. With rifle balls from the mountain men cracking through the air all around, he touched spurs to his broad-chested chestnut gelding and sprinted away from the battle that had become all too personal. Smoke Jensen instantly went after him.

Smoke didn't want to end it for Lathrop with a rifle. He shoved the Marlin into its saddle scabbard and nudged Dandy into a fast lope in pursuit. From behind and below, he heard the shouts, curses, and agonized cries of a fierce fight. The posse held their ground well, he noted in a quick glance behind which revealed the outlaw flatlanders streaming away once more.

A rifle cracked much nearer. "Got one," Monte Carson shouted, more in relief than in victory.

Gradually, Smoke gained on Lathrop. Wild-eyed with panic, Phineas Lathrop waved an empty .38 Colt Lightning at Smoke Jensen, then uselessly threw it at the gunfighter as Smoke closed to half a length. Smoke ducked it with ease and then found himself laughing at the terrified man who would be king. Sounds of yet another clash rose from the edge of the geyser field.

Short of an arm's grasp, Smoke Jensen readied himself for the difficult maneuver he had worked out in the closing moments of the pursuit. Boots free of the stirrups, he levered himself upright on his saddle pad, like a Roman rider.

Lathrop gawked at him in consternation as Smoke jumped outward, arms spread wide.

The shock of impact triggered the closing of those arms, like the jaws of a steel trap. Phineas Lathrop let out a pitiful wail as Smoke Jensen's momentum carried them both off the sweat-lathered gelding. They hit with stunning impact. Sour breath whooshed from Lathrop's lips and Smoke grunted as the body below him cushioned the shock of their landing.

For a long half minute the two men lay still. Then the long, powerful arms of Smoke Jensen flexed and levered him off Lathrop and the ground. It looked to Smoke to be an easy task now. Lathrop moaned softly. Smoke came to his boots. Lathrop's eyes blinked open suddenly and focused far faster than most men in his condition.

In the next instant, Lathrop aimed a vicious kick at Smoke's crotch. The blow of a pointy-toed boot nearly unmanned Smoke Jensen. Pain exploded in his groin and he found himself unable to take mental inventory of his treasured parts.

By the time he could move, and found the pain localized in the inside, upper part of his right thigh, Phineas Lathrop had come to his boots. A demented light glowed in his deepset, oddly walnut-colored eyes. His right hand groped uselessly at the shoulder holster under his coat, until he realized he had hurled his revolver at the man he faced. Visions of defeat clouded his features for a moment until he recalled he had followed Wade Tanner's advice.

He had a hideout gun concealed at the small of his back. Renewed hope brightened Lathrop's visage as he darted his hand behind him. He grasped the bird-head grips tightly and yanked the little .32 Smith free. Even if he could not beat the notorious gunfighter, his whirling mind told him, he could at least die like a man, fighting for what he believed in.

In that brilliant moment of revelation, Smoke Jensen took a quick step forward and denied Phineas Lathrop that privilege. A hard right to the jaw stunned and staggered Lathrop.

Where the hell had that come from? Before he could level his weapon, a sizzling left quickly followed, blurring Lathrop's vision.

Lathrop felt his gun hand seized. "Oh, no, Lathrop. It isn't going to be that easy."

Gasping, Phineas found the strength to form words. "Wh—what is it you want?"

"I'm going to pound the living hell out of you, then I'm taking you back to be hanged."

In renewed desperation and dawning horror, Lathrop swung an unaimed left that bounced off the point of Smoke's right shoulder. Lathrop followed with an upraised knee that also missed the target. Grinning, Smoke Jensen stepped back a pace and measured his opponent. Chin tucked in to protect his throat, Smoke feinted with a right, popped Lathrop hard with a left jab, then followed up with a one-two-three to the midsection. Unaccustomed to the rigors of a hard life, Lathrop's stomach muscles could not take the pounding. He crumpled like a wet newspaper.

Smoke Jensen felt no pity. He moved in again, raining lefts and rights on the sides of Lathrop's head. Dizzied, his vision flickering in and out of focus, Phineas Lathrop fought his rising pandemonium in an effort to make the right decision that would get him out of this terrible punishment. He brought up his hands to protect his head. An image slowly formed and danced behind his eyes.

The blade! That stiletto the Italian kid had given him. "A Sicilian equalizer," Nick diManfi had told him, snickering. He still had it, in a soft leather sheath suspended behind his back.

Phineas Lathrop found new strength and purpose. He forced himself backward, for the moment out of reach of the pounding fists of Smoke Jensen. The ground trembled under his feet. For a second, Lathrop thought Jensen had done some serious harm to his equilibrium. The moment passed. Lathrop reached behind his back

Fingers probed beneath his coat and shirt collar. He drew

on the leather thong to pull the hilt into reach. Suddenly the ground lurched again. Lathrop's heart all but stopped. New energy burst inside him as his fingers closed on the scale of the stiletto. With a cry of triumph, he yanked the blade free as the earth rumbled ominously all around.

Small vents of steam gave preliminary warning of the event about to occur. Lathrop ignored them as he lunged forward, the wicked tip of the thin-bladed knife aimed at Smoke Jensen's heart. To his utter surprise, Smoke Jensen did not shoot him.

Instead the thick, deep, long blade of a coffin-handled bowie appeared in Smoke's hand. A ringing sound broke through the growing subterranean growl as steel met steel. Smoke parried the attack easily. Then, instead of letting his powerful arm absorb the energy of Lathrop's charge, Smoke pivoted away and let Lathrop stumble past him.

A quick flick of his arm sent Smoke's blade downward to split the cloth of Lathrop's coat and shirt, and left a long, thin, pink line on his skin that quickly overflowed with bright red blood. Lathrop howled as a numbing fire-and-ice sensation spread through his body.

Certain he had been split open to his intestines, Phineas Lathrop sought only to exact as much punishment in return as he could. He spun on one heel and lashed out with the stiletto. Not designed for slashes, the weapon had little effect. Nick diManfi had not bothered to explain that the "old men" of the *Mano Niero* on Sicily usually drove the point into the throat of an unsuspecting victim. Ignorant of this, Phineas Lathrop fought for his life at a decided disadvantage. Smoke Jensen easily caught the blade on the false edge of his Bowie.

It skidded to the guard and Smoke gave a vicious twist that plucked the stiletto from Lathrop's hand. It flew in a high arc to land near a large black hole in the ground, which was surrounded by a cast-iron-pipe guardrail. With a desperate wail, Phineas Lathrop dashed after it.

Right then, the earth gave a final heave and a huge plume

of snowy steam belched from the opening. Fast behind it came a thick column of boiling water. The gigantic gout rapidly towered over the adversaries, a bull roar issuing from its base. Seething and churning, it continued to grow. Slowly its upper portion lost momentum. Scalding rain descended on the heads of Smoke Jensen and Phineas Lathrop.

Shielded by his sturdy Stetson, Smoke felt it through his thick leather hunting shirt as only a mild discomfort. For Phineas Lathrop it was a different matter. Bareheaded, he began to howl and slap at his scalded flesh. More pain erupted as the superheated water soaked through his cloth suit. Smoke saw this intervention of nature as a means of Lathrop escaping his just punishment.

He sheathed the bowie and rushed to the pain-racked Lathrop. Another powerful regurgitation sent steam and water upward again. A moment before Smoke reached him, Lathrop saw him coming. Biting back his agony, Lathrop bent hastily and snatched up the stiletto. He turned, snarling, on Smoke Jensen.

Smoke flexed his muscular thighs and launched himself at Lathrop, heedless of the danger of the knife. Arm extended, Smoke smacked the blade out of line. The impact of joined bodies knocked both men off their feet. They rolled over and over on the muddy ground, each grappling for the deadly blade. Lathrop found new purchase on the grip and flicked his wrist to bring the tip into contact with Smoke's chest. The wind shifted as it often did in this valley of smoke.

The feathery top of the tree-trunk-thick shaft of water wavered and then followed the inexorable pressure of the breeze. Hundreds of pounds of water at near-boiling temperature thundered down on the struggling men. Smoke Jensen wrestled himself around so that Phineas Lathrop wound up on top. He took the brunt of the scalding cascade.

Howling in agony, his knife forgotten, Lathrop sought only to get away. With a final burst of energy he wrenched free of Smoke's grasp. Fighting to keep upright on his boots, he slipped and slid over the untrustworthy ground. Foul minerals gave his mouth a sulphurous taste. Blinded by the waterfall effect of Old Faithful, he stumbled into the railing that had been erected to protect visitors.

He did a heels-over-head flip and landed with his lower legs directly in the boiling column of upthrust steam and water. Pain like none he had ever felt before roared up through Lathrop's thighs and withered the last reserves of his body. His shrieks rose above the thunder of Old Faithful. It took the last reserves of Smoke Jensen's strength to locate Phineas Lathrop and drag him to safety.

Hunter and hunted cleared the guardrail at the same time that Old Faithful ended its performance almost as abruptly as it had begun. In the shocking silence that followed, Smoke Jensen looked down at Phineas Lathrop and panted to gain the breath to form words.

"No—no, Lathrop. Even that's too good for you. I'm taking you back to hang."

"Tout alors, mon ami!" L'Lupe's raucous voice struck at Smoke's ears. "If you had told me you needed a bath, we could have found an easier way!"

"Hey, look, yourself, *cochon*. I'm parboiled and ready for the spit." Then Smoke recovered himself and looked around. "The others? How's the fight going?"

"She is over, my friend. And I see you have captured the prize pig—which I resent you calling me. Where to, now?"

Defeated in this exchange of banter, Smoke Jensen looked at his old friend with a jaundiced eye. "Haven't you had enough?" He considered the situation.

More than twenty good people killed, he enumerated. Among them, seven good friends. And there had been Ollie Johnson, so young and so wrapped up in his craft. He had come west for his story and died getting it.

Perhaps Sally could write the final episode for Ollie's sake. Smoke discounted his own aches and pains. They were nothing compared to what others had endured. He sighed heavily, then made a sweeping gesture.

"Monte and his posse can take care of any prisoners. I suggest you and our other old friends accompany Mr. Lathrop here as far as Big Rock. Then, I'm heading for the Sugarloaf. It's been far too long since I've seen Sally."

BETRAYAL OF THE
MOUNTAIN MAN

1

Smoke Jensen saw the calf struggling through a snow-drift. The little creature had separated from its mother and the rest of the herd, and was bawling now in fear and confusion. He also saw the wolves, two of them, about twenty-five yards behind the calf. They were inching up slowly, quietly, hunkered down on their bellies to reduce their presence.

Smoke snaked his Winchester from the saddle sheath, then jacked a round into the chamber. He hooked his leg across the saddle horn, rested his elbow on his knee, then raised the rifle to his shoulder and sighted on the lead wolf. He was about 150 yards away from the two wolves, and he was looking down on them so it would be a difficult shot. But he figured that even if he didn't kill them, he might at least be able to drive them away from the calf.

Smoke squeezed the trigger. The rifle kicked back against his shoulder as smoke bellowed from the end of the barrel. When the smoke rolled away, he saw the lead wolf lying on its side, a spreading pool of red staining the snow.

The other wolf turned and ran quickly toward the trees, kicking up little puffs of snow as it did so. Smoke jacked another round into the chamber and aimed at the second wolf. His finger tightened on the trigger; then he eased the pressure, and lowered his rifle.

"Don't reckon I should shoot you for doing what your instinct tells you to do," Smoke said quietly. "I just don't want you doin' it to my cows. Specially not this year."

Smoke rode down to the wolf he had killed, then dismounted. His bullet had hit the animal just behind his left foreleg, penetrated the heart, and killed it instantly. The wolf's eyes were still open, his tongue still hanging out of his mouth. Strangely, Smoke felt a sense of sadness.

"I'm sorry I had to do this, fella, but you didn't leave me any choice," Smoke said. "At least it was quick for you."

Smoke remounted, then rode on toward the calf. He looped his rope around the calf, then half-led and half-dragged it back to the herd. There, he removed the rope and watched as the calf hurried to join his mother.

What had once been a large herd was now pitifully small, having come through what they were calling the "Great Winter Kill." Hundreds of thousands of cattle had died out throughout the West this winter, and Smoke's Sugarloaf Ranch was no exception. He had started the winter with fifteen thousand head; he was now down to less than two thousand.

Smoke's only hope to save what remained of his herd was to push them into a box canyon and hope that it would shield them from any further winter blasts. He, Cal, and Pearlie were doing that very thing when he came across the wolves.

Looking up, Smoke saw Cal approaching him from the north end of the canyon opening, while at the same time Pearlie was approaching from the south. Even if he had not been able to see them, he would know they were coming toward him, because each of them was leaving a long, black trail in the snow.

Cal reached him first.

"What was the shootin'?"

"Wolves," Smoke answered.

"Yeah," Cal said. "Well, you can't much blame 'em, I guess. They're probably havin' as hard a winter as we are.

Same with all the other creatures, which is why they're goin' after cattle, rather than deer."

"Wolves?" Pearlie asked, arriving then.

"Yes, they were after a calf," Smoke said.

"Too bad you didn't see them a little earlier."

"What do you mean?"

Pearlie twisted in his saddle and pointed back down the black smear that marked his path through the snow. "Three calves back there, or what's left of 'em. Killed by wolves."

"Maybe we ought to put out some poisoned meat," Cal suggested.

Smoke shook his head. "I don't care to do that. Besides, there are enough animals around, frozen to death, that they probably wouldn't take the bait."

"You'd think they'd go after the dead ones, and leave the live ones alone," Pearlie said.

"The dead ones are frozen hard as a rock. They want something alive because it's warmer, and easier to eat," Smoke said.

"Speaking of something warm and easy to eat, you think maybe Miss Sally fixed us up any bear claws?" Pearlie asked.

"Does the sun come up in the east?" Cal asked.

Smoke chuckled. "I expect she did," he said. He stood in his stirrups and looked down toward the small herd. "We've got them in the canyon now; that's about all we can do for them. Let's head for the house."

The three started back toward the house, which was some five miles distant. A ride that, in good weather, would take no more than thirty minutes stretched into an hour because of the heavy fall of snow. The horses labored to cut through the drifts, which were sometimes chest high, and their heavy breathing formed clouds of vapor that drifted away into the fading light.

The three riders said nothing, lost in their own thoughts as they rode back toward the main house.

The oldest of the three, and the ranch owner, was Kirby "Smoke" Jensen. Smoke stood just over six feet tall, and had shoulders as wide as an ax handle and biceps as thick as most men's thighs. He had never really known his mother, and when he was barely in his teens, he went with his father into the mountains to follow the fur trade. The father and son teamed up with a legendary mountain man called Preacher. For some reason, unknown even to Preacher, the mountain man took to the boy and began to teach him the ways of the mountains: how to live when others would die, how to be a man of your word, and how to fear no other living creature. On the first day they met, Preacher, whose real name was Art, gave Kirby a new name. That name, Smoke, would one day become a legend in the West, and after a while, even Kirby thought of himself as Smoke Jensen.

Smoke was in his thirties, a happily married landowner whose ranch, Sugarloaf, had the potential to be one of the finest ranches in the state. For the last three or four years, Sugarloaf had lived up to its potential, so much so that Smoke had borrowed money to expand the ranch. He bought more land, built a new barn and bunkhouse, added onto the big house, and bought more cattle.

Then the winter hit. Blizzard followed blizzard as the temperature plummeted to record lows. All across the West cattle died in record numbers. Tens of thousands of cattle froze to death, thousands more died of starvation because they couldn't get to the food, while nearly as many died of thirst because the streams and creeks were frozen solid under several feet of snow.

Ironically, the smaller ranchers were better able to ride it out than the bigger ranchers, who had more land, more cattle, and much more to lose. In one terrible winter, Smoke Jensen had gone from being one of the wealthiest ranchers in Colorado to a man who was struggling to hang on to his ranch.

"Smoke, if you want, I'll take the lead . . . let my horse break trail for a while," Pearlie called up to him. The three men were riding in single file, the two behind the leader taking advantage of the lead horse breaking a trail through the snow.

"Sure, come on up," Smoke invited, moving to one side of the trail to let Pearlie pass.

A few years earlier, Pearlie had been a gunman, hired by a man who wanted to run Smoke off the land so he could ride roughshod over those who were left. But Pearlie didn't take to killing and looting from innocent people, so he quit his job. He had stopped by to tell Smoke that he was leaving when Smoke offered to hire him.

Since that time Pearlie had worked for Smoke and Sally. He stood just a shade less than six feet tall, was lean as a willow branch, had a face tanned the color of an old saddle, and a head of wild, unruly black hair. His eyes were mischievous and he was quick to smile and joke, but underneath his friendly demeanor was a man that was as hard as iron and as loyal to his friends as they come.

"I'll ride second," Cal said, passing with Pearlie. "That way I can take the lead in a few minutes."

Not too long after Pearlie had joined the ranch, a starving and destitute Cal, who was barely in his teens at the time, made the mistake of trying to rob Sally. Instead of turning him over to the sheriff, Sally brought him home and made him one of the family, along with Pearlie. Now Calvin Woods was Pearlie's young friend and protégé in the cowboy life.

The three men rode on in silence for the next fifteen minutes, frequently changing the lead so that one horse wouldn't be tired out. Finally they crested a hill, then started down a long slope. There, half a mile in front of them, the ranch compound spread out over three acres, consisting of the main house, bunkhouse, barn, corral, and toolshed.

In the setting sun the snow took on a golden glow, and the

scene could have been a Currier and Ives painting come to life.

The main house, or "big" house as the cowboys called it, was a rather large, two-story Victorian edifice, white, with red shutters and a gray-painted porch that ran across the front and wrapped around to one side. The bunkhouse, which was also white with red shutters, sat halfway between the big house and the barn. The barn was red.

A wisp of smoke curled up from the kitchen chimney, and as the three approached, they could smell the aroma of baking.

"Yep! She made some," Pearlie said happily. "I tell you the truth, if Miss Sally don't make the best bear claws in Colorado, then I'll eat my hat."

"Hell, that ain't no big promise, Pearlie," Cal said. "The kind of appetite you got, you eat anything that gets in your way. I wouldn't be that surprised if you hadn't already et your hat a time or two."

Smoke laughed.

"That ain't no ways funny," Pearlie complained. "I ain't never et none of my hats."

"But there ain't no danger of you eatin' your hat anyhow 'cause you're right," Cal said. "Miss Sally does make the best bear claws in Colorado."

Sally was a schoolteacher when Smoke met her, but she was far from the demure schoolmarm one most often thought of when picturing a schoolteacher. Sally could ride, rope, and shoot better than just about any man, and yet none of that detracted from her feminine charms. She was exceptionally pretty and her kitchen skills matched any woman and surpassed most.

The bear claws that Pearlie was referring to were sweet, sugar-coated doughnuts. They were famous throughout the county, and some men had been known to ride ten miles out of their way to drop by the Sugarloaf just on the off chance she'd have a platter of them made up and cooling on the windowsill.

* * *

The three men rode straight to the barn, where they unsaddled their horses, then turned them into warm stalls with hay and water. They took off their coats, hats, and boots on the enclosed back porch, dumping the snow and cleaning their boots before they went inside.

The house was warm and cozy, and it smelled of coffee, roast beef, fresh-baked bread, bear claws, and wood burning in the fireplace. Sally greeted Smoke with a kiss and the other two with affectionate hugs.

Around the dinner table the four talked, joked, and laughed over the meal. And yet, as Sally studied her husband's face, she knew that, just beneath his laughing demeanor, he was a worried man. It wasn't so much what he said, as what was left unsaid. Smoke had always been a man filled with optimism and plans for the future. It had been a long time since she had heard him mention any of his plans for improving and expanding the ranch.

Sally had no idea what time it was when she rolled over in bed, still in that warm and comfortable state of half-sleep. She reached out to touch Smoke, but when she didn't feel him in bed with her, the remaining vestige of sleep abandoned her and she woke up, wondering where he was.

Outside, the snow glistened under the bright full moon so that, even though it was the middle of the night, the bedroom was well lit in varying degrees of silver and black. A nearby aspen tree waved in a gentle night breeze and as it did so, it projected its restless shadow onto the softly glowing wall. Smoke's shadow was there as well, for he was standing at that very window, looking out into the yard.

"Smoke?" Sally called out in a soft, concerned voice.

"I'm sorry, darlin'," Smoke replied. "Did I wake you?"

Sally sat up, then brushed a fall of blond hair back from her face. "Are you all right?" she asked.

"I'm fine."

"You're worried, aren't you?"

Smoke paused for a long moment before he answered. Then, with a sigh, he nodded.

"I won't lie to you, Sally," he said. "We may lose everything."

Sally got out of bed and padded across the room. Then, wrapping her arms around him, she leaned into him.

"No," she said. "As long as we have each other, we won't lose everything."

2

The banker leaned back in his chair and put his hands together, making a steeple of his fingers. He listened intently as Smoke made his case.

"I'm sure I'm not the only one coming to you with problems," Smoke said. "I reckon this winter has affected just about everyone."

Joel Matthews nodded. "It has indeed," he said. "Right now our bank has over one hundred fifty thousand dollars in bad debt. I'll tell you the truth, Smoke. We are in danger of going under ourselves."

Smoke sighed. "Then it could be that I'm just wasting my time talking to you."

Matthews drummed his fingers on the desk for a moment, then looked down at Smoke's account.

"You have a two-thousand-dollar note due in thirty days," he said.

"Yes."

"What, exactly, are you asking?"

"I'm asking for a sixty-day extension of that note."

The banker turned at his desk and looked at the calendar on the wall behind him. The picture was an idealized night scene in the mountains. Below a full moon a train was crossing a trestle, its headlight beam stretching forward and every car window glowing unrealistically.

"Your note is due on April 30th," he said. "A sixty-day extension would take you to June 30th. Do you really think you can come up with the two thousand dollars by then?"

"I know that I cannot by April 30th, and I'll be honest with you, Joel. I don't know if I will have the money by June 30th either. But if any of my cattle survive the rest of this winter, I will at least have a chance."

"Smoke, can you make a two-hundred-dollar payment on your note? That would be ten percent."

Smoke shook his head. "Maybe a hundred," he said.

"A hundred?"

"That's about the best I can do right now."

Matthews sighed. "I'll never be able to convince the board to go along with it, unless you can at least pay ten percent on the loan."

Smoke nodded. "I understand," he said. He started to stand, but Matthews held out his hand.

"Wait a minute," he said.

Smoke hesitated.

"I know how you can come up with a hundred fifty dollars, if you are willing to do a job for me."

"A job for you?"

"Well, for the bank, actually," Matthews said. "It will take you about three days."

"Three days work for a hundred fifty dollars? I'll do it," Smoke said.

"Don't you even want to know what it is?"

"Is it honest work?"

"Oh, yes, it's honest all right. It might also be dangerous."

"I'll do it," Smoke said.

"Yes, I didn't think you would be a person who would be deterred by the possibility of danger. But just so that you know what you are letting yourself in for, we have a rather substantial money shipment coming by stagecoach from Sulphur Springs. If you would ride as a special guard during the time of the shipment, I will pay you one hundred fifty dollars."

Smoke gasped. "One hundred fifty dollars just to ride shotgun? It's not that I'm looking a gift horse in the mouth, Joel, but shotgun guards make about twenty dollars a month, don't they?"

"Yes."

"So why would you be willing to pay me so much?"

"We are bringing in over twenty thousand dollars," Matthews said. He sighed, then opened the drawer of his desk and pulled out a newspaper. "And the damn fool editor over at Sulphur Springs has seen fit to run a front page story about it."

Matthews turned the paper around so Smoke could see the headlines of the lead story.

HUGE MONEY SHIPMENT!

$20,000 In Greenbacks

TO BE TRANSPORTED

by Sulphur Springs Express Company

to BIG ROCK.

"Why in the world would he publish something like this?" Smoke asked.

"Well, if you asked the editor, I'm sure he would tell us that he is merely exercising his freedom of the press," Matthews said. "But I would call it idiocy. Anyway, the cat is out of the bag, and no doubt every outlaw in three states knows about the shipment now. Do you know Frank Simmons?"

"No, I don't think I do."

"Frank Simmons is the normal shotgun guard on this run. He's sixty-six years old and blind as a bat. Ordinarily it's not a problem. About the only thing the stage ever carries is a mailbag with letters from grandparents, a few seed catalogues, and the like. But this? Well, Frank just isn't up for the job."

"I see what you mean," Smoke said. "When do I go?"

"You can take the stage over Monday morning," Matthews said. "The money will arrive by train Tuesday night. Marshal Goodwin and a couple of his deputies will meet the train with the banker just to make sure it gets in the bank all right. Then, Wednesday, you'll take personal charge of it until you get it back here."

"Sounds easy enough," Smoke said.

Matthews laughed out loud. "For someone like you, I imagine it is," he said. "But I'll be honest with you, Smoke. If I had to guard that shipment, knowing that every saddle bum and ne'er-do-well from Missouri to California is after it, why, I'd be peeing in my pants."

Smoke laughed as well. "I'll have the money here Wednesday evening," he said. "And I'll be wearing dry pants."

"You want me to go with you?" Pearlie asked over the supper table that night.

"No, why should you?"

"Well, if it's like Mr. Matthews says, you're liable to run into some trouble between here and Sulphur Springs."

"No. I thank you for the offer, Pearlie. But I want you and Cal to stay here and look after what few cattle we have left. You'll have to take hay out to them, since they won't be able to forage. And you'll have to watch out for the wolves, and any other creatures that might have a yen for beef. The only chance we have of saving Sugarloaf is to keep enough cows alive that I can sell to raise the two thousand."

"All right, if you say so," Pearlie said as he reached for the last of the bear claws.

"That's four," Cal said.

"What's four?"

"That's four of them things you'n has had."

"Cal," Sally said sharply.

"What? You think I'm lyin', Miss Sally? I been a'countin' them."

"I'm not concerned about that. I'm talking about your grammar."

"That's four of *those* things *you have* had," Pearlie said, correcting Cal's grammar. "Not them things you'n has had."

"Have you had four of them, Pearlie?" Sally asked.

"Well, yes, ma'am, but I believe these are somewhat smaller than the ones you usually make," Pearlie replied.

Sally laughed, then got up from the table and, walking over to the pie saver, opened the door and pulled out an apple pie.

"Then you won't be wanting any of this, will you?" she asked, bringing the pie to the table.

"*I* sure do!" Cal said, licking his lips in anticipation as Sally cut a large slice for him.

"Maybe just a little piece," Pearlie said, eyeing the pie she was cutting. "With, maybe, a slice of cheese on top."

That night, Sally cuddled against Smoke as they lay in bed.

"You take care of yourself, Smoke," she said.

Smoke squeezed her. "I've spent a lifetime taking care of myself," he said. "I'm not likely to fall down on the job now."

"It was nice of Mr. Matthews to offer you the job," Sally said. "He did say we would get the extension?"

"Yes." Smoke sighed. "For all the good it will do."

"What do you mean?"

"We've got thirty days until the loan is due, with the extension ninety days. Then what? We are still going to have to come up with the money."

"You don't think we'll have enough cattle to sell?"

"What if we do?" Smoke said. "Then what? At best, we'll

just be buying time. A cattle ranch without cattle isn't much of a ranch."

They lay in the quiet darkness for a long moment before Sally spoke again.

"I know a way we might be able to come up with it," she said.

"Oh, no," Smoke said.

"Oh, no, what?"

"I'm not going to let you go on the line for me. I mean, I appreciate the offer, but I just wouldn't feel right, you becoming a soiled dove."

"What?" Sally shouted, sitting up in bed quickly and staring down at him.

Smoke laughed out loud. "I mean, I have given that very idea some thought too, but I wasn't sure you would do it. Then I figured, well, maybe you would, but I just wouldn't feel right about it."

"Kirby Jensen!" Sally said, laughing at him as she realized he was teasing. She grabbed the pillow, then began hitting him with it.

"I give up, I give up!" Smoke said, folding his arms across his face as she continued to pound him with the pillow. Finally, winded, she put the pillow down.

"Truce?" Smoke asked.

"Truce," Sally replied. Then, she smiled wickedly at him. "How much do you think I would make?"

"Sally!" Smoke gasped.

This time it was Sally's turn to laugh. "Well, you are the one who brought it up," she said between giggles.

Sally lay back down beside him and, again, they were quiet for a moment.

"How?" Smoke asked.

"How what?"

"You said you may have a way to raise the money. How would we do it?"

"Light the lamp," Sally said as she got out of bed, "and I'll show you."

Sally walked over to the dresser and opened the top drawer. Removing a newspaper, she returned to the bed just as a bubble of golden light filled the room.

"Read this advertisement," she said, pointing to a boxed item in the paper.

Smoke read aloud. "New York Company desires ranch land to lease. Will pay one dollar per acre for one-year lease."

"If we leased our entire ranch to them, we could make twelve thousand dollars," Sally said.

Smoke shook his head. "No," he said.

"Why not?"

"Sally, you know why not. If we lease this ranch to some outfit like this"—he flicked his fingers across the page—"they'll send their own man in to run things. We'll be tenants on our own land. Only the land won't even be ours, at least not for a year."

"Smoke, you said yourself we are in danger of losing everything," Sally said. "At least, this way, we could hang onto the ranch. All right, we won't make any money this year because everything we get will have to go toward the notes. But next year, we could start fresh."

"Start fresh with no money," Smoke said.

"And no debt," Sally added.

Smoke stared at the advertisement for a long moment. Then he lay back on the bed and folded his arm across his eyes.

"Smoke?"

Smoke didn't answer.

"Smoke, you know I'm right," Sally said.

After another long period of silence, Smoke let out a loud sigh.

"Yeah," he said. "I know you're right."

"Then you'll do it?"

"Is this what you want to do, Sally?"

"No, it isn't what I want to do," Sally admitted. "But I don't see any other way out of this. At least think about it."

"All right," Smoke agreed. "I'll think about it."

* * *

The man standing at the end of the bar had a long, pock-marked face and a drooping eyelid. He picked up his beer, and blew the foam off before taking a drink. His name was Ebenezer Dooley, and he had escaped prison six months ago. He was here to meet some people, and though he had never seen them, he knew who the three men were as soon as they came in. He could tell by the way they stood just inside the door, pausing for a moment to look around the main room of the Mad Dog Saloon, that they were here to meet someone.

The room was dimly lit by a makeshift chandelier that consisted of a wagon wheel and several flickering candles. It was also filled with smoke from dozens of cigars and pipes so that it took some effort for the three men to look everyone over. Dooley had told them that he would be wearing a high-crowned black hat, with a red feather sticking out of a silver hatband. He stepped away from the bar so they could see him; then one of them made eye contact and nodded. Once contact was made, Dooley walked toward an empty table at the back of the saloon. The three men picked their way through the crowd, then joined him.

One of the bar girls came over to smile prettily at the men as they sat down. She winced somewhat as she got a closer look at them, because they were some of the ugliest men she had ever seen.

Dooley had been in town for a few days, so she had already met him. He was tall and gangly, with a thin face and a hawklike nose. He was not handsome by any standard, but compared to the other three, he was Prince Charming.

"Girlie, bring us a bottle and four glasses," Dooley said.

The bar girl left to get the order, returned, picked up the money, then walked away. None of the men seemed particularly interested in having her stay around, and she was not at all interested in trying to change their minds.

"You would be Cletus, I take it?" Dooley said to the oldest

of the three men. Cletus had white hair and a beard and, as far as Dooley could tell, only one tooth.

"I'm Cletus."

"A friend of mine named McNabb told me you would be a good man to work with," Dooley said. "And that you could get a couple more."

"These here are my nephews," Cletus said. "This is Morgan." Morgan had a terrible scar that started just above his left eye, then passed down through it. He had only half an eyelid, and the eye itself was opaque. Morgan stared hard at Dooley with his one good eye.

"And this here'n is Toomey," Cletus continued. "Neither one of 'em's too quick in the mind, but they're good boys who'll do whatever I tell them to do. Ain't that right, boys?"

"Whatever you tell us, Uncle Cletus," Toomey said. "Mama said to do whatever you tell us to do."

"His mama is my sister," Cletus said. "She ain't none too bright neither, which is why I figure she birthed a couple of idiots."

Neither Morgan nor Toomey reacted to his unflattering comment about them.

"Can I count on them to do the job I got planned?" Dooley asked.

"I told you," Cletus said. "They'll do whatever I ask them to do."

"Good."

"You said this would be a big job?"

"Yes."

"How big?"

"Twenty thousand dollars big," Dooley said.

Cletus let out a low whistle. "That is big," he said.

"The split is fifty-fifty," Dooley said.

"Wait a minute, what do you mean, the split is fifty-fifty? They's four of us."

"I set up the deal, I'm in charge," Dooley replied. "I take half, you take half. How you divide your half with your nephews is up to you."

Cletus looked at his two nephews for a moment, then he nodded.

"All right," he said. "That sounds good enough to me. Where is this job, and when do we do it?"

"Huh-uh," Dooley replied.

Cletus looked surprised. "What do you men, huh-uh? How are we goin' to do the job iffen we don't know what it is we're a'supposed to be doin'?"

Dooley shook his head. "I'll tell you what you need to know when the time comes. I wouldn't like to think of you gettin' greedy on me."

"Whatever you say," Cletus replied.

3

Even though Smoke had nothing to do with the money yet, he was in the Sulphur Springs Railroad Depot when the eleven o'clock train arrived.

The depot was crowded with people who were waiting for the train. Some were travelers who were holding tickets, and some were here to meet arriving passengers, but many were here for no other purpose than the excitement of watching the arrival of the train.

They heard the train before anyone saw it, the sound of the whistle. Then, as the train swept around a distant curve, the few people on the platform saw the headlamp, a gas flame that projected a long beam before it.

The train whistled again, and this time everyone could hear the puffing of the steam engine as it labored hard to pull the train through the night. Inside the depot, Smoke stepped over to one of the windows, but because it was very cold outside, and warm inside, the window was fogged over. He wiped away the condensation, then looked through the circle he had made to watch the train approach, listening to the puffs of steam as it escaped from the pistons. He could see bright sparks embedded in the heavy, black smoke that poured from the flared smokestack. Then, as the train swept into the station, he saw sparks falling from the firebox and leaving a carpet of orange-glowing embers lying between the rails and trailing out behind the train. They glimmered for a moment or two in the darkness before finally going dark themselves.

The train began squeaking and clanging as the engineer applied the brakes. It got slower, and slower still, until finally the engineer brought his train to a stop in exactly the right place.

Much of the crowd inside went outside then, to stand on the platform alongside the train as the arriving passengers disembarked and the departing passengers climbed aboard. But Smoke and three men remained inside the depot. Smoke had met with the others earlier in the day when he had presented them with the letter from Joel Matthews, authorizing him to take possession of the money.

"Well, Mr. Jensen," the banker said, noticing Smoke for the first time that night. "On the job already, I see."

"I just came down to see if I would actually have a job tomorrow."

"That's probably not a bad idea," the young deputy said. "Coming down here now to watch us can give you a few pointers."

"Ha," the marshal said, laughing. "I can see Smoke Jensen picking up some pointers from the likes of us."

"Everybody can learn something," Smoke said.

The station manager stuck his head inside the door then.

"Mr. Wallace, you want to come sign for this now? The railroad is anxious to get rid of it."

"I'll be right there," the banker said.

The marshal and his deputy both drew their pistols, then followed Wallace out to the mail car. Smoke went outside with them, and he turned up the collar of his sheepskin coat as he watched Wallace take the money pouch from the express messenger. Then he followed the banker and his two guards down to the bank, where the money was put into the safe.

"There you go, Mr. Jensen," Wallace said when the money was put away. "All safe and sound for you tomorrow."

"Yes, well, I'll feel a lot better when it is safe and sound in the bank back in Big Rock," Smoke said.

Smoke was just finishing his breakfast the next morning, sopping up the last of the yellow of his egg with his last biscuit, when someone walked over to his table.

"You're Mr. Jensen?"

"Yes."

"I'm from the bank, Mr. Jensen. Mr. Wallace said to tell you to come over and get that . . . uh . . . package now," he said cryptically.

"All right," Smoke said, washing down the last bite with the end of his coffee. He put on his coat, turned up his collar, and pulled his hat down, then followed the messenger back to the bank.

"I didn't think the bank would be opened yet," Smoke said, his words forming clouds of vapor in the cold morning air.

"It isn't open yet," the young man said. "Mr. Wallace thought it would be better to give it to you before we had any customers."

"Sounds sensible," Smoke said.

Smoke thought they would go in through the front, but the young man walked alongside the bank until they reached the back. Then, taking a key from his pocket, he opened the back door and motioned for Smoke to go inside.

Wallace was sitting at a desk in his office when the young man brought Smoke in. The pouch that the money had come in was open, and there were several bound stacks of bills alongside.

"You want to count this money?" Wallace asked.

"It might be a good idea," Smoke replied.

"Jeremiah, pull that chair over here for Mr. Jensen."

"Yes, sir," the young messenger said.

Thanking him, Smoke sat in the chair and began counting. When he finished, half an hour later, he looked up at Wallace. "I thought it was supposed to be twenty thousand dollars."

"How much did you come up with?" Wallace asked.

"Twenty thousand four hundred and twelve dollars," Smoke replied.

Wallace smiled, and slid a piece of paper across his desk. "That exact amount is recorded here," he said. "It's good to see that you are an accurate counter. Sign here, please."

With all money accounted for, Smoke took the pouch and walked down to the end of the street to the stage depot. The coach was already sitting out front and the hostlers were rigging up the team.

Although it had not snowed in nearly a week, there were still places where snow was on the ground in many places, some of which could not be avoided. As a result, Smoke had snow on his boots, but he stomped his feet on the porch, getting rid of as much as he could.

The stage depot was warm inside, and he saw five people standing around the potbellied stove, a man, two women, and a young boy. There were three more men over by the ticket counter and one of them, seeing Smoke, came toward him. He was an older man, with white hair and weathered skin. He stuck his hand out.

"Good morning, Mr. Jensen. I'm Frank Simmons."

"Call me Smoke," Smoke said. "You would be the shotgun guard?"

"Yes, sir, normally that would be me," Simmons said.

"Normally?"

"Well, the truth is, if you have that much money to look after, ever'one figures it'd be better if you'd just go ahead and ride shotgun yourself." Simmons held out his hands and both were shaking. "I got me this here palsy so bad, why, I couldn't no ways hold a gun to shoot. Only reason I go along now is to keep Puddin' company. We don't never carry nothin' worth stealin'. That is, until now."

"Puddin'?"

"That would be me," another man said, coming over to shake Smoke's hand. "Puddin' Taylor is the name. I'm the driver. You'll be sittin' up on the high board with me, if you don't mind."

"No, I figure that's probably the best place for me," Smoke said. "Not looking forward to getting that cold," he said.

"Ah don't worry none 'bout gettin' too cold," Puddin' said. "We keep us a really warm buffalo robe up there. Why, you'll be as warm as the folks down in the box with their wool blankets."

"Puddin'," someone called from the front door. "Your team is hitched up, you're all ready to go."

"Thanks, Charlie," Puddin' replied. "All right, folks, let's get on the stage. I'm 'bout ready to pull out."

Smoke went outside with the others and watched as the passengers boarded the coach, then wrapped themselves in blankets to ward off the cold. Smoke climbed up onto the high seat alongside Puddin', who then released the brake and snapped the ribbons over the team. The coach jerked forward, then moved at a clip faster than a brisk walk through the town and onto the road.

Dooley stood on a rock and looked down the road.

"What we stayin' here for?" Cletus asked. "It's cold up here."

"We're here because by the time the coach reaches this point, the driver will have to stop his team to give 'em a breather. That's when we'll hit them," Dooley said.

Cletus, Morgan, and Toomey were sitting on a fallen log about forty yards away from the road. Morgan got up and walked over to a bush to relieve himself. He began to giggle.

"What are you laughin' at?" Toomey asked.

"Lookie here when I pee," Morgan said. "There's smoke comin' from it."

"That ain't smoke, you idiot," Dooley said. "It's vapor, same thing as your breath when it's cold."

"That don't make no sense," Morgan said. "There ain't no breath a'comin' offin' my pee."

"Wait," Tommey said. "I'm goin' to see if I can piss smoke too."

"Quiet!" Dooley said sharply. "I think I hear somethin'."

In the distance, Dooley could hear the whistle and shouts of the driver as he urged his team up the long grade.

"They're comin'. Ever'one get ready," Dooley said, climbing down from the rock.

"Git up thar, git on with ya'!" Puddin' shouted, urging the straining team up the grade. He leaned over to spit a chew, and a wad of the expectorated tobacco hit the right front wheel, then rotated down.

"Will you be stopping at the top of the grade?" Smoke asked.

"Yeah," Puddin' answered as he wiped his mouth with the back of his hand. "We got to, else the team'll give out before we reach the next way station."

Smoke pulled his pistol and checked the loads.

"What you doin' that for?" Puddin' asked.

"If I were planning to hold up this stage, this is where I would do it," Smoke said.

"Yeah," Puddin' said, nodding. "Yeah, you're prob'ly right."

It took another ten minutes before the team reached the crest of the grade.

"Whoa!" Puddin' called, pulling back on the reins.

The team stopped and they sat there for a moment, with the only sound being the heavy breathing of the horses. Vapor came, not only from their breath, but from their skin, as the horses had generated a lot of heat during the long pull up the hill.

Suddenly three armed men jumped out in front of the stage. One of the men fired and his bullet hit Puddin' in the arm.

Even before the echo of that shot had died out, Smoke was returning fire, shooting three times in such rapid succession that all three of the would-be robbers went down.

"Puddin', are you all right?" Smoke asked.

"Yeah," Puddin' replied, his voice strained with pain. "It just hit me in the arm, didn't do nothin' to any of my vitals."

"What's happening? What's going on up there?" someone from inside the coach called. The door to the coach opened.

"No!" Smoke shouted. "Stay inside!"

With his pistol at the ready, Smoke climbed down from the driver's seat, then moved slowly, cautiously toward the three men he had just shot. That was when he heard hoof-beats and looking toward the sound, he saw a rider bending low over the neck of his horse as he kept the horse at a gallop.

Smoke raised his pistol and started to shoot, but decided that whoever it was offered no immediate danger, so he eased the hammer back down and examined the three men.

All three were dead, their faces contorted in grimaces of pain and surprise.

"Did you kill the sons of bitches?" Puddin' called.

"Yeah," Smoke said.

"Good."

"Keep everyone on the stage until I have a look around," Smoke said.

Smoke followed the tracks of the three would-be robbers back into the edge of the woods. There, he saw a fallen log. There was also enough disturbed snow around the log that he knew this was where the men had been waiting. He also saw three horses tied to a branch. He walked over to the animals and patted one of them on the neck.

"Don't worry," he said. "I'm not going to leave you out here. You didn't try to hold up the stage."

Further examination showed that there had been a fourth horse, and Smoke was satisfied that that was the horse of the man he had seen running away. Nobody else was here, or had been here.

Smoke came back out of the tree line leading the three horses. He stopped at the bodies of the three outlaws.

"See anyone else back there?" Puddin' asked.

"No, it's all clear," Smoke said. He began putting the bodies on the horses, belly down. "Don't know which one of you belongs to which," he said to the horses. "But I don't reckon it matters much now."

Puddin' tied off the team, then climbed down. "You folks can come out now," he called to his passengers. "If you need to, uh, rest yourselves, well, there's a pretty good place for the ladies over there," he said.

"Let me take a look at your arm," Smoke said. He tore some of Puddin's shirt away, then looked at the wound.

"How's it look?"

"It went all the way through. If it doesn't get festered, you should be all right." Smoke tore off another piece of the driver's shirt. "Give me a chaw of tobacco," he said. "I'll use it as a poltice."

The driver chewed up a wad of tobacco, then spit it into the cloth.

"Here too. I'll need it on the entry and exit wound."

Puddin' complied, then Smoke wrapped the bandage around his arm, putting the tobacco over each wound.

"There was another'n, wasn't there?" the driver asked as Smoke worked.

"Yes. But I don't expect we'll have any trouble with him."

The passengers came back from their rest stop then, and the boy, who was about eleven, walked back to look at the bodies draped over the horses.

"Timmy, come back here," the boy's mother said.

"Wow," Timmy said to Puddin'. "There were three of them and just two of you, but you beat 'em."

Puddin' shook his head. "Not two of us, son," he said. "Just one." He nodded toward Smoke, who had already climbed back up into the seat. "He did it all by himself."

"What kind of man could take down three armed outlaws all by himself?" one of the male passengers asked.

"Well, a man like Smoke Jensen, I reckon," Puddin' replied.

Dooley rode his horse at a gallop until he feared that the animal would drop dead on him. Then he got off and walked him until the horse's breathing returned to normal.

He had told Cletus and his nephews to stay out of sight until he gave the word to confront the stage. He'd had it all planned out, which included staying separated so as to deny the stage guard any opportunity to react.

But before he knew it, all three jumped up in front of the stage. At first, Dooley couldn't understand why they would do such a damn fool thing. But as he was riding away from the scene, he began thinking about it, and he was fairly certain that he had figured it out.

Dooley was convinced that Cletus and his two nephews had planned to rob the stage, then turn on him, keeping all the money for themselves. But it didn't work out that way for them because the shotgun guard killed all three.

What sort of man could take on three gunmen and kill all three? Dooley wondered.

From the moment he had learned of the money shipment, he had begun planning this robbery. He'd even taken a trip on the stage, just to make certain that he knew the route it would travel. That's how he'd learned about the long grade and the necessity of stopping to rest the horses.

But the shotgun guard on the trip he took was an old man with the shakes. He wouldn't have presented any trouble at all. In fact, Dooley even watched the coach depart two more times, and it had been the same guard for each trip. This guard today was new and, as it turned out, deadly.

Dooley resented the fact that he didn't get the money, but he was just as glad that Cletus and his nephews got themselves killed. As it turned out, they were nothing but a bunch of double-crossing bastards anyway.

4

"Folks, can I have your attention please?" Sheriff Carson called.

At the sheriff's call, everyone in Longmont's Saloon grew quiet and turned to see what he had to say.

Sheriff Carson smiled, then nodded toward a table where Smoke was sitting with Sally, Pearlie, Cal, and Louie Longmont, owner of Longmont's Saloon.

"As you all know, our own Smoke Jensen here foiled a robbery last week, and that's why we're here celebratin' with him and Sally." Sheriff Carson turned toward Smoke, and held up his mug of beer. "Smoke, if those no-'counts had managed to steal the money you were guarding, the folks around here would be in a lot more trouble than we are. I thank you, and the town thanks you."

"Hear, hear," Longmont said, and the others in the saloon applauded.

"Mr. Longmont, another round of drinks if you please," Joel Matthews said. "The bank is buying."

"All right!" someone shouted, and there was a rush to the bar.

"I'll get ours," Pearlie said, getting up from the table.

"I'll have a beer," Cal said.

"He'll have a sarsaparilla," Sally declared.

"Miss Sally I . . ." Cal began, but Smoke cut him off with a steely gaze. Cal was about to say that he drank beer all the time when he was out with just Smoke and Pearlie, but he knew that if he told her that now, Smoke would curtail those privileges.

"May I join you?" Matthews asked, coming over to the table.

"Yes, please do," Sally said with an inviting smile.

Matthews sat down, then pulled an envelope from his inside jacket pocket.

"Smoke, the board voted to give you a reward of three hundred dollars, in addition to the one hundred fifty you earned," Matthews said, handing the envelope to Smoke.

"Smoke!" Sally said happily. "That will pay our interest, plus allow us to keep the money we were going to use."

Smoke nodded. "Thanks, Joel."

"I just wish it could be more," he said. "I wish it could be enough to pay off your entire note."

"Well, with the extension this will buy for me, maybe we'll come up with a way of handling that note," Smoke said.

At that moment, Emil Blanton came into the saloon, carrying a large pile of papers. Blanton was publisher of the local newspaper, the *Big Rock Vindicator*. Smiling, he brought one of the newspapers over to Smoke.

"Since you are the star of my story, I thought I might give you a free copy," Blanton said, holding it up for Smoke and the others to see.

SMOKE JENSEN
FOILS ROBBERY ATTEMPT.

On the 9th instant, the well-known local rancher Smoke Jensen volunteered his services as a shotgun guard for the Sulphur Springs Express Company. The reason for this was a special shipment of twenty thousand dollars, said money to be made available at the Bank of Big Rock in order to provide loans for those of the area who have been made desperate by the brutal winter conditions.

According to Mr. Puddin' Taylor, who was the driver of the coach, the would-be robbers accosted them just as they reached the top of McDill Pass. Before Taylor could question the intent of the three who had flagged down the coach, the highwaymen presented pistols, and opened fire with mixed effect. Mr. Taylor was wounded, but the other bullets missed. Smoke Jensen fired back, but not until after the robbers had fired first.

Smoke Jensen, as his reputation so nobly suggests, did not miss. Within scarcely more than the blink of an eye, all three outlaws were sent on their way to eternity, where they will be forced to plead their case before St. Peter and all the angels of heaven.

This newspaper joins other citizens of the fair city of Big Rock in congratulating Smoke Jensen for his quick thinking and courageous action.

Ebenezer Dooley was at the Cow Bell Saloon in the small town of Antinito, Colorado. A traveler had left a copy of the Big Rock newspaper in the saloon, and because Dooley had nothing else to do, he picked it up, took it over to an empty table, and began reading it.

The paper was over two weeks old, but that didn't matter because it had been several weeks since Dooley had read any news at all. He read about his botched robbery attempt.

"Smoke Jensen," Dooley said, scratching his beard as he read the weathered newspaper. "That's the name of the son of a bitch who stole my money."

Dooley folded the newspaper and put it in his pocket. "I'll be keepin' that in my memory."

"Beg your pardon?" the man at the next table over said.

"Nothin'," Dooley said. "I was just talkin' to myself, is all."

The man laughed. "I do that my ownself sometimes," he replied. "I guess when you're used to talkin' to your horse all the time, why, a man will sometimes just wind up talkin' to hisself."

"I guess so," Dooley said, not that interested in getting into a conversation with the man.

"You was readin' about Jensen, wasn't you? Smoke Jensen."

"Yeah," Dooley said. "Yeah, I was. How did you know?"

"You spoke his name."

"Oh, yeah, I guess I did."

"You know him?"

"No, I, uh, ran across him once," Dooley replied.

"So you wouldn't say he's a friend of yours?"

Dooley shook his head. "He ain't no friend. Do you know him?"

"Well, we ain't ever actual met, but I know who the son of a bitch is. He kilt my brother."

"He killed your brother? Why isn't he in prison for that?"

"Well, my brother was rustlin' some of Jensen's cattle at the time."

"Where were you when that happened?"

"I was in prison."

Suddenly Dooley smiled. "I'll be damned," he said. "I know who you are. You're Curt Logan, aren't you?"

Logan smiled, then picked up his glass and moved over to join Dooley. "I was wonderin' when you would recognize me. I mean, I recognized you right off. Course, we was in different cell blocks, so we didn't see each other all that many times. Then I done my time and got out." Logan looked puzzled. "What are you doin' out? I thought you was supposed to be doin' twenty years."

"Well, let's just say that the State of Colorado had its idea of when I should leave, and I had mine," Dooley said.

Logan chuckled. "I'll be damned. You escaped, didn't you?"

"Yes, I did. Fact is, you could get five hundred dollars just for turning me in to the law."

"Is that a fact?"

"It is," Dooley said. "But I'm not worried about you doin' that."

"Why not?"

"Because I know somethin' that would be worth a lot more than five hundred dollars to you. That is, if you are interested."

Logan nodded. "I'm interested," he said.

"What have you been doin' since you got out?" Dooley asked.

"Tryin' to make a livin'," Logan said. "I've punched some cows, worked at a freight yard, mucked out a few stalls."

"Haven't found anything to your likin', though, have you?"

Logan chuckled. "What's there to like about any of that?"

"I might have an idea," Dooley said, "if I can get enough men together."

"How many do you need?"

"Besides the two of us, I'd say about four more."

"Six men? Damn, what you plannin' to do? Rob a bank?"

Dooley smiled again. "Well, that's where the money is, ain't it?"

Smoke sat in his saddle and watched as his hands dragged the dead cattle into large piles, then burned them. It was the only way to clear away the carnage left from the brutal winter just passed. He and all the cowboys were wearing kerchiefs tied around their noses to help keep out the stench.

When the pile was large enough, Pearlie and Cal rode around the carcasses, soaking them with coal oil. Their horses, put off by the smell of death, were skittish, and would occasionally break into a quick gallop away. Cal's horse did that, reacting so quickly that Cal dropped the can of kerosene.

"Whoa! Hold it, hold it!" Cal shouted, fighting his mount. Cal was an exceptionally skilled rider who sometimes broke horses for fun. Because of that, he generally rode the most spirited horses, and not many of the other riders would have been able to stay seated. Cal rode easily, gracefully, until he got the horse under control again.

When the gallop was over, Cal brought his reluctant horse back to the task at hand, bending over from the saddle to retrieve the can he had dropped.

Finally, when the pile of dead cows had been sufficiently dosed with kerosene, Pearlie lit a match and dropped it onto one of the animals. The match caught, and within a few minutes, large flames were leaping up from the pile.

Pearlie and Cal rode back to where Smoke was, then reined up alongside him and turned to watch the fire.

"It's like a barbeque," Cal said.

"If it is, it's the most expensive barbeque you'll ever see," Pearlie said.

"Yeah," Smoke said, answering in one, clipped word.

"Sally," Smoke said that night as they lay in bed. There was agony in the sound of his voice.

"Yes?"

"I had to let all the men go today."

"I figured as much. I saw them all riding off."

"I even let Pearlie and Cal go."

"Oh," Sally said.

"Don't worry. They aren't going anywhere. I explained

that I cannot pay them, but they said they would stay anyway."

"Yes," Sally said. "I figured they would."

"We can't do it," Smoke said. He sighed. "We lost too many head. Even if we sold every cow we have left, we wouldn't make enough money to pay off the note on the ranch."

"Oh, Smoke," Sally said, putting her head on his shoulder.

"I've let you down," Smoke said. "I've failed you."

"No, you haven't let me down, and you haven't failed. You had no control over the weather."

"That's true, I had no control over the weather," Smoke said. "But if I hadn't borrowed so much money against the ranch, we could have ridden out this winter. Now, we're going to lose Sugarloaf. And I know how much you love this place."

"Oh, you silly darling," Sally said. "I do love this place, but don't you know that I love you much more? In fact, I love this place because of you. And no matter where we go, or what we have to do, it will be fine as long as we are together."

"Yeah," Smoke said. He tightened his arm around her. "That's good to know, but it doesn't make me any less a failure."

They lay in silence for a moment longer before Sally spoke again.

"We don't have to lose this place," she said.

"You have an idea as to how to save it?"

"Yes. Don't you remember? I told you about it last winter."

"You're talking about leasing the ranch, aren't you?"

"Yes."

Smoke sighed. "I don't want to do that. I don't want to give up control of my own place."

"But it would only be temporary. You would give up

control for one year. Surely that would be better than losing the ranch, and giving up control forever?" Sally insisted.

Smoke didn't answer for a moment, and Sally thought about pressing her case, but she held back. She had lived with Smoke long enough to know that he was thinking it through.

"All right," he finally said. "Suppose I decide to do this, what would be the first step?"

"There is a land broker's office in Denver," Sally said. "I saved the address. We can go there and talk to him."

"No, you stay here with the ranch," Smoke said. "It's ours for thirty more days. I wouldn't want to give anyone the wrong idea that we were abandoning it, and someone might think that is exactly what is happening if we both leave."

"All right, I'll stay."

"Besides, if we do lease the ranch, I expect the tenants will want to live in this house. So you, Pearlie, and Cal need to find someplace for us to go. The line shack over on Big Sandy might work. It's the biggest of all of them."

"We'll get it in shape while you're gone," Sally said.

"I hate having to ask you to live in such a place."

"It will be fine, Smoke, you'll see," Sally said. "I'll have it looking really nice by the time we move in. And it's only a year; then we'll be back in our own house."

"The Lord willing," Smoke said.

"Smoke, when you make the deal, don't forget that you must get the money in advance, in order to be able to pay the note."

"I know," Smoke said. "Don't worry, I will."

"It's going to be all right, Smoke," Sally said. "I know it will."

"Pearlie?"

Cal got no response.

"Pearlie?" he called again.

Although the bunkhouse had beds enough for twelve cowboys, Cal and Pearlie were the only two occupants at the present time.

Cal sat up in the darkness. He couldn't see Pearlie, but he could hear him snoring.

"Pearlie!" he said again.

"What?" Pearlie answered, sitting up quickly. "What's happening?"

"Are you asleep?" Cal asked.

Pearlie let out an audible sigh, then fell back in his bed.

"Well, I *was* asleep," Pearlie said.

"Oh. Well, then, I won't bother you."

Pearlie got out of his bunk, then walked over to Cal's bunk. He jerked all the covers off Cal.

"Hey, what did you do that for?" Cal shouted, reaching for the covers that Pearlie was holding away from him. "Give me my covers."

Pearlie handed him his covers, then sat back down on his bunk. "I'm listening now," he said. "So tell me what was so important that you had to wake me up." Pearlie ran his hand over the puff of purple flesh that was on his chest, the result of a bullet wound.

"We was goin' to bury you under the aspen trees," Cal said.

"What?"

"Last year, when we was down to the Santa Gertrudis Ranch, helpin' out Captain King, you got shot, remember?"

Pearlie laughed. "Well, Cal, that ain't somethin' that you just forget all that easy."

"Anyway, we didn't figure you'd live until we got you home, so we was already plannin' your funeral. We decided to, that is, Miss Sally decided to bury you under the aspen trees. That would'a been a real pretty spot too."

"Sorry it didn't work out for you," Pearlie said, teasing.

"Cal, please tell me you didn't wake me up just to tell me where you had planned to bury me."

"Miss Sally planned."

"All right, Miss Sally planned. Is that why you woke me up?"

"No."

"Then why did you?"

"I'm worried," Cal said. "What if Smoke can't get the money? I mean, he's got to come up with all that money in less than a month. I can't see no way he's goin' to be able to do that."

"He's been in some tough spots before," Pearlie said. "I reckon it'll work out all right."

"What if he don't?"

"What do you mean?"

"What if he don't get the money? Then he'll lose the ranch. And if he does, then where will we go? What will become of us?"

"Cal, are you worried about Smoke? Or are you worried about us?" Pearlie asked.

Cal ran his hand through his hair. "I guess I'm worried about both," he said.

"Well, at least you are honest about it," Pearlie said. "Truth is, I don't know what will become of us."

"You know what I think? I think we ought to leave," Cal said.

"Leave? You mean run out on Smoke and Miss Sally?"

"No, not run out on them," Cal said. "Just leave, so they don't have us to have to feed and worry about."

"Yeah," Pearlie said. "Yeah, I see what you mean."

"I think we ought to go now," Cal said.

"You mean just leave, without so much as a fare-thee-well?"

"Yes," Cal said. "Think about it, Pearlie. If we stick around long enough to tell them good-bye, you know what they are going to do. They are going to try and talk us into stayin' on."

"Maybe they need us to stay on."

Cal shook his head. "No, right now, we're a burden to

'em. I know how it is, Pearlie. I was on my own when I was twelve 'cause I didn't have no family to speak of, and I didn't want to be a burden to nobody."

"All right, we'll go," Pearlie said. "But I ain't goin' without leavin' 'em a letter. There ain't no way I'm goin' to just run out on 'em. Not after all the things they have done for us.'"

"I agree," Cal said. "The least we can do is leave 'em a letter tellin' 'em what happened to us."

5

"Smoke!"

Smoke was in the bedroom, packing for his trip, but the anguish in Sally's call to him caused him to drop the saddlebags on the bed and hurry to the kitchen. He saw her standing just inside the kitchen door, leaning against the counter. She was holding a letter in one hand, while her other hand was covering her mouth. Her eyes had welled with tears.

"What is it?" Smoke asked. "What has happened?"

"They are gone," Sally said in a strained voice.

"Who is gone? What are you talking about?"

"It's Pearlie and Cal," she said. "When I went out to the bunkhouse to call them in for breakfast, they weren't there, and all their stuff was gone. I found this lying on Pearlie's bunk." Sally handed Smoke a sheet of paper.

Smoke read the letter.

Dear Smoke and Miss Sally,

By the time you get this letter, me and Cal will be gone. We figure, what with all the problems you're havin' with the ranch and all, that you don't really need two more mouths to feed. And since you ain't got no cows to speak of, why, there ain't enough work to justify you keepin' us on just so's you can feed us.

*We are both grateful for all the good things you two
has done for us, and for all the good times we've had
together. I know you ain't either one of you old enough
to be our parents, but it's almost like that's just what
you are, the way you have took care of us and looked
out for us for all this time.*

*I hope you can save the ranch somehow. We'll be
looking in now and again to see how it is that you are
faring, and if we see that you got the ranch all put back
together again, why, we'll come back and work for you
again. Fact is, if we can find work now, why, me and
Cal has both said that we'll be sending some money
along to help you out.*

> *Your good friends,*
> *Pearlie and Cal*

"I can't believe they would do something like that to us,"
Smoke said.

"Oh, Smoke, I don't think they believe they are doing it
to us. I think they believe they are doing it for us."

"Well, that's just it. They didn't think," Smoke said. He
sighed. "That means you are going to be here all alone while
I'm gone. Will you be all right?"

"Why, Kirby Jensen," Sally said. "How dare you ask me
such a question?"

Smoke chuckled. "You're right," he said. "That was pretty
stupid of me. I pity the poor fool who would try and break
in here while I'm gone."

"Did you pack your white shirt and jacket? I think you
should wear that when you talk to the broker."

"I packed it," Smoke said. He put his hands on her shoulders. "It's a long ride to Denver," he said. "I'll be gone for at
least two weeks, maybe a little longer. I'll send you a
telegram when I get there, just to let you know that I arrived
all right. Then I'll send you another one when I get something worked out with the broker."

"I'll miss you terribly, but I'll be here when you get back,"

Sally said. "I'll spend the time while you are gone getting the line house ready for us. I intend to move some of my favorite pieces of furniture down there."

"How are you going to move them with Pearlie and Cal gone?"

"I'll go into town and ask Mr. Longmont to find someone to help me," Sally said. "Don't worry, I'll take care of it."

They kissed, and as the kiss deepened, Sally pulled away and looked up at him with a smile on her face.

"What would it hurt if you left an hour later?" she asked.

Smoke returned her smile. "Why, I don't think it would hurt at all," he said as he led her toward their bedroom.

It was just after dark when Pearlie and Cal rode into Floravista, New Mexico Territory. From the small adobe houses on the outskirts of town, dim lights flickered through shuttered windows. The kitchens of the houses emitted enticing smells of suppers being cooked, from the familiar aromas of fried chicken to the more exotic and spicy bouquets of Mexican fare.

A barking dog ended its yapping with a high-pitched yelp, as if it had been kicked, or hit by a thrown rock.

A baby cried, its loud keening cutting through the night.

A housewife raised her voice in one of the houses, launching into some private tirade about something, sharing her anger with all who were within earshot.

The main part of Floravista was a contrast of dark and light. Commercial buildings such as stores and offices were closed and dark, but the saloons and cantinas were brightly lit and they splashed pools of light out onto the wood-plank sidewalks and on into the street. As Pearlie and Cal rode down the street, they passed in and out of those pools of light so that to anyone watching, they would be seen, then unseen, then seen again. The footfalls of their horses made a hollow clumping sound, echoing back from the false-fronted buildings as they passed them by.

By the time they reached the center of town, the night was alive with a cacophony of sound: music from a tinny piano, a strumming guitar, and an out-of-tune vocalist, augmented by the high-pitched laughter of women and the deep guffaw of men. From somewhere in the Mexican part of town, a trumpet was playing.

Pearlie and Cal dismounted in front of the Oasis Saloon, tied their horses to the hitching rail, then went inside. Dozens of lanterns scattered throughout the saloon emitted enough light to read by, though drifting clouds of tobacco smoke diffused the golden light.

As they stood for a moment just inside the door, Cal happened to see a pickpocket relieve someone of his wallet. The thief's victim was a middle-aged man who was leaning over the bar, drinking a beer and enjoying his conversation. While he was thus engaged, the nimble-fingered pickpocket deftly slipped the victim's billfold from his back pocket. Instead of putting the billfold in his pocket, though, the thief walked down to the end of the bar and, casually, dropped it into a potted plant. Then the thief ordered a beer and stood there, drinking it casually.

"Pearlie, did you see that?" Cal asked.

"Yeah, I saw it," Pearlie answered.

"Maybe we should. . . ."

"Wait," Pearlie said. "Let's see what happens."

The victim ordered a second beer, then reached for his pocket to get the money to pay. That's when he realized that his billfold was gone.

Puzzled by the absence of his billfold, the man looked on the floor to see if he had dropped it. Then he picked up his hat, which was lying on the bar, to see if it was there.

"Hey," the man called. "Has anybody seen my billfold?"

"I know where it is," Cal said.

Cal and Pearlie were still standing in the middle of the floor, having just come in.

"You know where my wallet is?" the man replied in disbelief.

"Yes, sir, I know where it is."

"Well, where is it?"

Cal pointed to the potted plant that sat on the floor at the end of the bar.

"It's down there under that plant," Cal said.

The victim looked toward the plant; then he turned back toward Cal. "Now how in the hell would it wind up down there?" he asked. "I haven't moved from this spot since I got here."

The pickpocket, suddenly sensing danger, put his beer down and started walking toward the door. As he did, Pearlie stepped in front of him to stop him.

"Here, get out of my way," the pickpocket growled. "What are you doing?"

Cal pointed to the pickpocket Pearlie had stopped. "Your billfold is in that pot, because this fella put it there. Only, he didn't put it there until after he took all the money from it and stuck it down into his own pocket."

"What?" the pickpocket said. "Mister, are you crazy? I just come in here to have a beer."

"And steal some money," Pearlie added.

By now the confrontation had stopped all conversation as everyone looked toward Pearlie, Cal, and the pickpocket.

"I ain't goin' to stand around here and be accused of stealin'," the pickpocket said. He pointed toward the bartender. "What kind of place are you running here anyway? Do you just let anyone accuse an innocent person of picking someone's pocket?"

The barkeep brought a double-barrel shotgun up from under the bar, and though he didn't point it at anyone, its very presence lent some authority to his next comment.

"Mr. Thornton, you want to step down there and look in the potted plant and see if your wallet is there?" the bartender asked.

The men who were standing at the bar between Thornton and the potted plant stepped back to let him by. He walked to it, then looked down inside.

"I'll be damned!" he said. "He's right! My wallet is here!" Thornton reached down into the pot, then came up with the wallet, holding it high for everyone in the saloon to see.

There was an immediate reaction from all the other patrons.

"Any son of a bitch who would steal another man's wallet ought to be strung up," someone said.

"Or at least tarred and feathered," another added.

"I don't know what you are talkin' about," the pickpocket said, his voice and expression showing his anxiousness. "I didn't put that there."

"Is your money gone, Mr. Thornton?" Pearlie asked.

Thornton opened his wallet and looked inside.

"Yes!" he said. "Every dollar of it is gone."

Pearlie stuck his hand down into the pickpocket's vest pocket and took out some folded bills. He handed the bills to the bartender.

"Hey! That's my money!" the pickpocket said. "You all seen it. He just stole my money!"

"How much money did you have in your billfold?" Pearlie asked.

"I had nineteen dollars," Thornton answered. "Three fives and four ones."

The bartender counted the folded bills, then held them up. "Three fives and four ones," he announced to all.

The pickpocket tried to run, but two men grabbed him, then hustled him out of the saloon bound for the sheriff's office.

"Well, now, I would like to thank you two boys," the victim said, extending his hand. "The name is Thornton. Michael Thornton."

"I'm Pearlie, this here is Cal," Pearlie said, shaking Thornton's hand.

"Pearlie and Cal, eh? Well, I reckon that's good enough for me. Could I buy you boys a drink?"

"Later, perhaps, after we've had our supper," Pearlie

replied. "That is, if a fella can get anything to eat in here," he added to the bartender. "Do you serve food?"

"Steak and potatoes, ham and eggs, your choice," the bartender replied.

"Yes."

"Yes, which?"

"Yes, we'll have steak and potatoes, ham and eggs," Pearlie said.

Thornton laughed. "These young men are hungry," he said. "Bring them whatever they want. I'll pay for it."

"You don't need to buy our supper," Pearlie said. "We were just doin' what we figured was right."

"I know I don't need to. It's just my way of thanking you."

"If you really want to thank us, you can tell us where we might find a job in this town," Cal said.

"You two boys are looking for a job?"

"Yes, sir," Cal answered.

"You aren't afraid of hard work, are you?" Thornton asked.

"Not if it's honest."

"Good enough. I own the livery," Thornton said. "I can always use a couple of good men if you are interested."

"We're interested," Pearlie said.

"Then the job is yours."

6

Ebenezer Dooley turned in his saddle and looked at the five men who were with him. Buford Yancey, Fargo Masters, and Ford DeLorian were men he had worked with before. He had never worked with Logan, but he vaguely remembered him from their time together in prison. Curt Logan had brought along his brother, Trace, as the fifth man. Curt and Trace Logan were wearing identical red and black plaid shirts.

Dooley spit out a wad of tobacco as he stared at the two brothers.

"Logan, would you tell me why in the hell you and your brother are wearing those shirts? Don't you know they stand out like a sore thumb? Ever'one in town is goin' to see 'em, and remember 'em."

"There's likely to be some shootin', ain't there?" Curt Logan asked.

"I told you there might be. Robbin' a bank ain't like stealin' nickels off a dead man's eyes."

"Well, I already lost me one brother when he got hisself kilt by Smoke Jensen, and I don't plan to lose me another'n. That's why Trace 'n me is wearin' these here plaid shirts."

Dooley shook his head in confusion. "What's wearing a shirt like that got to do with it?"

"Things gets real confusin' when there's a lot of shootin' goin' on, and I don't plan for me'n my brother to shoot each other by mistake. As long as we're wearin' these here shirts, that ain't likely to happen."

"If you lead the posse to us 'cause of them shirts, I'll be doin' the shootin' my ownself," Dooley growled.

"Dooley," Fargo said. "The sun's gettin' on up. I figure it's nine o'clock for sure. The bank'll be open by now."

"Right," Dooley said. "All right, men, anybody got to take a piss, now's the time to do it."

Three of the men dismounted to relieve themselves, then all remounted and looked at Dooley.

"Fargo, you, Ford, and Yancey will ride into town from the south end. Me'n the Logans will come in from the north. That way, we won't be drawin' no attention on account of so many ridin' together."

"All right," Fargo said. "Come on, boys," he said to the others. "We'll need to get around to the other side."

Jason Turnball, the city marshal for the town of Etna, was a big man, standing almost six feet six and weighing well over two hundred pounds. He was sitting in a chair on the porch in front of Dunnigan's General Store. Dunnigan had reinforced the chair just for the marshal, because he liked having the marshal parked on his front porch. That tended to keep away anyone who might get the idea to rob the store, almost as if he had hired his own personal guard.

Marshal Turnball had his feet propped up on the porch railing, and his chair tipped onto the back two legs. He was peeling an apple, and one long peel hung from the apple all the way to the porch.

Billy Frakes, an eighteen-year-old who worked as a store clerk for Dunnigan, was sweeping the front porch.

"I tell you true, Marshal Turnball," Frakes said. "I believe that's about the longest peel you've ever pared."

"Nah," Turnball said as he cut it off at the end, then held

it up for examination. "I've done longer." He tossed the peeling to the bluetick hound that lived under the porch. The dog grabbed the peel, then backed up against the front wall to eat it.

"Look at them folks," Frakes said, pointing to the three riders who passed by in front of the store. "Two of 'em's got shirts just alike."

Turnball laughed. "Wouldn't think two of 'em would be dumb enough to wear a shirt that ugly, would you?"

Frakes laughed with him.

Fargo, Ford, and Yancey reached the bank just before Dooley and the Logan brothers. They stopped across the street from the bank and dismounted in front of a leather goods store. Yancey and Fargo examined a pair of boots in the window, while Ford dismounted and held the reins of the three horses. Dooley and the Logans arrived then, and Dooley nodded at Fargo, just before he and the Logans went into the bank.

"That's funny," Frakes said.

"What's funny?" Turnball replied.

"Them fellas over there in front of Sikes Leather Goods. How come you reckon that one is holdin' the horses, 'stead of tyin' 'em off at the hitchin' rail?"

"Maybe them other two just wanted to look at the boots and they was goin' to ride on," Turnball suggested.

"Well, if they're just wantin' 'em some boots, maybe one 'em would be interested in buyin' a pair of boots I just made," Frakes said. "I think I'll go down there an' see."

"If you go down there and sell your boots in front of Al Sikes's store, takin' business away from him, you never will get him to sell your boots for you," Turnball said.

"No, sir. I think it's just the opposite. If Mr. Sikes seen that folks would be willin' to buy boots that I've made, why, that might just make him want to sell 'em in his store," Frakes insisted as he stood the broom up against the wall. He stepped inside Dunnigan's for just a moment, then came back out carrying the boots he had made. He held them out for the marshal's inspection.

"What do you think of 'em?" he asked.

"They're good-lookin' boots all right," Turnball agreed. "Can't nobody say you don't do good work."

Smiling under Turnball's praise, Frakes started down the street toward Sikes Leather Goods.

Trace Logan stayed out front holding the horses, while his brother Curt and Dooley went into the bank. There were only two people inside the bank, Rob Clark, the owner, and Tucker Patterson, the teller. Both were just behind the teller's cage, and Patterson looked up as the two men came inside.

"Yes, sir," Patterson said. "Can I help you gent . . ." he began. Then he paused and gasped as he saw that both men were wearing hoods over their faces. They were also holding guns.

"This here is a holdup," Dooley said in a gruff voice. He held up a cloth bag. "Fill this bag with money."

"Mr. Clark?" Patterson said. "What shall I do?"

Dooley pointed his pistol at Clark and pulled the hammer back. It made a deadly-sounding click.

"Yeah, tell him, Mr. Clark," Dooley said. "What should he do?"

"T-Tucker," Clark said in a frightened voice. "I think you had better do what the man says."

"Yes, sir," Patterson said.

"Now you're getting smart," Dooley said.

Patterson started taking money from the cash drawer and putting it into the sack.

"Take a look out in the street," Dooley said to Curt. "Anybody comin' in?"

"Don't see nobody," Curt answered.

"That's all the money we've got," Patterson said, handing the sack back.

Dooley looked down into the sack. "There's not more'n a couple hundred dollars here," he said. "I know you got more'n that. I want the money from the safe."

"I . . . I don't have the combination to the safe," Patterson said. "Only the bank president has the combination."

"Where is the bank president?"

Patterson glanced toward Clark, but he said nothing.

"I see," Dooley said. "All right, Mr. Bank President, I'll ask you to open the safe."

Clark didn't move.

Dooley pointed his gun at Patterson. "Open the safe or I'll kill him right now," Dooley growled.

"Mr. Clark, please!" Patterson begged.

Nodding reluctantly, Clark walked over to the safe. Within a few minutes he had the door open. Dooley could see several small, filled bank bags inside.

"Damn!" Curt Logan said with a low whistle. "Have you ever seen so much money?"

"Put them bank bags in the sack," Dooley ordered, handing the sack over to Clark.

"What's takin' 'em so long?" Yancey asked, looking back toward the bank.

"Maybe there's lots of money and it's takin' 'em a while to get it all," Fargo suggested. "You don't worry about them; you just do the job you're supposed to be doin'. Keep a lookout all around you."

"There ain't nobody payin' no attention to the bank," Yancey said.

"Fargo, Yancey, there's someone comin'," Ford called from his position holding the horses.

"Where? Who?" Fargo asked.

"Up there," Ford said, nodding. "He's comin' right for us."

"He's carryin' a pair of boots," Yancey said. "Maybe he bought some boots here and he's bringin' 'em back."

"This is a hell of a time for him to be doin' that," Fargo said.

At that moment, Dooley and Curt Logan ran from the bank, still wearing hoods over their faces. Clark appeared in the front door of the bank, right behind them. He was carrying a pistol, and he fired it at the three men as they were getting mounted.

"Holdup!" Clark shouted. "Bank robbery! These men just robbed the bank!"

Dooley and both of the Logan brothers shot back at the banker, and Clark dropped his gun, then fell back into the bank.

"Shoot up the town, boys!" Dooley shouted. "Keep ever'one's head down!"

Frakes, who was nearly to the leather goods store by then, was surprised to see that the three men he was coming to see were also part of the robbery. He dropped his boots and ran as they began shooting up and down the street, aiming as well at the buildings. Window glass was shattered as the bullets crashed through.

One of the bullets hit the supporting post of the awning in front of the meat market, just as Frakes stepped up onto the porch. Frakes turned, and dived into the watering trough right in front of the meat market. Sinking to the bottom, he could hear the continuing sound of shots being fired, though now it was muffled by the water. Frakes held his breath as long as he could, then lifted his head up, gasping for air. By that time he could see the six men just crossing over the Denver and New Orleans railroad track. They galloped out of town, headed almost due west toward Thunder Butte, which rose some twenty miles away.

Frakes climbed out of the trough and stood in the street alongside, dripping water. The town was in a turmoil with men yelling at each other, dogs barking, and children crying. Several men were running toward the bank.

"Was anybody hit?" someone asked.

"Help me," Patterson was calling from the front of the bank. "Help me, somebody! Mr. Clark has been shot!"

By now there were several men gathered at the bank and as Frakes started toward it, he saw Dr. Urban going there as well. Urban was carrying his medical bag, and when he reached the bank he started shouting at the people to let him through.

"It's the doc," someone said. "Let him through."

Frakes went over as well, and because there were too many people crowded around for him to see, he climbed up on the railing. That gave him a good view, and he saw Dr. Urban kneeling beside Clark's prostrate form.

"How is he, Doc?" someone asked.

Dr. Urban put his fingers to Clark's neck, held them there for a moment, then shook his head.

"He's gone," Dr. Urban said.

"Somebody better go tell Mrs. Clark," Tucker Patterson said.

Dr. Urban looked up at Patterson. "Well, Mr. Patterson, I expect that should be you," he said. "You know her better than anyone else."

Gulping, Patterson nodded. "I expect that's so," he said.

"Did anyone get a good look at the ones who did this?" Turnball asked.

"Marshal, it was them same fellas we seen comin' into town," Frakes said. "The ones with them plaid shirts."

"Yeah, I seen them shirts too," one of the other townspeople said.

"That's right, Marshal," Patterson said. "Two of them were wearing red and black plaid shirts."

"Did you see their faces?" Turnball asked Patterson.

Patterson shook his head. "No, I didn't see their faces. They had their faces covered with hoods."

"The ones outside wasn't wearin' hoods," someone said.

"Yeah, well, wearin' hoods or not don't make no difference," one of the others said. "Near'bout all of us seen them shirts. You can't hide a shirt like that."

"You goin' after them, Marshal?"

"There are six of them," Turnball said.

"I don't care how many of 'em there is, they got our money. Hell, after this winter we just come through, that's near'bout all the money the town has left."

"I'll need a posse."

"I'll ride with you."

"Me too."

"You can count on me."

"I'll ride with you, Marshal," Frakes said.

"All right, men, get yourselves a gun, have your women put together two, maybe three days' food, get mounted, and meet me in front of my office."

"When?"

"I figure you should all be ready within an hour."

"An hour? Marshal, them outlaws can get a long ways in an hour," one of the men said. Like Turnball, he was wearing a badge, because this was Turnball's deputy.

"Pike, they've already got fifteen minutes on us," Turnball said. "If we go off half-cocked now, we ain't got a snowball's chance in hell of catchin' up to them. Best thing for us to do is be prepared. Now, are you plannin' on riding with the posse or not?"

"You know I'm goin'," Pike said. "I'm your deputy, ain't I?"

"Then get you some food, then get on back down to the office and wait until we are ready to go."

"All right, all right," Pike said. "I just don't want them sons of bitches to get away, that's all."

Turnball looked at the others, who seemed to be standing around awaiting further instructions. "What are you all a'waitin' on? Now!" he said gruffly, and with that, the posse scattered.

"Marshal, you want I should get some cuffs so we can cuff 'em when we find 'em?" Pike asked.

"Of course," Turnball said. "Unless you were plannin' on just askin' them not to try and get away."

"No, it's not that, it's just that I thought, well . . ." Pike hesitated.

"You thought what?"

"I wasn't all that sure we would be bringin' 'em back in, if you know what I mean."

"No, I don't know what you mean."

"I mean men like that, shootin' down Mr. Clark and stealin' all the town's money like they done. Well, some folks might think they don't have no right to be brought back in alive."

"Pike, I'm going to pretend I didn't hear that," Turnball said.

"It's not like I'm talkin' lynchin' or anything," Pike said. "I meant, uh, well, I meant, what if they put up a fight and we have to kill 'em? I mean, all legal like."

"Now, you get back down to the office and get ready, like I said."

"Sure, Marshal, sure," Pike said. "Like I said, I didn't really mean nothin' by it. I was just thinkin' on what might happen, is all."

"Do me a favor, will you, Pike? Don't think," Marshal Turnball said.

Smoke was riding north through a level forest. Just behind him a boulder-covered hillside rose almost ten thousand feet to the wooded and still-snow-covered peak of Thunder Butte. It was getting toward midday when Stormy started limping and Smoke had to stop. He had just lifted the left foreleg of his horse to look at the foot when he saw six men riding toward him.

Smoke didn't pay that much attention to them at first. He was on relatively level ground, which meant that anyone who was traveling through here would have to come in his general direction. Right now his biggest concern at the moment was the shoe. But the approaching horses made an obvious turn so that they began moving directly toward him.

Smoke had no idea what they wanted, so he kept an eye on them as he examined Stormy's hoof. He saw that the horse had picked up a rock between the shoe and the hoof, so he started working to get it out.

The riders came right up to him, then reined to an abrupt halt. Smoke looked up at them again.

"Howdy," he said.

"Howdy," one of the riders—a man with a long, pock-marked face and a drooping eyelid—said, swinging down from his horse. The other five riders dismounted as well.

There was something peculiar about the riders, the way they all dismounted and the way they stared at him. It was also curious how they let one man do all the talking. Two of the riders were wearing identical red and black plaid shirts, and as he looked at them more closely, he saw that they looked enough alike that they must be brothers. He didn't have a good feeling about the whole situation, and he decided that the quicker they left, the better it would be.

"Are you havin' any trouble?" the man with the pock-marked face and drooping eyelid asked.

"Nothing I can't handle," Smoke answered. He squinted at the men. "You folks headed anywhere in particular?"

"Yeah, we're lookin' for work," the man with the drooping eyelid said.

Smoke shrugged. "Don't know as you'll have too much luck there. The winter was pretty bad on most of the ranches. What few spring roundups there were are probably over now. Far as I know, none of the ranches are hiring. Maybe if you go farther south, down into New Mexico Territory where the winter wasn't so bad, you'll have some luck."

"What are you trying to do, mister? Put a shoe on a split hoof?" one of the men in a plaid shirt asked.

Smoke should have known better than to fall for an old trick like that, but out of concern for the horse, he looked at Stormy's foot. That was when one of the other riders stepped up and slammed the butt of his pistol down on Smoke's head. After that, everything went black.

7

Opening his eyes, Smoke discovered that he was lying facedown in the dirt. He had no idea where he was or why he was lying on the ground, though he sensed that there were several people standing around, looking down at him.

His head throbbed and his brain seemed unable to work. Who were these people and why were they here? For that matter, why was he here?

Smoke tried to get up, but everything started spinning so badly that he nearly passed out again. He was conscious of a terrible pain on the top of his head, and when he reached up and touched the spot gingerly, his fingers came away sticky with blood. Holding his fingers in front of his eyes, he stared at them in surprise. That was when he saw his shirt sleeve. He was not wearing the blue shirt he had started out with that morning. Instead, he was wearing a red and black plaid shirt . . . one of the shirts he had seen on the men who had accosted him.

"What happened?" Smoke asked. His tongue was thick, as though he had been drinking too much.

"I'll tell you what happened, mister. Looks to me like there was a fallin' out among thieves," a gruff voice said. "The other boys turned on you, didn't they? They knocked you out and took the money for themselves."

Smoke got up slowly, trying to make sense of things. He wasn't sure what the man was suggesting, so he just hesitated.

"That's right, ain't it?" the man asked. The man talking to him was a very big man, wearing a tan buckskin vest over a red shirt. Peeking out from just behind the vest was a lawman's star.

"I'm not sure I know what you are talking about, Sheriff," Smoke said.

"I'm not a sheriff, I'm marshal for the town of Etna. And lyin' ain't goin' to do you no good. Too many people seen you in that shirt you are wearing. And just because you wound up without any of the money, it don't make you no less guilty. You're going to hang, mister. I don't know which one of you killed Mr. Clark back there in Etna when you held up the bank, but it don't really matter none who pulled the trigger. Every one of you sons of bitches is just as guilty."

Smoke had been right in sensing that there were several people around him, because as he looked around now, he could see several more men glaring at him, all of whom were brandishing weapons, ranging from revolvers to rifles to shotguns.

Again, Smoke put his hand to the wound on his head. It was extremely painful to the touch, and he winced.

"Who are you?" Smoke asked.

"I'll be askin' the questions, mister," the big man replied. "But for your information, the name is Turnball." Turnball pointed to a thin-faced, hawk-nosed man who appeared to be in his mid-twenties. He was also wearing a star.

"This here is Pike, my deputy, and the rest of these men are temporarily deputized for posse duty. What is your name?"

"Jensen. Kirby Jensen, though most folks call me Smoke."

Turnball smiled broadly. "Smoke Jensen, eh?"

"You've heard of me?" Smoke said, relieved. Sometimes

having a reputation could be an intrusive aggravation. But in a case like this, it would be helpful in preventing a case of mistaken identity.

"Oh, yes, I've heard of you all right," Turnball said. "Fact is, I've got paper on you tacked up on my wall."

"Paper?"

"You're a wanted man, Mr. Jensen."

"No," Smoke said. "If you've got wanted posters on me, they are old. Very old. All the dodgers on me have been withdrawn. I'm not wanted."

"Well, if you wasn't wanted before, you're sure wanted now, seein' as how you robbed our bank. I reckon you and your friends figured you could get away with it 'cause Etna is so small. But you got yourselves another thing coming."

"I didn't rob any bank."

Turnball pointed to Smoke's shirt. "Anyone who would wear a plaid shirt while robbing a bank is just too damn dumb to be an outlaw," he said. "Hell, half the town of Etna described you."

"They may have described this shirt, Marshal, but they didn't describe me," Smoke said.

"Same thing."

"No, it isn't the same thing. This isn't my shirt."

Turnball laughed. "Oh, you mean you stole the shirt before you stole the money from the bank?"

"No. I mean whoever attacked me took my shirt and put this one on me."

Turnball and the others laughed.

"Now if that ain't about the dumbest damn thing I've ever heard. Why would anyone do that?"

"It's obvious, isn't it? They did it to throw the suspicion on me," Smoke explained. "I guess they figured the law around here would be dumb as dirt and buy into it. Looks like they were right."

Turnball laughed again. "You say I'm dumb, but you are the one who got caught. Quit lyin' and save your breath. I know what happened. You boys got into a little fight, and they lit out on you. I'm arresting you for the murder and bank robbin' you and the others done in my town," Turnball said.

Deputy Pike and one of the other riders grabbed Smoke roughly, and tried to twist his arms behind his back. Smoke broke loose.

"Oh, do it!" Pike said, cocking his pistol and pointing it at Smoke's head. "I'm just lookin' for an excuse to shoot you, you murderin' bastard!"

"Pike!" Turnball said gruffly. "I told you, we're takin' him back alive. You kill him here, we never will find the others."

Smoke glared at Pike. "If you want to shackle me, just ask," he said. "No need for you to pull my arms out of their sockets."

"Put your hands behind your back," Pike ordered.

"Shackle his hands in front of him," Turnball said. "He's got to ride his horse back into town."

Smoke held his hands out in front, and Pike shackled them together.

"Help him on his horse," the marshal ordered. "And pick up them empty bank wrappers. Like as not, we'll be needing them as evidence."

"Marshal Turnball, my horse picked up a stone," Smoke said. "I was working on his foot when the bank robbers jumped me. He'll go lame if it isn't taken care of."

"Check it out, Frakes," Turnball said.

Frakes, who was the youngest of the bunch, had been staring unblinkingly at Smoke from the very beginning. He made no effort to move.

"Frakes?" the marshal said again.

Frakes blinked, as if just aware he was being spoken to. "What?"

"He said his horse picked up a stone. Check it out."

"Left foreleg," Smoke said.

Frakes lifted the horse's left foreleg. "Yeah, there's a stone here, all right," he said. He took a knife from his pocket and, after a moment, got the stone out.

"Thanks," Smoke said.

"You're welcome," Frakes said.

Pike held the reins as Smoke got mounted.

"You're making a big mistake," Smoke said. "I did not hold up any bank. I was on my way up to Denver to meet with a land broker. I own Sugarloaf Ranch down in Rio Grande County. I haven't even been in Etna before today."

"You want to explain these empty bank wrappers here?" Turnball asked, holding one of them out for Smoke to examine. Printed on the side of the wrapper was $1,000,00 BANK OF ETNA.

"They must've been left here by the men who jumped me. They're the ones you are looking for."

"Jumped you, you say?"

"Yes, I told you, I was seeing to my horse when they rode up. They started talking to me, and the next thing I knew, they knocked me out. That must have been when they took my shirt and left this one. That's also when they left these bank wrappers lying around. They set me up."

"You got any witnesses to that?"

"Well, no," Smoke answered. "The only witnesses are the ones who did it, and they certainly wouldn't testify against themselves."

"Too bad you got no witnesses, mister. 'Cause I do have witnesses. At least half a dozen of 'em. And they'll ever'one of 'em swear they seen you and the other robbers ridin' out of town."

"Your witnesses are wrong, Marshal. They are either mistaken, or they are lying."

"Mister, I am one of them witnesses," Turnball said. "And I don't cotton to being called a liar. So, don't you go tellin' me what I did and what I did not see." He pointed at Smoke's chest, adding, "I remember them plaid shirts you and one of the other robbers was wearin' like as if there was a picture of 'em drawn on my eyeballs."

"I told you, this isn't my shirt," Smoke said again. "You are making a huge mistake."

"No, friend," the lawman responded. "The only mistakes made around here was made by you. And you made three of 'em." Ticking them off on his fingers, he enumerated: "Your first mistake was in pickin' a bank in my town to rob. Your second was in havin' a fallout with the other thieves, and your third was in getting yourself caught. Now, let's go."

The ride back to town took about two hours, and as Turnball and his posse rode into town, several of the town's citizens turned out along either side of the street to watch.

"They caught one of 'em!" someone yelled.

"Good job, Marshal!" another said.

"Hang 'im! Let's hang the son of a bitch now!" yet another shouted. "Ain't no need for a trial! Hell, the whole town seen him kill Mr. Clark!"

The last citizen had several others in the town who agreed with him, and the mood grew much uglier by the time Turnball got Smoke back to the jail.

"What you goin' to do with him now, Marshal?" someone asked as the riders all dismounted.

"I'm going to put him in jail and hold him there until Judge Craig can get down here and hold a trial," Turnball said.

"Hell, there ain't no need in wastin' the judge's time or our time," one of the citizens said. "If you ask me, I say we hang the son of a bitch now, and get it over with."

"Fremont, I hope you are just mouthin' off to hear yourself talk," Turnball said. "I hope you aren't really talkin' about lynchin'."

"Come on, Jason, you seen what he did to poor old Mr. Clark. His wife has been grievin' something pitiful ever since it happened," Fremont said. "It ain't right that poor Mr. Clark is dead and the son of a bitch that killed him is still alive."

"Pike," Turnball said gruffly. "Get the prisoner in the cell."

"These folks are pretty worked up," Pike said. "Maybe Fremont's got a point. I mean, why should the town pay to feed the prisoner when he's just goin' to hang anyway?"

"Get the prisoner in the cell like I told you to," Turnball said. Turnball pulled a shotgun from the saddle boot of his horse. "The rest of you," he said to the crowd. "Get on about your business and let me get about mine."

"Marshal, you know damn well if we try him, the judge is goin' to find him guilty. Then we'll hang him anyway," Fremont said.

"Then you can afford to be a little patient."

"To hell with patience. I say let's do it now and get it over with," Fremont insisted, still undeterred by Marshal Turnball's chastising.

Turnball pointed the shotgun at Fremont. "You aren't listenin' to me, are you?" Turnball asked menacingly.

"Whoa, hold on there!" Fremont said, his voice showing his fright. Fremont held his hands out in front of him and took a couple of steps back. "What are you doin', Turnball? You'd shoot an innocent man to save a murderer?"

"There's nothin' innocent about a lynchin', or about anyone who would suggest one," Turnball said. He pulled the hammer back on one of the barrels of the double-barrel shotgun he was holding. "Now if these here people don't leave in the next ten seconds, I'm goin' to blow your head off."

"Wait a minute! What do you mean you're going to blow my head off? I'm not the only one here," Fremont said, obviously frightened at having the gun pointed at him.

"No, you aren't. But you are the one doin' all the big talk, and you are the one I'm going to kill if the others don't leave."

"Why would you shoot me if *they* don't leave?" Fremont asked.

"'Cause I won't be able to kill all of them," Turnball said impatiently. "One, two, three . . ."

"Let's go!" Fremont said to the others. "Let's get out of here!"

Turnball watched as the townspeople left. Then he looked at the men who had ridden with him in the posse.

"You folks can go too," he said. "I thank you for ridin' with me."

The posse members left as well, some of them remounting and riding away, others leading their horses. Frakes remained behind.

"You may as well go on too, Frakes."

"You think the town would really lynch Jensen?" Frakes asked.

"It sounded for a few minutes there like they were giving the idea some thought," Turnball said. "But I don't intend to let it happen. I can't say as I blame them, though. Mr. Clark was a good man, and he carried a lot of people through the winter, givin' 'em time on their loans and all."

"What if we don't have the right man?" Frakes asked.

Turnball laughed. "What do you mean, what if we don't have the right man? Hell, you was right over there on Dunnigan's porch with me when they rode in. We commented on the shirts two of 'em was wearin', remember?"

"Oh, yes, sir, I remember all right," Frakes said.

"Then what makes you think we ain't got the right man?"

"I remember the shirt," Frakes said. "But I don't know as I remember the face. I know for a fact he wasn't the one standin' out front. And when the other two come out of the bank, why, they was both wearin' hoods."

"Well, don't worry about it. We got the right man, all right. And soon as he gets his day in court, why, we'll prove he is the right one. Then we'll build a gallows right here on Front Street, and all these people that's got a bloodlust out will have their hangin'. Only by then, it'll be legal."

"Yeah," Frakes said. "Yeah, I guess you're right." Frakes climbed onto his horse, then started riding it toward the livery.

Turnball watched him for a moment, then went inside. He

saw Pike standing over at the utility table by the wall. Pike was leafing through all the wanted posters.

"You got him into the cell with no problem, I take it?" Turnball asked.

"No problem," Pike said as he continued to page through the wanted posters. "I reckon his kind knows better than to mess with me."

"No doubt," Turnball replied sarcastically.

"Aha! You was right!" Pike said, suddenly holding up one of the posters. "We do have some paper on a fella named Smoke Jensen. Hey, Marshal, did you know there's a five-thousand-dollar reward on him!"

"No. I just remember having seen the name on a dodger, that's all."

Pike whistled. "Five thousand dollars," he said. "Damn that's a lot of money. Just think what we can do with that money."

"It don't do us any good to think about it," Turnball said.

"What do you mean it don't do us any good to think about it? We're the ones that caught him. I'd like to know who has a better claim on it."

"It ain't a point of havin' a better claim on it. We're the law," Turnball explained. "If you're the law, you can't collect on a reward. That's just the way of it."

"Well, that ain't right," Pike said, crestfallen. "That ain't no way right."

"Marshal," Smoke called from the cell at the back of the room. "Check the date on that poster."

Turnball looked at the poster, front and back. "There ain't no date," he said.

"Well, take a good look at the poster then," Smoke said. "Can't you see how the paper has already turned color? That alone should tell you how old it is."

Turnball shook his head. "It don't matter how old it is. I've never received anything cancelin' it."

"All right. It tells what county issued it, doesn't it?"

Smoke asked. "Doesn't it say it came from Hinsdale County?"

"Hinsdale County, yes."

"Then it is easy enough for you to check," Smoke said.

"Check, how?"

"All you have to do is send a telegram to the sheriff of Hinsdale County and ask if the poster is still good."

Turnball stroked his chin for a moment. "I could do that, I suppose, but what difference would it make?"

"What do you mean, what difference would it make? It would prove that I'm not a wanted man."

"Oh, it might prove that you aren't wanted for this crime anymore," Turnball said, pointing to the poster. "Whatever the crime was. But that don't have anything to do with why you are in jail now. You are in jail now because you robbed a bank and killed a good man, and near half the town seen you do it. That's somethin' you can't get out of."

"I didn't do it," Smoke said.

"Yes, well, I guess we'll just have to let a judge and jury decide that, won't we?"

Dooley, the Logan brothers, Fargo, Ford, and Buford Yancey had watched from an elevated position near the place where they had encountered Smoke. They saw the posse arrive, confront Smoke, then ride away with him as their captive.

"Ha!" Yancey said. "That was smart leavin' them empty bank wrappers like that. They think he done it."

"Yeah, but this is what gets me. They got to know that there was more'n one person," Fargo said. "How come they're all goin' back with him? Why ain't they still searchin' for the rest of us?"

"Come on, Fargo, you know how posses is," Curt Logan explained. "When they first get started, why, they're all full of piss and vinegar, ready to chase a body to hell and back. But they run out of steam just real quick. Especially if they find just enough success to make 'em feel good about themselves. And what we done was give 'em somethin' to make 'em think they done good."

"Let's go," Dooley said, turning away.

Dooley led them up into the high country and through a pass that was still packed with snow.

"Damn, Dooley," Curt Logan said. "Couldn't you find a place that's easier to get through? The snow here is ass-deep to a tall Indian."

"Nobody who's looking for us will expect us to come this way," Dooley said. "And if they do come this way, it'll be just as hard for them as it is for us."

"Well, you seen 'em. They ain't even comin' after us at all," Curt Logan said. "I sure don't see no need to be workin' so hard just to get away from a posse that ain't even chasin' us."

"If you don't like followin' me, just go your own way," Dooley offered.

"Well, hell, we ain't got no choice now but to keep on a-goin' this way," Curt Logan said. "Now it'd be as hard to go back as it is to keep goin'."

"Besides which, we ain't divided up the money yet," Yancey said.

"We'll divide it up soon as we get through the pass," Dooley said. "Then we can all go our separate ways."

8

"Come on, Pearlie, why won't you go with me?" Cal asked.

"I just don't care that much about travelin' shows, that's all," Pearlie said.

"But they say that Eddie Foy is really funny."

"You go, Cal," Pearlie said. "Have a good time."

"You're sure you don't want to come? I mean, I won't go if you . . ."

"Go," Pearlie said. "We aren't joined at the hip. You can do something by yourself if you want to."

Cal smiled. "All right, if you're sure." He started down the street toward the music hall. A large banner that was spread across the front of the music hall read: EDDIE FOY— DANCER—HUMORIST.

"Cal?" Pearlie called.

Cal turned toward him.

"If you hear any good jokes, tell me tonight, will you?"

Cal nodded. "I will!" he said.

Pearlie watched his young friend walk away; then he headed for the saloon. It wasn't that he didn't want Cal's company, or even that he didn't enjoy his company. It was just that he intended to play a little poker tonight and he knew how Sally felt about such things. He didn't want to be blamed for getting Cal mixed up in a card game.

There was another reason Pearlie wanted to play cards tonight. On the few nights he had come in for a beer, which was all he could afford before his first payday working in the livery stable, he had noticed that the Oasis Saloon employed a woman as dealer for the card games.

The woman's name was Annie, and through the week, Pearlie and Annie had flirted with each other. She had invited him into the game several times, and Pearlie sometimes got the idea that the invitation might be for more than just a game of cards.

He had turned her down every time, not because he didn't want to, but because he couldn't afford to. Tonight, he felt like he could, so he nursed a beer at the bar, then went straight to the table the moment a seat opened up.

"My, my," Annie said, smiling up at him. "Look who has finally come around."

"I thought I might give it a try," Pearlie said, sitting in the open chair.

"New player, new deck," Annie said. She picked up a box, broke the seal, then dumped the cards onto the table. They were clean, stiff, and shining. She pulled out the joker, then began shuffling the deck. The stiff, new pasteboards clicked sharply. Her hands moved swiftly, folding the cards in and out until the law of random numbers became king. She shoved the deck across the table.

"Cut?" she invited Pearlie. She leaned over the table, showing a generous amount of cleavage.

Pearlie cut the deck, then pushed the cards back. He tried to focus on her hands, though it was difficult to do so because she kept finding ways to position herself to draw his eyes toward her more interesting parts.

"You aren't having trouble concentrating, are you?" Annie teased.

"Depends on what I'm concentrating on," Pearlie said.

Annie smiled. "You naughty boy," she said.

"Here, what's goin' on here?" one of the other players asked. "You two know each other?"

"Not yet," Annie answered. She licked her lips. "But I have a feeling we are going to. Five-card?" She paused before she said the next word. "Stud?"

"Fine," Pearlie said.

The cards started falling for Pearlie from the moment he sat down. He won fifteen dollars on the first hand, and a couple of hands later he was ahead by a little over thirty dollars. In less than an hour, he had already tripled the money he'd started with.

Eddie Foy, wearing a broad, outlandish black and white plaid suit, along with a bright red shirt and a huge bow tie, pranced and danced across the stage. He was a very athletic dancer who often twisted his body into extreme positions, but did so gracefully.

Sometimes he would stop right in the middle of his dance and look at one of his legs in a seemingly impossible position. When he did so, he would assume a look of shock, as if even he were surprised to see his leg there. Then, with that same shocked expression on his face, he would stare at the audience, as if asking them how this had happened.

The audience would react in explosive laughter; then the music would start again and his dance would resume.

Sometimes in the middle of his dance, the music would stop and Eddie would walk to the front of the stage, turn sideways, then stare out at the audience, almost as if surprised to see them there. He was carrying a cane, and he had a method of holding the cane behind him in such a way as to cause his hat to seem to tip on its own.

As he spoke, he affected a very pronounced lisp.

"Yethterday wath thuch a nith day that I went for a thmall thtroll," he began.

The audience grew quiet, and Cal leaned forward in anticipation of the upcoming joke.

"I took mythelf into the bank and gave the teller a twenty-dollar bill. My good man, I thaid, I would like to trade thith bill for two ten-dollar billth.

"The teller complied with my requeth.

"I then thaid, my good man, tho well did you perform that tathk, that now I would like to trade my forty-year-old wife for two ladieth of twenty."

Eddy Foy tipped his hat as the audience exploded with laughter.

Cal decided that would be one of the jokes he would have to remember to tell Pearlie.

Back in the Oasis Saloon, most of the other players were taking Pearlie's good luck in stride, but the one who had asked if Annie and Pearlie knew each other, a man named Creedlove, began complaining.

"Somethin' kind'a fishy is goin' on here," Creedlove said.

"Fishy, Mr. Creedlove?" Annie asked sweetly.

Creedlove looked at Annie, then nodded toward Pearlie. "I think you'n him's workin' together," he said.

"And just how would we be working together?" Annie asked. Almost instantly, the smile had left her face and her words were cold and measured.

"You think I believe that him winnin' all the time is just dumb luck?" Creedlove asked.

"It's not luck, it's skill," Pearlie said. "And the only dumb person in this card game is you. You need to calculate the odds so as to know when to bet and when to fold. That's somethin' you haven't figured out."

"You think you have me pegged, do you?" Creedlove asked. He stared across the table through narrowed eyes. "Suppose me'n you have a go at it? Just the two of us."

"Don't ask me," Pearlie said. "Ask the others if they'd be willing to sit it out."

"I come to play cards," one of the others said. "I don't plan to sit nothin' out."

"Twenty-five dollars to sit in," Creedlove said.

"That's too rich for my blood."

"Anyone else?"

"Play your game, Creedlove. I'll just drink my beer and watch," one of the others said.

"How about you?" Creedlove asked Pearlie.

"All right, I'll play. Name your game," Pearlie said.

"Five-card stud."

"I'm in," Pearlie said, sliding twenty-five dollars to the middle of the table.

Creedlove reached for the cards, but Pearlie stuck his hand out to stop him. "You don't think I'm going to let you deal, do you? We'll let the lady deal."

"Huh-uh," Creedlove said, shaking his head. He nodded toward one of the other players. "We'll let Pete deal."

"How do I know that you and Pete aren't in cahoots? Suppose we get someone who isn't at this table right now," Pearlie suggested.

"Who?"

Pearlie looked around the saloon and saw that there were at least four bar girls working the tables. "How about one of the ladies?" Pearlie asked. "You can choose."

"All right," Creedlove said. He looked over toward the nearest one. "You, honey, come here," he called.

The girl looked up in surprise at being summoned in such a way.

"It's all right, Sue," Annie said. "It'll just take a minute."

"We want you to deal a hand of cards," Creedlove said to Sue when she came over.

"She gets ten dollars from the pot," Annie said.

"What? Why should she get ten dollars?"

"If she gets ten dollars from the pot, it won't make any difference to her who wins," Annie said. "It will guarantee you that it's a fair game."

"That's fine by me," Pearlie said. "How about you?"

"All right," Creedlove agreed.

Sue dealt a down card to each, then an up card. Creedlove showed a king, Pearlie a five of hearts.

Creedlove laughed. "Not lookin' that good for you, is it? Bet five dollars."

Pearlie matched the bet.

The next card gave Creedlove a pair of kings showing. Pearlie drew a six.

"Bet ten dollars," Creedlove said.

Pearlie called the bet, and Creedlove's next card was a jack. Pearlie drew another six, giving him a pair of sixes.

Creedlove bet another ten dollars and Pearlie called.

Creedlove's final card was another jack. Pearlie drew another six.

"Well, now," Creedlove said. "I have two pair, kings and jacks, and you have three of a kind." Creedlove lifted his down card. "So the big question is, do I have a jack or a king as my hole card? Or do your three little sixes have my two pair beat?" He chuckled, and put twenty dollars in the pot. "It's going to cost you twenty to find out."

Pearlie called and raised him twenty.

The smile left Creedlove's face. "You're puttin' quite a store in them three sixes, aren't you? How do you know I don't have a full house?"

"I'm betting you have two pair, and I have you beat," Pearlie said.

Creedlove hesitated for a second, then, with a big smile, he pushed twenty dollars into the center of the table. "All right, I've got you right where I want you. I call." He smiled and flipped over his down card to disclose a king. "Well, lookie here, a full house, kings over jacks. It looks like you lost this one, friend. A full house beats three sixes."

Creedlove reached for the pot as Pearlie turned up his down card showing another six.

"Yes, but it won't beat four sixes," he said, reaching for the pot and pulling it toward him.

"What?" Creedlove gasped. He pointed at the table. "That's not possible!" he said.

"Of course it's possible," Pearlie said. "There are four of everything in a deck. Or hadn't you ever noticed that?" he added innocently.

By now, everyone in the saloon was aware of the high-stakes game and they had all gathered around to watch. They laughed at Pearlie's barb.

Creedlove slid the rest of his money to the center of the table. "I've got thirty-six dollars here," he said. "What do you say we cut for high card?"

Pearlie covered his bet, then Sue fanned the cards out.

"I'll draw first," Creedlove said.

Creedlove drew a queen.

"Ha!" he said triumphantly.

Pearlie drew a king.

"What the . . ." Creedlove shouted in anger. "You cheated me, you son of a bitch! Nobody is this lucky!"

"How did I cheat?" Pearlie asked. "You had the same chance I did."

"I don't know how you cheated," Creedlove said. "I just know that, somehow, you cheated."

Pearlie stood up then, and stepped back from the table. "Now, mister, you might want think about that for a moment," he said in a quiet but ominous voice. "You can always get more money, but you can't get another life."

"No," Creedlove said, shaking his head and holding his hand out in front of him as he backed away. "No. I ain't goin' to draw against you. But I ain't takin' back my words either. You are a card cheat."

"Both you gents just hold it right there," someone said loudly and, looking toward the sound of the voice, Pearlie saw the bartender pointing his shotgun toward them.

"Callin' someone a cheat is the kind of thing that can get a man killed if he can't back it up," the bartender said. "Annie, Sue, you been watchin' this. Was there any cheatin' goin' on?"

"Not a bit of it, Karl," Annie replied. "The game was aboveboard in every respect."

"All right, then that leaves you at fault, Creedlove. So I reckon you'd better get on out of here."

"You got no right to run me out of here," Creedlove said.

The bartender pulled back the hammers of the shotgun.

"This here scattergun gives me the right," the bartender said. "Now, you can either walk out, or your bloody carcass will be pulled out. Which is it going to be?"

Creedlove glared at the bartender for a moment. Then he glared at Pearlie.

"This ain't the end of it," Creedlove said to Pearlie. "Me'n you will run in to each other again sometime."

"I can hardly wait," Pearlie replied.

"Don't let the door hit you in the ass on your way out," Annie called to him.

A thunderous laughter from the saloon patrons chased Creedlove out of the saloon.

"Marshal?" Smoke called from the cell.

"What do you want, Jensen?"

"I appreciate you standing up to the mob like that."

"That wasn't a mob," Turnball said. "That was a group of concerned citizens. Maybe you don't realize this, Jensen, but folks around here had a hard winter."

"We all had a hard winter," Smoke said.

"Yes, well, a lot of the folks hereabout wouldn't have their homes or businesses if not for Mr. Clark. You picked the wrong man to kill."

"I didn't kill him."

"And you expect me to believe that?"

"Marshal, send a telegram to Sheriff Carson, back in Big Rock. He can tell you who I am."

"I might just do that," Marshal Turnball said. Turnball walked away from the cell and saw Deputy Pike standing at the front window.

"What are you lookin' at?" Turnball asked.

"Them fellas you run away is all standin' down there in front of the Bull's Head."

"I don't have any problem with them as long as they're standin' down there talkin' and not up here makin' trouble," Turnball said.

"That wasn't right, you runnin' 'em off like that," Pike said. "Ever'one of 'em is our friend. I can't believe you would'a shot Mr. Fremont over somethin' like this."

"I didn't shoot him, did I?"

"Would you have shot him?"

"I didn't shoot him, did I?" Turnball repeated.

9

"And then he said, 'I walked into thith church,'" Cal was saying.

"Thith?"

"This," Cal explained. "But that's how he talked. He would say words like Mithithippi instead of Mississippi. It was real funny the way he talked."

"All right, go on with the joke," Pearlie said. It was the morning after, and Cal and Pearlie were mucking out stalls in the stable.

"All right. So Eddie Foy says, 'Thith cowboy went into thith church and took a theat on a long bench, neckth to a pretty woman.' And then Eddie Foy asked everyone in the audience, 'What do you call that long bench that people thit on in a church?'

"And everyone in the audience yells back at him, 'Pew!'"

Cal laughed. "So then Eddie Foy says . . . he says, 'No, thath what the pretty woman thaid when the cowboy that down bethide her. Pew.'"

"So the pretty woman told him what the bench was called?" Pearlie asked.

"No!" Cal said in exasperation. "Don't you get the joke? She said 'Pew' 'cause the cowboy was stinkin' up the place."

"Oh," Pearlie said. He laughed. "Yes, that is funny."

"He was real funny," Cal said. "He told a lot of funny stories and I can remember most of 'em, but they aren't as funny when I tell them."

"Well, that's 'cause Eddie Foy does that for a livin', and he's good at it," Pearlie said. "You're a cowboy who . . ." Pearlie paused and looked at the rakes he and Cal were holding. "No, *we* are cowboys," he corrected, "who muck out horse manure for a living."

Cal laughed. "I reckon that's so."

"Cal, how would you like to go back?"

"Go back? Go back where?"

"To Sugarloaf."

"I thought we wasn't going to go back there as long as we were a burden on Smoke and Miss Sally," Cal said.

"Miss Sally would correct you and say weren't," Pearlie said.

"Well, but didn't you say we *weren't* going back to be a burden on Smoke and Miss Sally?"

"That's what I said all right," Pearlie said. "But if we go back now, we won't be a burden."

"How do you figure that?"

Pearlie stopped mucking and looked around the stable to make sure no one was close enough to overhear him.

"I played some cards last night," Pearlie said. "And I won some money."

"How much did you win?"

"Two hundred seventeen dollars," Pearlie replied with a broad smile.

"Two hundred dollars?" Cal asked in amazement.

"Two hundred seventeen," Pearlie corrected.

"That's a lot of money!"

"It sure is," Pearlie said. "It's enough to go back and help out."

"When do we leave?"

"Today," Pearlie said.

"Have you said anything to Mr. Thornton?"

"Yes, I told him we would be leaving today. In fact, we

could leave right now if we wanted to, but I promised him we would finish with the stalls before we left."

"Yeah," Cal said. "That's only right."

The two men began raking with renewed vigor. Then, after a few minutes, Cal looked up.

"That's why you didn't want to go see Eddie Foy last night, isn't it?"

"Yeah," Pearlie said. "I just had a feelin' I was going to be lucky. And it turns out that the feelin' was true."

Creedlove sat nursing his drink in the back of the saloon in the little town of Solidad. He had left Flora-vista shortly after his run-in with Pearlie at the card game in the Oasis Saloon. He had lost so much money in the card game that he barely had enough money to get by, and wouldn't have any if he hadn't stolen twelve dollars from a stage way station.

That was three days and fifty miles ago, and he didn't figure he would ever see Pearlie again. But when he looked up as two men came in, there he was—Pearlie, and another cowboy who was even younger.

Because Creedlove was sitting alone, at a table in the back of the saloon, he was blocked from Pearlie's direct view by the cast-iron stove, which, though cold now, still smelled of its heavy winter use.

Creedlove watched as Pearlie said a few words to the bartender, then Pearlie and his friend took their beers to a nearby table.

Creedlove got up from the table, pulled his gun from his holster, then, holding it down by his side so it wouldn't be obvious that he had already drawn his weapon, stepped around the stove and started across the floor.

Pearlie was just pulling the chair out from the table when out of the corner of his eye, he saw Creedlove moving toward him. Pearlie wondered, briefly, what Creedlove was doing this far north of Floravista.

"Draw your gun, you son of a bitch! I aim to shoot you dead!" Creedlove shouted, raising his own pistol at the same time he was challenging Pearlie.

"Pearlie, he already has his gun out!" Cal shouted.

Pearlie didn't need Cal's warning because even as Creedlove was bringing his pistol to bear, Pearlie drew his own pistol and suddenly the room was shattered with the roar of two pistols exploding.

The other patrons in the saloon yelled and dived or scrambled for cover. White gun smoke billowed out from both guns, coalescing in a cloud that filled the center of the room. For a moment, the cloud obscured everything.

As the cloud began to roll away, Creedlove stared through the drifting white smoke, glaring at Pearlie.

Creedlove smiled and opened his mouth, but before he could say anything, there was an incoherent gagging rattle way back in his throat. His eyes glazed over, and he pitched forward, his gun clattering to the floor.

That threat over, Pearlie looked around the saloon, checking to see if there was anyone else laying for him. Pearlie's pistol was cocked and he was ready to fire a second time, if a second shot was needed. He saw that Cal had drawn his own pistol and was also looking around the room for any potential danger.

Satisfied that there was no further danger, Pearlie holstered his pistol. Cal holstered his as well, and seeing them put their pistols back in the holsters, the other patrons began, slowly, to reappear from under tables, behind the bar and stove, and even from under the staircase.

A lawman came running in then, but seeing that it was all over, he put his gun away. He looked toward the body on the floor.

"Anybody know this man?" the lawman asked.

"His name is Creedlove," Pearlie said.

"Did you shoot him?"

"I did."

"It was a fair fight, Sheriff," the bartender said. "The fella on the floor drew first."

"That's right, Sheriff," one of the others said. "Fact is, this Creedlove fella not only drew first, he already had his gun out before he even challenged this man."

After that, several men at once began telling the story, each adding embellishments from his own perspective. When they were finished, the lawman came over to Pearlie and Cal.

"You got 'ny idea why he would come after you like that?"

"I won some money off him playing cards the other night," Pearlie said.

"Were you cheatin'?"

"No, sir, I wasn't."

"What's your name, mister?"

"Smith," Pearlie said. "John Smith."

Cal looked at Pearlie in surprise, but said nothing.

"Are you staying in town for the night, Mr. Smith?"

"I hadn't planned on it," Pearlie said. "My friend, Bill Jones, and I are heading toward California."

The sheriff realized then that Pearlie hadn't given his right name, and he sighed and shook his head.

"All right," he said. "No need for you to give me your right names, if what everyone here says is true. And there's no need for you to stay in town any longer. Fact is, it might be better all around if you just kept passing through."

"Soon as we finish our beer, we'll be on our way," Pearlie said.

The sheriff looked over at the bartender. "I'll get someone to come down here and get the body out of here," he said.

"Thanks, Sheriff," the bartender said. Looking around the saloon, he saw that several new customers had come in, drawn by the excitement. The bartender smiled.

"No big hurry, though," he said. "It seems to be good for business."

Carrying the wanted poster on Smoke Jensen, Marshal Turnball walked down toward the telegraph office.

"Good job catchin' that murderer and bank robber, Marshal," one of the townspeople said.

"Thank you," Turnball replied.

"Too bad he didn't have any of the money with him."

"Yes, it is. But at least we have him," Turnball said.

When Turnball stepped into the telegraph office, a bell on the door announced his entrance. Rodney Wheat, wearing a green visor and red suspenders, was sitting behind the counter reading a penny-dreadful novel. Wheat looked up as the marshal entered.

"I hear you caught one of the bank robbers," Wheat said.

"Yes," Turnball answered. He showed Wheat the poster. "It was this fella."

Wheat looked at the poster.

PROCLAMATION
$5,000.00
REWARD

For the Apprehension

DEAD OR ALIVE

Of the Murderer
KIRBY "SMOKE" JENSEN.

This Notice Takes the Place
Of All Previous
REWARD NOTICES.

Contact: *Sheriff,* Hinsdale County, Colorado
IMMEDIATELY.

"I want you to send a telegram to the sheriff out in Hinsdale County, telling him that we have this fella in custody," Turnball said.

Wheat shook his head. "I can't do that," he said.

"What do you mean you can't do that? Why can't you do it?"

"The telegraph line is down. It's been down for a couple of days now."

"Well, when do you think you'll get it back?"

Wheat shook his head. There's no way of telling. Last time it took two weeks."

"Two weeks?"

Wheat nodded. "Two weeks," he said. "And it might even take longer this time. If the line is out up in the higher elevations, there will still be so much snow that the line crew might not be able to get to it."

Turnball stroked his jaw as he contemplated the situation. Then he nodded. "All right. I'll send a letter. What's the county seat of Hinsdale County?"

"Lake City," Wheat answered. "But I don't know if you are going to have any more luck with the letter than you are with sending a telegram. That's on the other side of the mountains, and I'm sure none of the high passes are open yet."

"Maybe not," Turnball replied. "But I'm going to try."

Smoke was lying on the bunk in his cell with his hands laced behind his head, staring at the ceiling. He had to admit that the cell was solidly built. The bars didn't go all the way to the ceiling, but came up only about six feet. Between the top of the bars and the ceiling itself was a two-foot wall of solid brick. At the back of the wall there were three small windows, enough to let in light and air, but not one of the three large enough for a man to pass through, even if there were no bars.

When he heard the marshal come back into the office, he sat up.

"Marshal?" he called.

"What do you want, Jensen?" Turnball answered.

"Did you send a telegram to Sheriff Carson, back in Big Rock?"

"No."

"What about the Sheriff of Hinsdale County? Did you contact him about whether or not the poster was current?"

"I told you, it doesn't matter whether or not the poster is current," Turnball said. "I'm only interested in the man you killed here, and the bank that you robbed here."

"I didn't do it," Smoke said. "I told you, contact Sheriff Carson. He'll vouch for me."

"I'll send him a letter," Turnball said.

"A letter?"

"The telegraph wire is down," Turnball explained. "Fact is, if Judge Craig wasn't scheduled to come into town tomorrow, we wouldn't even be able to send for him. At least, we can have us a fair trial."

"Hold on there, Marshal," Smoke said. "You aren't planning on holding a trial before you can check up on my story, are you?"

"We're holding your trial tomorrow," Turnball said. "We don't get that many visits from a judge, and I don't intend to waste this one."

"What about a lawyer?" Smoke asked. "Do I get a lawyer?"

"We got two lawyers in town," Turnball said. "If it's the way they normally do it, they'll flip a coin to see who prosecutes and who defends. It seems to work out all right."

10

There was no courthouse in the town of Etna, so the trial was held in the school. At the top of the blackboard in the front of the room, the alphabet was displayed in both cursive and block letters, in capital and lowercase. On the side panel of the blackboard were the work assignments for each of the six grades that attended the single-room schoolhouse. A stove sat in a sandbox in the corner of the room, and artwork of the children was pinned on the wall.

Two tables had been placed in the front of the classroom. One table had two chairs, and that was for Smoke and his lawyer. The other table was the prosecutor's table, and it had only one chair. The jury occupied the two first rows of desks in the classroom, while the citizens of the town squeezed into the remaining desks. Others were standing along the two side walls and the back wall. The judge's bench was the schoolteacher's desk, while Miss Garvey, the school-teacher, was pressed into service as the court reporter.

Smoke felt a sense of melancholy as he looked around the schoolroom. His Sally had been teaching at a school exactly like this one when he met her. It was a cruel irony that his fate was about to be decided in a place like this.

"All rise!" Marshal Turnball shouted. In his capacity as city marshal, Turnball was also acting as the bailiff.

At Turnball's call, everyone seated in the classroom cum courtroom stood to await the arrival of the judge.

Judge Arlie Craig was a short, fat man who filled out his black robes. He was bald, except for a tuft of white over each ear. He took his seat at the bench, then looked out over the courtroom.

"The court may be seated," he said.

As the people sat, Judge Craig removed his glasses and cleaned them thoroughly. Then he put them back on, hooking them very carefully over one ear at a time. During this process the courtroom was very quiet, almost as if mesmerized by it. The only sound came from outside the courtroom, and that from a barking dog.

"Bailiff, would you call the case, please?" Judge Craig said.

"Your Honor, there comes before this honorable court one Kirby Jensen," Turnball said. "Mr. Jensen is charged with the murder of Robert J. Clark, said murder committed during the act of robbery of the Bank of Etna."

"Was this charge issued by a grand jury?"

"It was, Your Honor. The grand jury met this morning."

"Thank you," Judge Craig said. "And is the accused now represented by counsel?"

"He is, Your Honor," the lawyer sitting beside Smoke said. "I am Asa Jackson, duly accredited by the bar of the State of Colorado to practice law."

The judge looked over at Smoke.

"Is the defendant satisfied with counsel?"

"I am not, Your Honor," Smoke said.

His response surprised the judge and startled many who were in the court. Several reacted audibly, and one man shouted, "At least you have a lawyer! That's more than you gave Rob Clark!"

Others shouted out as well, and Judge Craig had to bang his gavel several times to restore order.

"Mr. Jensen, what complaint do you have against Mr. Jackson?"

"Your Honor, I have no complaint against Mr. Jackson personally. But I would prefer to select my own lawyer."

"There are only two lawyers in town," Judge Craig replied. "Would you rather have the prosecutor act as your defense counsel?"

"No, Your Honor. I ask for a delay so that I may get a lawyer from my own hometown of Big Rock."

"Mr. Hagen, you are the prosecutor," Judge Craig said. "How say you to this request?"

"Your Honor, the crime is still fresh upon the minds of all the witnesses. I fear that any delay may cloud their memories, perhaps even to the detriment of the defendant. All that is required by the law is that he be provided with counsel, and we have done so. I move that his request for a delay be denied."

Judge Craig nodded, then looked back at Smoke. "Due to my own busy schedule, it would be several weeks before I could return to Etna. And, as Mr. Hagen has pointed out, the closer the trial is held to the event, the sharper the memories of the witnesses who are called. Therefore, your request for a delay in the trial is denied. Has there been voir dire of the jury?"

"There has, Your Honor, and both defense and prosecution have accepted the jury as it is now constituted," Hagen said.

"Very good," Judge Craig replied. "Now, Mr. Jensen, how do you plead to the charge against you?"

"Not guilty," Smoke said.

"Very well," Judge Craig said. He cleared his throat. "The defendant represented and the jury accepted, I declare this case in session. Mr. Hagen, make your case."

Lester Hagen was a tall, gangly-looking man with a wild shock of hair and prominent ears. Standing, he turned to face the jury, which was seated just behind him.

"It won't take me long to do this," he said, speaking so quietly that those in the back had to strain to hear. "Practically everyone in this town was a witness to the robbery of the Bank of Etna on the sixth day of this very month. I could call any of them, and all would give compelling and damning testimony. Ten thousand dollars was taken, money that belonged to the fair people of this town."

Turning back to the table, he picked up the red and black plaid shirt Smoke had been wearing when he was arrested.

"Look at this shirt," he said. "It is not a shirt one can easily forget. And if you see this shirt on a man who is in the act of killing another, then the shirt becomes even more vividly burned into your memory. This shirt alone is enough to convict the defendant. No matter what he or his lawyer may say to obfuscate the issue, the facts are indisputable. A man wearing this very shirt killed Rob Clark. This man," he said, with a dramatic pointing of his finger toward Smoke, "was captured wearing this very shirt. I think that when this trial is finished, you will have no difficulty in finding Mr. Kirby Jensen guilty as charged."

As Hagen took his seat, there was a spontaneous outbreak of applause from the gallery.

"Hear, hear, there will be no such demonstration in this courtroom!" Judge Craig said with an angry bang of his gavel.

The court grew quiet, then all turned their attention to Asa Jackson. Like Hagen before him, Jackson stood to address the jury. Considerably shorter than Hagen, and with eyes made almost buglike by his thick glasses, Jackson made less of an impression by his appearance.

"The law states that before you can find someone guilty, you must be convinced beyond the shadow of a doubt that he is guilty. You will hear the witnesses say that there were three men shooting into the bank. Since three men were shooting, it's impossible to say that Kirby Jensen was the one who actually murdered Mr. Clark."

Jackson sat back down and Smoke leaned over toward him.

"The way you presented that, it made it sound as if I was there," Smoke complained.

"It's going to be hard to say you weren't there, with the evidence that the prosecutor has," Jackson said. "Our best hope is to sew doubt as to who actually did the shooting."

"Prosecution, you may call your first witness," Judge Craig said.

"Prosecution calls Mr. Tucker Patterson," Hagen said.

Tucker Patterson walked to the front of the room and put his hand on the Bible.

"Do you swear to tell the truth, the whole truth, and nothing but the truth, so help you God?" Turnball asked.

"I do."

"The witness may be seated," Judge Craig said.

Hagen approached the witness chair. "For the record, Mr. Patterson, what is your employment?"

"I am the head teller of the Bank of Etna," Patterson replied.

"Hell, Tucker, you're the only teller," someone shouted from the gallery, and everyone laughed.

Judge Craig slammed his gavel down, then, with an angry scowl, addressed the gallery. "If there is one more outbreak, I will hold the person responsible in contempt of court. You will be fined, and you will spend time in jail."

Patterson looked at Hagen. "Mr. Barnes is right," he said, identifying the person who spoke up. "There is only one teller, but Mr. Clark had assured me that, if we were ever to hire a second teller, I would be the chief teller. Therefore my position, technically, was that of head teller."

"Mr. Patterson, were you in the bank on the sixth instant?"

"I was."

"Tell the court what happened that day."

"Mr. Clark and I were both behind the teller's cage, counting the money to make certain that the books were balanced, when two men came in."

"Can you describe the two men?"

"One of the men was wearing a shirt like that one," Patterson said, pointing to the shirt that was still lying on the prosecutor's table.

"Let the record show that the witness identified the prosecution exhibit as the shirt worn by one of the robbers."

"Object, Your Honor," Jackson said. "The witness said it was a shirt like that one. He didn't say he was wearing that one."

"I stand corrected, Your Honor," Hagen said. "Mr. Patterson, you said there were two men?"

"Yes. The other man was wearing a white shirt."

"I object!" Smoke called out. "He is describing the clothes, not the men."

"Mr. Smoke, if your attorney cares to make that objection, he may do so," Judge Craig said. "But as the defendant, you are not allowed to object."

Smoke turned to Jackson. "Are you going to object?" he asked.

Jackson nodded. "I object," he said. "Mr. Jensen is correct. The witness is describing clothing, and not the men themselves."

"Sustained," the judge said.

"Mr. Patterson, could you see the men's faces?" Hagen asked.

"No, they were covered by hoods," Patterson replied.

"So, by looking at the defendant, you cannot say, as a matter of actual fact, that he was not one of the robbers, can you?"

"I object," Jackson said. "He just said that the men's faces were covered."

"Listen to the question, Counselor," Judge Craig said. "He asked if he could positively say that Jensen was *not* one of the robbers."

"Oh," Jackson said.

"Objection is overruled."

"So, since you cannot positively say that he was not one of the robbers, it is possible that he was one of them?"

"Yes."

Hagen continued with Patterson, eliciting from him the

details as to how Clark got a gun, then ran to the front door to challenge the bank robbers as they were leaving.

"I told him not to go, that there were too many of them," Patterson said. "But Mr. Clark was a brave man, and he wouldn't hear of it. He ran to the front door and started to shoot, but got shot instead."

"Thank you, Mr. Patterson. Your witness," Hagen said as he sat down.

Jackson stood, but didn't approach the witness. "Did you see who actually did the shooting?"

"No, I was inside the bank. I saw Mr. Clark get shot, but from where I was, I couldn't see who shot him."

"So even though you saw Mr. Jensen wearing this shirt in your bank, once the robbers got outside, you have no idea who did the actual shooting?"

"I object!" Smoke said loudly.

"You are objecting your own lawyer?" Judge Craig asked.

"Your Honor, I ask the court's permission to act as my own lawyer."

"Are you saying you wish to dismiss counsel?"

"Yes, Your Honor, that is exactly what I am saying."

"Court is going to stand in recess for half an hour," Judge Craig said. "Marshal Turnball, clear the courtroom of everyone except you and the defendant."

"Yes, sir," Turnball said. "All right, people, you heard the judge. Everyone out."

"Your Honor, if there is going to be a sidebar, I request permission to remain," Hagen said.

"Permission denied," Craig said. "You will leave with everyone else."

"What about me?" Jackson asked. "Since the defendant is my client, shouldn't I be present?"

"You heard the defendant, Mr. Jackson," Craig said. "You have just been dismissed."

It took less than a minute for everyone to leave. Then Turnball, who had been standing at the door watching them leave, came back to the front of the room.

"They are all gone, Judge," he said.

Craig removed his glasses and cleaned them again. Watching him, Smoke realized that it was more of a nervous action than because the glasses actually needed cleaning.

"Mr. Jensen, there is a saying in the legal profession that a person who defends himself has a fool for a client." He put the glasses back on, again looping them very carefully over each ear, one at a time. "Do you know what I am saying to you?"

"Yes, sir, I believe I do," Smoke replied.

Judge Craig pointed at Smoke, and began shaking his finger. "Disabuse yourself of any idea that I will go easier on you because of your inexperience or lack of knowledge of the law. Regardless of your competence or incompetence, this case will be tried under the rules of law. Do you understand that?"

"Yes, sir, I do."

"Very well. Mr. Jackson is dismissed, and I hereby declare you sui juris."

"I beg your pardon?"

"Sui juris," the judge repeated. "It is a Latin term meaning that you have the capacity to act for yourself in legal proceedings. You are hereby acting as your own counsel."

"Thank you, Your Honor," Smoke said.

"Marshal Turnball, you may reassemble the court."

"All right, our take come to ten thousand dollars," Dooley said after he counted out the money. "That's a thousand dollars apiece for each of you."

"Wait a minute," Yancey said. "You think they can't none of us cipher? I make that over sixteen hundred dollars for each of us."

Dooley shook his head. "I set it up, I take half," he said.

"That ain't right," Yancey protested. "We all of us took our chances when we robbed that bank. We should all of us get the same amount of money."

"Tell him, Curt," Dooley said.

"Maybe you ain't never done nothin' like this before," Curt said to Yancey. "But the one that gets the job set up is always the one that gets the most money."

"There didn't nobody say nothin' like that when I got asked to join up," Yancey said. "And I don't intend to just stand by and get cheated like this."

"Look at it this way," Curt said. "You got a thousand dollars now, which you didn't have before. You know how long you'd have to cowboy to make a thousand dollars?"

Yancey shook his head. "I don't care; that ain't the point. I don't intend to be cheated like that."

While Yancey was talking, Dooley pulled his pistol. Yancey didn't notice it until he heard the click of the hammer being pulled back.

"Then I reckon you can't be reasoned with, can you?"

"What? What are you doin' with that gun?"

"Go, Yancey," Dooley said.

"Go? Go where?"

"Anywhere," Dooley said. "I don't want you around anymore."

"All right," Yancey said. "It ain't right, but give me my money and I'll be on my way."

Dooley shook his head. "No money for you."

"What do you mean no money for me?"

"One thousand dollars wasn't enough for you, so you get none. Now, get out of here."

Yancey glared at Dooley, then he started toward his horse.

Dooley pulled the trigger, the gun roared, and Yancey's horse dropped in its tracks.

"What the hell did you just do?" Yancey shouted. "You son of a bitch! You just killed my horse!"

"You're lucky I didn't kill you," Dooley said. "Curt, get his gun."

Curt walked up to Yancey and pulled his pistol from his holster.

"All right, Yancey, start walkin'," Dooley said, making a motion with his pistol.

"This ain't right," Yancey said.

"I thought we already had that settled," Dooley said. "I decide what's right."

Dooley shot again and the bullet hit the ground right next to Yancey's feet, then ricocheted through the valley, whining as it did so. Even before the echo died, Yancey was running back down the trail, chased by Dooley's evil laughter.

"Dooley," Fargo said. "Leavin' him out here without a horse or a gun . . . he could die."

"Yeah, he could," Dooley said. "Now, each one of you boys is two hundred dollars richer. That is, unless you don't want the money."

"Hell, I want the money," Ford said.

"Me too," Curt said.

"I'll take my share," Trace said.

"Fargo, that just leaves you," Dooley said. Dooley had not yet put his pistol back in its holster when a little wisp of smoke curled upward from the end of the barrel. The implication was obvious to Fargo.

"Yancey was a troublemaker," Fargo said. "You was right to do what you done."

"I thought you might see things my way," Dooley said as he counted out the money.

11

As the trial continued, the prosecution called witness after witness to the stand to testify as to what they saw on the morning of the robbery. In every case the testimony was the same. They had seen two men leaving the bank, then they'd heard Clark shout out the warning that the bank had been robbed. They talked about seeing and hearing the exchange of gunshots, and seeing Mr. Clark go down.

"Did all of the robbers shoot at Mr. Clark?" Hagen asked a witness.

"No, sir, just the two who come out of the bank, and the one that was holdin' the horses in front of the bank. There was three more men across the street, waitin' in front of Sikes Leather Goods, but they didn't shoot at Mr. Clark."

"How do you know that those three men were involved with the robbery?" Hagen asked.

"'Cause they all left town together, and all of 'em was shootin' and hollerin' as they rode away."

"I see," Hagen said. "But as far as who actually shot Mr. Clark, it was the two men, who were wearing red and black plaid shirts, and the one man who was wearing a white shirt. Is that what you are saying?"

"Yes, sir."

"From your point of observation, could you tell which one of the three actually killed Mr. Clark?"

"No, sir, I could not."

"In fact," Hagen continued, "if I told you that there were four bullets in Mr. Clark's body, would you be able to believe that all three may have had a hand in killing him?"

"Yes, I would say so."

"Mr. Jensen," Judge Craig said quickly. "Counsel is leading the witness. Are you not going to object?"

"I'm not going to object, Your Honor, because I don't care which of the three, or if all three, killed him. I wasn't one of the three."

"Very well, I will disallow it myself. Jury will disregard counsel's last comment. You may continue, Mr. Hagen."

"I'm through with this witness, Your Honor."

"Did you see me in the street in front of the bank that day?" Smoke asked.

"Yeah, I seen you. I seen you in that shirt," the witness replied.

"I've no doubt but that you saw the shirt," Smoke said. "But I want you to look at my face closely. Is this the face of the man you saw in front of the bank?"

"No, you ain't the one that was standin' in front of the bank," the witness said. "But I done told you, and everyone has done told you. The faces of the two that come out of the bank was covered by masks."

"Thank you, that's all," Smoke said.

"But I seen that shirt you was wearin'," the witness added.

"Thank you, that is all," Smoke repeated.

Billy Frakes was Hagen's next witness.

Frakes was pointed out as having had a unique perspective on the robbery, because he had gone down to try and sell a pair of boots to three men who were waiting across the street from the bank, and who subsequently turned out to be in collusion with the robbers.

As the prosecutor had done with all the other witnesses, Hagen held up the red and black plaid shirt.

"Have you ever seen this shirt before, Billy?"

"Yes, sir."

"Where did you see it?"

Frakes pointed to Smoke. "He was a'wearin' it when we found him," he said.

"Let the record show that the witness has pointed out that the defendant was wearing this very shirt when he was captured," Hagen said.

"Had you ever seen the shirt before?"

"Yes, sir."

"When and where did you see it before?"

"I seen it on the sixth of this month," Frakes said. "I seen it when the two men who was wearin' them come ridin' into town. Then, I seen it again when the two bank robbers come runnin' out of the bank."

"Wait a minute," Hagen said in sudden interest. "Are you saying that you saw him when he rode into town?"

"Yes, sir."

"And this was before the robbery?"

"Yes, sir."

"So, you saw him without the mask?"

"Maybe," Frakes said.

"Maybe? What do you mean, maybe?"

"I seen their faces, but I didn't look at them that long. I couldn't tell you if this was one of the men or not."

"But you do remember the shirt, right?"

"Yes, sir."

"You saw this shirt on one of the men who came into town?"

"Yes, sir."

"And you saw it again when you were with the posse as they arrested him?"

"Yes, sir."

"No further questions. Your witness, Mr. Jensen."

"Did you get a good look at the man who was standing in front of the bank, the man wearing a shirt just like that one?" Smoke asked.

"Yes, sir, I got a good look at him."

"Am I that man?"

"No, sir, you ain't that man."

Smoke turned away as if to sit down. Then, getting an idea, he stopped and turned back toward the witness.

"You said you were going to try and sell a pair of boots to one of the robbers?"

"Yeah, I was. See, I make boots and I figured if I could sell a few pair, well, maybe Mr. Sikes would carry 'em in his store," Frakes said. "And I thought maybe one of them might buy my boots since I seen 'em lookin' at boots in Sikes's window."

"You make boots, do you?"

"Yes, sir."

"So, you must know quite a bit about boots."

Frakes smiled. "I know more'n most folks do, I reckon."

"Do you take notice of the kind of boots people wear?"

"Oh, yes, sir, I'm always lookin' at folks' boots."

"Can you tell me what kind of boots I'm wearing?" Smoke asked. He started to stick his boot out so Frakes could see it, but Frakes waved it off.

"You don't have to show me," he said. "I've done looked at 'em. Them boots you're wearin' is what's called black cherry brush-off boots. They're real nice boots, and kind of expensive."

"Were any of the bank robbers wearing boots like these?" Smoke asked.

"Ha!" Frakes said. "Are you kidding? None of 'em had boots like those."

"Not even the two men who were wearing the red and black plaid shirts?" Smoke asked.

Frakes shook his head. "No, sir." He chuckled. "They was wearing old, scruffed-up boots, the kind you can buy anywhere for no more'n two dollars."

Suddenly, the smile left Frakes's face, and he looked over at the judge. "That's right," he said. "They wasn't none of 'em wearin' boots like these here boots."

"Thank you. No more questions," Smoke said.

In redirect, Hagen tried to get Frakes to say that he couldn't be sure about the boots, that maybe one of them could have been wearing boots like the boots the defendant was wearing, but Frakes couldn't be budged.

"They was all six wearin' scruffed-up boots," he insisted.

When the prosecution finished its case, Judge Craig invited Smoke to call any witnesses he might have for his defense.

"Your Honor, in order to call any witnesses for defense, I would have to bring some people here from Big Rock."

"Could any of the people from Big Rock testify that you were somewhere else on the day of the robbery?" Judge Craig asked.

"No, sir. They would be more on the order of character witnesses," Smoke said.

"I see. Mr. Jensen, is there any witness, anywhere, who could testify that they were with you on the sixth of this month?"

Smoke shook his head. "No, Your Honor," he said. "I was on the trail for that entire day. I did not see a soul until I encountered the bank robbers."

Craig removed his glasses and polished them vigorously for a moment. Then he put them back on.

"If you cannot find a witness who can testify in direct contradiction to any of the witnesses the prosecution has brought to the stand, then I see no reason for granting a stay on this trial. I'll give you half an hour to compose your thoughts. Then I will expect you to make your closing arguments." Judge Craig slammed the gavel down on the desk. "This court stands in recess for one half hour."

As Smoke sat back down at his table, he saw the prosecutor summon Pike over to him. Hagen and the deputy spoke for a moment, then Pike left.

"Do you want me to help you with your closing argument?" Jackson asked.

Smoke shook his head. "No, thanks," he said. "I'm sure you mean the best, Mr. Jackson. But seeing as this is my life we're talking about here, I think I'd feel better if I did it myself."

"All right," Jackson said. He got up and started to leave. Then he turned and looked back at Smoke. "Mr. Jensen, don't try to make a speech. Just talk to the folks in the jury as if you were telling a friend what happened."

Smoke nodded. "Thanks," he said. "I appreciate the tip."

All too soon, it seemed, Marshal Turnball stepped up to the front of the room.

"All rise," he shouted.

Again, the gallery stood as Judge Craig came back into the court and took his seat.

"Mr. Jensen," Craig said after everyone was seated. "You may begin your closing argument."

"Thank you, Your Honor," Smoke said. He turned to face the jury.

"I must say that I am a little surprised that nobody in this town knows me," he began. "I guess this is a little far from Big Rock, so it's out of my home area. But I am well known back home. And, I'm proud to say, that I am known as a man of honesty and integrity. One of my closest friends in Big Rock is Sheriff Carson. I own a ranch there, a rather substantial ranch, and I am what you might regard as a pillar of the community.

"Now, normally, it isn't my style to blow my own horn, so to speak. But, since I don't have anyone over here to blow it for me, well, I reckon I don't have much choice." Smoke smiled broadly, and tried not to let it show when nobody returned the smile.

"I did not rob the bank here. I did not kill Mr. Clark. I did not know Mr. Clark, but from some of the testimony I've heard today, I'm sure he was a very good man. I can understand how having a good man killed so senselessly could get a town upset. But wouldn't it be better for you to find the person who actually did it?

"I wish I could tell you that I know who did it, but I don't. I was set upon by six men, two of whom were wearing shirts identical to the one prosecution is using as his evidence. While I was distracted, one of them knocked me out, and when I came to, I saw that my own shirt was gone, and I was wearing that shirt." He pointed toward the shirt.

"I was angry that someone had stolen my shirt, and puzzled as to why they would do it. But when Marshal Turnball and his posse came along a little later, I learned the reason. One of the bank robbers, perhaps even the killer, put this shirt on me to throw suspicion my way.

"Before you vote on your verdict, I want you to think about two things. Number one, nobody saw the face of the second man who was wearing the plaid shirt, and number two . . ." Smoke held out his foot. "We heard Mr. Frakes say that not one of the six was wearing boots like these."

Satisfied that he had done his best, Smoke sat down. Just as he did so, he saw Pike, smiling from ear to ear, come back into the school cum courthouse. He was carrying a bag, which he showed to Hagen. The two spoke about it for a moment, then looked over at Smoke.

Pike chuckled.

"Mr. Hagen?" the judge said.

"Please the court, I'd like one minute," Hagen said.

"Make it quick."

Hagen took the sack over to Frakes and showed it to him. Frakes looked into the bag, then nodded.

"Thank you," Hagen said. Hagen returned to the front of the room, facing the jury.

"Gentlemen of the jury," he began. "In Kirby Jensen's closing argument, you heard him say that he owned a large ranch near Big Rock. That is true, he does own a large ranch. However, according to papers found on him when he was arrested, that ranch is encumbered by a mortgage note of two thousand dollars, due in just over one month. If he fails to make that payment, he will lose his ranch.

"That, I submit, is incentive enough to make an otherwise honest rancher rob a bank.

"Where is that money, you may ask? Why was it not found on him? That is a good question, and the answer is as simple and as old as the sin of thievery itself. There is no honor among thieves, and he had none of the money when he was arrested because Jensen was beaten and robbed by his own fellow thieves.

"Did Kirby Jensen kill Mr. Clark? There were four bullets found in Mr. Clark's body, so it is likely that one of the bullets was his. But according to the law, it doesn't matter whether any of those bullets came from Jensen's gun or not. According to the law, everyone who was there is equally guilty of his murder.

"Now there comes only the question, was he there? You have heard witness after witness testify that they saw this shirt on the back of one of the killers. You also heard Billy Frakes testify that he saw the faces of the two men when they rode into town, and, having seen the faces, cannot rule out the possibility that Kirby Jensen was one of them. And not even Jensen can produce one witness who can testify that he wasn't there.

"So, what did Jensen do? He showed Billy Frakes a pair of fancy boots, and asked if any of the robbers were wearing such boots. Billy Frakes said no."

Hagen reached down into the sack and pulled out a pair of boots.

Smoke felt his heart sink. He had brought along those old and worn boots, intending to wear them to keep his better boots from getting scuffed. But they were uncomfortable as riding boots, so he kept them rolled up in his blankets.

"Mr. Pike took these very boots from Kirby Jensen's bedroll about half an hour ago," Hagen said, continuing with his closing argument. "You all saw me show these boots to Billy Frakes. Billy just told me that, if need be, he is prepared to testify that the two men in the red and black plaid shirt were wearing boots exactly like these.

"Gentlemen of the jury, your task is solemn, but it is simple. Your task is solemn, because you are charged, by your fellow citizens, with the responsibility of bringing justice to our fair town. But your task is simple, because there is overwhelming and irrefutable evidence to help you come to the right decision. And the right decision is to find Kirby Jensen guilty of murder in the first degree."

Hagen turned and started back toward his seat.

"Good job, Hagen, you got the son of a bitch!" a man shouted, and several others cheered and applauded.

It took Judge Craig several seconds of banging the gavel until he was able to restore order in the court. Finally, when the gallery was subdued, he charged the jury.

The jury filed out through the back door of the schoolhouse, then gathered under a shade tree to discuss the case. They returned in less than half an hour.

"Who is the foreman of the jury?" Judge Craig asked.

"I am, Your Honor. The name is Jeff Colfax."

"Mr. Colfax, has the jury reached a verdict?"

The jury foreman leaned over to spit a wad of tobacco into a spittoon before he answered. He wiped his mouth with the back of his hand.

"We've reached a verdict, Your Honor," he said.

"Would you publish the verdict, please?"

"We, the jury, find this here fella"—he pointed to Smoke—"guilty of murder and bank robbin'."

"So say you all?"

"So say we all."

"Thank you, Mr. Foreman," the judge said. "The jury is dismissed. "Mr. Turnball, you are hereby relieved of your duty as court bailiff, and may resume your duties as city marshal. Now, Marshal Turnball, bring your prisoner before the bench to hear his sentencing."

Marshal Turnball stepped over to the defense table and looked down at Smoke.

"Stand up and hold your hands out," he ordered.

Smoke did as he was directed, and Turnball clamped the manacles on his wrists before leading him up to stand before the judge.

"It is the sentence of this court that a gallows be constructed in the city street so that all may bear witness to the inevitable result that befalls a person bent on following the path of crime. Then, on Thursday next, at ten o'clock of the morning hour, you will be removed from your jail cell and taken to this public gallows where a noose will be placed around your neck, a lever will be thrown, a trapdoor will fall from under your feet, and you will be hurled into eternity.

"May God have mercy on your evil, vile, and worthless soul, sir, because I have none."

The judge ended his pronouncement with the banging of his gavel, and Marshal Turnball and one of his deputies led Smoke out of the court and down to the jail.

12

"One hundred dollars!" the big man with the white, handlebar mustache shouted above the din in the saloon. "I'll bet one hundred dollars that no man can stay on Cannonball for one whole minute."

Pearlie and Cal were on their way back to Big Rock, but had stopped in the town of Jasper. They were having a quiet beer together in the Good Nature Saloon when they heard the offer.

"That ain't much of a bet, Stacey," one of the others in the saloon said. "Hell, there ain't nobody ever stayed on him for more'n ten seconds. Can't nobody stay on him for a full minute."

"I'll try it, if you give odds," another cowboy said.

"What kind of odds?" Stacey asked.

"Two to one," the cowboy answered. "I'll put up twenty. If I can stay on for a whole minute, you'll pay me forty."

"You got twenty dollars, cowboy?" Stacey asked.

"I got twenty," the cowboy answered.

"Take 'im up on it, Stacey. I'd like to see if anyone really could ride Cannonball."

"Yeah, give us a show," another shouted.

Stacey stroked his mustache for a second, then he nodded.

"All right," he said. "Put up the twenty dollars. Let's see what you can do."

"Yahoo!" one of the others shouted, and everyone poured out of the saloon to see the ride.

"Come on, Cal, let's go see this," Pearlie said, standing and tugging on Cal's arm.

There had been no more than twenty men in the saloon when the challenge was issued, but as they started down the street toward the corral, word spread through the rest of the town so that many more joined. By the time they reached the corral, which was at the far end of the street from the Good Nature Saloon, there were nearly one hundred spectators.

Pearlie and Cal found a seat on the top rail of the corral fence and watched as they saddled Cannonball.

Cannonball was a big horse with a well-defined musculature. He was also a very aggressive horse, fighting even against being saddled.

"Hey, Stacey, if Pete can't do it, can I give it a try?" one of the cowboys shouted.

"Have you got 'ny money?" Stacey replied.

"I've got money."

"All right, you're next."

When, at last, they got the saddle on Cannonball, Pete climbed up on the top rung of the fence and crouched there, ready. Pete nodded toward the two men who were handling Cannonball, and they led the horse over.

Pete pounced onto the horse's back, and the two handlers let go, then jumped out of the way. Cannonball exploded away from the fence, then went through a series of gyrations, bucking, twisting, coming down stiff-legged, and ducking his head. Pete was thrown in less than ten seconds.

"Whoowee, that's some horse!" someone shouted.

"My turn," the one who had put in the bid to be second said. But like Pete, he was thrown in a matter of seconds.

"I'll try it for twenty dollars," another said, and Pearlie and Cal watched as the third rider was thrown even faster than the first two.

"Look," Cal said to Pearlie as still a fourth man tried to ride the horse. "See how he ducks his head to the left there, then sort of leans into it? If a man would sort of jerk his head back to the right, he could stop that."

"You think you could ride him, Cal?" Pearlie asked.

Cal didn't answer right away. Instead, he watched another rider try and get thrown.

"Yeah," Cal said. "I think I could."

"Do you think you could a hundred dollars' worth?"

"Ha! Are you kidding? I don't have a hundred dollars."

"*I* do. I'll give it to you to bet, if you think you can ride him."

Cal shook his head. "No, Pearlie, that's your money. That's money you said you were going to give to Smoke and Miss Sally."

"Yes, it is," Pearlie said. "But if you could win two hundred dollars more, don't you think that would be even better?"

"Well, yeah, sure, but . . ."

"Do you think you can ride him, or don't you?"

Cal looked at the horse just as it threw another rider.

"Yeah," Cal said. "I think I can ride him."

The two wranglers grabbed Cannonball and brought him back to the end of the corral.

"Anybody else?" Stacey called, holding up a fistful of money, all of it won from would-be riders within the last few minutes.

Nobody responded.

"This is your last chance, boys. Anybody else want to try before we put Cannonball back in his stall?"

There was still no answer.

"All right, men, get the saddle off him," Stacey said to his wrangler.

"Here, Cal, here's the money," Pearlie said.

Cal hesitated but for one second, then he called out loudly.

"I'll have a go at it for one hundred dollars," he said.

Several had started to leave the corral, but when they heard Cal call out, they stopped and came back.

"What did you say?" Stacey asked.

Call held up the one hundred dollars that Pearlie had given him.

"I said I would ride him," Cal said. "And I'm betting one hundred dollars that I can stay on him for an entire minute."

"Who is that fella?" one of the men in the crowd asked.

"I don't know," another answered. "I think he must've just come into town. I ain't never seen him afore now."

"Where did you get a hundred dollars?" Stacey asked.

"What difference does it make where I got it?" Cal answered. "You didn't ask anybody else where they got the money."

"And you want to wager that one hundred dollars that you can stay on Cannonball for a minute?"

"Yes, sir."

"That's one whole minute, mind you," Stacey said. "Not fifty-nine seconds."

"An entire minute," Cal agreed.

"All right, I'll bet you a hundred," Stacey said.

"Huh-uh," Cal replied, shaking his head.

"What do you mean, huh-uh? That's what you're wantin', ain't it? To bet a hundred dollars?"

"I am betting one hundred dollars," Cal said. "You are betting two hundred dollars."

"Two hundred dollars is a lot of money," Stacey said.

"The boy's right, though, Stacey," Pete said. Pete was the cowboy who was the first to try to ride Cannonball. "That's what you said. You said you was givin' two to one. If the boy bets a hunnert and he stays on the horse for a whole minute, you give him two hunnert."

"Pete's right," one of the others called out.

"All right," Stacey said. "All right, it don't matter none. There ain't no way this boy, or anyone, can stay on Cannonball for a whole minute."

"Ride 'im, boy!" someone shouted.

"Yeah! Let's see you take Stacey's money!" another called.

"Who is this fella Stacey anyway?" Pearlie asked as several men gathered around Cal to offer him their best wishes.

"He owns the mercantile here in town," someone said. "He got rich during the winter by sellin' his goods at about three or four times what they was worth."

"They ain't nobody here but what wants to see him ride that horse and take some of his money away from him," Pete said to Pearlie.

"Well, come on, boy!" Stacey called. "Are you goin' to ride or not?"

"I'll ride," Cal said. He gave the one hundred dollars back to Pearlie. "Hold on to it."

"Well, get over here and do it," Stacey said.

"Ride 'im, cowboy," the others said by way of encouragement.

Cal walked down to the other end of the corral, climbed up on the fence, then dropped down onto Cannonball's back.

Cannonball leaped away from the fence, throwing Cal into the air as he did so. The others groaned as they saw the saddle slipping to one side. Then Cal did an amazing thing. Instead of coming back down on the saddle, he came back on the horse's hindquarters, just behind the saddle. He held on as the saddle slipped off; then he moved forward and riding bareback, stayed with the animal.

The horse tried every maneuver to throw Cal off. He porpoised and sunfished; he twisted and turned; he reared on his hind legs, then jumped up on his forelegs; he dipped his head and leaned, a maneuver that had been successful with all previous riders. Cal countered that move just as he told Pearlie he would, by jerking the horse's head back and kneeing him in the neck on the opposite side.

Unable to lose his rider any other way, Cannonball began galloping around the corral, running close to the fence trying to rake him off. Those who were on the fence had to jump back to get out of the way.

When the horse reached the end of the corral, he leaped

over the fence, and continued his bucking out in the street. The spectators hurried out into the street to watch.

Cannonball leaped up onto the front porch of Stacey's Mercantile Store.

"No!" Stacey shouted, running out into the street in front of his store. "Get him down from there!"

Cannonball twisted and kicked, and when he did, he kicked out one of the front windows of the store. A second kick took out the door and a third kick took out the other window. Then, coming down off the porch, Cannonball hit the pillars, causing the porch roof to collapse.

Cannonball came out into the street and, seeing Stacey, started galloping toward him.

"No!" Stacey shouted again. He leaped to the left just in time to keep from being run down, and he landed face-first in a pile of horse apples. He screamed in anger and frustration as he stood up with gobs of manure sticking to him.

Cannonball ran at full speed to the far end of the street, then came to a sliding stop. Cal stayed on his back.

Everyone watched as horse and rider remained motionless at the far end of the street. Then Cal turned Cannonball around, and they walked back up to the corral at a leisurely pace. When they got back, Cal was sitting sideways on the horse's back.

"How long has it been?" Cal asked.

"One minute and thirty-seven seconds," the timer said.

"You owe me two hundred dollars," Cal said as he slid down. He reached up and patted the horse, which stood calmly beside him.

"I never thought you would be able to stay on," Stacey said.

"Yeah," Pete said. "Especially after you loosened the saddle.

"I did not loosen the saddle."

"Then I guess you did it on your own, huh, Jerry?" Pete asked one of the two wranglers.

"I . . . I . . ." Jerry began nervously. Then he looked over at Stacey and pointed. "I didn't do it on my own," he said. "Mr. Stacey, he told me to do it."

"You're fired, Jerry," Stacey said with an angry growl.

"No need for you to be firin' me," Jerry replied. "I quit." Jerry looked at Cal. "Sorry, fella, I ought'n to have done that. I reckon I was just tryin' to hang on to my job."

"No need to apologize," Cal said. "I won't be holdin' on to any hard feelings. I just want my money, that's all."

Stacey stared at Cal for a long moment. Then, with a loud, audible sigh, he pulled a roll of money from his pocket and counted off two hundred dollars. "Here!" he said angrily. "Here's your damn money!"

"Hey, Mr. Stacey," one of the cowboys called out. "Does that bet still hold? I think I could ride ole Cannonball now."

"You go to hell!" Stacey said gruffly as all the cowboys laughed.

"Four hundred twenty-six dollars," Pearlie said as he and Cal counted their money that night.

"That ain't the two thousand Smoke needs to save the ranch," Cal said.

"Maybe it ain't," Pearlie agreed. "But it ain't no small potatoes either. And it might help him. If nothin' else, it'll give 'em a little money to start with, if they have to start all over again."

"Yeah," Cal said.

"You're all right with this, ain't you, Cal?" Pearlie asked. "I mean, givin' our money to 'em and all. When you think about it, this is a lot of money to be givin' away like this. In fact, I don't know as I've ever had that much money on my own before."

"I know I ain't," Cal said.

"Are you goin' to be able to give it up? 'Cause if you don't, I don't think anyone would fault you."

"I'm goin' to give it up," Cal said.

Pearlie smiled, then reached out his hand and took Cal's hand in his.

"Good man," he said. "Good man."

13

Smoke was lying on the bunk in the small, hot, and airless cell, listening to the sound of the carpenters at work as they were busily constructing a gallows.

The hammers banged and the saws ripped through the lumber.

"Joe? Hey, Joe, hand me up that two-by-four, will you?"

"You are going to need more than one two-by-four there. Jensen is a big man. Hell, he could fall through the floor and break his neck," Joe called back.

Smoke heard the exchange, as well as the laughter that followed it.

Turnball stepped up to the cell.

"Sorry 'bout all the noise out there," Turnball said.

"Yeah, well, it's not like it's keeping me awake," Smoke replied.

Turnball chuckled. "I'll say this for you. For a man who's about to be hung, you've got a sense of humor. Anyway, your lunch will be here in a few minutes. The jail has a deal with Emma's Café to furnish meals for the prisoners."

"Thanks," Smoke said.

"Oh, and I also have some paper and a pencil here," Turnball said. "If there's anyone you'd like to write a letter to, I'll see to it that it gets mailed."

"Any chance of sending a telegram?" Smoke asked.

Turnball shook his head. "The line is still down. If you want to send word out to anyone, a letter is the only way you can do it."

"All right, let me have the paper and pencil," Smoke said.

Turnball nodded, walked over to his desk and got the paper and pencil, then brought them back and passed them between the bars. Smoke took them, then returned to his bunk and sat down. He lifted the pencil to write, but didn't begin right away.

He didn't want to hurry into the letter. He realized that by the time Sally got this letter, he would be dead. Because of that, he needed to think, very carefully, about what he would say.

His lunch came before he started writing, so Smoke ate the ham, fried potatoes, and biscuits while he contemplated what he would say to Sally. Then, with his lunch eaten and the sound of construction still ringing in his ears, he began to write.

My Dearest Sally,

If you are reading this letter, it means I am dead.

That's a very harsh thing to be telling you, so maybe you should pause for a minute so you can catch your breath.

I know this isn't the kind of opening sentence you would expect to read in a letter from me, and believe me, it's not one I wanted to write. But there is no other way to say it, other than to come right out and say it.

I also realize that some explanation is in order so, as well as I can, I will bring you up on just what has happened to me since I left home a week ago.

The trip up from Sugarloaf was a lot more difficult than I expected, as there is still a lot of snow in some of the higher elevations. Coming through Veta Pass, which normally should take only a matter of hours, took two days. Stormy had to break through snow that was up to his chest, and by the time we did get through, I had to give both him and me a pretty long breather.

We did not see another living soul for those two days. And that is bad, because if we had seen anyone else, anyone at all, I probably wouldn't be in this fix.

It's time now for me to explain just what kind of fix I am in. I am, as of this writing, sitting in a jail in Etna, Colorado. It seems that the Bank of Etna was robbed on the morning of the sixth of this month. As it happens, on the sixth I did see someone else. But by pure coincidence, and the worst luck, the people I encountered were the very men who had robbed the Bank of Etna.

Stormy had picked a stone, and I was in the process of taking it out of his shoe when the six men rode up. I was not expecting anything out of the ordinary from my encounter with them, so I was not nearly as vigilant as I should have been. As a result, I was caught off guard and knocked out.

Sally, I know this was a dumb, you might even say a tenderfoot, thing for me to do. And you know me better than that. You know that, normally, I am much more alert.

I suppose my only excuse is that I was tired from the travel. And to be honest, I wasn't in the best of spirits, due to the fact that I was on my way to Denver to lease our ranch. That is something I know we needed to do, but it wasn't something I was looking forward to.

Anyway, thanks to my own dumb poor judgment, I was knocked out. But the story gets even stranger, Sally, because when I came to, I realized that I was wearing the shirt of one of the men who had waylaid me. I didn't have time to wonder about it, though, because almost from the moment I came to, I was face-to-face with a posse from Etna.

It was then that I found out what the shirt was all about, because the posse, seeing me in that very shirt, assumed that I was one of the ones they were looking for. I was arrested, and taken into town.

I was certain that I would be able to prove my innocence, but because I had not encountered anyone during my time on the trail, I was unable to establish an alibi. The posse had not believed me when they picked me up, and neither did the jury. I was found guilty, not only of the robbery, but of the murder of the banker, a man named Rob Clark.

That brings us back to the opening line of this letter. As a result of the verdict, I was sentenced to death by hanging. And now, as I write this letter, I can hear them building the gallows out in the street.

Putting down the tablet and pencil, Smoke climbed up onto the bunk so he could look out through the high window. He couldn't actually see the gallows, though as it was now late afternoon, he could see its shadow against the side wall of the apothecary. The men had quit work for the day, but Smoke could tell from the projected shadow that they had completed the base of the gallows.

When Pearlie and Cal rode into Big Rock, Pearlie pointed to a buckboard and team that was parked in front of the telegraph office.

"Isn't that rig from Sugarloaf?"

"Yes," Cal said. "Smoke must be sending a telegram."

"Let's go surprise him," Pearlie suggested.

Dismounting alongside the buckboard, Pearlie and Cal stepped into the telegraph office. Rather than surprising Smoke, they were themselves surprised to see Sally there.

"Hello, Miss Sally," Cal said.

There was a look of concern on Sally's face when she turned, but that was replaced by a big smile the moment she saw Pearlie and Cal.

"Pearlie! Cal!" she said happily. Opening her arms, she embraced each of them in turn. "Oh, I'm so happy to see you. I am so glad you are back!"

"Where's Smoke?" Cal said. "We've got something for him."

The smile left Sally's face to be replaced, once more, by a look of concern.

"I don't know where he is," she said. "He is supposed to be in Denver, meeting with a land broker. He was going to send me a telegram to tell me that he had arrived safely, but I haven't heard anything."

"Well, maybe the telegraph lines are down," Pearlie suggested. "You know, this was an awful bad winter."

"The direct lines are down," Sally said. "But Cody was able to get a message through by relaying it through Wichita. And if I can get through to Denver that way, you know he can get through to me."

Pearlie was quiet for a moment, then he nodded. "Yes, ma'am, I reckon if there was a way to send you a telegram, Smoke would figure it out," he said. "I was just tryin' to keep you from worryin' too much, that's all."

"You say you got through to Denver?" Cal asked.

"Yes. I sent a telegram to the broker, asking if Smoke had arrived. I'm waiting now for the reply."

Behind them, they heard the telegraph begin clacking. The telegrapher hurried over to the instrument, sat down in front of it, grabbed the key, then sent something back.

"Cody, is that my telegram?" Sally asked.

"Yes, ma'am, I believe it is," Cody replied.

The machine began clacking again, and Cody picked up a pencil and started recording the message on a little yellow tablet. The instrument continued for several seconds while Cody wrote. Then the machine grew silent.

Once again, Cody put his hand on the key to send a message back. Then, clearing his throat, he tore the page from the tablet, stood up, and brought it over to Sally.

"I wish I had somethin' better to report, Miss Sally," Cody said as he handed the message to her.

HAVE NOT SEEN SMOKE JENSEN STOP EXPECTED HIM
TWO DAYS AGO STOP WILL HAVE HIM SEND MESSAGE
IF HE ARRIVES STOP

"Now I am beginning to get worried," Sally said.

"You want us to go look for him?" Pearlie asked.

"I don't want you to go without me," Sally said. "But I want to give it a couple more days. I would hate to be out looking for him, and not be here to get his telegram when it comes."

"All right," Pearlie said.

"Thank you, Cody," Sally called back to the telegrapher.

"Miss Sally, if anything comes for you in the next day or so, I promise I'll get it out to your ranch," Cody said.

"I appreciate that," Sally said. Then to Pearlie and Cal: "Well, I take it you two are back. Shall we go home?"

"We're back," Cal said. "And guess what we brung you."

"What you *brung* me?" Sally scolded.

"Uh, what we brought you?"

"That's better. And it doesn't matter what you brought me. I'm just happy to see the two of you back where you belong."

"Four hunnert dollars," Cal said.

"What?" Sally responded with a gasp, surprised by the comment.

"We brung . . . uh, that is, we brought you four hunnert dollars," Cal said. "To help save the ranch."

"Where on earth did you get . . . no, never mind, it doesn't matter where you got it. However you got it, it's your money. Please don't feel any obligation toward Sugarloaf."

"Miss Sally, you don't want to hurt our feelings, do you?" Pearlie asked.

"What? No, of course not."

"Well, then, you must know that we consider Sugarloaf our home too. I know we don't own any of it, or nothin' like that. But it is our home nonetheless. And like you said, this here money is our money, which means we can pretty much do with it as we please. Ain't that right?"

Sally sighed. She wasn't even going to consider the poor grammar.

"Yes," she said. "It's your money to do with as you like. And yes, Sugarloaf certainly is your home."

"Then, we want to give you this money to help save it."

"Thank you," Sally said. "I couldn't be more touched."

Smoke did not finish writing the letter the first day. For a while, he considered scrapping the entire letter, but realized that, while he was actually writing, it almost seemed as if he were with Sally. So, late in the afternoon of the second day, he picked up the tablet and continued the letter.

As I am sure you have learned by now, I did not get to Denver to see the broker, so I have not been able to rent out Sugarloaf. Maybe you can make all the arrangements by telegraph. Or maybe it would even be better for you to sell Sugarloaf. You should be able to get a lot more money than we owe on the ranch. Then you could move into town somewhere and live comfortably on the money you would get from the sale.

I know that right now, as you read this letter, money is probably the furthest thing from your mind. But it is one of the foremost things on my mind. If something like this had to happen, I wish it could have happened last year, or even the year before. The ranch was solvent then, and you would not have been as foolish as I was to risk so much on the greedy ambition of growing even larger. My only comfort now is in knowing that you are smart enough to be able to salvage what value there remains of the ranch.

I hope Pearlie and Cal return sometime soon. I think having them around will help you deal with this. Or maybe you will help them deal with it. For some reason, women seem to be stronger than men about such things.

    I have been writing this letter for two days now, not because I am having a hard time in writing it, but because while I am writing it, I feel myself closer to you.

When Smoke heard the sound of construction halt for the day, he put the letter aside and, once more, climbed up onto his bunk to see what he could see. The sun was low in the west, and as it had done the day before, it projected the shadow of the gallows-in-progress onto the wall across the alley from the jail. Today he could see the base and the steps, and just the beginning of the gibbet.

On the third day, Smoke finished his letter.

Sally, I have faced death many times before, and just as I was not afraid then, I am not afraid now. You cannot spend your life in this magnificent country and not be aware that death is a part of life, or that there is something higher than we are. And because I believe in that higher power, I do not think this is the end. It is only a door from this life into whatever God has in store for me. If there is a balance sheet of my life, I am comfortable with the idea that I will be received into His Glory.

    My only regret is that I did not have more time to spend with you. You, Sally, have been the purpose and the love of my life. Know that, even though you may not see me, I will find a way to be with you from now on.
                      Your loving husband,
                          Smoke

At about the same time Smoke finished his letter, the hammering and sawing stopped, and when he climbed up on his bunk to look at the shadow against the wall, he could see the entire gallows. The instrument of execution was complete, to include the gibbet and dangling rope. The hangman's noose was already tied.

Having faced death many times before, Smoke was convinced that he had come to an accommodation with it. But he was about to be hanged for something he did not do, and there was something about that prospect that bothered him even more than the actual dying. It wasn't just that he was going to be executed, though that was bad enough. It was that those who actually were guilty were getting away with it.

Smoke folded his letter and put it in the envelope Turnball had given him. He had just finished addressing it when Deputy Pike stepped up to the cell and looked in.

"Who'd you write that letter to?" Pike asked.

"I wrote it to my wife."

"Your wife, huh?" Pike said. He giggled. "Is your wife a good-lookin' woman? I mean, bein' as she's goin' to be a widder-woman, why, just maybe I'll go meet her."

"Why don't you do that?" Smoke said.

"Hah! You want me to go meet your widder?"

"Yes," Smoke said. "Tell her how much you enjoyed watching me die." Smoke smiled, a cold, hard smile. "Then I suggest you duck."

"Why? Is she goin' to hit me with a fryin' pan?"

"No. She is more likely to shoot you with a forty-four," Smoke said.

"Really?"

"Really."

"Well, we'll just see about that." Pike stuck his hand in through the bars of the cell. "If you'll give me your letter, I'll see to it that it gets mailed."

"No, thanks."

"What do you mean no, thanks? Don't you want it mailed?"

"Not unless I'm dead."

"Well, don't you be worryin' none about that. You're goin' to be dead by a little after ten o'clock tomorrow mornin'."

"You can mail it then," Smoke said.

"Pike, get away from that cell and quit bothering the prisoner," Turnball called from his own desk.

"I was just . . ." Pike started.

"I don't care what you was just," Turnball said. "Just get away from the cell like I told you to."

"All right, Marshal, whatever you say," Pike replied.

That night, Deputy Pike was on duty. As it grew dark, he lit a kerosene lantern, but the little bubble of golden light that the lantern emitted barely managed to light the office. Although the cell was contiguous to the office, very little of the light from the lantern reached it. The cell, while not totally dark, was in deep shadows.

Just as the clock struck ten, Pike came over to the cell. Smoke was lying on the bunk with his hands laced beside his head. Because Pike was backlit by the lantern, Smoke could see him quite clearly. However, the dark shadows inside the cell made it more difficult for Pike to see Smoke.

"Hey, Jensen," Pike called. "Jensen, you awake in there?"

"I'm awake," Smoke replied, his low, rumbling voice floating back from the shadows.

"It's ten o'clock," Pike said. He giggled. "You know what that means, don't you? That means you only got twelve hours left to live."

Pike put his fist alongside his neck, representing a hangman's noose. Then he jerked his fist, tipped his head over to one side, and made a gagging sound in his throat.

"Shhhiiick!"

Laughing, Pike walked back into the office.

He came back at eleven. "Eleven hours," he said.

"Thanks so much for reminding me," Smoke said sarcastically.

"Oh, don't you worry none about that," Pike said. "I plan

to come here ever' hour on the hour all night long. What's the good of hangin' somebody if you can't have a little fun with it?"

True to his word, Pike came back at midnight, and again at one. And each time, he told Smoke the time left with particular glee.

As it so happened, Smoke had a good view of the clock from his cell, so, just before two o'clock in the morning, he climbed up to the very top of the cell and hung on with feet and hands. As he expected, Deputy Pike came to the cell just as the clock was striking two. But because Smoke was in the shadows at the top of the cell, Pike didn't see him.

"Jensen?" Pike called. "Jensen, where are you?"

Smoke was in an awkward and uncomfortable position, and he didn't know how much longer he would be able to hold on. He watched Pike's face as the deputy studied the inside of the cell, and he could tell that Pike was both worried and confused.

"Where are you?" Pike asked again. "Where the hell did you go?"

Pike hurried back to get the key, then he returned and opened the door to step inside.

Smoke wasn't sure if he could have held on for another moment, but he managed to hold on until Pike was well inside the cell and clear of the door.

Then Smoke dropped down behind him.

"What the hell?" Pike shouted, turning around quickly to face Smoke. That was as far as he got. Before his brain had time to register what was going on, Smoke took him down with a powerful blow to the chin.

Working quickly, Smoke dragged the deputy over to the bunk. Then he pulled off the deputy's socks and stuffed them in his mouth to keep him from shouting the alarm after he left.

"Whew," Smoke said as he pulled the socks off Pike's smelly feet. "Those socks are pretty strong. Sorry about stuffing these in your mouth like this, Pike, but maybe you should think about washing your feet a little more often."

Smoke handcuffed the deputy to the bunk so he couldn't get rid of the socks. Then he closed and locked the door.

By then, Pike was conscious, and he lay on the bunk, glaring at Smoke with hate-filled eyes. He tried to talk, but could barely manage a squeak.

"Deputy Pike, it has been fun," Smoke said. "We'll have to do this again sometime."

14

Smoke retrieved his guns and saddlebags from the office. Then, almost as an afterthought, he took the red and black plaid shirt that had played such a role in his trial. After that, he let himself outside. The cool night breeze felt exceptionally refreshing to him, especially after several days of being cooped up in a cell.

As he stepped out into the street, he saw in actuality what he had only seen in shadow before now. The gallows was rather substantial, consisting of thirteen steps leading up to a platform that was about ten by ten. He didn't go up the steps for a closer examination, but he knew there would be a trapdoor at the center of the platform. Gabled over the top of the platform was the gibbet, and hanging from the gibbet was the rope and noose.

There was a sign in front of the gallows:

TO BE HUNG
AT TEN O'CLOCK OF THE MORNING
ON THE 15TH INSTANT

FOR THE MURDER OF ROBERT CLARK
KIRBY JENSEN

PUBLIC INVITED.PUBLIC INVITED.

Taking out the pencil he had used to write his unsent letter to Sally, Smoke drew a large X across the sign. Then at the bottom he added:

HANGING CANCELLED

Chuckling to himself, Smoke hurried down to the livery stable. Although the night was moon-bright, it was very dark inside the stable where his horse was being kept.

He knew that Stormy was in here because he overheard Turnball telling someone that the town of Etna was going to sell Smoke's horse in order to pay for the expense of his trial and hanging.

As he moved down through the center corridor of the stable, he could smell straw and oats, as well as the manure, urine, and flesh of a dozen or more horses. The animals were being kept in stalls on either side of the center passage, but in the darkness of the building they were little more than large, looming, indecipherable shadows and shapes to him. He would have to depend upon Stormy to help him.

"Stormy?" Smoke called quietly. "Stormy, are you in here?"

Smoke heard a horse whicker in response, and going toward the sound, he found his horse with his head sticking out over the door of the stall.

"Good boy," Smoke said, rubbing his horse behind its ears. "Did you miss me?"

In response, Stormy nudged his nose against Smoke.

Smoke saw that his saddle was draped over the side of the stall. With a silent prayer of thanks for it being so convenient to him, he picked up the saddle and put it on his horse. Then, very quietly, he opened all the other stall doors in the stable and, clucking at the horses, called them out. Mounting Stormy, he then rode around to the corral and opened the gate. Within moments he had gathered a small herd of some thirty horses, and he started moving them out of town. He kept the herd going until he was at least two miles away.

Then he pulled his pistol and fired into the air, causing the horses to break into a gallop.

The lead stallion started running in a direction that would take the herd farther away from Etna, and the others followed instinctively. Smoke was certain that after they tired of running, the herd would dissipate and the horses would probably return, one at a time, to the corral.

But for now they were in a panic, following the leader, and he knew it would be at least one day, maybe more, before the horses got back. He was certain that this wasn't every horse in town, but it represented a sizable number of them, enough to make the immediate raising of a posse difficult.

Once Smoke escaped from jail, he knew better than to go back home to Sugarloaf, or to even try to get in touch with Sally. There was no doubt in his mind but that Turnball would have notified Sheriff Carson back in Big Rock. And while Smoke and Carson were close friends, Carson was a man of great integrity, and Smoke's presence there under these circumstances would be very difficult for him.

The only way Smoke could avoid going back to jail, and keeping a date with the hangman, would be to find the real bank robbers and murderers. And it was that, his determination to find the real outlaws and clear his own name, that drove him now.

Tracking six riders on a trail that was a week old would be a task so daunting for most men that they would never even think to try. But Smoke wasn't most men, and he never gave the task before him a second thought. He had learned his tracking skills from a master tutor. The classes began during his days of living in the mountains with the man called Preacher,

"He's a good one to learn from," another mountain man once said to Smoke, speaking of Preacher. "Most anyone can track a fresh trail, but Preacher can follow a trail that is a month old. In fact, I've heard some folks say that he can track a fish through water, or a bird through the sky. And I ain't one to dispute 'em."

Now, as Smoke started on the trail of the bank robbers, the words of his tutor came back to him.

"Half of tracking is in knowin' where to look," Preacher told the young Smoke. *"The other half is looking.*

"Reading prints on a dirt road is easy. But if you know what you are doing, you can follow the trail no matter where it leads. Use every sense God gave you," Preacher explained. *"Listen, look, touch, smell. Taste if you have to."*

Smoke never was as good as Preacher, but if truth be told, he was second only to Preacher, and he could follow a cold trail better than just about anyone. Returning to the place where he had encountered the bank robbers, he managed to pick up their trail.

It was difficult, the trail being as old as it was, but he was helped by the fact that the robbers were trying to stay out of sight. Because of that, they avoided the main roads, and that made their trail stand out. The funny thing is, if they had stayed on the main roads, Smoke might not have been able to find them because their tracks would have been covered over, or so mixed in with the other travelers that he wouldn't be able to tell which was which.

But cutting a trail across fresh country the way they did led Smoke just as straight as if they had left him a map. Also, since they were isolated from the other traffic, Smoke was able to study each individual set of hoofprints. To the casual observer, all the prints would look alike, just the U shape of the horseshoes. But a closer examination showed that each set had its own peculiar identifying traits. That would be very helpful to him once they got back onto a major trail, for then he would be able to pick out the individual prints from among many others.

Tracking became even easier once he reached high country because there was still snow on the ground, and it was almost as if they were leaving him road signs.

Then, just on the other side of a large patch of snow, the riders went their separate ways. When that happened, Smoke had to choose which trail he was going to follow.

"What the hell?" Marshal Turnball said when he came into his office the next morning and found Deputy Pike gagged and handcuffed to the bunk and locked in the cell.

"Uhhnnn, uhhhnn," Pike grunted. He was unable to speak because of the socks that were stuffed in his mouth.

"Oh, shut up your moaning," Turnball said, his irritation showing in his voice. "Where are the damn keys?"

"Uhnnn, uhnnn," Pike grunted again.

"Oh, shut up," Turnball repeated.

Finding the keys lying on his desk, Turnball unlocked the cell door, then pulled the socks from Pike's mouth.

"Now, Deputy Pike, would you please tell me just what the hell happened?" Turnball asked as he started looking through the key ring for the one that would unlock the handcuffs.

Pike coughed and gagged for a moment after the socks were removed. "The son of a bitch got away!" he finally blurted out.

"I can see that, Pike," Turnball said. "The question is, how did he get away? When I left last night, he was locked in this cell. Now I come in here this morning and what do I find? Jensen? No! I find you all trussed up like a calf to be branded. Now I want to know how that happened."

"He jumped me," Pike said.

"He jumped you?"

"Yes, sir."

"You were outside, he was locked in the cell, and he jumped you?"

"I, uh, wasn't exactly outside the cell when he jumped me."

"Go on."

"Well, you see, I come into the cell," Pike said. He went on to explain how he had looked in the cell and, not seeing the prisoner, went in to investigate. He left out the fact that he had been harassing the prisoner every hour on the hour.

The front door to the jail opened then, and Syl Jones came in. Jones was the owner of the corral.

"Marshal, the horses is gone," Jones said.

"The horses? What horses?"

"Your horse, my horse, just about ever' horse in town. They're all gone."

"What the hell are you talking about? Gone? Gone where?"

"I don't know gone where. All I know is, when I come to work this mornin' the stable door was open, all the stalls was open, and the corral gate was open. They ain't one horse left."

"Jensen," Turnball said angrily.

"Jensen? Are you talkin' about Smoke Jensen? The fella we're goin' to hang this mornin'?" Jones had been a member of the jury that had convicted Smoke.

"Yes, that's exactly who I mean. The fella we *was* goin' to hang this morning," Turnball said. He looked at Pike, the expression on his face showing his anger. "That is, we was goin' to hang him before Pike, here, just opened the door and let 'im go."

"You let 'im go? What the hell did you do that for?" Jones asked.

"Shut up, Jones," Pike growled. "You think I done it of a purpose?"

"Well, even if he did escape, why would he steal ever' horse in town?" Jones asked.

"He didn't steal them, he just ran them off," Turnball said. "He figured it would keep us from comin' after 'im."

"Oh, yeah, I guess that's right," Jones said. "Well, if he just run 'em off, like as not they'll all be back before the day's out."

"In the meantime, that gives him a full day's head start." Sighing audibly, Turnball ran his hand through his hair. "Damn you, Pike," he said.

Turnball started for the front door.

"Where you goin'?" Pike asked.

"To the telegraph office. There has to be some way to get a message out."

"Yes, we've got a line through to Omaha," James Cornett said. "Just got put back up yesterday."

"Could you send a message to the sheriff of Hinsdale County through Omaha?"

"Well, if they are connected to anyone, I suppose we can. We could go through Omaha to Wichita to Denver to . . ."

Turnball waved his hand. "I don't need you to build the telegraph line for me, Cornett. Just send the message."

"All right," Cornett replied. "What's the message?"

"I'll write it out for you," Turnball said as he began writing. "Actually, two messages, one to the sheriff of Hinsdale County and one to Big Rock, down in Rio Grande County."

Half an hour later, just after Turnball got through explaining to a disappointed crowd that there would be no hanging today, Cornett came into his office with a message.

"We heard back from the sheriff of Hinsdale County," Cornett said, handing the message to Turnball.

Turnball read it, then shook his head. "What have we gotten ourselves into?" he asked.

"What is it?" Pike asked.

Without a word, Turnball handed Pike the telegram.

ANY SUCH REWARD POSTER ON KIRBY JENSEN AS MAY
EXIST HAS LONG BEEN RESCINDED STOP KIRBY JENSEN IS
ONE OF THE LEADING CITIZENS OF THE STATE STOP IT IS
HIGHLY UNLIKELY THAT JENSEN WOULD PARTICIPATE IN A
BANK ROBBERY STOP EXPECT INVESTIGATION FROM STATE
ATTY GENERAL OFFICE STOP GOVERNOR PITKIN PERSON-
ALLY INTERESTED IN CASE STOP

Cody Mitchell, the Western Union operator in Big Rock,
Colorado, was sweeping the floor of his office when the instrument began clacking to get his attention. Putting the
broom aside, he moved over to the table, sat down, and responded that he was ready to receive.

Cal was filling a bucket at the water pump when he saw a
boy of about fifteen riding toward the house.

"Can I help you with somethin'?" Cal called out to him.

"This here's the Jensen spread, ain't it?" the boy replied.

"It is."

"I got a message for Mrs. Jensen from Mr. Mitchell."

"Mitchell?" Cal asked.

"Mr. Cody Mitchell, the telegrapher."

"Oh!" Cal said. He smiled broadly. "It must be from
Smoke. Give the telegram to me, I'll take it to her."

The boy shook his head. "I ain't got no telegram. All I got
is a message, and Mr. Mitchell says I'm to tell it to her personal."

"All right," Cal said, picking up the bucket. "Come on, I'll
take you to her."

An hour after the message was delivered, Sally, Pearlie,
and Cal were in Sheriff Carson's office.

"You didn't have to come into town, Miss Sally," Carson
said. "I was goin' to come out there to see you."

"What's this all about, Sheriff?" Sally asked.

Sheriff Carson stroked his chin. "All I can tell you is what I heard from the marshal up in Etna. He said that they arrested Smoke for murder and bank robbery, and they tried him and found him guilty. He was supposed to hang this mornin', but he got away."

"Thank God," Sally said, breathing a sigh of relief.

"Yes," Carson said. "Well, he did get away, but it's my understanding that Marshal Turnball has sent word out all over the West sayin' Smoke is a wanted man."

"Sheriff, you know there is no way Smoke would hold up a bank, or murder someone," Sally said. "How could a fair jury find him guilty of such a thing?"

"I reckon they don't know him like we do," Carson said. "Sally, uh, they want me to arrest him if he comes back. I'm legally and morally bound to do it, so if he comes to the ranch first, you tell him to just keep on going and not to come into town."

"Don't worry, Sheriff," Sally said. "I don't think Smoke will come back until he has this mess all cleared up."

That night in the bunkhouse, Pearlie woke up in the middle of the night. When he awoke, he saw Cal sitting at the window, just staring outside.

"Damn, Cal, what time is it?" Pearlie asked from his bed.

"I don't know," Cal answered. "It's some after midnight, I reckon."

"What are you doin' up?"

"Can't sleep."

"You're thinking about Smoke, ain't you?"

"Yeah."

"Smoke will be all right. He can take care of himself; you know that."

"Yeah, I know it."

"And he'll find out who done this and get that set right too."

"Unless . . ." Cal answered, allowing the word to hang, pregnant with uncertainty.

"Unless what?"

Cal turned to look at Pearlie for the first time. "Pearlie, have you stopped to think that maybe Smoke, that is, maybe he . . ."

"Did it?" Pearlie responded.

Cal nodded his head, but said nothing. His eyes were wide, worried, and shining in the moonlight.

"Cal, believe me, I've known Smoke longer than you have. He didn't rob that bank and he didn't kill that banker."

"I mean, if he did, why, I wouldn't think no less of him," Cal said. "What with the winter we just come through, and the danger of him maybe losin' Sugarloaf an' all."

"He didn't do it," Pearlie said again.

"How can you be so sure?"

"I told you how I can be so sure. It's because I know him."

"Pearlie, you know how I come to be here, don't you? I mean, how I tried to rob Miss Sally that time? If it had been anyone else but her, I would of probably got away with it. Then, there's no tellin' where I would be now. I might even be a bank robber. But I ain't, 'cause she took me in."

"Yes, I know that."

"The point is, I ain't a thief. I mean, I ain't no normal thief, but I was pretty desperate then, so I done somethin' I never thought I would do. I could see how Smoke might do the same thing if he thought he had to."

"All right, Cal, do you want me to tell you how I know he didn't do this?"

"Yes."

"It's easy," Pearlie said. "The sheriff said there were six of 'em robbed the bank, right?"

"Right."

"If Smoke was going to rob a bank, he wouldn't need no five other men to help him get the job done. He would'a done it alone."

Cal paused for a minute, then he broke into a big smile.

"That's right!" he said. "He would'a done it alone, wouldn't he? I mean, Smoke, there ain't no way he would need someone else to help him do a little thing like rob a bank."

"Are you satisfied now?"

"Yeah," Cal said. "Yeah, you're right. Smoke didn't rob that bank."

"So, you'll go to bed now and let me get some sleep?"

"Yeah," Cal said. "Good night, Pearlie."

"Good night, Cal."

15

It was just growing dark when Smoke rode into the little town of Dorena. He passed by a little cluster of houses that sat just on the edge of town and as he came alongside them, he could smell the aroma of someone frying chicken. That reminded him that he was hungry, not having eaten anything for the entire day.

Smoke had never been in Dorena before, but he had been in dozens of towns just like it, so there was a familiarity as he rode down the street, checking out the false-fronted buildings: the leather goods store, the mercantile, a gun shop, a feed store, an apothecary, and the saloon.

The saloon was called Big Kate's, and when Smoke stopped in front of it, he reached down into the bottom of his saddlebag, moved a leather flap to one side, and found what he was looking for. He had put one hundred dollars in the saddlebag before he left Sugarloaf, keeping it in a way that a casual examination of the pouch wouldn't find it. Fortunately, it had escaped detection when he was arrested and his horse and saddle were taken.

The smell of bacon told him that Big Kate's offered an opportunity for supper, so he went inside.

One of the amenities the customers could enjoy at Big Kate's was a friendly game of cards. On the wall there was a sign that

read: THIS IS AN HONEST GAMBLING ESTABLISHMENT—
PLEASE REPORT ANY CHEATING TO THE MANAGEMENT.

In addition to the self-righteous claim of gambling integrity, the walls were also decorated with animal heads and pictures, including one of a reclining nude woman. There was no gilt-edged mirror, but there was an ample supply of decent whiskey, and several large jars of pickled eggs and sausages placed in convenient locations.

From a preliminary observation, Big Kate's appeared to be more than just a saloon. It was filled with working girls who all seemed to be attending to business. Smoke saw one of the girls taking a cowboy up the stairs with her.

The upstairs area didn't extend all the way to the front of the building. The main room, or saloon, was big, with exposed rafters below the high, peaked ceiling. There was a score of customers present, standing at the bar talking with the girls and drinking, or sitting at the tables, playing cards.

A large, and very bosomy, woman came over to greet Smoke.

"Welcome to Big Kate's, cowboy," she said. "I don't believe I've seen you before. Are you new in town?"

"I am," Smoke answered. "I take it that you are . . ." He hesitated, then left out the descriptive word. "Kate?"

Big Kate laughed, a loud, guffawing laugh. "It's okay, honey, you can call me big. Hell, I've got mirrors and I ain't blind. Now, could I get you something to drink?"

"Yes," Smoke answered.

"Wine, beer, or whiskey?"

"Beer," Smoke said. "And something to eat, if you've got it."

"Beans and bacon is about it," Big Kate replied. "And cornbread."

"That'll be fine," Smoke said

"Kim, do keep the cowboy company while I get him something to drink," Big Kate said, adroitly putting Smoke with one of her girls.

Kim was heavily painted and showed the dissipation of her profession. There was no humor or life left to her eyes.

"You were in here last week, weren't you?" Kim asked. "Or was it last month?"

Smoke shook his head. "You've never seen me before," he said.

"Sure I have, honey," Kim answered in a bored, flat voice. "I've seen hundreds of you. You're all alike."

"I guess it might seem like that to you."

"Would you like to come upstairs with me?"

"I don't think so," Smoke said. He smiled. "I'm just going to have my dinner and play some cards. But I appreciate the invitation."

"Enjoy your dinner, cowboy," Kim said in a flat, expressionless voice that showed no disappointment in being turned down. Turning, she walked over to sit by the piano player.

The piano player wore a small, round derby hat and kept his sleeves up with garter belts. He was pounding out a rendition of "Little Joe the Wrangler," though the music was practically lost amidst the noise of a dozen or more conversations.

"What's the matter? You didn't like Kim?" Big Kate asked, returning with Smoke's beer.

"Kim was fine," Smoke said. "I've just got other things on my mind, that's all."

"It must be somethin' serious to turn down a chance to be with Kim. She's one of our most popular girls," Big Kate said, laughing. "If you'll excuse me now, I see some more customers just came in and I'd better go greet them. Oh, there's a table over there. Your food will be right out."

"Thanks," Smoke said.

Ebenezer Dooley had stepped out through the back door to the outhouse to relieve himself. He was just coming back in when he saw Smoke Jensen talking with Big Kate.

What the hell? he thought. How the hell did he get out of jail?

Dooley backed out of the saloon before he was seen.

Kim brought Smoke another beer and supper, then left to ply her trade among some of the other customers. Smoke ate his supper, then, seeing a seat open up in a card game that was in progress, took the rest of his beer over to the table.

"You gents mind if I sit in?" he asked.

"We don't mind at all. Please, be our guest," one of the men said effusively, making a sweeping gesture. "The more money there is in a game, the better it is, I say."

"Thanks," Smoke said, taking the proffered chair.

Some might have thought it strange for Smoke to play a game of cards under the circumstances, the circumstances being that he was a man on the run. But he was also a man on the hunt, and he had learned, long ago, that the best way to get information was in casual conversation, rather than by the direct questioning of people. He knew that when someone started questioning people, seriously questioning them, the natural thing for them to do was to either be very evasive with their responses, or not say anything at all.

Smoke had already drawn his first hand before he saw the badge on the shirt of one of the other men who was playing.

"You the sheriff?" Smoke asked.

"Deputy," the young man answered with a broad smile. "The name is Clayton. Gideon Clayton. And you?"

"Kirby," Smoke replied, using his first name that no one ever used. Then, in a moment of inspiration, he decided to make that his last name. "Bill Kirby," he added.

For a moment, Smoke felt a sense of apprehension, and part of him wanted to just get up and leave. But he knew that doing something like that would create quite a bit of suspicion.

On the other hand, with Deputy Clayton being here, he might learn right away if any telegraph message of his escape had reached the sheriff's office. But when Deputy Clayton made no move toward him, nor gave any indication of being suspicious of him, Smoke knew that, for now, he was safe to continue his search.

To the casual observer it might appear that Smoke was so relaxed as to be off guard. But that wasn't the case, as his eyes were constantly flicking about, monitoring the room for any danger. And though he was engaged in convivial conversation with the others at the table, he was listening in on snatches of dozens of other conversations.

"I believe it is your bet," Deputy Clayton said to Smoke. Smoke missed the challenge when it was first issued because he was looking around the room to see if he could spot any familiar faces. "Kirby?" the deputy said again.

"I beg your pardon?"

"I said, I believe it is your bet," Clayton said.

"Oh, thank you," Smoke said. He looked at the pot, then down at his hand. He was showing one jack and two sixes. His down card was another jack. He had hoped to fill a full house with his last card, but pulled a three instead.

"Well?" Clayton asked.

Smoke could see why Clayton was anxious. The deputy had three queens showing.

"I fold," Smoke said, closing his cards.

Two of the other players folded as well, and two stayed, but the three queens won the pot.

"Thank you, gentlemen, thank you," Clayton said, chuckling as he raked in his winnings.

"Deputy Clayton, you have been uncommonly lucky tonight," one of the other men said good-naturedly. Smoke had gathered from the conversation around the table that the one speaking was Doc McGuire.

"I'll say I have," Clayton agreed. "I've won near a month's pay just sittin' right here at this table."

"What do you think, Beasley?" Doc asked one of the

other players. "Will our boy Clayton here give up the deputy sheriffin' business and go into gambling full-time?"

"Ho, wouldn't I do that in a minute if I wasn't married?" Clayton replied.

"Where's Sheriff Fawcett tonight?" Beasley asked.

"The sheriff's taking the night off," Clayton said. "I'm in charge, so don't any of you give me any trouble or I'll throw you in jail," he teased. The others laughed.

"Where you from, Mr. Kirby?" Doc McGuire asked as he shuffled the cards.

"Down in Laplata County," Smoke lied.

"Did you folks have a hard winter down there?"

"Yes, very hard."

"I was reading an article in the Denver paper a few weeks ago," Clayton said. "According to the article this was the worst winter ever, and it was all over the West. Hundreds of thousands of cows were lost."

"It was a bad one all right," Beasley said as he dealt the cards. "Some folks think that bad weather only hurts the farmers and ranchers, but I can tell you as a merchant that it hurts us too. If the farmers and ranchers don't have any money to spend, we can't sell any of our goods."

"I reckon it was the winter that made those folks hold up the bank over in Etna," Smoke said, taking a chance in bringing up the subject.

"There was a bank robbery in Etna?" Beasley asked. "I hadn't heard that."

"Yes," Deputy Clayton said. "We didn't get word on it until yesterday. Six of 'em held up the bank and killed the banker."

"They killed the banker?" Beasley asked. "Wait, I know that banker. His name is Clark, I think."

"Yes, Rob Clark," Clayton said. "But I understand they caught one of the ones who did it."

"Good. I hope they hang the bastard," Beasley said. "From what I knew of him, Clark was a good man."

"Oh, I expect the fella that killed him is already hung by now," Clayton said.

"You haven't heard anything on any of the others, have you?" Smoke asked.

"No, as far as I know they're still on the run," Clayton said as he pulled in another winning hand.

Smoke won the next hand, which brought him back to even, and the way the cards were falling, he decided he had better stop now. When Clayton started to deal, Smoke waved him away.

"Are you out?"

"Yeah, I'd better quit while I have enough money left to pay for my hotel room," Smoke said, pushing away from the table and standing up. "I appreciate the game, gentlemen, but the cards haven't been that kind to me tonight. I think I'll just have a couple of drinks, then turn in."

Ebenezer Dooley was standing just across the street from the saloon, tucked into the shadows of the space between Lair's Furniture and Lathum's Feed and Seed stores. He had been there for just over an hour when he saw Smoke step outside.

"Well now, Mr. Jensen," Dooley said quietly. "It's time I settled a score with you, once and for all."

Dooley pulled his pistol and pointed it, but just as he did so, a wagon passed between him and Smoke. By the time the wagon had cleared, he saw Smoke going into the hotel.

"Damn!" he said, lowering his pistol.

16

The hotel clerk was reading a book when Smoke stepped up to the desk. He looked up.

"Yes, sir, can I help you?"

"I'd like a room."

"Would you prefer to be downstairs or upstairs?"

"Upstairs, overlooking the street if possible."

"Oh, I think I can do that for you," the clerk said. He turned the book around. "The room will be fifty cents."

Smoke gave him the half-dollar, then signed the book, registering as Bill Kirby.

The clerk turned the book back around, checked the name, then wrote the room number beside it. He took a key down from the board and handed it to Smoke.

"Go up the stairs, then back to your left. The room number is five; you'll see it right in front of you."

"Thanks," Smoke said, draping his saddlebags over his shoulder.

The stairs were bare wood, but the upstairs hallway was covered with a rose-colored carpet. The hallway was illuminated by wall-sconce lanterns that glowed dimly with low-burning flames, putting out just enough light to allow him to see where he was going.

The number 5 was tilted to one side, but Smoke didn't

have any difficulty making it out. He unlocked the door, then went inside. The room was dark, illuminated only by the fact that he had left the door open and some light spilled in from the hall. He saw a kerosene lamp on the bedside table, as well as several matches.

Dooley was frustrated that Smoke had managed to go into the hotel before he was able to take a shot at him. He put his pistol back in his holster while he contemplated what to do next.

Dooley had a room in the hotel himself. Maybe the best thing to do would be to wait until much later, then sneak down the hall into Smoke's room and kill him in the middle of the night.

Dooley had just about decided to go back to the saloon and have a few drinks while he was waiting, when he saw a lantern light up in one of the windows facing the street on the second floor of the hotel. That had to be Smoke Jensen.

As it happened, the stable was just across the street from the hotel, so Dooley ran back to the alley, then down to the stable, coming in through the back door. Going to the stall where his horse was boarded and his saddle waited, he snaked his rifle from the saddle holster. Then, with rifle in hand, he climbed into the hayloft and hurried to the front to look across the street into the hotel. He smiled broadly when he saw that the shade was up and the lantern was lit. Just as he had thought it would be, the occupant of the room was Smoke Jensen.

He had an excellent view from the hayloft.

It was a little stuffy in the room, so Smoke walked over to the window, then raised it to catch the night breeze. That was when he saw a sudden flash of light in the hayloft over the livery across the street.

Instinctively, Smoke knew that he was seeing a muzzle

flash even before he heard the gun report. Because of that, he was already pulling away from the window, even as the bullet was crashing through the glass and slamming into the wall on the opposite side of the room.

Smoke cursed himself for the foolish way he had exposed himself at the window. He knew better; he had just let his guard down. He reached up to extinguish the lantern, and as he did so, a second shot came crashing through the window.

He extinguished the lamp, and the room grew dark.

"Damn!" Dooley said aloud. He jacked another round into the chamber of his rifle and stared across the street into the open, but now dark, window of Smoke Jensen's room.

Dooley was very quiet, very still, and very observant for a long time, and it paid off. He saw the top of Jensen's head appear just above the windowsill. He fired a third time.

This bullet was closer than either one of the other two, so close that he could feel the concussion of the bullet. But this time he had seen the muzzle flash from across the way, so he had a very good idea of where the shooter was, and he fired back.

Dooley hadn't expected Jensen to return fire. For one thing, Dooley was well back into the loft, so he was convinced that he couldn't be seen at all. He hadn't counted on Jensen being able to use the muzzle flash of his rifle to locate his position.

The bullet from Jensen's pistol clipped just a little piece of his ear, and he cried out and slapped his hand to the shredded earlobe.

"You son of a bitch," he muttered under his breath.

* * *

"What was that?" Smoke heard someone shout.

"Gunshots. Sounded like they came from down by the . . ."

That was as far as the disembodied voice got before another shot crashed through the window.

"Get off the street!" another voice called. "Everyone, get off the street!"

Smoke heard the command, loud and authoritative, floating up from below. "Everyone, get inside!"

Smoke recognized the voice. It belonged to Deputy Clayton, the man he had been playing cards with but a few minutes earlier. On his hands and knees so as not to present a target, Smoke crept up to the open window and looked out again. He saw the deputy running up the street.

"Clayton, stay away!" he shouted down to him. Clayton headed for the livery stable with his pistol in his hand. "Clayton, no! Get back!"

Smoke's warning was not heeded. A third volley was fired from the livery hayloft, and Clayton fell facedown in the street.

With his pistol in his hand, Smoke climbed out of the window, scrambled to the edge of the porch, then dropped down onto the street. Running to Clayton's still form, he bent down to check on him. Clayton had been hit hard, and through the open wound in his chest, Smoke could hear the gurgling sound of his lungs sucking air and filling with blood.

"Damnit, Clayton, I told you to get down," Smoke scolded softly.

"It was my job," Clayton replied in a pained voice.

At that moment, another rifle shot was fired from the livery. The bullet hit the ground close by, then ricocheted away with a loud whine.

"He's still up there," Clayton said.

"Yeah, I know," Smoke said.

"What's going on?" someone shouted.

"What's all the shootin' about?" another asked.

"Get back!" Smoke yelled. "Do what the deputy told you! Get back!"

"Is the deputy dead?"

Another shot from the loft of the stable did what Clayton and Smoke had been unable to do. It forced all the curious onlookers away from the street and out of the line of fire.

Smoke fired back, shooting once into the dark maw of the hayloft. Then, taking Clayton's pistol and sticking it down in his belt, he ran to the water trough nearest the livery, diving behind it just as the man in the livery fired again. He heard the bullet hit the trough with a loud popping sound. He could hear the water bubbling through the bullet hole in the water trough, even as he got up and ran toward the door of the livery.

Smoke shot two more times to keep the shooter back. Then, when he reached the big, open double doors of the livery, he ran on through them so that he was inside.

Once inside, he moved quietly through the barn itself, looking up at the hayloft just overhead. Suddenly he felt little pieces of straw falling on him and he stopped, because he realized that someone had to be right over him. That's when he heard it, a quiet shuffling of feet. He fired twice, straight up, but was rewarded only with a shower of more bits and pieces of straw.

"That's six shots. You're out of bullets, you son of a bitch," a calm voice said.

Smoke looked over to his left to see a man standing in the open on the edge of the loft. It was one of the bank robbers.

"Well," Smoke said. "If it isn't the pockmarked droopy-eyed son of a bitch who set me up."

"How the hell did you get out of jail, Jensen?" he asked. "I figured they'd have you hung by now. I must confess that I was some surprised when I seen you come in the saloon tonight."

"You're going to shoot me, are you?" Smoke asked.

"Seems like the logical thing to do, don't you think?"

"What's your name?"

Dooley laughed. "What do you need to know my name for?"

"I don't know. Maybe because I'd like to know the name of the man that wants to kill me."

"It ain't just wantin' to, Jensen. I'm goin' to kill you. And to satisfy your curiosity, my name is Dooley. Ebenezer Dooley."

"Since you are in a sharing mood, Mr. Dooley, where are the others?" Smoke asked.

Dooly laughed. "You got some sand, Jensen," he said. "Worryin' about where the others are when I'm fixin' to shoot you dead."

"Where are they?"

"I don't know where they all went, but the Logan brothers was goin' to Bertrand. Not that it'll matter to you. You got 'ny prayers, now's the time to say them."

Slowly, and deliberately, the outlaw raised his rifle to his shoulder to take aim.

Smoke raised his pistol and fired.

Dooley got a surprised look on his face as he reached down and clasped his hands over the wound in his chest. He fell forward, tumbling over once in the air, then landing on his back in a pile of straw in the stall right under him. The horse whinnied and moved to one side of the stall, barely avoiding the falling body.

Smoke stepped into the stall and looked down at Dooley. The outlaw was gasping for breath, and bubbles of blood came from his mouth.

"How did you do that?" Dooley asked. "I counted six shots."

Smoke held out the pistol. "This is the deputy's gun," he said. "I borrowed it before I ran in here."

"I'll be go to hell," Dooley said, his voice strained with pain.

"I expect you will," Smoke said as Dooley drew his last breath.

Smoke saw that the horse was still pretty agitated, and he petted it on the neck to try and calm it down.

"I'll be damned," he said. "No wonder you are upset. You're his horse, aren't you?"

The horse continued to show its agitation.

"Don't worry, I'm not going to shoot you. You can't help it because your owner was such a bastard."

As Smoke continued to try and calm the horse, he saw a twenty-dollar bill lying in the straw over by the edge of the stall, just under the saddle.

"Hello, what's this?" he said, leaving the horse and going over to retrieve the bill. That's when he saw another bill sticking out of the rifle sheath.

Smoke stuck his hand down into the rifle holster and felt a cloth bag. Pulling the bag out, he saw that it was marked BANK OF ETNA. There were five packets of bills in the bag, each packet wrapped by a band that said $1000. Four of the packets were full, and one was partially full.

Smoke looked back toward the door of the stable to make certain that he wasn't being watched; then he took the money bundles from the bag and stuck them inside his shirt. After that, he stuffed the empty bag back down into the rifle boot, then walked out into the street.

The street was still empty.

"It's all right, the shooter's dead!" Smoke called. "Someone get Doc McGuire to come have a look at the deputy!"

At his call, several people began appearing from inside the various buildings and houses that fronted the street. One of the first to show up was Doc McGuire, who, carrying his bag, hurried to the side of the fallen deputy. Kneeling beside the deputy, Doc McGuire put his stethoscope to the young man's chest. He listened for a moment, then, with his face glum, shook his head.

"He's dead," he said.

One of the others to hurry to the scene was the sheriff. The sheriff, who had gotten out of bed, was still tucking his shirt into his trousers as he came up. His badge gleamed in the moonlight.

"Damn," he said as he saw his deputy lying on the ground. "Anybody know who did this?"

"His name was Dooley. Ebenezer Dooley, and you'll find him in the barn," Smoke said.

"In the barn?" the sheriff said, pulling his pistol.

"It's all right. He's dead."

The sheriff looked at Smoke. "Did you kill him?"

"Yes."

"And who might you be?"

"The name's Kirby. Bill Kirby," Smoke said, continuing to use his alias.

"Tell me, Kirby, did you have a personal grudge with this fella?" Sheriff Fawcett asked.

"No."

"Then how come it was that you and him got into a shootin' war?"

"You'd have to ask Dooley that, Sheriff," Smoke said. "He's the one that started the shooting."

"What are you pickin' on him for, Sheriff?" one of the townspeople asked. "He's right, the man in the barn started the shootin' and Deputy Clayton come after him, only he got hisself kilt. Then this fella"—he pointed at Smoke—"went in after him. "I seen it. I seen it all."

"Did you know this man?" Sheriff Fawcett asked Smoke.

"No."

"Then, how'd you know his name was Dooley?"

"He told me his name before he died."

Sheriff Fawcett had a handlebar mustache, and he curled the end of it for a moment. "Seems to me like I've heard that name before. There may be a wanted poster on him. Are you a bounty hunter?"

"I'm not a bounty hunter. I just happened to be here when this all started happening."

"Mr. Kirby would you be willing to stop by my office tomorrow and answer a few questions for me?"

"I don't mind," Smoke said.

"In the meantime, if some of you fellas would get these

bodies over to the undertaker, I'll go see Mrs. Clayton and tell her about her husband." Sheriff Fawcett sighed. "I'd rather take a beating than do that."

Smoke hung around until the two bodies were moved; then he walked back across the street and into the hotel. The hotel clerk was standing at the front door when Smoke went inside.

"Mister, that's about the bravest thing I ever seen, the way you run into that barn like that. It was the dumbest too, but it sure was brave."

"You're half right," Smoke said with a little chuckle. "It was dumb."

When Smoke went up to his room, he took the money out of his shirt, counted it, then put it in his saddle bags. He'd counted 4,910 dollars, which was nearly half of what had been stolen. He wasn't exactly sure how he was going to handle it, but he had it in mind that, somehow, returning the money might help him prove his innocence.

But this was only half the money. For his plan to work, he would have to track down every remaining bank robber and retrieve whatever money was left.

17

The next morning Dooley's corpse was put on display in the front window of Laney's Hardware Store. He was propped up in a plain pine box, and was still wearing the same denim trousers and white shirt he had been wearing at the time of his death.

Dooley's eyes were open and opaque, and his mouth was drawn to one side as if in a sneer. When the viewers looked closely enough, they could see that, although the undertaker had made a notable effort, he had not been able to get rid of all the blood from the repaired bullet hole in the shirt.

A sign was hanging around the corpse's neck.

EBENEZER DOOLEY
THE MURDERER OF
DEPUTY GIDEON CLAYTON
SHOT AND KILLED BY BILL KIRBY
ON THE SAME NIGHT

After the money was divided, the five remaining bank robbers went their separate ways. Dooley went off by himself, but the Logan brothers left together, and so did Fargo Masters and Ford DeLorian, who were first cousins.

Ford was relieving himself while Fargo remained mounted, his leg hooked around the saddle horn.

"Hey, Fargo," Ford called up from his squatting position. "You know what I been thinkin'?"

"Ha," Fargo teased. "I didn't even know you could think, let alone what you were thinkin'."

"I'm thinkin' it don't do no good to have this here money if we ain't got no place to spend it."

"Yeah, I've give that a little thought myself," Fargo replied.

Ford grabbed a handful of leaves and made use of them. "So, how about we go into the next town and spend a little of this money?" he said as he pulled his trousers back up.

"Sounds fine by me," Fargo replied. "Where is the closest town?"

"Closest town is Dorena," Ford said, "But we can't go there."

"Why not?" Fargo asked.

"'Cause that's where Dooley was goin'."

"So?"

"I thought he said it wouldn't be good for us to all go to the same place."

"We won't all be in the same place," Fargo said. "Just you'n me and Dooley."

"Yeah, you're right," Ford said as he remounted. "Ain't no reason he gets to go to the closest town and we got to ride over hell's half acre, just to find us a place to spend some money."

"That's what I was thinkin'. You been to Dorena before?" Fargo asked.

"Yeah, once, a long time ago."

"I've never been there. What's the best way to get there from here?" Fargo asked.

"It's just on the other side of that range of hills there," Ford said, pointing. "We should be there by noon."

"First thing I'm goin' to do when we get there is get me a big piece of apple pie," Ford said. "With cheese on top."

Fargo laughed. "You just give me an idea about what I aim to get me."

"What is that?" Ford asked.

"A cold piece of pie and a hot piece of ass," Fargo called back over his shoulder as he slapped his legs against the side of his horse, causing it to break into a trot.

Ford laughed, then urged his horse into a trot as well.

The sun was high in the sky as Fargo and Ford reached Dorena. A small, hand-painted sign on the outer edge of the town read:

Dorena
Population 515
Come Grow With Us

No railroad served the town, and its single street was dotted liberally with horse apples. At either end of the street, as well as in the middle, planks were laid from one side to the other to allow people to cross over when the street was filled with mud.

The buildings of the little town were as washed out and flyblown up close as they had seemed from some distance. The first structure they rode by was a blacksmith's shop.

TOOMEY'S BLACKSMITH SHOP

Ironwork Done.

Tree Stumps Blasted.

That was at the east end of town on the north side of the street. There, Ford and Fargo saw a tall and muscular man bent over the anvil, the ringing of his hammer audible above all else. Across the street from the blacksmith shop, on the south side of the street, was a butcher shop, then a general store and a bakery. Next were a couple of small houses, then a leather shop next door to an apothecary. A set of outside stairs climbed the left side of the drugstore to a small stoop that stuck out from the second floor. A sign, with a painted hand that had a finger pointing up, read:

Roy McGuire, M.D.

Next to the apothecary was the sheriff's office and jail, then the bank, a barbershop and bathhouse, then a hotel.

On the north side of the street, next to the blacksmith shop, was a gunsmith shop, then a newspaper office, then a café, then several houses, followed by a seamstress shop, then a stage depot, the Brown Dirt Saloon, several more houses, then the stable, which was directly across from the hotel.

Fargo pointed to the café. "There!" he said. "Let's go in there 'n get us somethin' good to eat."

"All right," Ford agreed. The two men cut their horses to the side of the street toward the café, then dismounted and tied them off at the hitching rail. When they stepped inside the building, some of the patrons reacted visibly to the filth and stench of the two visitors.

They found a table and sat down. A man and woman who were sitting at a table next to them got up and moved to another table.

"What you reckon got into them folks?" Ford asked.

"I guess they don't like our company," Ford answered.

A man wearing an apron came up to them. "You gentlemen just coming into town, are you?" he asked.

"Yeah, and we're hungry as bears," Fargo said. "What you got to eat?"

"Oh, we have a lot of good things," the man replied. "But, uh, being as you just came in off the trail, perhaps you would enjoy your meal better if you cleaned up first? There is a bathhouse just across the street."

"Yeah, we seen it," Ford said. "But we're hungry. We'll eat first, then we'll go take us a bath."

"Go take a bath first," the waiter said. "Trust me, you will enjoy your meal much more."

"How do you know?" Ford asked.

"Because in your present condition, you are offensive to my other customers, and I don't intend to serve you until you have cleaned up."

"The hell you say," Ford replied angrily.

The waiter turned away from the table and started back toward the kitchen.

"Look here, mister, don't you walk away while I'm a'talkin' to you!" Ford called after him, reaching for his gun.

Fargo reached across and grabbed Ford's hand, preventing him from drawing.

"You don't want to do that, Ford," he said sternly, shaking his head.

"I ain't goin' to let no son of a bitch talk to me like that," Ford said angrily.

"Come on, let's go take a bath," Fargo said. "Our money ain't goin' to do us no good if we're in jail."

"You heard what . . ."

"Come on," Fargo said again, interrupting Ford's grumbling. "We'll board our horses, then take a bath."

As the two left the livery, they saw a crowd of people gathered in front of the hardware store, about halfway down the street.

"What do you reckon that's all about?" Fargo asked, pointing toward the crowd.

"I don't know," Ford said. "What do you say we go down there an' take a look?"

"All right," Fargo agreed.

The two men started down the street toward the hardware store, but stopped when they got close enough to see what everyone was looking at.

"I'll be damned," Ford said as he spit a stream of tobacco,

then wiped the dribble from his chin. "That's ole Dooley up there in that pine box."

"It sure as hell is," Fargo replied.

"How'd he wind up there?" Ford asked.

"It tells you right there on the sign they got hangin' around his neck," Fargo said.

"Hell, Fargo, you know I can't read," Ford said. "What does the sign say?"

"It says he was kilt by a fella named Bill Kirby."

"Bill Kirby? I ain't never heard of no Bill Kirby, have you?"

Fargo shook his head. "Can't say as I have," he said.

"What for do you think this fella Kirby kilt 'im?"

"I don't know. Says on the sign that Dooley kilt a deputy sheriff, then this Kirby fella kilt him."

Ford studied the corpse for a long moment.

"What you lookin' at?" Fargo asked.

Ford chuckled. "Hell, the son of a bitch is even uglier dead than he was while he was alive."

Fargo laughed as well. "He is at that, ain't he?" He paused for a moment before he spoke again. "Wonder where at is his share of the money," Fargo said.

"He prob'ly spent it all already," Ford said.

"He couldn't of spent it this fast," Fargo insisted.

"Then he must'a hid it," Ford said.

"What do you say we hang around town long enough to find out just what happened?" Fargo suggested. He smiled. "Ha, the son of a bitch got most of the money; now he ain't even around to spend it. What do you say we find it and spend it for 'im?"

"Yeah," Ford agreed. "I would like that."

When Sally, Pearlie, and Cal rode into Etna, they saw a gallows in the middle of the street, just in front of the marshal's office. A rope was dangling from the gibbet, the noose at the end ominous-looking.

"That kind of gives you chills lookin' at it, don't it?" Cal said. "I mean, knowin' it was for Smoke."

"It wasn't used," Sally said, "so it doesn't bother me."

"Where do we start?" Pearlie asked.

"Why don't you two go on down to the saloon and see what you can find out?" Sally asked. "I'll check in the marshal's office."

"Uh, you want me'n Cal to go on down to the saloon?" Pearlie asked.

"Yes. Smoke always says you can find out more about what's going on in a saloon than you can from the local newspaper."

Pearlie smiled broadly. "Yes, ma'am, I've heard 'im say that lots of times. All right, me 'n Cal will go on down there and see what we can find out. We'll all get together later," Pearlie added.

Pearlie and Cal continued to ride on down to the saloon, while Sally reined up in front of the office, dismounted, then went inside. A man with a badge was sitting at the desk, dealing poker hands to himself. He looked up as she entered.

"Somethin' I can do for you, little lady?" he asked with a leering grin.

"Are you Marshal Turnball?"

"No, I'm his deputy. The name is Pike."

"Where can I find Marshal Turnball?" Sally asked.

"What for do you need him?" Pike asked. "I told you, I'm his deputy." Pike moved around to the front of the desk, to stand uncomfortably close to Sally. "You want anything done . . . why, all you got to do is just ask."

"All right," Sally said. "I want you to tell me where I can find Marshal Turnball."

"I tell you what," Pike said, putting his hand on Sally's shoulder. "Maybe if you'd be nice to me, I'll be nice to you."

Pike moved his hand down to her breast.

* * *

Pearlie and Cal stepped up to the bar and ordered a beer apiece. When they were delivered, Pearlie blew some of the foam away, then took a long, Adam's apple-bobbing drink.

"You're pretty thirsty, cowboy," the bartender said.

"We rode a long way today," Pearlie answered.

"That'll make you thirsty all right," the bartender agreed.

"Say, we noticed the gallows out in the street as we came into town," Pearlie said. "You folks about to have a hangin'?"

"Well, we thought we was," the bartender said. "But the fella we was goin' to hang, a man by the name of Kirby Jensen, got away."

"How did he do that?"

The bartender laughed. "Hey, Marshal Turnball," the bartender called across the room. "Here's two fellas wantin' to know how Jensen got away."

"Ain't nobody's business how he got away," Turnball replied gruffly.

Pearlie and Cal turned toward the man who had answered the bartender. They saw a big man filling a chair that was tipped back against the wall. He was wearing a tan buckskin vest over a red shirt. The star of his office was nearly covered by the vest, though it could be seen.

Pearlie took his beer and started back to talk to the marshal. Cal followed him.

"Mind if we join you?" Pearlie asked when he reached the table.

"It's a free country," the marshal replied, taking in the empty chairs with a wave of his arm. "What can I do for you?"

"We're looking for Smoke Jensen," Pearlie said.

"Who?"

"Kirby Jensen," Pearlie clarified.

"Ha," Turnball said. "Ain't we all? What do you want him for?"

"We don't want him for nothin'," Cal said. "He's our friend."

"Your friend, huh? Well, mister, your friend robbed a bank and killed our banker."

"Was he caught in the act of robbin' the bank?" Pearlie asked.

"Near'bout," Turnball said.

Turnball explained how he and the posse found Smoke out on the prairie. "There was some of them empty wrappers, like's used to bind up money, on the ground around him, and they was marked 'Bank of Etna.' Besides which, he was still wearin' the same plaid shirt he was wearin' when he robbed the bank."

"Plaid shirt?" Cal said. He chuckled. "Smoke ain't got no plaid shirts. He don't even like plaid."

"Yeah? Well, he was wearin' one when he robbed the bank, and he was wearin' that same shirt when we caught him."

"Did he confess to robbin' the bank?" Pearlie asked.

"No." Turnball laughed, a scoffing kind of laugh. "He said he was set upon out on the prairie by the ones who actual done it, and one of 'em changed shirts with him."

"But you didn't believe him," Pearlie said. It was a statement, not a question.

"It wasn't just me that didn't believe him," Turnball said. "Your friend was tried legal, before a judge and jury, and found guilty."

"Did you think to send a telegram back to Rio Grande County to check with Sheriff Carson?" Pearlie asked.

"We couldn't. The telegraph line was down."

"If the line was down, how is it that you was able to send a telegram a few days ago sayin' that Smoke had escaped?"

Turnball squinted. "Are you fellas deputies to Sheriff Carson?"

"We ain't regular deputies, but we've been deputies from time to time," Pearlie said. "So I'll repeat my question. How is it that you could send a telegram after he escaped, but you didn't think to send one to check on him?"

"They got a line put up that we was able to use," Turnball explained.

"If you had just waited, I think the sheriff would have told you that Smoke couldn't have done what you said he done."

"Let me ask you this," Turnball said. "Is it true that Jensen is bad in debt? That he's about to lose his ranch?"

"He owes some money, yes," Pearlie said. "But he wasn't about to lose the ranch. He was goin' to Denver to make arrangements to lease Sugarloaf out for the money that he needed."

"That's what you say. But sometimes folks change. Especially if they get desperate."

"How did Smoke escape?"

"What do you mean, how did he escape? He escaped, that's all. I had him in jail, then when I come back to the jail the next mornin', he was gone."

"Was there anyone guardin' him while he was in jail?" Pearlie asked.

"Yeah, my deputy was. Why?"

"A few minutes ago you said that Smoke robbed your bank and killed a banker. But you didn't say anything about him killin' your deputy."

"I didn't say that 'cause he didn't kill 'im," Turnball said.

"If Smoke is the killer you think he is, don't you think he would have killed the deputy when he was getting away?"

"What? I don't know," Turnball said. He was silent for a moment. "Maybe he would have."

"Marshal, we brung Mrs. Jensen with us," Cal said. "Would you like to meet her?"

"What do I want to meet her for?"

"She rode a long way to get here, Marshal," Pearlie said. "It wouldn't hurt you to meet her."

Turnball sighed and stroked his chin, then he nodded and reached for his hat.

"All right," he said. "I'll meet her. Where is she? At the hotel?"

"We left her down at your office," Cal said. "She might still be there."

"Oh, damn," Turnball said. "I hope she didn't tell Pike who she is."

"Pike?"

"Pike is my deputy," Turnball said. "He is as dumb as dirt, and he was . . . well, he was . . ."

"He was what?"

"He was ridin' Jensen pretty hard while he was in jail, carryin' on about how he was goin' to go back to Jensen's ranch and tell his widow first-hand what happened to him."

"That would be all the more reason for Smoke to kill your deputy, wouldn't it?" Pearlie said. "But he didn't do it, did he?"

"No, he didn't," Turnball said. "But now I'm worried about the woman bein' down there with Pike. There's no tellin' what that dumb son of a bitch might do if he knows who she is."

"Might do?" Pearlie asked.

"To Mrs. Jensen."

Pearlie and Cal looked at each other, then both laughed.

"What is it?" Turnball asked. "What's so funny?"

"What's funny is you worryin' about Miss Sally," Cal said.

When Pearlie, Cal, and Turnball stepped into Turnball's office a few minutes later, they saw Sally sitting at the desk, calmly dealing out hands of cards. She looked up and smiled.

"Hello, Pearlie, Cal," she said. She turned her smile toward Turnball. "And you must be Marshal Turnball," she said.

"Yes, ma'am, I am," Turnball said. "I'm sorry you had to wait here all alone. My deputy was supposed to be here."

"Oh, he is here," Sally said.

"He is? Where?"

"I'm afraid Mr. Pike was a bad boy," Sally said. "So I had to put him in jail."

Looking toward the jail cell for the first time, Turnball saw Pike, handcuffed to the bed. His socks had been stuffed into his mouth.

"I'm sorry about sticking his socks in his mouth like that," Sally said. "But his language was atrocious. I just didn't care to listen to it anymore."

18

Fargo and Ford were in adjacent bathtubs. They had agreed to spend some of their money on new duds, so a representative of the mercantile store came to the bathhouse to show some of the clothes the store carried. He was standing alongside the two tubs, displaying his shirts.

"Them's just ordinary work shirts," Ford said. "Ain't you got nothin' fancier than that?"

Like Fargo, Ford was wearing his hat, even though he was in the tub. And like Fargo, he was smoking a cigar.

"These are very good shirts, sir," the store clerk said defensively.

"I was just lookin' for somethin' a little fancier is all."

"We only had one dress shirt in stock," the clerk said. "And the merchants all went together to buy it and a suit of clothes for Deputy Clayton to wear for his funeral."

"Oh, yes, that's the man Bill Kirby shot, ain't it?" Fargo asked.

The clerk shook his head. "No, Mr. Kirby shot the man who shot the deputy. Dooley, his name was. Ebenezer Dooley."

"Do you know this here fella Bill Kirby?" Fargo asked. "Does he live here in town?"

"I don't know him. I believe he is just passing through," the clerk said. "He has a room down at the hotel."

"Hand me that bottle of whiskey," Ford said, pointing, and the clerk complied.

"Will you gentlemen be making a purchase then?" the clerk asked.

"Yeah," Fargo said. He pointed to the pile of dirty clothes they had been wearing. "I tell you what, you take them old ones, and leave us the new ones, and we'll call it an even trade."

The store clerk looked shocked. "I beg your pardon, sir?"

Fargo laughed out loud at his joke. "I was just funnin' you," he said. He reached down on the floor beside the tub and picked up a billfold, then took out some money and handed it to the clerk. "This here ought to do it."

"Yes, thank you," the clerk said.

"And you can also have the old clothes," Fargo said.

The clerk looked at the old clothes with an expression of distaste on his face. "You, uh, want me to take the old clothes?" he asked. "And do what with them, sir?"

"Do anything you want to with them," Fargo said. "Clean them up and wear them if you want to. Or burn them."

"Burn them, yes. Thank you, I'll do that," the clerk said. Looking around, he saw a stick and he used the stick to pick the clothes up, one item at a time. Then he dropped them into the paper in which the new clothes had been wrapped. "I'll take care of them for you," he said.

After the clerk very carefully and hygienically collected the old clothes, he wrapped them in the packing material, then left the bathhouse. Ford took a big drink of the whiskey, then tossed the bottle into an empty tub.

"Did you see the way he got into a piss soup when you told him you wanted to trade even for them duds?" Ford asked, laughing out loud.

"Yeah," Fargo said, laughing with him. "He was so old-maidish the way he was handlin' them clothes, I should'a made him put them on and wear them out of here."

Ford lifted his arm and began rubbing the bar of soap against his armpit. "Hey, Fargo, how do you figure we ought to go about lookin' for Dooley's money?" he asked.

"We could start by goin' over to the hotel where he was stayin' at and lookin' through his room," Fargo suggested.

"Ha! Like they're goin' to let some strangers look through his room."

"We ain't strangers," Fargo said. "We're Dooley's brothers."

"What? No, we ain't," Ford said.

"We are if we say we are," Fargo said. "And who's going to know the difference?"

"Oh," Ford said. Then, as he understood what Fargo was saying, he smiled and nodded. "Oh!" he said again.

"Five hundred dollars?" Smoke said.

"Yes, sir," Sheriff Fawcett said. "Turns out I was right. I had heard Dooley's name before. There's a reward poster on my wall right now offerin' five hundred dollars for anyone who kills or captures him. By rights, that money should go to you. Unless you have something against taking bounty money."

"No, believe me, I don't have anything against it," Smoke said.

"Well, then, if you hang around town for another twenty-four hours, I'll have authorization from the governor's office to pay you the reward," the sheriff said.

"Thanks," Smoke smiled. "You've got a nice, friendly town here. I don't mind staying another twenty-four hours."

Ford belched loudly as he finished eating. A plate filled with denuded chicken bones told the story of the meal he had just consumed. In addition to fried chicken, mashed potatoes, biscuits, and gravy, he had also eaten two large pieces of apple pie, each piece topped by melted cheese.

"Let's go get drunk," he suggested.

"Not yet," Fargo said. "First things first."

"Yeah? What could possibly come before getting drunk?"

"Finding the money," Fargo said.

"Oh, yeah. So, where do we start?"

"We start at the hotel."

"Will that be all, gentlemen?" the waiter asked, approaching their table then.

"Yeah."

"And don't you both look so nice now that you are all cleaned up?" the waiter said obsequiously. Using a towel, he bent over Ford and began to brush at his shirt.

"Here? What are you doing?" Ford said in an irritable tone of voice.

"I'm just brushing away a few of the crumbs," the waiter said. "It is part of the service one performs when one is in a position to receive gratuities."

"Receive what?" Ford asked.

"Gratuities."

"What is that?"

"Tips?" the waiter tried.

Ford shook his head. "I don't know what you are talking about."

"Oh, well, then, let me explain, sir," the waiter said. "It is customary in a place like this that when one provides a service that is satisfactory, the customer will leave a gratuity, that is, leave some money as a"—the waiter struggled for the word—"gift, as a token of his appreciation for that service."

"What you are sayin' is, you expect us to give you some money above the cost of the meal," Fargo said. "Is that it?"

The waiter broke into a wide smile. "Yes, sir. I'm glad you understand, sir. Ten percent is customary."

"A gratuity?"

"Yes, sir."

"But that's not part of the bill, is it? I mean, if we don't leave you anything, that's not against the law?" Fargo asked.

"Oh, no, sir, not at all. That's why it is called a gratuity."

"Well, if the law don't say I've got to, I ain't goin' to," Fargo said. "Come on, Ford, we've got work to do," he added.

"Good-bye, gentlemen," the waiter said with a forced smile. He watched them until they stepped out into the street. Then the smile left his face. "You cheap bastards," he added under his breath.

Fargo and Ford were standing in front of the registration desk at the hotel.

"Would you tell me what room Mr. Ebenezer Dooley is a'stayin' in?" Fargo asked. "He's our brother."

The clerk blinked a few times in surprise.

"I beg your pardon," he said. "Who are you asking for?"

"Mr. Ebenezer Dooley," Fargo said. "We was all supposed to meet up here in this hotel today, and we figured he'd be down here in the lobby waitin' for us by now, but he ain't here." Fargo chuckled. "Course, as lazy as ole Eb is, like as not he's lyin' up there sleepin' like a log."

"Oh," the clerk said. "Oh, dear, this is very awkward."

"Ain't nothin' awkward about it," Fargo said. "He's our brother, and he's expectin' us. Tell you what, just give me the key and we'll go wake him up our ownselves."

"You haven't heard, have you?"

"We ain't heard what?" Fargo replied, playing out his role. "What are you talkin' about? Look, just give us the key so we can go wake up our brother and then we can get on our way."

The hotel clerk shook his head. "I'm talking about your br . . . uh, about Mr. Dooley. I can't believe you haven't heard yet."

"What's there to hear?"

"I'm sorry to have to tell you gentlemen this, but Mr. Dooley was killed last night."

"Kilt? Did you hear that, Ford? Our brother was kilt," Fargo said, feigning shock and concern.

"That's real bad," Ford said, though neither the expression in his voice nor his face reflected his words.

"How was he kilt? What happened?" Fargo asked the hotel clerk.

"He was involved in a shoot-out," the clerk answered. "It seems that your brother killed our deputy sheriff; then he was killed himself."

Fargo pinched the bridge of his nose and shook his head. "Oh," he said. "Mama ain't going to like this, is she, Ford?"

"No," Ford said, his voice still flat and expressionless. "She ain't goin' to like it."

"You can, uh, view your brother down the street if you'd like," the hotel clerk said. "His remains are on display in the window of the hardware store."

"What? What kind of town is this that they would put our brother in the window for ever'one to gape at?" Fargo asked.

"Believe me, sir, it wasn't my doing," the clerk said, frightened. He held up his hands and backed away, as if distancing himself from the issue.

"Where at's our brother's things?" Fargo asked. "We'll just get them and be on our way."

"Your brother's things?"

"His saddlebags, or suitcase, or anything he might have had with him. I want to take 'em back to Mama. You got 'em down here?"

"No, they are still in the room. I'm waiting for the sheriff to tell me it is all right to take them out."

"What's the sheriff got to do with it? I told you, we're his brothers. If Brother Eb's still got some things in his room, then we're the ones should get them, not the sheriff."

"Well, I don't know," the clerk said. "I'm not sure about this."

"Just give me the key to his room," Fargo said, more forcefully this time. "We'll go up there and have a look around our ownselves."

"Sir, how do I know you are his brother?"

"How do you know? 'Cause I told you I am his brother."

"Just the fact that you tell me that doesn't validate it."

"Doesn't what?"

"Doesn't prove it."

"Well, hell, why didn't you say you needed proof? Ford, tell him I'm Dooley's brother."

"Yes, sir, he's Dooley's brother all right," Ford said.

"And Ford is his brother too," Fargo said. "So there, you've got all the proof you need."

"That's not really proof, that's just the two of you vouching for each other," the clerk said. "Maybe we should wait for the sheriff. I could send for him if you like."

"Tell you what," Fargo said. "My brother had a drooping eye right here." Fargo put his hand over his right eye. "Now, how would I know that if I wasn't actual his brother?"

The clerk sighed. The two men were getting a little belligerent with him and they were frightening-looking to begin with. What was he protecting anyway? As far as he knew, there was nothing up there but a set of saddlebags anyway.

The clerk took a key from the board and handed it to Fargo. "Very well, Mr. Dooley. This goes against my better judgment, but go on up there and look around if you must."

"Thanks," Fargo said.

Fargo took the key; then he and Ford went up to the room. Dooley's saddlebags were hanging over a hook that stuck out from the wall.

Fargo grabbed the bags and dumped the contents onto the bed. One shirt, one pair of denim trousers, a pair of socks, and a pair of long underwear tumbled out.

"You pull out all them drawers and have a look," Fargo ordered, and Ford started pulling out the drawers from the single chest.

Finding nothing, Fargo stripped the bed, then turned the straw-stuffed mattress upside down.

"Nothin' here," Fargo said angrily. "Not a damn thing!"

Ford started to put the drawers back in the chest.

"What are you doin'?"

"Puttin' these back."

"To hell with 'em, just leave 'em," Fargo said. "We can't be wastin' no more time here."

When the two men came back downstairs, the clerk looked up. He was surprised to see that they weren't carrying anything with them.

"You didn't find his saddlebags?" he asked.

"We found 'em, but there weren't nothin' there that Mama would want," Fargo said as they left.

"What'll we do now?" Ford asked when the two men went out into the street.

"I don't know," Fargo said, taking his hat off and running his hand through his hair. "I figured for sure he would have had the money hid out in his room somewhere," Fargo said.

"Maybe he had it with him, and the undertaker took it," Ford suggested.

"Good idea. Let's go down there and talk to him," Fargo said.

"You think the undertaker would keep the money if he found it?" Ford asked.

"We'll soon find out."

19

Gene Prufrock, the undertaker, had done nothing to prepare the outlaw's body but wash the shirt, then put him in a pine box. He didn't like the idea of making a public show of the dead, no matter how despicable a person he might have been. So when the sheriff asked him to stand Dooley's body up in the hardware store window, Prufrock tried to talk him out of it. But the sheriff prevailed, and Dooley's body was now on display.

It was a different story with Gideon Clayton, though. The young deputy had been very popular among the citizens of the town, and Prufrock was taking his time to do as good a job as he possibly could. Several of the merchants had gotten together to buy a special coffin for Clayton. It was finished with a highly polished black lacquer and fitted with silver adornments. Those same merchants had also bought him a suit, so that Gideon Clayton's body lay on Prufrock's preparation table, dressed in a suit and tie that he had never worn in life. The undertaker made the final touches, combing Clayton's hair and powdering and rouging his cheeks.

Prufrock had just stepped back to admire his work when he was suddenly surprised by the entry of two men.

"Is there something I can do for you gentlemen?" Prufrock asked.

"Yeah, we want to ask you some questions," Fargo said.

"Could the questions wait? As you can see, I'm working on a subject."

"Is that what you call them? Subjects? Why don't you just call them what they are? Dead meat?" Ford asked with a laugh.

"I'm sorry, sir, but I do not find your joke at all funny. I believe, very strongly, in maintaining the dignity of the departed," Prufrock said.

"I hear that when somebody dies, you take all the blood out of them," Ford said. "Is that true."

"Yes."

"What do you do that for?"

"So we can replace the blood with embalming flood. It preserves the body."

"What do you do with the blood?"

"We dispose of it," Prufrock said impatiently. "Gentlemen, please, I don't like people back here. Is there something I can do for you?"

"Who is this fella you're workin' on here?" Fargo asked, pointing to the body on the table. "Was he rich or somethin'?"

"No. Why would you think he is rich?"

"Well, look at him. He's all decked out in a new suit. And I'm lookin' at that real pretty coffin over there and figurin' you're about to put him in it. Is that right?"

"That's right."

"Then he must'a been rich."

"He wasn't rich, he was just well respected. He was our deputy sheriff."

"Your deputy sheriff, huh? So what you are saying is that this is the man our brother killed."

Prufrock gasped. "Good heavens! Mr. Dooley is your brother?"

"Yeah," Fargo said.

The mortuary was in the same building as the hardware store, but behind it. Fargo pointed toward the front. "The man you have standin' up in that window out there, showin' him off like a trussed-up hog, is our brother. Is that what you mean when you say you like to maintain the dignity of the departed? Our brother is a departed, ain't he? Where at's his dignity?"

"I . . . I'm sorry. I don't think anyone knew that he had kin in town."

"We just come into town this mornin'," Fargo said, indicating himself and Ford. "Didn't find out about our brother until we saw him standin' there in that store window for all the world to see."

"I'm sorry about your brother," Prufrock said.

"Yes, well, like I say, he was our brother. So that means that anything you found on him is rightly our'n."

"I beg your pardon?" Prufrock said, surprised by the sudden change in the direction of the conversation.

"His belongin's," Fargo said. "Ever'thin' he had on him is rightly our'n now. Well, 'cept he can keep them clothes on he's a'wearin'. Wouldn't want him to have to show up in hell butt naked."

Both Fargo and Ford laughed.

"That'd be funny all right," Ford said. "Ole Dooley walkin' around in hell naked as a jaybird."

"Dooley?" Prufrock said.

"What?"

"You called him Dooley."

"Well, hell, that's his name," Ford said. "What else am I supposed to call him?"

"It's just that, within the family, people normally use first names."

"Yeah, well, Eb, bein' the oldest, was just always called Dooley," Fargo said, trying to smooth over Ford's mistake. "Now what about his belongings? Do you have any of 'em here?"

"Well, of course there's his gun and his boots," Prufrock said. "Only other thing he had was the clothes he is wearing.

But of course, you have already indicated that you don't want those."

"What about the money?"

"Yes, I'm glad you brought that up," Prufrock said. "That will be five dollars."

"Five dollars? That's all he had on 'im, was five dollars?" Fargo asked.

"Oh, no, you misunderstand. He had less than one dollar on him. The five dollars is what you owe me."

Fargo looked confused. "Why the hell should I owe you anything?"

"You did say that he was your brother, did you not? That means that someone owes me for the preparation of his body. As you two gentlemen are his next of kin, you are responsible for his funeral."

"Far as I'm concerned, he ain't goin' to have no funeral," Fargo said. "We may be his next of kin, but you ain't goin' to get no money from us."

"Then, what do you propose that I do about burying your brother?"

"What would you do about buryin' him if I hadn't'a come along today?"

"He would be declared an indigent, and I would collect the fee from the town council. Of course, that would also mean that he will be buried in a pauper's grave."

"That's fine with me. Go ahead and get your money from the town," Fargo said. "Come on, Ford, let's go."

"Aren't you even interested in when and where he is to be buried?" Prufrock called out as Fargo and Ford left the mortuary.

"No," Fargo yelled back over his shoulder.

"My word," Prufrock said quietly as the men left.

"The only place we ain't looked yet is the stable," Ford said. "Are we goin' to tell the fella watchin' the stable that Dooley was our brother?"

"No," Fargo said. "If Dooley owes any money for boardin' his horse, the son of a bitch might try to make us pay."

"Then how are we goin' to look?"

"We'll just have to find another way," Fargo replied.

Fargo and Ford hung around the stable until they saw the stable attendant go into the corral to start putting out feed for the outside horses. Then the men slipped into the barn.

"How will we find what stall he was in?" Ford asked.

"You know his horse, don't you?"

"Yeah, sure I know his horse."

"We'll just look around until we see whichever horse is his."

The two men started looking into the stalls. Then, at the fifth stall they examined, Ford said, "There he is. I'd recognize that horse just about anywhere."

Opening the door, they stepped inside, then Fargo picked up a pitchfork and handed it Ford. "Get to work," he said.

"Get to work doin' what? What's this here pitchfork for?"

"Start muckin' around in the straw, make sure he don't have it hid there."

"Yeah, well, while I'm shovelin' straw and shit, what are you going to do?"

"I'm going to look at his saddle and blanket roll."

"How come you get to look in his saddle, while I have to muck around in the straw and horseshit?"

"That's just the way it is," Fargo said.

Grumbling, Ford began tossing the straw aside while Fargo examined the saddle. Finding nothing there, he unrolled the blanket. When his search of the blanket turned up nothing, he stuck his hand down into the empty rifle sheath.

"Ha!" he said happily. "I feel somethin' here! I think this is it!"

Ford tossed the pitchfork aside and hurried over to watch Fargo as he retrieved a bag. But as soon as he brought the bag out for a closer examination, his smile changed to a frown.

"What the hell?" he said. "The bag is empty. There ain't no money here!"

"Well, where is it?" Ford asked. "Somebody's got it. He wouldn't of just kept an empty bag."

"Bill Kirby," Fargo said.

"Who?"

"The man they say shot Dooley. His name is Bill Kirby. And I'd bet you a hunnert dollars to a horseshoe that he's the one that got the money."

"So what do we do now?"

"We find the son of a bitch," he said.

20

When Fargo woke up the next morning, he saw that he was in one of the rooms upstairs over Big Kate's saloon. There was a whore sleeping beside him and as he looked at her in the harsh light of day, he marveled at how different she looked now from the way he'd thought she looked last night. There was a large and disfiguring scar on one cheek. She was missing three teeth, and her breasts were misshapen and laced with blue veins.

"Damn," he said to himself. "How'd you get so ugly so fast? I must'a been pretty damn drunk last night."

Turning the covers back, he stepped out on the floor, put on his hat, and then, totally naked except for the hat, walked over to the window and looked at the back of the building behind the saloon. Feeling the need to urinate, he lifted the window and let go, watching as a golden arc curved down. A cat, picking through the garbage below, was caught in the stream and, letting out a screech, started running down the alley.

"Ha!" Fargo laughed out loud.

At that moment the door to the room opened and Ford came in.

"Son of a bitch!" Ford DeLorian said. "I seen 'im! I seen 'im when he come out of the sheriff's office."

"You seen who?" Fargo asked.

"I seen the fella that kilt ole Dooley."

"You seen Kirby?"

Ford smiled broadly. "Yeah, I seen 'im," he said. "Only his name ain't Kirby."

"What do you mean, his name ain't Kirby?"

"I mean his name ain't Kirby 'cause it's Jensen. He's the same fella that we put Logan's shirt on," Ford said. "Smoke Jensen, Dooley said his name was then. You recollect him, don't you, Fargo? He's a big man."

"Yes, I recollect him all right," Fargo said. "But how do you know he's the one that kilt Dooley?"

"Well, he's the one they give the reward for doin' it," Ford said. "They was talkin' about it downstairs, how Kirby was goin' to get a reward from the sheriff this mornin'. That's why I went down there so I could see what he looked like."

"You went down to the sheriff's office?"

"Yeah. I was out workin' this mornin', while you was in here layin' up with the whore."

"Well, you had her first. If you hadn't been so tight about it, we could'a each had our own whore 'stead of sharin' one."

"Is she still asleep?" Ford asked, looking toward the bed.

"Yeah, she's either asleep or passed out," Fargo replied.

"She did drink a lot last night," Ford said.

"She couldn't of drunk as much as we did. Otherwise, we wouldn't of brought her up here. Did you get a good look at her? She is one ugly woman."

"Yeah, well, me'n you ain't exactly what you would call good-lookin'," Ford replied. "Damn, Fargo, you just goin' to stand there naked all day?"

"Oh, yeah," Fargo said. "I guess I'd better get dressed."

"You know what I don't understand?" Ford asked as Fargo began pulling on his long underwear. "I don't understand what Jensen's doin' here. How come he ain't in jail?"

"He must'a broke out."

"Yeah, well, that's the trouble with jails these days," Ford said. "Hell, a citizen can't even count on 'em to keep the outlaws locked up."

"Are you sure it was Jensen you saw?"

"Yeah, I'm sure. And if you don't believe me, you can see for yourself. He's downstairs right now. But you better hurry, 'cause he ain't goin' to be there long."

"How do you know?"

"'Cause I heard him askin' someone how to get to Bertrand."

Fargo look up sharply. "Bertrand, you say?"

"Yeah."

"That's where the Logans was goin'."

"Yeah, that's what I was thinkin' too," Ford said. "You reckon Jensen is goin' after them?"

"Of course he is. Damn, you know what I think the son of a bitch is doin'?"

"No, what?"

"Well, what he is plannin' on doin' is runnin' us down and killin' us one at a time," Fargo said.

"For revenge?"

"Probably some revenge," Fargo agreed. "But more'n likely, it's to get his hands on the money that we stole."

"Damn! That mean he plans to kill *us*, don't it?"

"Yeah," Fargo replied. "Unless we kill him first."

"How we goin' to do that? We can't just walk downstairs and shoot him where he's sittin'."

"No, but if he's goin' to Bertrand, we can set up an ambush along the way."

As Smoke rode out of Dorena, he thought about the reward money he had received from killing Ebenezer Dooley. Five hundred dollars was still quite a way from having enough money to pay off the note on his ranch, but it was a start. If there had been a reward for Dooley, maybe there was a reward on the others. If each of them was worth five hundred dollars, finding them all would be worth three thousand dollars. Three thousand dollars would not only pay off the note on his ranch, it would give him a little operating capital to start the next year with.

Smoke had never been a bounty hunter, had never even considered it. But this was a different situation from hunting men just for the bounty. He needed to find each of these men in order to prove that he was innocent of the bank robbery in Etna.

On the first night on their way back to Sugarloaf Ranch, Sally, Pearlie, and Cal made camp on the trail. They found a place next to a fast-flowing spring of clear water where there was abundant wood for their fire and grass for the horses. Cal had gathered the wood, Pearlie had made the fire, and now Sally was cooking their supper.

Pearlie started laughing.

"What ever are you laughing about?" Sally asked.

"I was thinkin' of the way you had the deputy all trussed up and gagged like that."

"Yeah," Cal said. "And what was real funny was the way the marshal was laughin' at it. He said Smoke done the same thing to him."

"*Did* the same thing," Sally corrected.

"Yeah," Cal said. "But you have to admit, whether he done it or did it, it was funny, especially you doin' it too."

"He had such a dejected look about him that I almost felt sorry for him," Sally said.

The others laughed again, then Cal inhaled deeply. The aroma of Sally's cooking permeated the camp.

"They ain't nothin' no better'n bacon and beans when you're on the trail," Cal said as he walked over to examine the contents of the skillet that was sitting on a base of rocks over the open fire. A Dutch oven of biscuits was cooking nearby. "It sure makes a body hungry."

"Cal, you are incorrigible," Sally said, shaking her head.

"What you mean is, there isn't *anything* better than bacon and beans," she said, correcting him.

"Yes, ma'am, I reckon that is what I meant," Cal said contritely.

"And when have you not been hungry?" she added with a chuckle.

"Well, you're right about that, Miss Sally," Cal said. "But there ain't . . . isn't," he corrected, "anything any better than bacon and beans cooked out on the trail."

"'Ceptin' maybe bear claws," Pearlie said. "Too bad you can't make us a batch of them out on the trail."

Sally smiled. "Well, maybe I will make some tomorrow night," she suggested.

Pearlie smiled broadly. "That would be . . ."

"Help me, somebody," a voice called, interrupting Pearlie in mid-sentence.

"What was that?" Sally asked.

"Help me," the voice called again.

"Can anyone see him?" Cal asked, looking all around them.

"Who is it? Who's out there?" Pearlie called. He pulled his pistol and cocked it. "Answer up. Who's out there?"

"Don't shoot," the voice called. "I ain't got no gun."

"Come toward the camp," Pearlie said. "Come slow, and with your hands up in the air, so we can see you as you come in."

"I'm comin'," the man's voice answered.

The three campers looked toward the sound of the voice until a man materialized in the darkness. As he came toward them, he kept his hands raised over his head, just as Pearlie had ordered.

"That food sure smells awful good," he said. "It's been near a week since I've et 'nything other'n some roots and bugs."

"Who are you?" Sally asked.

"The name is Yancey, ma'am," the man said. "Buford Yancey." His hands were still raised.

"You can put your hands down, Mr. Yancey," Sally said. "And you are welcome to some of our beans."

"Thank you, ma'am, that's mighty decent of you," Yancey said.

"What happened to your horse?" Cal asked.

"He stumbled and broke his leg," Yancey said. "I had to put him down."

"How'd you do that? You don't have a gun," Pearlie said.

"Oh," Yancey replied. "Well, I, uh, lost my gun. It must'a fell out of my holster. Uh, if you don't mind, I'm goin' to go over there an' get me a drink of water."

Yancey went over to the side of the stream, lay on his stomach, stuck his mouth down into the water, and drank deeply.

A few minutes later Sally took the food off the fire, then distributed it to the others. Pearlie noticed that she took less for herself than she gave anyone else.

After they had eaten, Pearlie found a moment to talk to Sally without being overheard.

"Miss Sally, what do you aim to do about this man?" he asked.

"Do? What do you mean what do I aim to do about him?"

"What I mean is, he's eaten. Don't you think it's time to send him on his way?"

"Look at the man," Sally said. "He's half dead. We can't just send him away."

"Well, what do you plan to do with him?"

Sally sighed. "I don't know exactly," she said. "As far as I know, the closest town is still Etna. I guess we should take him back there."

"That'll make it two extra days before we get back to the ranch," Pearlie said.

"I realize that, but it can't be helped."

"So that means you're going to let him spend the night here with us?"

"Pearlie, I told you, we can't just run him off," Sally insisted.

"I don't like it. There's somethin' about him that I don't trust."

"I'll tell you what," Sally suggested. "We can take turns staying awake all night. That way, someone will always be watching him. Do you think that would make you feel better?"

"Yes, ma'am," Pearlie said. "I think that would be a good idea."

"All right, I'll take the first watch. I'll stay awake until midnight. You take the second watch, from midnight to four, and we'll get Cal to take the watch from four until dawn."

"You know your problem, Miss Sally? Your problem is you are too decent to people," Pearlie said. "Your first notion is to just take ever'one at their word. But that hasn't been my experience."

"Pearlie?" Sally said. She put her hand on his shoulder and gently shook him. "Pearlie?"

"What?" Pearlie asked groggily.

"It's your time on watch," Sally said.

"Oh," Pearlie groaned.

Sally chuckled. "Don't blame me. You said we shouldn't trust our visitor, remember?"

"Yes, ma'am, I remember," Pearlie said. He sat up and stretched, then reached for his boots. He nodded toward Yancey, who was wrapped up in a spare blanket. "Has he been quiet?"

"Sleeping like a log," Sally replied.

"It don't seem—"

"It doesn't seem," Sally corrected.

"Yes, ma'am. It doesn't seem fair that he gets to sleep all night, while we have to take turns lookin' out for him."

"Don't forget to wake Cal at four," Sally said.

During Pearlie's watch he sat very still, just listening to the snap and pop of the burning wood. For the first hour he stared into the fire. He looked at the little line of blue flame that started right at the base of the wood, watching as the blue turned to orange, then yellow, and finally into twisting ropes of white smoke as it streamed up from the fire. Orange sparks from the fire rode the heat column high into the night sky, where they added their tiny, red glow to the blue pinpoints of the stars.

Pearlie didn't know when he fell asleep, but he did know when he woke up. He woke up when he heard the metallic click of a pistol being cocked. Opening his eyes, he saw Buford Yancey standing in front of him, holding a pistol that was pointed directly at him.

"I figured if I stayed awake long enough, I'd catch one of you asleep," Yancey said.

"Where did you get the pistol?" Pearlie asked.

Yancey pointed to one of the two bedrolls.

"The boy over there had it lying on the ground alongside him. It wasn't hard to get. No harder than it's goin' to be for me to take one of them horses."

"You don't need to do that," Pearlie said. "Miss Sally was plannin' on us takin' you into Etna tomorrow. She figured you could get back on your feet there."

"Ha!" Yancey said, laughing out loud. "Now that would be a fine thing, wouldn't it? For you to take me back into Etna, after I just robbed the bank there little more'n a week ago."

"You?" Pearlie said. "You are the one who robbed the bank?"

"Yeah, me'n some pards," Yancey said. "Only they ain't much my pards now. The stole my share of the money from me."

"Was one of your pards Smoke Jensen?" Pearlie asked.

"Who? No, he ain't . . . wait a minute," Yancey said. "I think Jensen was the name of the fella we put Curt's plaid shirt on. Leastwise, that's what Dooley said his name was."

"So you admit you framed him?"

"Slick as a whistle," Yancey said with a laugh.

"Thank you, Mr. Yancey," Sally's voice said. "I will expect you to tell Marshal Turnbull that."

"What the hell?" Yancey said, spinning around quickly, only to see Sally holding her pistol on him.

"Drop your gun," Sally ordered.

Yancey smiled. "You think I'm going quake in my boots and drop my gun just because some woman's holding a pistol on me? Why, you'd probably pee in your pants if you even shot that thing." Yancey reached for her gun. "Why don't you just hand that over to me before you hurt yourself?"

Sally fired, and the tip of Yancey's little finger turned to blood and shredded flesh.

"Oww!" Yancey shouted, dropping his gun and grabbing his hand. "What the hell? You shot my finger off."

"Just the tip of it," Sally replied. "And I chose your little finger because I figure you use it less. It could be worse."

"Are you trying to tell me that you aimed at my little finger? That it wasn't no accident that you hit it?"

"Miss Sally always hits what she aims at," Pearlie said, picking up the pistol Yancey dropped.

"Get over there and sit down," Sally ordered.

"Miss Sally, I'm sorry about this," Pearlie apologized. "I must've fallen asleep. The next thing I knew, he was holding a gun on me."

"That's all right," Sally answered. "I'm sorry I didn't pay more attention to you. You said there was something about him you didn't trust. It turns out that you were right."

21

Ford lay on top of a flat rock, looking back along the trail over which he and Fargo had just come.

"Do you see him?" Fargo asked.

"Yeah, he's back there, comin' along big as you please. He's trailin' us, Fargo. I mean he's stickin' to us like stink on shit. We can't get rid of him."

"I don't want to get rid of him," Fargo said.

"What do you mean you don't want to get rid of him? You said yourself that you thought he was trackin' down ever'one of us to kill us."

"Why did I suggest that we come through Diablo Pass? It's twenty miles farther to Bertrand this way than it would have been by going through McKenzie Pass."

"I thought it was to throw him off our trail," Ford said.

"No. It was to get him to come through here. I can't believe the son of a bitch was dumb enough to take the bait. We're playin' him like you'd play a fish."

"If you say so," Ford said, though it was clear that he still didn't understand what Fargo had in mind.

"Think about it, Ford," Fargo said. "This is the perfect place to set up an ambush. I'll stay on this side of the pass, you go on the other side. When he gets between us, we'll open up on him. We'll have him in a cross fire."

"Why do I have to go over the other side?" Ford asked. "That means I've got to climb down, go over, then climb back up."

"Want the money he took from Dooley, don't you?"

"Yeah."

"Then just do what I tell you without all the belly-aching."

"All right," Ford answered. "But after all this trouble, he better be carryin' that money with him, is all I can say."

"He's got the money," Fargo said. "It couldn't be anywhere else. But even if he didn't have it, we'd have to kill the son of a bitch before he killed us. Remember?"

"Yeah," Ford said. "I remember. All right, I'll go over to the other side."

"Get a move on it. Looks like he's comin' along pretty steady," Fargo ordered.

Smoke had noticed the hoofprints shortly after he left Dorena. Because he had identified each set of prints from his original tracking, he recognized these prints as belonging to two of the bank robbers.

Smoke was actually going to Bertrand to follow up on Dooley's declaration that two of the robbers had gone there. He had not expected to cut the trail of two of the very people he had been tracking.

Could these tracks belong to the Logan brothers? At first he thought they might. Dooley had told him they were in Bertrand, but clearly, these tracks were fresh. In fact, they were made within the last hour. If they belonged to the Logan brothers, what were they doing out here? Especially if they were holed up in Bertrand? These tracks didn't seem to be going to Bertrand, or at least, if they were going there, they weren't going by the most direct route.

As a result of having come across the fresh hoofprints, Smoke's journey to Bertrand changed from a normal ride to one of intense tracking. But within an hour after he first came across the trail, he realized, with some surprise, that they weren't trying to cover their tracks. On the contrary, it was almost as if they were going out of their way to invite him to come after them.

Why would they do that? he wondered.

Then, as he contemplated the question, the answer came to him.

They wanted him to find them, and they wanted him to find them so they could kill him. They must have been in Dorena while he was there. That meant that they probably knew that he killed Dooley. They probably also knew that he took Dooley's share of the loot.

Smoke saw that the trail was leading to a narrow draw just ahead of him. He had never been in this exact spot before, but he had been in dozens of places just like this, and he knew what to expect.

He stopped at the mouth of the draw and took a drink from his canteen while he studied the twists and turns of the constricted canyon. If the two men he was following were going to set up an ambush, this would be the place for them to do it.

Smoke pulled his long gun out of the saddle holster, then he started walking into the draw, leading his horse. Stormy's hooves fell sharply on the stone floor and echoed loudly back from both sides of the narrow pass. The draw made a forty-five-degree turn to the left just in front of him, so he stopped. Right before he got to the turn, he slapped Stormy on the rump and sent him on through.

Stormy galloped ahead, his hooves clattering loudly on the rocky floor of the canyon.

"Ford, get ready!" Fargo shouted. "I can hear him a-comin'!"

"I see 'im!" Ford shouted back.

The canyon exploded with the sound of gunfire as Ford

and Fargo began shooting from opposite sides. Their bullets whizzed harmlessly over the empty saddle of the horse, raising sparks as they hit the rocky ground, then ricocheted off the opposite wall, echoing and reechoing in a cacophony of whines and shrieks.

"Son of a bitch!" Ford shouted. "Did we get him? We must've got him! I don't think I saw nobody on the horse!"

"I don't know," Fargo replied. "I didn't see him go down. Look on the ground. Do you see him anywhere?"

"No," Ford replied. "I don't see him. Where is the son of a bitch?"

From his position just around the corner from the turn, Smoke looked toward the sound of the voices, locating one of the two ambushers about a third of the way up the north wall of the canyon. The man was squeezed in between the wall itself and a rock outcropping that provided him with a natural cover.

"Fargo, where is he?"

The one who called out this time was not the one he had located, so looking on the opposite side of the draw, toward the sound of this voice, Smoke saw a shadow move.

Smoke smiled. Now he had both of them located, and he not only knew where they were, he knew who they were. At least, he knew their first names.

"Fargo? Ford?" he called. "I'm right here. If you're looking for me, why don't you two come on down?"

"You know our names?" Ford called down to him. "Hey, Fargo, the son of a bitch knows our names! How does he know our names?"

"Oh, I know all about you two boys," Smoke called back. "I know that you robbed the bank back in Etna. I know that you killed the banker."

"Weren't us that killed the banker," Ford called back. "It was Ebenezer Dooley and Curt and Trace Logan that done that. We was across the street from the bank."

"Ford, will you shut the hell up?" Fargo called across the canyon.

"Dooley cheated the rest of you, didn't he?" Smoke called. "There was ten thousand dollars taken from the bank, but he kept half of it."

"How do you know he kept half the money?" Fargo called down to him.

"Well, now, how do you think I know, Fargo?"

"You took it, didn't you? You've got the money with you right now."

"That's right," Smoke said.

"You son of a bitch!" Fargo said. "By rights, that's our money."

Smoke laughed. "It's not your money. It belongs to anyone who can hold on to it. And right now I'm holding on to it. You know what I'm going to do now?"

"What's that?"

"I'm going to take *your* money," Smoke said.

"The hell you are," Fargo replied. "You might'a noticed, mister, they's two of us and they's only one of you."

All the while Smoke was keeping Fargo engaged in conversation, he was studying the rock face of the wall just behind the outlaw. Then he began firing. His rifle boomed loudly, the thunder of the detonating cartridges picking up resonance through the canyon and doubling and redoubling in intensity. Smoke wasn't even trying to aim at Fargo, but was, instead, taking advantage of the position in which his would-be assailant had placed himself.

Smoke fired several rounds, knowing that the bullets were splattering against the rock wall behind his target, fragmenting into deadly missiles.

"Ouch! You son of a bitch, quit it! Quit your shootin' like that!" Fargo shouted.

As Smoke figured it would, the ricocheting bullets made Fargo's position untenable and Fargo, screaming in anger, stepped from behind the rock. He raised his rifle to shoot at Smoke, but Smoke fired first.

Fargo dropped his rifle and grabbed his chest. He stood

there for a moment, then pitched forward, falling at least fifty feet to the rocky bottom of the canyon.

"Fargo?" Ford shouted. "Fargo?"

"He's dead, Ford," Smoke shouted. "It's just you and me now."

Smoke watched the spot where he knew Ford was hiding, hoping to see him, but Ford didn't show himself. Smoke took a couple of shots, thinking it might force him out as it did Fargo, but he neither saw nor heard anything except the dying echoes of his own gunshots.

"Ford? Ford, are you up there?"

Then, unexpectedly, Smoke heard the sound of hoofbeats.

Damn! he thought. He should have realized that they would have their horses on the other side. Ford had slipped away.

Smoke started to step around the turn, then halted. Ford could have sent his empty horse galloping up the trail, just to fool him.

He looked cautiously around the corner, then saw that his caution, though prudent, was not necessary. Ford was galloping away.

Smoke also saw Stormy standing quietly at the far end of the draw. He whistled and Stormy ducked his head, then came trotting back up the draw toward him.

A second horse joined Stormy, and Smoke realized that it must be Fargo's horse.

In a saddlebag on Fargo's horse, Smoke found a packet of bills bundled up in a paper wrapper. The name of the bank was printed on the wrapper, along with the notation that the wrapper held one thousand dollars.

The bills were so loosely packed within the wrapper that Smoke knew there was considerably less than one thousand dollars, which, he knew, had been Fargo's share of the take.

Smoke put the roll in his saddlebag where he was keeping the money he had taken from Dooley. After that, he led the horse over to Fargo's body.

"Sorry to have to do this to you, horse," Smoke said as he

lifted Fargo up and draped him over the saddle. "I know this is none of your doing, but we can't just leave him out here."

Marshal Turnball, with his chair tipped back and his feet propped up on the railing, was ensconced in his usual place in front of Dunnigan's Store. He was rolling a cigarette and paying particular attention to the task at hand when he felt Billy Frakes's hand on his shoulder.

"That's one of 'em," Billy said.

"What?"

"That's one of the bank robbers," Billy said excitedly. "He was one of the fellers that was in front of Sikes Leather Goods lookin' at the boots when the bank was robbed."

When Turnball looked in the direction Billy Frakes had pointed, he saw four people coming toward him. There were four people, but only three horses. The woman, whom he recognized as Sally Jensen, was riding double with Cal, the younger and smaller of the two men who had come to Etna to see about her husband.

The fourth person, the one Frakes had pointed out, was riding alone. He also had a rope looped around his neck, and riding next to him, holding on to the other end of the rope, was Pearlie.

"Damn," Turnball said with a long-suffering sigh. "I thought they had left town."

Turnball tipped his chair forward and stood up.

"Maybe they come back to bring the bank robber," Frakes said.

"You're sure that fella with them is one of the bank robbers?"

"I was standin' not more'n twenty feet from him when it all happened," Frakes said. "And I got a good look at him 'cause he wasn't wearin' no mask like the ones that went into the bank. But he was waitin' outside and, when the robbers rode out of town, all of 'em shootin' and such, he was ridin' along with 'em, shootin' his gun and screamin' like a wild Indian."

The riders, seeing Turnball standing on the porch in front of Dunnigan's Store, headed his way.

"Mrs. Jensen," Turnball said politely, touching the brim of his hat. "Gents," he said to the others.

"Marshal," Sally replied.

"Who have you got here?" Turnball asked.

"This man's name is Buford Yancey," Sally said.

"Yancey has something to tell you," Sally said.

"Arrest this woman, Marshal," Yancey said. He held up his little finger, which was covered by a bandage. The bandage was reddish brown with dried blood. "She shot my finger off."

"You're lucky she didn't shoot something else off," Pearlie said. "Now tell the marshal what you told us."

"I don't know what you're talkin' about," Yancey said. "I ain't got nothin' to say."

"Are you sure about that?" Pearlie asked as he gave a hard jerk on the rope.

"Easy there," Yancey said fearfully. "You could break my neck, messin' around like that."

"Get down off my horse, Yancey," Cal said.

Scowling, Yancey got down.

"You're goin' to tell the marshal what you told us, or I aim to drag you from one end of this street to the other," Pearlie said, backing his horse up and putting some pressure on Yancey's neck.

"All right, all right," Yancey said. "I'll talk to him."

"You was one of them, wasn't you?" Frakes said. "You was one of the bank robbers. I seen you."

Yancey looked over at Sally. "I don't reckon I need to say much," he said. "The boy here's done said it for me."

"He hasn't said it all," Sally said.

"You got more to say, Yancey?" Turnball asked.

"I wasn't one of 'em what went inside," Yancey said.

"Like the boy here said, he seen me standin' in front of the store across the street from the bank. I didn't go inside."

"What about the others? The ones who did stay inside? Who was they?" Turnball asked.

Yancey thought for a moment, then he nodded. "Yeah," he said. "Hell, yeah, you want to know who they was, I'll tell you. Ain't no need in coverin' up for them. Them sons of bitches stole my share of the money, and you better believe I don't intend to go to jail while they're wanderin' around free."

"First, Mr. Yancey, tell them who was not with you," Sally demanded.

"Who was not with me?" Yancey replied, a little confused by Sally's remark. Then, realizing what she was saying, he nodded. "Oh, yeah, I know what you mean. You're talkin' about Jensen," Yancey said. Yancey looked back at the marshal. "Jensen wasn't with us. He wasn't no part of the robbin' of the bank."

"What do you mean he wasn't with you? I saw him," Turnball said. "We all saw him. Nobody is likely to miss that shirt he was wearing."

"Yeah, that was Dooley's idea," Yancey said. "We put Curt Logan's shirt on him. Then we dropped a couple of them paper things that was wrapped around the money by him. We seen you and the posse when you found him. You took the bait like a rat takin' cheese." Yancey laughed. "Dooley's an evil son of a bitch, but he sure is smart."

"Dooley," Turnball said. "Would that be Ebenezer Dooley?"

The smile left Yancey's face. "Yeah, Ebenezer Dooley. He was the one behind it all, and he's the one that stole from me. I tell you true, I hope you catch him."

"We don't have to catch him," Turnball said. "He's dead."

"He's dead? The hell you say," Yancey said.

"It came in by telegram," Turnball said. "He was shot by a man named Kirby."

"Kirby?" Sally said.

"That's the name that was on the telegram," Turnball said. "Seems that Dooley shot the deputy sheriff over in Dorena, and this fella Kirby shot Dooley."

"This man Kirby," Sally said. "Is he another deputy, or something?"

"Not unless it's someone they've put on recently," Turnball said. "I've never heard of him."

"I see."

"Come on, Yancey," Turnball said. "Oh, and Mrs. Jensen, you might want to come down to the jail with me."

"Why?" Sally asked.

Turnball chuckled. "Don't worry, I ain't arrestin' you or nothin'. But I've got a feelin' that there's a reward out on Yancey. I thought you might be interested in it if there was."

"You thought right, Marshal. I would be very interested in it," Sally said.

Deputy Pike was standing by the stove, pouring himself a cup of coffee, when he heard the door open.

"You want some coff . . . ," Pike began, speaking before he turned around. He stopped in mid-sentence when saw that Turnball had a prisoner. "Who is this?" he asked.

"This is one of the bank robbers," Turnball said. "Put him in jail."

"Yes, sir!" Pike said. "Come on, you, we've got just the place for you." Grabbing the key from a wall hook, Pike took the prisoner back to the cell, opened the door, and pushed him in. "Where'd you catch 'im?" Pike asked as he closed the door.

"I didn't catch him," Turnball answered. "She did."

"What?" Pike asked. Turning back again, he saw Jensen's wife and the two men who were traveling with her. "You!" he said. "What are you doing here?"

"Why, Mr. Pike," Sally said. "Aren't you happy to see me?"

"I'd be happy if I never saw you again," Pike said.

Turnball chuckled. "Don't worry. I won't let her throw you in jail again."

"She tricked me," Pike said.

"Yeah, I'm sure," Turnball said. He began going through several circulars. Then finding what he was looking for, he held it up for Sally. "I was right. Mr. Yancey is worth five hundred dollars."

"You said somethin' about the town offerin' two hundred and fifty dollars as well?" Pearlie said.

"I did say that, didn't I? Mrs. Jensen, it looks like you'll be getting out of here with seven hundred and fifty dollars. That ought to make you feel a little better about us."

"I'll feel much better when you send out telegrams informing everyone that my husband is no longer wanted for bank robbery and murder."

"Yes, ma'am, all the lines are open now, so I'll do that right away," he said.

"Do you think there was a reward for Ebenezer Dooley?"

"I'm sure there was."

"Good."

"Why do you say good? He's already been killed."

"I said good because I'm sure Smoke is the one who killed him."

Turnball shook his head. "No, ma'am. I told you, it was somebody named Kirby." Then he stopped. "Wait a minute. Your husband's name is Kirby, isn't it? Kirby Jensen."

"Yes."

"Do you really think it was him?"

"If Smoke was found guilty for something he didn't do, I've no doubt but that he is hunting down the bank robbers right now in order to clear his name."

"Well, I tell you what, Mrs. Jensen. If your husband is the one who took care of Dooley, and he can have the sheriff of Dorena vouch for him, we'll be sending on another two hundred fifty dollars reward on him as well."

"Thank you," Sally said. "When will I get the reward due me?"

"I'll get a telegram off to Denver today. I figure by tomorrow we'll have authorization back. You should get all your money then."

"Hey, Marshal, if you're through talkin' about how much money you're goin' to give this woman for shootin' my little finger off, maybe you'll get the doctor to come take a look at it," Yancey called from his cell.

"Looks to me like Mrs. Jensen did a pretty good job of doctorin'," Turnball said.

"I know my rights," Yancey insisted. "I'm your prisoner. That means I got a right to have a doctor treat me."

"All right, I'll get the doc down here for you," Turnball said. "I ought to tell you, though, he likes to amputate. More'n likely he'll chop that finger clean off. Maybe even your hand."

"What?" Yancey gasped. He stepped back away from the bars. "Uh, no, never mind. She done a good enough job on me. I won't be needin' no doctor."

"I didn't think you would," Turnball said.

Pearlie and Cal were laughing at Yancey as they left the marshal's office.

"You know what, Miss Sally? With your reward money and what we have, there's almost enough money to save Sugarloaf right there," Pearlie said.

"Yes, there is."

"I tell you this. The trip back home tomorrow is going to be a lot more joyful than it was when we started out yesterday," Cal said.

"It would be if we were going back home. But we aren't going to Sugarloaf yet," Sally said.

"Where are going?"

"We're going to find Smoke."

"How are we going to find him? I mean, where will we start?" Cal asked.

"We'll start in Dorena," Sally said. "First thing tomorrow, after we collect the reward money."

"Do you think Smoke is the one who killed Dooley?" Cal asked.

"I'd bet a thousand dollars he was," Sally said.

22

Smoke looked back over his shoulder as he led the horse across the swiftly running stream. The horse was carrying Fargo's body, belly down, across his back. The horse smelled death and he didn't like it one little bit.

Stormy and Fargo's horse kicked up sheets of silver spray as they trotted through the stream. Smoke paused to give them an opportunity to drink. Smoke's horse, Stormy, was a smart horse and knew from experience that he should take every opportunity to drink when he could. He put his lips to the water and drank deeply, but Fargo's horse just tossed its head nervously. The horse was obviously anxious to get to where it was going so it could rid itself of its gruesome cargo.

Smoke reached over and patted Fargo's horse on the neck a few times.

"Hang on just a little longer, horse," Smoke said gently. "If what they told me back in Dorena is right, it won't be much longer, then you'll be rid of your burden."

The horse whickered, as if indicating that it understood.

"Come on," Smoke said when Stormy had drunk his fill. "Let's be on our way."

* * *

Sheriff Fawcett was sitting at his desk with a kerosene lantern spread out before him. He was cleaning the mantle when Sally, Pearlie, and Cal stepped through the door. Seeing a beautiful woman coming into his office, the sheriff smiled and stood.

"Yes, ma'am," he said. "Is there something I can do for you?"

"I hope you can help me find my husband," Sally said.

The smile left, to be replaced by a troubled frown. "Is he missing?"

"Well, not missing in that he is lost," Sally said. She smiled to ease his concern. "He is missing in that I don't know where he is."

"You think he is here in Dorena?"

"I think he has been here," Sally said. "His name is Kirby Jensen, though most people call him Smoke."

"Jensen?" Sheriff Fawcett said. "Jensen? Wait a minute. I just heard something about someone with that name." He walked over to a table that was up against the wall and started shuffling papers around. He picked up a yellow sheet of the kind that was used for telegrams. "Here it is," he said. He read the message, then his face grew very concerned and he looked up at Sally.

"Did you say Jensen was your husband?"

"Yes. My name is Sally Jensen."

"And you are looking for him?"

"I am."

Sheriff Fawcett shook his head and sighed. "Well, evidently, so is every lawman in Colorado," he said. He held up the paper. "According to this, he is an escaped prisoner, convicted of murder and robbery."

"No, he ain't!" Cal shouted in a bellicose voice.

"Cal," Sally said, holding up her hand as if to calm him down, "it's all right." She maintained her composure as she smiled at the sheriff. "What my young friend is trying to say is that the wanted notice has been rescinded."

"It's been what?"

"It has been canceled," Sally explained. "Marshal Turnball, back in Etna, sent out telegrams rescinding the notification that my husband was a wanted man."

"Why would he do that?"

"'Cause Smoke wasn't guilty, that's why," Cal said, his voice holding as much challenge as it had earlier.

"It seems that one of the bank robbers was caught," Sally said.

"Ha! It wasn't the law that caught him. Tell the sheriff who it was that caught 'im, Miss Sally," Pearlie said.

"*She* caught him," Cal answered, pointing proudly to Sally. "She caught 'im, and we took him in and got a reward for him."

"His name was Buford Yancey," Sally said.

Sheriff Fawcett nodded. "Yancey," he said. "Buford Yancey. Yes, I've heard that name. He's a pretty rough customer, all right."

"He ain't so rough now," Cal said. "He's over in Etna behind bars."

"And he has not only confessed to the robbery," Sally said, "he has also confessed that my husband was not involved. The actual bank robbers framed him so people would think he was guilty."

"And you say that word has been sent out to all the law agencies around the state calling back the wanted notice?" Sheriff Fawcett asked.

"He was supposed to have sent word out by telegraph," Sally said.

Again, Fawcett began looking through all the papers on his desk. After a moment or two of fruitless search, he shook his head.

"I'm sorry. There's nothing here."

"What about your telegraph service? Is your line still up?"

"As far as I know it is," Fawcett answered. "If you'd like, Mrs. Jensen, we could walk down to the telegraph and check this out."

Sally nodded. "Yes, thank you, I would like that," she said.

The four walked from the sheriff's office down to the Western Union office. The group was unremarkable enough that no one paid them any particular attention as they passed by, other than to take a second glance at the very pretty woman who was obviously a stranger in town.

The little bell on the door of the Western Union office caused the telegrapher to look up. He stood when he saw the sheriff, and smiled when he saw the pretty woman with him.

"Can I help you, Sheriff?"

"Danny, have you got any telegrams you haven't brought down to my office yet?" Sheriff Fawcett asked.

"As a matter of fact, I have," the telegrapher said. "I didn't think there was any rush to it, so I hadn't gotten around to it yet."

The telegrapher picked up a message from his desk, then handed it to Sheriff Fawcett. Fawcett read it, then nodded.

"You're right, Mrs. Jensen," he said. "Your husband is no longer wanted."

"Except by me," Sally said. "I have to find him. You see, he doesn't know that he is no longer a wanted man."

"I see. And you are afraid of what he might do while he thinks he is wanted?"

"I'm sure that whatever he does will be justified by the law," Sally said. "For example, I am sure that he killed a man called Ebenezer Dooley right here in your town."

Sheriff Fawcett shook his head. "No, that was a man named Kirby. We have eyewitnesses who say they saw Bill Kirby engage Ebenezer Dooley . . . in self-defense, I hasten to add . . . and shoot him down."

"Was he a big man with broad shoulders, a narrow waist, blue eyes?"

"Well, yes, that sounds like him, all right," Sheriff Fawcett said.

"That's him."

"So his name isn't Kirby?" Sheriff Fawcett asked. Then he stopped in mid-sentence and chuckled. "Wait a minute, I get it now. He's calling himself Kirby from Kirby Jensen, right?"

"That's right," Sally said. "Did you say you paid him a reward?"

"Yes. Dooley had a five-hundred-dollar reward on him."

"Seven hundred fifty," Sally corrected.

"No ma'am, it was only five hundred," Sheriff Fawcett said.

"Dooley was one of the bank robbers," Sally explained. "The town of Etna added two hundred fifty dollars to the reward."

"Uh, Mrs. Jensen, if you are asking me to pay the additional two hundred fifty dollars, I got no authority to do that," the sheriff said.

"I don't need the money from you, just your verification that my husband is the one who killed Dooley."

"Well, uh, I don't know as I could actually . . ." Fawcett began, but Sally interrupted him.

"Is this the man?" she asked. She was holding an open locket in her hand, and Fawcett leaned down to look at the picture. He studied it for a moment, then nodded.

"Yes, ma'am, that's him all right," he said.

"You'll write the letter validating that he is the one who killed Dooley?"

"Yes, ma'am, I'll be glad to do that," the sheriff said. He smiled. "I'll do better than that. Danny," he called to the telegrapher.

"Yes, Sheriff?"

"Send a telegram to the city marshal in Etna, Colorado," he said. "In the message, say that Kirby Jensen is the man who killed Ebenezer Dooley. As this was a justifiable killing, there are no charges against Jensen, and he was paid a reward for bringing Dooley to justice. Then put my name to it."

"Yes, sir," the telegrapher said as he sat down to his instrument.

"You know," the sheriff said with a smile. "Now that I

know who you are talking about, I think I might even be able to help you find him. At least, I can tell you where he went from here."

"Where?"

"Bertrand," the sheriff answered.

"How far is it to Bertrand?"

"Well, there are two ways to go. Some folks go through Diablo Pass because the pass isn't quite as high. But most folks go through McKenzie Pass, which is about ten miles closer."

"Thanks," Sally said.

23

After several hours of riding on a bumping, rattling, jerking, and dusty stagecoach, the first view of Bertrand could be quite disconcerting to its passengers. Especially to someone who had never seen the town before. Experienced passengers were often called upon to point out the town, for from the top of the pass it looked like nothing more than a small cluster of the brown hummocks and hills common to this country.

Five years after founding the town, a saloon keeper named John Bertrand was shot down in the street of his own town. The drunken drifter who killed him was lynched within an hour of his foul deed. Now, without the entrepreneurial spirit of its founder, the little town was dying, bypassed by the railroad and visited by the stagecoach but two times per week. Its only connection to the outside world was a telegraph wire, and though it was recently restrung, even it had been down for most of the winter.

Smoke stopped on a ridge just above the road leading into Bertrand. He took a swallow from his canteen and watched the stage as it started down from the pass into the town. Then, corking the canteen, he slapped his legs against

the side of his horse and sloped down the long ridge, leading the horse over which Fargo's body had been thrown.

Smoke was somewhat farther away from town than the
coach, but he knew he would beat it there because he was
riding down the side of the ridge, whereas the coach had to
stay on the road, which had many cutbacks as it came down
from the top of the pass.

Smoke passed by a sign that read: WELCOME TO BERTRAND.
Behind it, another sign said: THE JEWEL OF COLORADO.

Smoke wasn't at all sure that the person who wrote that
sign was talking about the same town he was riding into
about then. He didn't see much about the little town that
would classify it as the "Jewel of Colorado."

Two dirt roads formed a cross in the middle of the high
desert country. The town consisted of a handful of small
shotgun houses, and a line of business buildings, all false-
fronted, none painted. The saloon was partially painted,
though, with LUCKY NUGGET painted in red high on its own
false front.

As he rode into town, the fact that he was bringing in a
corpse caused him to be the center of attention. Several
people, seeing him, began to drift down the street with him
to see where he was going.

Smoke was heading for one particular building, identified
by a black letters on a white board sign that said:

TATUM OWENS, *Sheriff*.
Bertrand, Colorado.

By the time he reached the front of the sheriff's office,
more than twenty people had gathered around. Even the
sheriff had come out of his office, summoned by someone

who had run ahead to tell him about the strange sight of someone riding into town bringing with him a dead body.

As Smoke dismounted and tied Fargo's horse to the hitching rail, Sheriff Owens lit his pipe.

"Did you kill 'im?" the sheriff asked around the puffs that were necessary to get his pipe started.

"I did."

"I figure you must think you had a good reason to kill 'im," the sheriff said. "Otherwise, you would have left him."

"He was trying to kill me," Smoke said.

"Sounds like reason enough," Sheriff Owens said. "And if there ain't nobody to back you up, there ain't nobody here to say any different. What you plannin' on doin' with him?"

"I figured the sheriff's office was as good a place as any to leave him," Smoke replied.

"Would you happen to know his name?"

"I don't know his last name. But I heard him called Fargo," Smoke said. "He robbed a bank in Etna," Smoke added.

The sheriff nodded. "Ah, then that would be Fargo Masters." Smoke looked up in surprise.

"How do you know that?" he asked.

The sheriff nodded. "The telegraph is up again, and word come through this mornin' tellin' about the robbery. It also named all the robbers, and put out a reward of two hundred fifty dollars for each one of them. That means you've got money comin', if we can prove this is who you say he is."

"What if I show you the money he had on him?" Smoke asked.

"You got the money from him?"

Smoke nodded. "From him, and from Ebenezer Dooley."

"If you've got the money, I'd say that's pretty good proof."

"Sheriff, what do you want me to do with the body?" a tall, skinny man asked. His long black coat and high-topped hat identified him as an undertaker.

"Find a pine box for him," the sheriff said. "If nobody claims him within a few days, you can bury him."

"Is the town going to pay?"

"Five dollars, Posey," the sheriff said. "Same as with any indigent."

"Sometimes the town don't pay," Posey complained as he took the horse by the reins and started leading it down the street to the mortuary.

"I admit we're late sometimes," Owens called after Posey. "But when you get down to it, we've always paid."

Having satisfied their curiosity as to who the corpse was, most of the gathered townspeople began moving away. The coach that Smoke had seen several minutes earlier was just arriving in town now, and it pulled to a stop at the stage depot, which was next to the sheriff's office.

"Hey, Walt, how was your trip?" the sheriff called up to the driver.

"The trip was fine, no problems," Walt replied as he set the brake and tied off the reins of his six-horse team. "Folks, this is Bertrand!" he called down.

The door to the coach opened and the passengers stepped outside. One of them glanced over toward the sheriff, then seeing Smoke, smiled broadly.

"Why, Smoke Jensen!" the passenger called over to him. "What are you doin' here? You're a long way from home, aren't you?"

Smoke knew the passenger only as Charley. Charley was a salesman who from time to time had come into Longmont's Saloon when he was in Big Rock.

Smoke considered pretending that he didn't know what the passenger was talking about, but decided it would be less noticeable to just respond and get it over with.

"Hello, Charley," Smoke said. "I haven't seen you in a while."

"No, Big Rock isn't my territory anymore," Charley replied. "But I sure had me some friends over there. Listen, when you get back over there, you tell Louie Longmont and Sheriff Carson that ole Charley Dunn said hi, will you?"

"Sure, Charley, I'll do that," Smoke replied. He was aware that Sheriff Owens was staring hard at him.

"You're Smoke Jensen?" the sheriff asked. "Is your real name Kirby Jensen?"

"Yes," Smoke said. He poised for action. He didn't want to kill the sheriff, but he wasn't going to go back to jail either. Especially for a crime he didn't commit.

"Oh, then you must've already got the word. Otherwise, you'd still be running."

"I've already got the word?" Smoke asked. "Got what word?"

"Why, that you've been cleared," the sheriff said. "That message that come in this morning also canceled the wanted notice that went out on you." Owens laughed. "But, since we didn't have a telegraph line through to anyplace else until just the other day, we wasn't gettin' much news anyway. I found out that you was wanted and not wanted on the same day."

Smoke smiled broadly. "Well, that's good to know, Sheriff," he said.

"So, what are you going to do now? Go back home?" Sheriff Owens asked.

Smoke shook his head. "You say there is a two-hundred-fifty-dollar reward for every one who took part in the bank robbery?"

"That's right."

"That's good to know," Smoke said. He smiled. "It's also good to know that I don't have to worry about you wanting to lock me up while I go about my business."

"What business?"

"Finding the other bank robbers."

Bidding the sheriff good-bye, Smoke started toward the saloon, as much to slake his thirst as to find out more information. He tied his horse off in front, then on a whim, took the plaid shirt out of his saddlebag and put it on.

Pulling his pistol from its holster, Smoke spun the cylinder to check the loads, then replaced the pistol loosely and went inside. He had long had a way of entering a saloon, stepping in through the door, then moving quickly to one side to put his back against the wall as he studied all the patrons. Over the years he had made a number of friends, but it seemed that for every friend he made, he had made an enemy as well. And a lot of those enemies would like nothing better than to kill him, if they could. He didn't figure on making it easy for them.

As Smoke stood there in the saloon with his eyes adjusting to the shadows, he saw one of the men he was looking for. He might not have even noticed him had the man not been wearing the shirt Smoke was wearing when the men jumped him. It was a shirt that Sally had mended when Smoke tore it on a nail in the barn.

As Smoke thought about it, he began to get angrier and angrier. He was not only angry with the man for being one of those who framed him, he was angry because the man was wearing a shirt that Sally's own hands had mended and washed.

What right did that son of a bitch have to be wearing, next to his foul body, something that Sally had touched?

The man was talking to a bar girl, and so engaged was he that he noticed neither Smoke's entrance, nor his crossing the open floor to step up next to him.

"Would you be Curt or Trace Logan?" Smoke asked.

"I'm Curt. Do I know you?"

"Let's just say that's my shirt you are wearing," Smoke said.

"What?" the man replied. For a moment he was confused; then, perhaps because Smoke was wearing the very shirt *he* had been wearing, he realized who Smoke was. Smoke saw the realization in the man's eyes, though he continued to protest.

"What do you mean I'm wearing your shirt? I don't know what are you talking about."

"You know what I'm talking about," Smoke said. "You, your brother, and four others set me up to take the blame for a bank you robbed in Etna. I've already taken care of two of your friends. You and Trace are next. Where is Trace, by the way?"

Curt's eyes widened, then he turned toward the bartender. "Bartender, send somebody for the sheriff," he said. "This man is an escaped convict."

"Go ahead, send somebody for the sheriff," Smoke said. "I just left his office." Smoke gave a cold, calculating smile. "I'd like him to come down here and take charge. According to the sheriff, Curt Logan is worth two hundred fifty dollars to me."

The bartender looked back and forth between the two men, not knowing who to believe.

"Dan, this man is Smoke Jensen," someone called out from the door. Although Smoke didn't realize it, Charley, the salesman, had followed him to the saloon from the sheriff's office, and was now standing just a few feet away. "I've known Mr. Jensen for years, and I'll vouch for him. And I was just down at the sheriff's office while Jensen and the sheriff were talking. Jensen's telling the truth. This man," he said, pointing toward Curt, "is lying."

"You're crazy," Logan said.

"I don't know that he is so crazy," the bartender said to Logan. "I've been wonderin' where you and your brother got all the money you two been throwing around ever since you come to town. Besides which, Jensen is wearing a shirt just like the shirt your brother is wearing. To me, that means that the story he's tellin' makes sense."

"We . . . we sold some cows, that's where we got the money. And the shirt's just a coincidence."

"Where is your brother?" Smoke asked.

Suddenly Curt went for his pistol. Smoke drew his as well, but rather than shooting him, he brought it down hard on the top of his head.

Logan went down like a sack of feed.

Smoke stared at the man on the floor. "Do you have any idea where his brother is?"

"Yeah, I know. He's upstairs," the bartender said. "Like I

told you, they been spendin' money like it was water. He and this one have been keepin' the girls plumb wore out ever since they got here."

"Which room is he in?"

"Well, he's with Becky, so that'd be the second room on your left when you reach the head of the stairs. And you better watch out for Becky too. She's some taken with him now, I think. Though to be truthful, I think it's more his money than it is him."

"Thanks."

The altercation at the bar had caught the attention of all the others in the saloon, and now all conversation stopped as they watched Smoke walk up the stairs to the second floor.

When Smoke reached the room at the top of the stairs, he stopped in front of the door, then raised his foot and kicked it open.

Becky screamed, and Trace called out in anger and alarm.

"What the hell do you mean barging in here?" he shouted.

"Get up and get your clothes on," Smoke said. "There's a two-hundred-and-fifty-dollar reward out for you for robbing a bank, and I aim to collect it. I'm taking you down to the sheriff."

"The hell you are."

Smoke should have been more observant. If he had been, he would have noticed that Trace had a gun in the bed with him. From nowhere, it seemed, a pistol appeared in the outlaw's hand.

Trace got off the first shot, and Smoke could almost feel the wind as the bullet buzzed by him and slammed into the door frame.

Smoke returned fire and saw a black hole suddenly appear in Trace's throat, followed by a gushing of blood. The outlaw's eyes went wide, and he dropped the gun and grabbed his throat as if he could stop the bleeding. He fell back against the headboard as his eyes grew dim.

Becky's screaming grew louder and more piercing.

"You killed him! You killed him!" Becky shouted. She picked up the outlaw's gun and, pointing it at Smoke, fired at him.

Becky's action surprised him even more than the fact that Trace had had the gun in bed with him. Stepping quickly toward her, he stuck his hand down to grab the gun, just as she pulled the trigger again. The hammer snapped painfully against the little web of skin between Smoke's thumb and forefinger. It brought blood, but it didn't hit the firing pin, so the gun didn't go off.

Smoke jerked the pistol away from Becky, then threw it through the window. Then, just to make certain there were no other hidden weapons, he picked up one side of the bed and turned it up on its end, dumping Trace's body and the naked bar girl out on the floor.

Becky curled up into a fetal position and began crying. Smoke looked at her for a moment, then left the room. When Smoke reappeared at the top of the stairs, he saw that everyone in the saloon was looking up to see how the drama had played out. They watched in silence as he descended the stairs, then several rushed toward him to congratulate him.

Smoke smiled back and nodded at them, but he was very subdued about it. He didn't consider killing a man to be anything you should be congratulated for. Looking toward the floor, he saw that that Curt Logan was gone. Silently, he cursed himself for not tying him up before he went upstairs.

"Where did he go?" he asked.

The bartender looked toward the floor where Curt Logan had been lying, and was genuinely surprised to see that he was no longer there.

"I . . . I don't know," the bartender said. "We was all lookin' upstairs to see what was goin' to happen. I reckon he must've left when nobody was payin' attention to him."

"That's real brotherly love for Curt to leave and let Trace face me alone," Smoke said.

He walked over to the bar. "I'll have a beer," he said.

"Yes, sir, and it's on the house," the bartender replied. As the bartender took an empty mug down to the beer barrel to fill it, Smoke happened to glance toward the mirror that was behind the bar. That was when he got a quick glimpse of the reflection of Curt Logan just outside the front window. The outlaw had a gun in his hand, and he appeared to be sneaking up toward the front door.

When Smoke leaned over the bar for a better look, he happened to see the double-barrel, ten-gauge, sawed-off Greener shotgun that the bartender kept handy. Picking it up, Smoke pulled both hammers back, then turned toward the door just as Curt Logan came through the batwings with his pistol in his hand.

"You son of a bitch!" Logan shouted, shooting toward Smoke. His bullet crashed into one of the many bottles that sat in front of the mirror, shattering the bottle and sending up a spray of amber liquid. The other customers at the bar, suddenly finding themselves in the line of fire, dived to the floor and scooted toward the nearest tables.

Smoke pulled both triggers on the shotgun and it boomed loudly, filling the saloon with smoke. Curt Logan was slammed back against the batwing doors with such force as to tear them off the hinges. He landed on his back at the far side of the boardwalk with his head halfway down the steps just as Sheriff Owens, drawn by the sound of the first shots, was arriving.

When Owens came into the saloon, he saw Smoke standing at the bar, still holding the Greener. Twin wisps of smoke curled up from the two barrels.

The sheriff looked back through the broken door at the body lying on the porch; then he stepped up to the bar.

"Give me a beer, Dan," he said.

Dan drew the beer, then with shaking hands, held it toward the sheriff.

"Better let me take that before you spill all of it," the sheriff said, taking the beer. He blew the foam off, and took a drink before he spoke to Smoke, who by now had put the shotgun down and picked up his own beer.

"Let me guess," the sheriff said. "You've just earned your-self another two hundred fifty dollars."

"Five hundred," Smoke replied. "That's Curt Logan. His brother Trace is upstairs."

Suddenly there was a commotion at the door and, as fast as thought, Smoke drew his gun and turned toward the sound.

"Hello, Smoke," Sally said. "How've you been?"

Sally had a gun in her hand, having just used it as a club. Ford DeLorian was lying facedown on the floor, uncon-scious. His right arm was stretched out before him, his fin-gers wrapped around a pistol.

Pearlie bent down and took the pistol from Ford's hand.

Cal came in right behind Sally and Pearlie, and Sally came over quickly to embrace Smoke.

"Sheriff Owens, this is my wife, Sally."

"Sheriff," Sally said, smiling sweetly. "I hope you aren't planning on arresting my husband for bank robbery. Be-cause I'm here to tell you that he has been cleared."

"Yes, ma'am, I know that," Sheriff Owens said. "I was just tellin' him that the state owes him seven hundred fifty dollars."

"Make that a thousand dollars," Smoke said, nodding toward the man who was just beginning to regain conscious-ness. "His name is Ford DeLorian."

"I guess that explains why he was planning to shoot you," Sheriff Owens said. "All right, I stand corrected. The state owes you one thousand dollars."

"No," Sally said. "You were right the first time. It's just seven hundred fifty."

"What are you talking about?" Smoke asked. "He was one of the bank robbers, and there is a two-hundred-fifty-dollar reward for each of them."

"I know," Sally said. She smiled at Smoke. "But this two hundred and fifty dollars is mine."

As Ford came to, he looked around in confusion, wonder-ing what everyone was laughing at.